I0634930

The Nesbit Trilogy

The Nesbit Bunch

Chasing Shadows
The Gray Ladies
Endpoint?

The Nesbit Bunch

by

Rob G Lerner

Cover by PJ Hines

Pomanjer Publishing Co., LLC

ISBN-13: 978-0999251119 (Pomanjer Publishing Co., LLC)
ISBN-10: 0999251112

Published 2018
Pomanjer Publishing Co., LLC

Pomanjer Publishing Co., LLC, publishes fiction and non-fiction books that speak to our hearts and catch the idiosyncratic attention of the Pomanjers.

Pomanjer Publishing Co., LLC
P.O. Box 986, Vienna VA 22183 USA

The Nesbit Bunch

by
Rob G Lerner
Cover by PJ Hines

The Nesbit Bunch brings together for the first time all three of the Nesbit novels. Each novel is complete and unabridged, and together they detail the saga of the American Interpol Agent Nesbit, the Scotland Yard Constable Tom Thwait, and the Scotland Yard Inspector Grace Sedgwick.

About the author

Rob G. Lerner is the author of four novels (seven, if you count the stories in this volume). He is currently working on another book of fiction that he hopes to complete sometime in the near future. Lerner still plays pool, although not with the same dedication he had while writing his previous books, and he continues to enjoy Heifetz, Formula One, Titian, and baseball. Whenever feasible, Lerner lives in Virginia with his loved ones, and there are rare moments when he can be reached through the Pomanjer Publishing Co., LLC.

Find out more about the author at
https://www.amazon.com/author/robglerner

Please leave a review of Rob G. Lerner's books on the Amazon pages.

Previously by Rob G. Lerner:

Snapshot
Lerner's fourth novel, *Snapshot*, is a departure from his previous works and announces his intention to delve deeper into the human psyche. The unnamed narrator of the story is living in the San Francisco Bay area when he meets and falls in love with the strange and passionless Luce. Certain that he cannot live without her, the narrator orchestrates a series of tests to find out if she is capable of loving him. San Francisco, Carmel, and even Lake Tahoe crop up in this bizarre tale, and it only when everything seems lost that he finds the very thing he has been seeking. (2016)

Changers
Book one of the *Changers'* series, *Changers* covers the lives of five young friends who discover a secret ability – the ability to turn themselves into animals. It is a wonderful, exhilarating ability, but it also proves to have some unforeseen consequences for the community, the legal system, and ultimately their friendship. (2013)

Minders
Book two of the *Changers'* series, *Minders* continues the story started in book one. The once solid friendship of the five young people appears irreparably damaged when Luke unexpectedly learns of the whereabouts of the young woman Iowa. Against the advice of his former friends, and in violation of Changer law, he embarks on a journey to find her and rekindle what was once a blossoming relationship. But what begins as a test of his love for Iowa and his loyalty to the Changers quickly evolves into a challenge to his sense of reality and the ultimate truth. (2015)

The Boy Who Loved Dolphins
Timmy is a young boy whose presence is a burden to his parents. His beloved grandfather, his only friend, fires his imagination with wild tales of life beneath the shimmering sea. After his grandfather unexpectedly dies, Timmy and his family vacation at a small, coastal town where Timmy discovers wild dolphins and learns about love, family, and tragedy. (2012)

To Pamela and Alex

Contents

Chasing Shadows

Chapter 1

"Agent Nesbit?" he asked and immediately stuck out his hand. The question was a formality. Even though he had never met the man, he was well acquainted with him through internal reports and external media.

"You must be Constable Thwait," the other replied somewhat cautiously. The beaming young man in the ill-fitting suit was something of a mystery to Nesbit.

Nesbit grabbed Thwait's thick paw and gave it a firm shake. Nesbit was a good head taller than Thwait and, although he was well past the half-century mark, he was thin (not the slightest bulge above his belt) and still retained a full head of dark, albeit slightly graying, hair. It had been a long flight, but Nesbit arrived clean-shaven, his hair meticulously in place, and his suit (midnight blue offset by a white shirt and a yellow power tie) wrinkle-free.

"Yes, sir. We're pleased Interpol could spare you. I'm told you've had positions around the world but are now working from home...I mean from the United States." Thwait was familiar with Nesbit's background and reputation, and he was genuinely enthusiastic to be working with him on the upcoming investigation.

Nesbit nodded and reached down to pick up his suitcase.

"No, please," Thwait insisted and practically snatched it from the other's hand. The suitcase was surprisingly small and light, which suggested to Thwait that Nesbit didn't need much time in London to wrap up things.

"Thanks, Tom. We're only too happy to lend a hand to the London Metropolitan Police. So how long do you think it'll take to get through customs? I don't think I've ever seen it so crowded." He glanced around at the vast crowds of jostling people cramming the mammoth customs hall.

Thwait was a junior officer in his mid-twenties. Having recently gained weight, his official black suit was now straining at the seams while his narrow, red tie appeared to be constricting his neck as if it were an inverted noose. Thwait smiled at Nesbit, and his smooth, almost juvenile cheeks puffed out, giving his face a warm, jovial appearance unlike Nesbit's official, scowl-like smile.

"Follow me," Thwait said and immediately began squeezing between people and sidestepping luggage crowding the opening of the hall. With a quickness and agility that belied his bulk, he led Nesbit around and through lines of people queuing up for the customs agents. Reaching the front of one interminable line of tired, angry visitors, he pushed in front of an elderly foreign couple and their four grown daughters just as they were about to present their passports to the customs agent. Thwait winked at Nesbit and then flashed his badge at the impassive agent behind the counter.

"Wait the minute," the elderly man said in broken English, "We are in line for all day. You cannot have right to step in front of us like this." The customs agent silenced the man and his suddenly vocal wife and daughters by pointing an index finger at the man's forehead, after which he waved Thwait and Nesbit through with a sweep of the index finger on his other hand. Once the officers were out of sight, the elderly man's wife and her daughters began pointing their index fingers at the agent and hollering at him in their native tongue.

"Probably quicker than the last time you were here, sir."

"True, my friend, but right now I think there are a few things more important than patting ourselves on the back for getting through the lines quickly."

"Yes, sir," Thwait replied, and this time he led Nesbit outside into the cool, late-afternoon air to an unmarked, black sedan that was parked in a specially reserved spot next to the terminal entrance. Placing the suitcase carefully inside the boot, both men walked around to the sides of the car and got in, and it was at that point that Thwait noticed Nesbit's briefcase.

They were silent for several minutes while Thwait deftly maneuvered the sedan through the congested streets, speeding around slower vehicles and tapping on the horn at pedestrians who were either in the street or who looked as if they were about to enter it. When he had finished slipping around one particular knot of traffic, Thwait glanced at Nesbit and said, "I have the room next to yours. The station thought it might speed the investigation if I took a room, too. Normally, I commute from the outskirts."

"Sounds fine to me, Tom. It's Tom, right?"

"Yes, sir. Constable Thomas Thwait."

Nesbit nodded and yawned. "Sorry," he said. "I came here directly from the 'Big Apple.'"

"Sir?"

"New York, Tom, and a bloody long flight, I don't mind telling you."

"Oh, I see." Thwait hit the brakes briefly and then swerved around a couple of young women crossing the street. "If you'd like, sir, you can take a nap until we get to the hotel. We have a good fifteen minutes or so until we're there."

"I'll be fine. Actually, I'm more interested in hearing what you know about Angelique Dubois."

"Yes, sir. Well, we don't know a lot, but she's definitely in the country and undoubtedly up to something, so I'm told."

"Do you have her under surveillance now? No? That's okay. We'll put her on the radar quickly enough. I went through the material the station sent me. The picture is definitely her, and I believe your assumption that she's up to something is spot on. She's been in the UK how long? Two weeks? I can tell you from my experience that she doesn't like to cool her heels in the EU for any extended period of time. We'll have to hit the road running, my friend, because she's likely on the verge of pulling off whatever it is she has planned."

"That's what HQ thinks, and I believe that's why your services were requested. You're the world's expert on Ms. Dubois, and we're all anxious for you to find out what she's up to and put a stop to it."

"Yes, yes. As I said, I got the information, although I'm a little surprised no one at your station thought to inform me sooner."

"We're close to the hotel, sir. Since it's getting late, perhaps you like to get something to eat and continue the conversation after dinner? There are a lot of good restaurants near the hotel."

Nesbit started to respond, but immediately stopped when Thwait suddenly swerved to avoid an erratic driver. Tapping lightly on the horn two times, he sped past the car and reentered the lane several car lengths ahead of the slower vehicle. "It's hard to believe these drivers."

"The traffic seems to be worse every time I'm here," Nesbit replied, forgetting what he initially wanted to say.

Thwait stretched his thick neck and rolled his puffy shoulders while tightly gripping the wheel. "As you know from the report, sir, a confidential source told us that Ms. Dubois is planning to steal a valuable book. The source

3

had nothing on the book, and so we can't say where she's going to get it or how she's going to get it out of the country. I shouldn't think someone with her skills would have trouble getting just about any book out of the country."

"Who's your source? What's your level of confidence in him?"

"My deepest apologies, sir, but I'm not at liberty to disclose the name. Well, to be honest, I really don't know the name. HQ only gave us that much. They did indicate that they had the highest confidence in the individual."

"That's fine, Tom. There are things that I can't disclose, either. However, for her to get involved in something like this, it's got to be big time – Shakespeare, Beowulf, Gutenberg, or some other monument of British heritage – otherwise it lacks the thrill factor she constantly seeks." He paused momentarily while Thwait threaded his way between two cars on a narrow, one-way street.

"Yes," Nesbit continued, "There are a couple things you need to know about our Angelique. One, she comes from a wealthy family who apparently denied her nothing while she was growing up. Expensive clothes, jewelry, fast sports cars, as well as the best boarding schools and universities, she had it all. But instead of using her advantages and education for some greater good, she launched on a life of crime, not petty thievery, mind you, but big-time crime, the kind of crime that puts her in a different class than most of your smugglers, cat burglars, and the like. Perhaps you might slow a little in this traffic."

The car bounced over something in the road and continued on.

Nesbit coughed slightly in his hand. "As I was saying, Angelique loves thefts and swindles, that is, as long as everyone else thinks they're impossible, and as long as she can use the jobs to tout her elite criminal status. She'd rather steal the Washington Monument for nothing if it brought her notoriety in certain criminal circles than reap the benefits of something twice as valuable if no one knew about her theft."

"She's never been caught, am I right, sir? She must be very good…"

"Good, my friend? There's no one in her class. The police throughout Europe and the United States have done everything they could to apprehend her, but she's as slippery as grease on a rainy street. Just when they think they have her, she's gone and there's hardly a trace left behind. A few years ago, she was apprehended in Egypt, but at the last minute the government was forced to let her go because they didn't have anything on her and didn't have enough time to manufacture something. Jewels, antiques, rare items of all kinds, she takes it all, and so far there hasn't been much that anyone could do about it."

"What's the other thing, sir?"

"The other thing?"

"Yes, sir, you said there were a couple things about her that I needed to know. You mentioned one."

"Hmm, yes, yes, let me see. Now, where was I? Yes, of course, the second is that she possesses great organizational skills. She runs such a well-oiled organization that she could steal the smile off the Mona Lisa and ship it outside the country before anyone knew something was wrong and without leaving the slightest trace of Mona's lipstick behind. Angelique's marvelous, my friend, one of the all-time greats, and that's why she can charge a premium for her services."

"She doesn't work alone?" Thwait hammered the horn, this time at an elderly pedestrian who wasn't crossing the street fast enough.

Nesbit jerked upright. Straining to see the gesticulating pedestrian over his shoulder, he turned back to the street ahead and cleared his throat. "You can look at Angelique as a kind of independent contractor. She'll get an order from, say, a sleazy financier or a criminal cartel, after which she'll find the best means of fulfilling the order. It's kind of an interesting process. Once she has the order in hand, she'll scope out the place where the desired item is located, develop a detailed plan for its acquisition, and then assemble a team to execute her plan. As far as we can tell, the team members are different for every job, and the only person that any of these individuals has in common is apparently Angelique herself. She's extremely effective, and almost impossible to pin anything on."

"Why doesn't the cartel assemble its own team and cut out the middleman or, in this case, the middle woman? Seems to me it could simplify matters and save some money. Bloody hell! Sorry, sir, that car came out of nowhere."

"It happens, I suppose. Anyway, for most collectors, an acquisition takes the kind of time, effort, and specialized resources they don't have or want to expend, not to mention the fact that if something goes wrong, their collection efforts could be severely curtailed. My friend, Angelique has earned a five-star criminal rating, if you will, because her clients know that she can accomplish the most complicated job in an efficient and timely fashion, while at the same time keeping people like you and me and the press off their doorsteps. Should Angelique make a mistake, it's her lovely neck on the chopping block."

Thwait hesitated and momentarily checked his speed. He wanted to ask Nesbit one question but didn't know how to frame it without possibly insulting the man. "Tell me, sir," he began hesitantly, "How come nobody's put her in jail yet? You and others have been tracking her for at least ten years, you know what she looks like, you understand her modus operandi, and yet we're still on her trail right now. I know you said she's one of the greats, but even the greatest criminals get caught sooner or later. I apologize, sir, if I'm missing something or out of line."

Nesbit glanced at Thwait and smiled at him as if he were smiling at a child who asked a silly question. "You're young, my friend, but not out of line." He paused for a moment as if he were trying to explain something that couldn't be adequately explained in mere words. Shaking his head at last, he said matter-of-factly, "I nearly apprehended her twice. One time she slipped across the border before I could get the authority to move, and another time her attorneys intervened just as I was about to slap the cuffs on her. Tom, her legal beagles can make the best judges believe two and two equals five. That's a fact, my friend. But while she seems untouchable to some people, to me she's... Let's just say that sooner or later I'll be the one putting nails into her coffin."

"What? You don't mean kill..."

"Just a figure of speech. I'd like to kill her career, though."

Thwait smiled and nodded as if he had understood all along. Glancing out the window and noticing some dark clouds in the distance, he said, "We're close, maybe another five minutes to the hotel."

"Great. I need to stretch my legs. So let me ask you a few questions, my friend. You said that Angelique's been in the country for two weeks. How come no one reached out to me sooner?"

"We really didn't know she was here until one of our officers spotted her on the street a few days ago. We requested her customs records shortly thereafter, but it took some time for them to arrive. I guess it works that way sometimes. At any rate, we greatly appreciate the fact that you were able to come here on such short notice."

"Let me get this straight. One of your officers ran into her a couple of days ago, and yet neither he nor anyone else at the station seems to know where she is now? That doesn't sound like efficient police work to me."

"Well, I'm not sure it's exactly like that. She gave one of our officers the slip when he tried to follow her. Even so, there's not a lot we can do, since she's not currently wanted for a crime in the UK. If I'm not mistaken, Interpol doesn't have any Red Notices on her. Why is that, sir?"

"We're hamstrung just like you." Nesbit casually relaxed against the car door.

"Careful, sir, I don't think the door's closed all the way. We can talk more in a few minutes. We're here."

Chapter 2

The car came to an abrupt halt in front of an elegant, 19th century hotel near the financial district. Before any of the hotel attendants could reach the car, Thwait jumped out and pulled Nesbit's suitcase from the boot. He handed the arriving attendant the car keys, but wouldn't let him or anyone else touch Nesbit's property, which he quickly carried up the hotel's steps, through the revolving glass doors, and into the lobby. Standing on the plush carpet next to wide, ornate pillars beneath an arched and frescoed ceiling, Thwait again fended off the hotel's staff while he waited for Nesbit to appear.

"Please," Nesbit said with a pleasant smile when he emerged from the doors and met Thwait with a gracious smile. "I can take it from here."

The men walked to the front desk and, after Nesbit checked in (Thwait had checked in earlier), they took the elevator to the eleventh floor and proceeded to their respective rooms, which were connected by a door with a double lock. Thwait said that as soon as Nesbit was ready, they could go out for a bite (it was already past dinner time, and there was an Italian restaurant a few minutes away that he was eager to try). Nesbit, however, noted that he was more tired than he thought after the long trip and suggested room service instead. There was a large, circular table in his room, and he nodded toward it and said that they could eat there while going over the case. One hour later, Thwait and Nesbit were seated at the table, eating steak and lobster while reviewing the material from Nesbit's briefcase.

Thwait was especially interested in the photographs of Angelique that Nesbit had curated over the years. He was studying each one for clues when he paused at one particular image of Angelique standing at a busy street corner in some nameless city. Shaking his heavy head, he put this picture with the others and reordered them as if he were mixing a deck of cards. When he was done, he started from the topmost picture and slowly worked his way down to the middle of the stack, looking carefully at each image for something that he might have missed during the first pass. He stopped when he came to a photo of Angelique apparently shopping at an upscale boutique. "She's stunning," he said quietly to himself, his eyes riveted on a picture of a young woman in a tight-fitting dress. Thwait's expression took a serious turn, and he looked across the table at Nesbit. "These photographs…they were obviously taken at various places around the world, some during the day, some at night, and yet in each one Ms. Dubois is elegantly dressed. In practically every picture she looks like she's heading out to a fancy ball or some other formal event. I don't get it, sir."

Nesbit smiled and nodded. Everyone seemed to have a strong reaction to the woman. "She always dresses as if she had just walked out of a fashion magazine. There's no question that her looks inspire confidence and perhaps a little trepidation."

Thwait nodded, but now there was something hovering in the back of his mind. "Blast!" he suddenly stammered out. "I'm sorry, sir. I just remembered I had something to tell you but, for the life of me, I don't recall what it is. It had something to do with Ms. Dubois."

Nesbit was troubled that he didn't yet have a full understanding of the case, and so it was irritating that anyone should let some possibly significant fact slip through his mental fingers. "It happens, I suppose. Let me know immediately when you remember, even if it's in the middle of the night. I do have one more question for you, though." He pulled what appeared to be a passport photo of a middle-aged man from papers that Thwait had earlier pushed to one side of the table.

Thwait was slightly embarrassed by his lack of professionalism compared to the neat piles of information that Nesbit had contributed.

"I printed this out from an email, but no one said why they sent a picture of this chap. Is there some relevance to it, or was this just another mistake by your team?"

Thwait leaned over and looked at the image. "I'm sorry, sir. I don't know where my mind's been. This is what I wanted to tell you."

"Probably with Angelique. Now, about this photograph…is there any significance to it?"

"Yes, I think so. What I mean to say is, well, that is…"

"Out with it man. Don't tell me you have a stutter."

"No, sir, not at all, or at least I don't think I do. What I was going to say is that the man you're holding by the ear is Charlie Saunders, the proprietor of a shop called Antiquarian Books. It's an interesting connection, don't you think? I mean, she's after a special book, and he sells those kinds of special books. He's Canadian, and he's been in London for at least a year, although he may have been living in the country longer than that."

Nesbit waited silently for Thwait to clarify his statement. When he didn't respond, Nesbit shook his head and said, "Yes, he looks like a Canadian. There are a lot of bookshops in this town, and I wouldn't be surprised if more than a few are manned by Canadians. We have the same problem in the States. But what does this have to do with our lady friend here?"

"I'm sorry, sir. I guess I wasn't making myself clear. One of our off-duties spotted her leaving this gentleman's shop. Well, he was close enough to the shop to think that she may have been leaving it. I don't exactly know. It happened a few days ago. We pulled some records on his shop and came up with the picture. Pretty good, don't you think, sir?"

Nesbit's eyes narrowed in on Thwait's. "The off-duty is certain it was her?"

"Oh, yes, sir, he's seen a picture of Ms. Dubois. He's confident of the attribution."

"All right, then, this is interesting. What do you have on the proprietor? The picture, I presume, derives from his passport. Do you have anything else? Immigration records, criminal files, life records, any of that? What do you have that will help us understand the connection between them?"

"We haven't got much. To be perfectly honest, we've been a little pressed for…"

"Fine, fine, let's back up a moment. Where did she go after leaving the shop?"

"We don't exactly know, sir. The off-duty didn't follow her."

Nesbit stared at his British colleague. "What? He didn't follow her? This is one of the most important cases your station will ever have, and you're telling me that your off-duty didn't follow Angelique even though he recognized her? I don't understand. He should have stuck to her like glue. What's the problem here?"

"Well, sir, he was off duty. He was taking his baby to the doctor, and the baby was screaming at the time and so… Anyway, the off-duty identified her, Ms. Dubois, when she turned to see all the commotion. He called it in as soon as he could, but Ms. Dubois was gone by the time our officers arrived."

Nesbit grimaced slightly and rubbed his chin. Reaching across the table, he grabbed a piece of bread and began to chew it absently. "That's all? All right, I suppose we can connect the dots, if there are any. Tell me, has anyone spoken to this proprietor?" Nesbit looked closely at the paper to get the right name. "This Charles Saunders fellow?"

"Charlie Saunders, sir. No, we decided to wait until you arrived. We thought it best if you questioned him first, and then you can tell us if he's connected to Ms. Dubois."

"I guess that's reasonable, Tom," Nesbit said and reached for another piece of bread. "You don't mind, do you?" he asked as he dipped it into his coffee.

"Please, sir," Thwait responded, waving a thick hand to relinquish all rights to the food still on the table.

"Okay, let's go back to where we started. You said you had some things on this Charlie character? Where are they? Never mind, can you at least summarize what you have?"

"One of our officers did, sir. I'm afraid there wasn't a lot of information available. Obviously, we came up with a copy of his passport photo, and we're certain that he's the proprietor of the shop, but there's not much beyond this. We haven't been in the shop, so we don't know what's going on in there. Oh, we do have one more thing. Inspector Sedgwick, the officer who was doing background, was able to check his tax records..."

"Now we're getting somewhere."

"And Mr. Saunders hasn't generated more than a few pounds from his shop. He's been in business for nearly a year, and..."

"No sales?"

"No customers. Inspector Sedgwick finds this remarkable, sir, since the shop is located in an excellent part of town for this kind of business. She says that there are numerous commercial establishments in the same general area and that the foot traffic near his doorstep is quite substantial. Inspector Sedgwick is going to canvas the shop's neighbors to see if she can uncover anything derogatory about the man or his shop."

Nesbit rubbed the back of his neck with his right hand and then stood up. Placing his hands behind his back, he began to walk from one side of the room to the other. "I wish we could use my ex-wife's private investigator. There isn't a thing he can't dig up – or make up, when he doesn't have the facts."

"Do you have children, sir?" Thwait asked, not knowing what else to say.

Nesbit stopped and looked over his shoulder at him. "Yes, one, but he's grown and on his own. I haven't seen him in years, not since the divorce."

"Sorry to hear that, sir."

"No need," Nesbit replied and began walking with his head down. "I wish...do you want to know something? He took my ex-wife's side on everything. He stood up in court, he stood up in front of me and everyone else in God's green earth, and puppeted all the nonsense she had accused me of doing. Would it surprise you to know that one of my greatest faults was being dedicated to my work?" He stopped again and breathed deeply. "I'm sorry, Tom," he said shaking his head. Turing back to Thwait, he said, "You don't need to bear my heavy burden. Say, you don't have any children, do you? Not married, huh? Too young? Take your time, my friend, take your time – and don't spend your life nursing regrets. Anyway, sounds like we need to pay this Charlie and his shop a visit tomorrow morning."

"I was hoping you'd say that, sir," he replied and immediately began to pull all the material together in a big, unorganized mound. Noticing Nesbit staring at him, he smiled and quietly began to sort everything into stacks according to size. Once done, he handed them to Nesbit, who carefully placed them back into his briefcase.

Chapter 3

Charlie's shop was located on a narrow side street near the Ravenswood Museum and tucked into the shadows between two larger businesses. One of the businesses was a bridal shop, the other a travel agency, and, unlike Charlie's shop, both of them were clearly doing landmark business, judging by the numbers of people going in and out of their doors.

At Nesbit's insistence, Thwait parked a couple blocks away so that they could get a better sense of the neighborhood before speaking to Charlie. While they didn't expect to find escape routes (hidden alleys, broken fences, impenetrable shadows, and the like), they were concerned about other, unsuspected dangers should he prove to be their man. It was a little after nine on a cold and overcast morning when one of the men finally grasped the handle of the door and peeked through the window into Antiquarian Books.

The shop was essentially one, large open room. It was lined on three sides with tall, nearly empty bookshelves, while on the back wall were a door (shut) and a desk, which held a decrepit-looking cash register. The back door led to a storeroom that Charlie used to stage his acquisitions before he shelved them. This was little more than an oversized closet, although it was big enough for a small table and a couple of nondescript chairs. As he did most days, Charlie sat on the stool behind the register, facing the street door and impassively reading one of the numerous tabloids that he kept in one of the desk's side drawers.

There was an OPEN sign in the door's window. A high-pitched, mechanical bell above the door tinkled when Nesbit and Thwait entered, causing Charlie to look up briefly from his tabloid. "May I help you?" he asked the strange gentlemen, who were both dressed in dark suits.

"No," Nesbit replied. "Just looking, I'm afraid. You don't mind, do you?"

"No, be my guest. On your left are books printed before 1800, behind you books printed between 1800 and 1900, and on your right books printed after 1900, including modern firsts. Please let me know if you can't find something or if you're looking for something in particular. Most of our business is done through special order."

Thwait smiled in his large, gentle way, while Nesbit frowned, nodded, and walked stiffly over to the books on his left. Thwait took the opposite side of the room. Charlie returned to his tabloid, seeming to ignore his visitors while keeping a cautious eye on their movements.

Charlie Saunders was in his mid-fifties, slightly taller than average, and quite thin. Although his jowls were beginning to look heavy, his face was still smooth overall and he sported a full head of closely cropped hair, most of which was a dull gray. On the back of his right hand was a noticeable, star-like scar that was nearly two inches in length. Complementing his hair, Charlie favored gray suits, white shirts, and bland ties (usually the plain, undifferentiated black ones).

While Thwait and Nesbit casually glanced at the books (unlike his colleague, Thwait actually picked up one book, a slender volume that he remembered reading as a child), Charlie adjusted his tabloid so that he could follow their movements more carefully. Attuned to suspicious behavior, he could tell that Nesbit was the person in charge (Nesbit kept glancing around the shop as if he were casing the place, although Charlie knew that no self-respecting robber would have any interest in his establishment) and that the last thing this character had on his mind was a book purchase. Thwait was clearly inexperienced (he seemed quite taken by the book he was holding), and therefore Charlie wasn't overly concerned about what he was doing. Suspicious that the men were police officers, Charlie finally put his tabloid back into the drawer and directed his full attention to Nesbit.

"Are you sure you're not looking for something in particular?"

Nesbit stopped and turned to Charlie. "Just looking, that's all. Are you sure you don't mind? I'm not interrupting your business, am I?"

Charlie smiled as if Nesbit's words and attitude confirmed his suspicions. "I see you're interested in books before 1800. Do you have a preferred period? How about the English Renaissance? It's one of my favorites."

"Sure," Nesbit replied. His experience told him that Charlie was playing a cat-and-mouse game with him, and he was going to show the proprietor that he knew far more about such child's play than a mere bookseller, even if the bookseller was a master criminal. "Sure, what do you recommend? Something valuable, I hope."

"They're all valuable. It just depends on what you want. I have an original facsimile of Shakespeare's First Folio. The Folio is very rare and dates from the mid-nineteenth century. You're familiar with the First Folio, aren't you?"

14

Thwait was beginning to get worried. He didn't know anything about a Shakespeare folio (or even what a folio was), and he sensed from Charlie's smirk that something wasn't quite right.

"A little. Where's this volume – folio, right? – and how much do you want for it?"

"It's a little on the pricy side. It's rare, of course. Are you genuinely interested, or is there something else on your mind?"

"No, I'm interested. You're interested, too, aren't you, Tom," he added, nodding in Thwait's direction.

"Yes, I'm interested." Thwait re-shelved the book he was holding and moved closer to Nesbit.

"It's a little slow today, but you guys look like real connoisseurs. I'll tell you what. I'll let you have it for a thousand. It's worth fifty percent more, you know. Just don't tell anyone about the discount, right? I'll be forced out of business if other gentlemen like yourselves start demanding price cuts."

"Sounds good. I won't say a thing if it's as good as you claim. Are you sure it's an original fac…what did you call it?"

"Here, let me get it," Charlie said and got off his stool and went over to where Thwait was now standing. He pulled a large volume out from one of the shelves and brought it over to Nesbit, handing it to him as if it were a valuable treasure when in fact it was merely one of the countless modern editions of Shakespeare's plays. "I keep it over there for special customers like you and your friend."

Nesbit thumbed through its pages and then examined its cover. "Valuable, huh?"

"Absolutely. Look at the condition of the book – pristine, I might add – and notice how well the pages are printed and annotated. It's practically from the Bard's own mouth."

"Who? But I thought you said that it dated from the 1800s. It says here that the book was published in 1972. Care to see for yourself?"

"I know. It's valuable because it's based on a pre-1850 edition."

"And you want to charge me how much for it?"

Charlie smiled, revealing deep lines at the corners of his eyes and mouth. "It's negotiable."

Thwait watched the two without knowing what to make of the strange conversation. Since he didn't know Nesbit very well, he could only assume that he didn't know anything about the volume he was holding, and therefore he hoped that he wasn't going to shell out anything for a book that looked exactly like the one he used in school.

"Okay," Nesbit said and began to examine the book more carefully, slowly turning one page after another and touching certain passages as if they had some special significance.

Increasingly uncomfortable, Thwait mentally fished around for a way to intervene before his colleague went off the deep end. But just as he was about to interrupt their conversation with a fit of coughing (he couldn't come up with anything else), Nesbit tossed the book to Charlie, who barely caught it before it hit the floor.

"I don't know what kind of fool you take me for, Charlie," Nesbit said, scowling, "But that book's not worth horse piss. The First Folio was printed in the 1700s, and the whereabouts of every authentic edition still in existence is fully documented. Now, I don't recall having seen anything from your shop on the list, and so I can only assume that if you really do have a valuable edition, it isn't exactly yours. Oh, yes, a facsimile is a reproduction of something, am I right?"

Charlie kept his cool eyes on Nesbit and didn't notice Thwait, who was beaming from ear to ear over his colleague's exposure of the con. Thwait wasn't certain that Nesbit was correct, but he knew enough to feel that Charlie didn't know any more.

"Charlie, unless you want to discuss the early editions of Shakespeare's plays, I'd suggest we get down to something a little more interesting, a little closer to our own era."

Charlie glowered at Nesbit as if he indeed had exposed his game. Without another word, he returned to the stool behind the cash register and, after he made himself comfortable, calmly informed Nesbit in so many words that the ball was now in his court. "What do you want to talk about?"

Nesbit smiled and walked over to the front of the desk. Thwait followed, but kept a couple feet behind him and to one side. "Let's start with the shop," he said, standing directly in front of Charlie. "I'll admit I haven't seen everything, but what I have seen isn't very impressive. I don't even have to touch the books to see that they're little more than a bunch of cheap, secondhand editions. I'll let my colleague speak for the moderns, but I know there's no way a serious book buyer will be fooled by this crap. But then, you don't do a lot of business, do you, Charlie? We've been here for thirty minutes and not a single person has come through your door."

"It's morning. The afternoon rush hasn't come yet."

"I know for a fact that you haven't had any real sales since you first opened the doors of this august establishment. How do you stay in business, Charlie?"

Charlie hesitated and glanced over to Thwait, who was glad that Nesbit didn't make him say something about the moderns. "Okay, what's the deal? Who are you? Despite your accent, you've got to be among London's finest, otherwise you wouldn't know my name and wouldn't be asking these stupid questions. That being the case, I'd like to see some identification before we go any further."

"You're a Canadian, aren't you? Maybe you've seen too many American movies. I don't have to show you anything, Charlie boy. And don't start telling me about your rights, because as my friend here will attest, you don't have any rights while you're in this country."

Charlie stepped off his chair and faced the men. "What? Let me tell you something," he said to Nesbit, staring him in the eyes, "I don't have to say a word to you. And if you want something other than information on cheap, secondhand editions, as you call them, you better go next door and get a ticket back to wherever you came from."

"You know, Charlie, my colleague can make a call and within the hour a couple of gentlemen from Scotland Yard will be scouring this place from top to bottom."

"Tell them to get the grime in the lavatory."

Nesbit smiled, although the angelic expression on Thwait's face was completely gone (he resented the manner in which Charlie spoke to his esteemed colleague and dismissed the police). "Fine, fine, have it your way, Charlie. We'll be seeing you again." He turned to leave, motioning with his head for Thwait to follow. But when he grasped the doorknob, he didn't pull it open and instead stopped and appeared to be contemplating something. Turning around, he walked back to Charlie, forcing Thwait to take a large step to one side to avoid a collision. Staring at Charlie, although this time he wasn't smiling, Nesbit said, "There's something else I'd like to know about your bookshop, as you call it."

"As I call it? It's true I don't have an extensive inventory, but you certainly aren't in a position to judge its quality. You didn't pick up a single book, much less examine one and make an assessment of its value. If you had, you might have noticed the fine Beaumont and Fletcher folio over there, next

17

to your boyfriend," he said, gesturing toward a shelf next to where Thwait was standing. "It's the 1676 edition, the first complete edition of the playwrights' plays. A little lower in the same bookcase is a lovely little quarto, the 1592 edition of Thomas Kyd's *The Spanish Tragedy*. One of the more interesting features in this play is the 'play within the play,' which Shakespeare either wrote or ripped off for *Hamlet*." Glancing at Thwait and then back at Nesbit, both of whom looked puzzled, he added, "And you're wrong to presume I'm ignorant when it comes to Shakespeare. The First Folio was published in 1623, and, if you're interested in how Shakespeare became Shakespeare, I'd recommend reading something about his 18th century editors. So if you're interested in buying a book, I'm all ears. But if all you want to do is talk about my income, then you can go to the tax bureau."

Thwait's eyes were wide open, and he wondered if Nesbit was going to counter Charlie's claims, refute all the mistakes that he must surely have made.

Nesbit, however, merely nodded. "Okay," he said, "So you have a decent memory. That being the case, tell me, Charlie, what was Angelique Dubois doing in your shop two days ago?"

"Who's Angelique Dubois? I don't know her. I don't keep track of the people coming into my shop. But when they do come in, I generally assume they're looking for fine books, unless of course their behavior suggests they have something else on their mind."

"Would it help if I described her? Hmm, let's see. She's tall, elegantly dressed, and, as everyone says, drop-dead gorgeous. Do I need to say more?" Nesbit smiled as if Charlie had the same opinion about Angelique's looks. "Come on, you know the person I'm talking about. Apart from us, you haven't had anyone else in your shop for months. I find it hard to believe you can't remember someone like that, someone as fine looking as she is."

Charlie looked at Nesbit without responding.

"Think hard, Charlie." Nesbit paused but didn't turn away from Charlie. "Okay, you're a Canadian, and Canadians are kind of like Americans. I suppose they all want to be Americans. Tom, please show Charlie your credentials."

Thwait glanced on either side and discretely displayed his identification. Nesbit smiled again and then flashed his.

"Now that we can put the formalities aside, do you remember Angelique? I don't mean to put words in your mouth, Charlie, but she is a looker, isn't she?"

"Interpol?" Charlie said, emitting a half chuckle. "You don't have any authority here."

"Perhaps more than you think. Nonetheless, my colleague does, and we can take you in on his word alone. Isn't that right, Tom?" Nesbit motioned toward Thwait, who nodded ominously, his heavy cheeks bouncing as he moved his head. "Now, let's try this once more. Do I need to repeat myself or is your memory coming back? The door chime rang and this good-looking woman strolls into the shop."

Charlie frowned and, after glancing from one man to the other, reluctantly confirmed Angelique's visit. "Yeah, a woman came into my shop a few days ago. But she didn't tell me her name, and I didn't ask because she wasn't buying."

"What do you mean?"

"I mean she came into the shop, looked around for a few minutes, and left. Nothing else."

"You greeted her, right? Didn't you say anything else? You said more to us when we entered, and we aren't half as good looking as she is."

"What do you want from me? I told you exactly what happened."

Nesbit tugged at his earlobe and glanced at Thwait, who respectfully remained slightly behind Nesbit. "This is curious, Charlie. I mean, this beautiful woman...okay, let's forget that. Of all the book shops in town, Angelique comes into yours. Not only does she go out of her way to come inside, but once inside, she glances around and then leaves without a word. Is that what you're saying? How do you explain that?"

"That's what I'm saying, and I don't have to explain anything."

"Charlie, it's better if you cooperate. If you make our job harder, we're going to make things harder for you – and I'm not talking about tax authorities and all that other stuff."

"What're you saying?"

"I'm saying, Charlie, that I want the truth. You give me that in all its excruciating detail, and we're out of your hair...unless, of course, you're tangled up in something else. Even then, if you level with us, we might be able to help you a little. Now, Charlie, the truth and nothing but the truth, so help you God."

Charlie leaned back against his desk and folded his arms. "Okay," he began after a few moments of intense silence. "The door chime rang, just as you said, and in walks this lady, blonde hair, fancy clothes, spiked heels, the whole package. It was almost like a scene out of a movie. She's gorgeous, and she looks around without saying a single word. I could see her smile from time to time – her nose has that little crinkle when her lips move – but not a single word, at least not at that moment. At first, I keep my mouth closed. I try to be cool. I mean, I don't have a lot of customers, certainly none that look like her, and so I'm not going to chase her out by pressuring her to look at this or that. Most of it is crap, as you know.

"Anyway, after a few minutes of browsing – mainly at the pre-1700s stuff, and she even pulled a couple of the better volumes and thumbed through them – she turns to me and she says, 'Goodbye.' That's it. 'Goodbye.' Not another word, and she leaves. I kid you not. Okay, so maybe I went to the window to get a good look at her sashaying down the street. Man oh man – we say stuff like that in Canada, just like the Americans. Man oh man..." Charlie wagged his head and grinned at Nesbit. "Do you get the picture now? Do you want more? She came into the shop, looked around, and left. We didn't talk philosophy or anything else. And what you might have trouble understanding is that she didn't disclose her criminal plans, if that's you're trying to sniff out. Why else would you come here and ask about her? Now, I have one more word for both of you – beat it, or I'll call the cops."

Nesbit smiled and emitted a forced laugh. Thwait, on the contrary, was stone-faced, and one word from Nesbit and he would have cuffed Charlie and hustled him downtown, as the Americans say.

"Okay, Charlie," Nesbit said, not laughing this time. "Okay, I get the picture. I'm willing to take your word that things happened exactly as you described. But if she tells us a different story, I'm going to be upset. Last chance: Is there anything else you want to say?"

"Maaaan oh maaaan..."

Nesbit nodded as he and Thwait left the shop.

A few minutes after the door shut, Charlie walked to the window and glanced up, down, and across the street. When he was certain that he wasn't being observed, he locked the door and turned over the OPEN sign. Stepping across to the pre-1700 shelves, he retrieved the Beaumont and Fletcher folio. Charlie had always been fond of some of their plays, especially Beaumont's *The Knight of the Burning Pestle*, which seemed funnier and far less conventional than Shakespeare's comedies. Carefully opening the book, he ran his fingers across the title page, and then carried the book into the backroom and shut the door behind him. A few minutes later, he emerged from the room, flipped the CLOSED sign over, and took his stool behind the register. He retrieved a tabloid from his drawer and settled down for a long and uneventful day.

Chapter 4

Nesbit and Thwait went to the station after leaving the shop, crossing the city in record time, as Thwait boasted. Once there, they met with other officers and debriefed them on the case and their meeting with Charlie. The meeting took place in a fairly large, nondescript, windowless conference room. There were no pictures or decoration of any kind in the room, which was dominated by a long, wooden table, on either side of which all the officers were sitting. Nesbit sat at one end of the table, with Thwait next to him, and on the opposite end sat the Chief, the head of the station. On the table in front of the Chief was a neat stack of papers, a manila folder, a pencil, and a glass of water. The same items were on the table in front of all the other officers in the room, but unlike the others the Chief hadn't touched any of these things, not even the water. The Chief was tapping the eraser end of his pencil on the folder as Nesbit finished talking, having described Angelique, detailed her methods, and offered an analysis of the meeting with Charlie at his shop.

"What's your gut feeling on this Saunders chap, Constable Thwait?" the Chief asked when Nesbit had finally finished speaking. "Is he hardboiled or in cahoots with Dubois? That kind of behavior rubs me the wrong way."

"It's clear there's more to him than meets the eye," interjected Nesbit. "He knows too much. Besides, people don't come on hard-nosed unless they're trying to hide something. And what could he be trying to hide? Most likely his relationship with Angelique and the heist she's planning."

"Is that right, Constable Thwait?"

"Absolutely," replied Nesbit. "Angelique was spotted leaving his shop. This would be extraordinary if she weren't planning something with him. You see, she's all business, and she likes to travel light."

The Chief looked at Nesbit and then at Thwait. "Travel light? What does that mean, Constable Thwait?"

"It means she doesn't like any extra weight or baggage when she's working," answered Nesbit. "Anything extra – a souvenir, reading material, whatever – could slow her down and limit her mobility. This is also why she travels alone. People are simply another form of baggage."

The Chief was a little over six feet tall and, because of his closely-cropped hair and his trim, muscular physique, he had the look and bearing of a military officer. If the Chief had one quirk, it was his tendency to squint (usually with his left eye) as if he was having trouble seeing or was a heavy smoker, neither being the case. Squinting at Thwait, he asked, "So you're positive that she's on the job and not visiting the sights or looking for a small gift for a relative or friend? We get millions of people here every year, and even some of the worst of these individuals can think of things other than their crimes."

"Without a doubt," Nesbit said. "I've been watching her for years, and I can tell when she's working and when she's on vacation. And I can assure you she didn't come to the UK for vacation."

"Do you agree with this, Constable Thwait?"

"He does, and furthermore he agrees that she's after a piece of British heritage, a rare artifact of some kind."

"Okay, I've already heard that. I just need to be certain you two aren't chasing shadows."

"She's no shadow," Nesbit replied.

The Chief adjusted his tie, which was a little loose on his muscular neck, after which he resumed tapping his pencil against the folder. "Thwait, are you positive about Saunders? He's working with Dubois, right?"

"I have a gut feeling that's never wrong," said Nesbit. "I'm afraid we don't know much about him, but I'm convinced it's because he's trying to fly under the radar, which only supports our contention that he's connected to Angelique. She doesn't work with high-visibility people. Angelique likes to operate in the shadows where she can move freely and safely, and the last thing she wants is a light shining on her business."

"You mentioned Saunders is a Canadian."

"We pulled a copy of his passport," said one of the officers to the left of the Chief. "It's in your folder." The Chief turned and squinted at the officer, who immediately became silent.

"All right, so he's Canadian. Do you know anything else about him? Do you have background that might shed light on his motivations and methods of operation? Can you or anyone else tell me why he's been in the country so long – several months, right? – if he's only here to pull off something with Dubois? Constable Thwait, I have to tell you that this is one of most troubling aspects of this case, at least insofar as his involvement in concerned." The Chief scanned the officers around the table, all of whom looked down or avoided his squinting gaze, except Nesbit. "Constable Thwait, do you have anything else to add?"

"Clearly, we need some more information on Charlie," Nesbit offered. "It would be helpful if we could get some background checks on the man – criminal history, work permits, immigration records, and the like. The Canadian embassy must have some information. As for his time in country, it's not unusual for Angelique to connect with persons who are familiar with the region where the job is going down. Such people offer her a particular kind of experience and cover needed to pull off a job – pull it off successfully, that is. My gut feeling is that whatever she's doing, it's so big that she sent a vanguard – Charlie – ahead of her to establish the necessary bona fides, contacts, and so forth to enable her to purloin this monument of British heritage when the time comes. Remember," he added, as the Chief and all the other officers were looking in his direction, "Angelique doesn't do the small stuff. She's only after the big items, the irreplaceable items, the priceless objects, and these often require long-term planning to pull off successfully."

Okay," said the Chief, nodding his head as if in thought. "Okay, we can pull some background, but let me emphasize one thing. We need to tread lightly with respect to Charlie. You're certain he's not from the States? We don't need some stupid mistake turning this into an international incident. And that goes for Dubois, too, since she isn't a British subject. Are we all clear on this?" He scanned the officers, who all nodded their heads in agreement. "Inspector Sedgwick," he added, turning to the trim, well-dressed young woman on his right, "One of your officers pulled Saunders' passport?"

"Yes, Chief, but I haven't had a chance to look carefully at it. I haven't verified…"

"Don't worry about it. Pull some additional material on Saunders. Constable Thwait, I presume you have what you need on Dubois?"

Thwait glanced at Nesbit, and Nesbit nodded his head to him.

"Good, then I'll expect regular reports from you and Agent Nesbit. The Chief dropped his pencil and pushed his chair back.

"Excuse me," Nesbit said as the Chief was about to stand, "We could use some additional resources. This is a big case, and Angelique is the slickest operator you'll ever see. Tom and I are certainly up to the task, but we need extra support to ensure that we stop her in time."

"Maybe Inspector Sedgwick could offer some assistance." He scooted his chair back up to the table and picked up his pencil. Squinting at Nesbit, he resumed tapping his pencil against the folder in front of him.

24

Nesbit glanced at Sedgwick. Grace Sedgwick (and no one ever called her by her first name) was a few years older than Thwait and one of the station's rising stars. Tall, athletic, and attractive, she was an enigma to Thwait because she wore nothing but nondescript business suits, allowed her lifeless hair to hang straight to her shoulders, and never used makeup, not even to mask the slight droop of the left side of her mouth. Turning to the Chief, her lip betraying a more noticeable droop than usual, she looked at him as if he were asking her to do something inexplicable. While she was happy to help the investigation in almost any way, she was at the same time hesitant to work with Nesbit because of the man's cocky demeanor, although neither he nor anyone else could cow her.

"Yes," Nesbit asserted. "We need eyes on Charlie. We need 24/7 on his shop and the same on his flat, if Seggy finds his address." He nodded at Sedgwick to assure her that this was going to be the biggest case of her career. "Charlie's lines will need to be tapped as well."

The Chief squinted at him without comment.

"Once we locate Angelique, which could happen through the tap on Charlie's line or when she comes into his shop again, we'll need several officers on her. Though the best criminals only need one maybe two bodies, Angelique is better than the best. At a minimum I would suggest three or four at all times, more if you have them. Seggy could help manage them."

The Chief's squint became more prominent, practically turning his eyes into horizontal slits of skin. Without moving his head, he flipped his pencil around and began tapping its point on the table's surface.

"Furthermore, I'll need a command and control center – this room will do nicely – to coordinate our efforts both in the field and in the office. I'm sure you can appreciate how big this case is and what it will do to everyone's career when I arrest Angelique and, of course, Charlie."

There were snickers from a couple officers near Thwait. Thwait nervously glanced in their direction and then back at the Chief, who had also shot a quick look in their direction.

The Chief was silent for a moment. Squinting at Nesbit and then at Thwait, he said, "Is that all, Constable Thwait?"

"For now," said Nesbit. "But things are capable of changing any second. If we flush her out of hiding, we may need more officers. I would also add that we need officers at border control. At some point, Angelique's going to slip out of the country as fast as she can, and Charlie is likely to be right on her heels. Remember, she doesn't want to leave behind any evidence that could implicate her, and so we have to assume that she chose Charlie in part because he's as slick as she is, or nearly so."

There were some more faint snickers from the other side of the table, but these were quickly muffled by an abortive cough when the Chief glanced at the source.

The Chief put his pencil down on the table with deliberation and then leaned back in his chair. Once again eyeing Nesbit and then Thwait, who practically quailed each time the Chief squinted at him, he shook his head slowly. "Agent Nesbit, I think we all recognize the relative importance of this investigation – I suppose that's why HQ requested Interpol's assistance – but what you and Constable Thwait need to recognize is that we're not dealing with a murder or an attempt on a Royal or an MP." There was another cough, which immediately died out when the Chief hesitated. "While you and I may think this case merits the highest attention, I can assure you that others are not of a similar mind. There's no way to get a tap on anyone's line unless, as I suggested, there's an attempt on a Royal or an MP, and even then we couldn't get one this side of six months, if that. As for officers" – he made a sweeping gesture to the individuals seated around the table – "what you see here is practically the entire station, and each of these men and women has at least twenty open investigations on their desks as we speak – and each one a major investigation to someone. Agent Nesbit, even if I wanted to, I couldn't give you anything close to what you're asking for. For now, Constable Thwait can remain on the case – with the understanding that I might pull him at any time for other duties – and Inspector Sedgwick will spend a couple hours later this afternoon on background. I wish I could do more." The Chief pushed his chair back again and hesitated. "As for a command and control center, this room is not available. Constable Thwait's desk or your hotel room, which I understand has a nice table in it, will have to do for now."

One of the officers began to cough and quickly left the room.

Nesbit hesitated and scanned the faces of the officers around the table, as if he expected one of them to object and plead his cause. When no one seemed so inclined, he raised his left hand and said, "With all due respect, I'm not sure you understand the implications of what I'm saying. Angelique is skittish, and once she gets it into her pretty head to leave, she's gone and there won't be a thing we can do about it. Case closed, and all our efforts – not to mention the crown jewel of British heritage – are down the drain."

"Constable Thwait, I can assure you that I fully understand what you're saying, but I don't think you understand the implications of what I'm saying, or whose saying in this instance matters most." This time a couple of the officers adjusted themselves in their chairs. The officer who had been coughing returned, but immediately left again when his coughing came back. The Chief paused and squinted at both Nesbit and Thwait, neither of whom was entirely certain whom he was squinting at. "If I gave you a quarter of what you're asking for, this station would be unable to fulfill the duties that it has been sworn to fulfill. I truly would like to do more, but until someone donates a few million spare pounds to the investigation, I'm afraid I can only give you what I noted earlier." He paused in thought. "I will offer you this, however: Any of the officers here are free to help out as they see fit, provided that it is done on their own time and that their efforts in no way affect station resources or any other investigation."

Nesbit glanced down and then at Thwait and the other officers. "I completely understand," he began, as if he finally understood the Chief's position. "I may have seemed a little out of line, but I can assure you that I was motivated purely by the implications to the Crown, British heritage, and British pride should Angelique and Charlie succeed."

The Chief placed his pencil back on the table but continued to squint at Nesbit and Thwait.

"Yes, Tom and I will take whatever we can get." Nesbit looked at Thwait and winked as if both he and Thwait knew that this wouldn't be the end of it. "And we'll keep you updated, as I think you rightly requested."

The Chief got up, after which all the other officers except Nesbit slid their chairs back and got up from the table.

"May I ask one more question?" Nesbit said loud enough to be heard over the din of the moving chairs. "Does anyone know the publication date of Shakespeare's First Folio or what a…" He paused while a couple officers were looking at him and pulled out a small notebook from his breast pocket. After thumbing through a few pages, he added, "Yes, yes, here it is. Can someone tell us what's so special about Shakespeare's 18th century editors?"

Chapter 5

When the meeting was over, Nesbit and Thwait began walking through the dim and bland hallways toward the main entrance of the building. Nesbit was calm and confident. There was even a slight, contemptuous smile at the corners of his mouth. Thwait, though, was visibly concerned.

"What do you think, sir?" he asked, hesitant to offer his own opinion.

"I think it went well. Your Chief is naturally reluctant to apply the appropriate manpower to the case – it's his job to be reluctant – but I'm certain that once he truly understands what's happening under his very nose, he'll give us what we need. However," he added, stopping and facing Thwait. "However, we will need to keep on him from time to time, otherwise he's likely to think that we can do it all by ourselves."

Thwait eyed him as if he and Nesbit had been in different meetings. "The resources," he began reluctantly, "the resources…they don't exist. The Chief was right that most of our officers were at the table."

"My friend, yours is one group, and there are hundreds like them in other buildings throughout the city. You can't protect London with only a handful of officers. But if your group is maxed out, the Chief can obtain them elsewhere. It's done all the time."

"I suppose that makes sense, but I don't think he'd give us everything. Maybe in a best-case scenario half…"

Nesbit eyed him raised his eyebrows. "A wise man once said, 'If you want five, demand ten.'

"What? I don't get it, sir. Who said that?"

"Me. I'm only hoping for half. If I had only asked for what he could reasonably procure, I might have got half of that, maybe less. Trust me, Tom, I know exactly what I'm doing." He continued down the hallway and after a few more steps said over his shoulder to Thwait, who was now a few feet behind him, "They can laugh all they want. And, yes, I could tell a couple of your boys were laughing. We'll see how funny everything is when we arrest Angelique, Charlie, and all the others conspiring with her." He was quiet for a moment as they approached the entrance. Before Nesbit pushed the heavy, glass door, he stopped and turned again to Thwait. "One more thing. I want to know if Charlie is right about the folio and those editors. Do you think you could pressure one of your officers, maybe Siggy, to get on that, too?"

"Inspector Sedgwick."

"Whatever."

Chapter 6

Charlie couldn't help puzzling over the inexplicable arrival of the men. It was obvious that they were probing him for something, but what was less clear was whether he or the woman Angelique was object of the probe. It was somewhat troubling to think that he might be the object, but since he had experience in these kinds of things, he wasn't ready to panic, at least not yet. He knew they couldn't prove anything. If they had the goods on him, they would have arrested him right away and wouldn't have wasted everyone's time with their inane chatter and stupid questions. And where did they get the idea that he came from Canada?

Angelique was another matter. He remembered her clearly (and the lead officer was right: He couldn't forget the woman both because of her beauty and the fact that she was practically the only person to visit the shop for quite some time), and he tried to envision a scenario in which someone like her could be involved in something of such importance that London's finest would be following her. Of course, he had seen a few good-looking women involved in crime, but by and large most of the women were hard looking and unattractive, as if crime itself had made them unfit for modeling agencies or fine dresses. That being said, he had trouble imagining what she could have done – robbery, extortion, murder? None of it made sense with her looks. Later that evening after picking up several slivers of old paper and flushing them down the toilet in his flat, Charlie promised himself that he would find out what the woman was up to if she ever came back to his shop.

Charlie was at his shop the following day as if he had never seen the men or heard of Angelique. The cold, drizzly weather outside made the windows gray and there were fewer people on the streets than normal. But while the gloomy weather matched to some extent his gloomy thoughts, he knew enough not to brood over things unless one planned to take action – brooding pointlessly made one careless, neurotic, and often vulnerable. Seated behind the register, tabloid in hand, he was prepared for a long and hopefully uneventful day. Sometime in the early afternoon, a delivery man brought a small box of books and placed it on the floor near the register. After signing for the delivery, Charlie followed the brown-uniformed man to the door and locked it after he exited. Turning over the OPEN sign, he casually took the box to the back room, where he examined its contents. There were several small books, each carefully wrapped, along with a brief note from the sender, stating that the contents were of "high value."

Charlie shelved all the books but one (a 1612 quarto of one of John Webster's masterpieces, a play titled *The White Devil*), which he slipped into his coat pocket, and then reopened the shop. Positioning himself on his chair behind the cash register, he picked up his magazine and began to read. "The pathetic fools," he mumbled as he finished one article and then started another. Finishing the latter article, one with more pictures than text, he closed the magazine and tossed it into a small wastebasket near his feet. "I can't believe anyone's interested in idiots who do nothing," he added.

Feeling the slight tug of the small book in his pocket, Charlie decided to leave for the day. It was still early, of course, but he knew that he wasn't sacrificing any sales. Even if the stars were aligned and he could reasonably expect one or two sales by day's end, he also realized that a couple of sales wouldn't be enough to keep the shop afloat or, more importantly, offset the pleasure he would have examining the book. Indeed, he looked forward to touching the pages, caressing the lines of the very book that was published in Webster's lifetime, and doing so alone and without fear of interruption. After locking the door (and glancing at the window to make sure he flipped the OPEN sign over), he quickly walked six blocks to the Underground and hopped onto the train for an hour's ride to his neighborhood.

Charlie lived alone in a small, two-room flat on the third floor in a nondescript building about three and a half blocks from the Underground. The place was as unpretentious as the neighborhood, but it was only temporary and he was certain that he would be able to afford a bigger place in a couple of years or so. Besides, he had lived in smaller, less comfortable places, and there was a lot to say for having one's own kitchenette and a bathroom that one could safely use any time day or night. There was also a lot to be thankful for with respect to his immediate neighbors, working-class families who left him alone and didn't ask any questions.

After gently placing the book on the small table next to the wall and yanking the chain to the overhead light, Charlie pulled up a chair and began examining the book. The cover, which was made from a fine-quality, red Moroccan leather (he could tell by its texture and smell), was a later addition, most likely from the early 19th century, judging by its condition. The pages, on the contrary, appeared genuine. They had the same feel and smell as those from other English publications of the early 17th century, and the watermark on one of the pages was dated 1612, the correct date of the play's first publication. Charlie also examined the type face on several pages (checking for indentations from the weight of the press and tracking certain letters for signs of increasing wear or breakage as they were reused throughout the text), which had been set by an anonymous compositor. His examination wouldn't be the final word – for that a chemist would have to determine if the composition of the paper matched authenticated books of the same period – but it was enough to convince him that he had the genuine article and that he could get some decent money from it with the right buyers.

Satisfied that the purchase had been a sound one, Charlie turned to the title page and examined the engraving, which showed a delicately drawn profile of a waterfowl standing near a lake. There was a handful of reeds on the shore of the lake, mainly behind the bird, while smaller tufts of grass were being crushed under the animal's feet. He also noticed, in the right-hand corner of the engraving, a strange deformation – it looked as if the engraving plate had cracked during the impression – which not only added to the aesthetic quality of the image but would also increase its value to prospective purchasers. Smiling, moved by the beauty of the image, Charlie reached across the table and retrieved a razor blade from a stack of old tabloids in the corner. Blade in hand, he repositioned the book so that the covers lay flat on the table while he held the page with the waterfowl perpendicular to the front and back covers and, placing the edge of the blade as close as he could to the binding's stitching, carefully cut the entire length of the page. Once the page was free, he put it aside and trimmed the remnants that were left in the book so that it was difficult to tell that a page had been removed. Picking up the page and momentarily admiring its beauty, he slipped it into a plastic sleeve and dropped the sleeve in a large, cushioned mailer, which he sealed and addressed, and stuck both the mailer and the book into his coat pocket. Charlie made a mental note to drop the mailer in a box on his way to the shop and to place the book on the shelf next to others of the same period and in a similar condition.

From time to time, Charlie received other old books at his shop. In almost every case, he either pocketed the book or placed it in a briefcase and brought it home to be subjected to similar operations. It seemed ironic that whatever value he lost when the books were deprived of their engravings, he more than recouped the lost value by selling the engravings individually. For example, one could take a folio that was worth, say, 1,000 pounds, deprive it of its engravings and thus reduce the value to about 900 pounds. The engravings, however, could bring in as much as 500 pounds each, which would easily make up for the loss on the book, especially if one were able to retrieve several engravings from a single book. You couldn't get a better return on your investment.

This is not to suggest that there weren't risks involved in damaging valuable artifacts, but the gains outweighed the risks, especially if the gains enabled him to remain in business until he could develop a steady client base. Charlie sold the engravings to unscrupulous dealers and organizers of antiquarian book shows, and his profits enabled him to acquire additional books that he could slice up for a steady, under-the-table revenue stream. But while he received a fairly regular supply of books at his shop, he generally avoided such operations in his shop. He knew that if he were caught in the act, he would have to endure a number of unpleasantries that he preferred to avoid.

Chapter 7

One unusually bright morning nearly a week after Nesbit and Thwait spoke to Charlie, an attractive young woman entered his shop. She was tall and slim, and she had shimmering blonde hair and an equally striking string of pearls that adorned her long, graceful neck. Although she was dressed in an elegant white dress (silk?) and wore spiked heels, she didn't appear to be a straggler from an upscale party that had wandered into the shop by mistake. On the contrary, the confident manner in which she entered and checked out the contents on the shelves suggested that she was either a potential customer or someone from a nearby shop sizing up the competition.

Charlie didn't immediately recognize the woman, but when she smiled briefly at him and waved off his offer to help (her glistening red nails and sparking gold bracelet were giveaways), he remembered the woman in the dark dress and sunglasses who had come into his shop several days ago, and he was nearly certain that the two women were one and the same. For a few moments, Charlie considered addressing her by name (didn't the police call her Angelique?), but he decided to wait until he found out what the woman, Angelique or her double, wanted before becoming familiar. If it was Angelique, he was keenly interested in what she was doing to draw the interest of the Metropolitan police.

Slowly moving from bookcase to bookcase, the woman ran her fingers across the bindings of several books and occasionally picked up one and carefully examined it. Charlie was impressed by the way she handled the books – retrieving them by the center of the binding to prevent damage to the cover and cradling each one in her left hand while carefully turning pages with her right to protect the integrity of the spine – and then by the seriousness with which she considered their contents. Neither Nesbit nor Thwait knew enough about books to pull off a decent charade. When she had examined five or six books from different sections, she walked over to within a few feet of the register behind which Charlie was impassively seated and inquired about American books, specifically mid-19th century first editions.

"Hawthorne? Emerson? Twain? Howells? Perhaps you're interested in poetry? Longfellow, Whitman, Poe? We don't have any at the moment, but I get them all from time to time. However, they go as quickly as they come in. Maybe if you're looking for something specific I may be able to procure it.

34

We have connections with dealers and estate sales all around the world. Recently…"

"That's fine," she interrupted and smiled vaguely, alluringly. "Let me think about it and maybe we can talk."

She turned and went back to the shelves, this time to the older books, the pre-1800 section. Pulling out the Webster, the very book he had operated on, she thumbed through it and then, turning and holding it in the air, told him that the book was damaged.

"The front plate is missing. And, if I'm not mistaken, it looks as if it had been removed recently. Without the plate, I'd say this book is worth considerably less than what you're asking."

Charlie smiled uneasily. "What would you consider a fair price?"

He stepped out from behind the register and walked over to where the woman was standing. Seeing her up close, he couldn't help admiring the gentle curve of her eyebrows, the manner in which they arched upward when she spoke, and her nose, which was almost too narrow to be attractive but which somehow looked beautiful on her stunning face. He also noticed the lines of her red lips, especially on the right, which continued to smile slightly even when the rest of her face was not. If all this weren't enough, her perfume began to permeate his senses, filling him with the desire to touch her left cheek with the back of his right hand. He kept his distance, of course.

"No, I'm not interested because of the damage, and I wouldn't recommend asking such a high price if you want customers to think you're a knowledgeable, reputable dealer."

Charlie took the book from her hand. Hesitating for a moment, he smiled and thanked her for noticing. Before he was halfway back to the register, the woman called out to him over her shoulder, "Here's another one. The plate is missing in this one, too, and again you're asking full price."

Charlie retrieved that book as well. He wasn't able to move before she spotted another book with the same problem and then another. Turning and facing him, she smiled and slowly shook her head. "I'll bet there are lots more here, Mr. Sanders. If you engage in this kind of practice, I don't see how you'll stay in business much longer."

"It's Saunders. I buy books wherever I can, often in bulk, and sometimes I get these volumes. They still have their value, regardless of whether or not you think I'm offering a fair price. But how did you get my name?"

The woman smiled again, although this time her expression was friendly, as if she were speaking to someone she knew. "I'm sorry, Mr. Saunders…"

"Charlie."

"I'm sorry, Charlie. I was only trying to point out something that might hurt your business. I suppose many people wouldn't notice or even care. I think you do, though."

Charlie was about to thank her for her concern, but she suddenly turned and walked to the other side of the shop and began examining other books.

"I still don't know how you got my name. Is there something I can help you with?" he asked, although she wasn't facing him.

"Don't worry, Charlie, I'm not with the book police, if there is such a thing."

"I didn't think so." Charlie went toward the door to glance out the window. It was a natural move, not unlike licking one's lips when people are staring, but when he looked up the street, he noticed the two officers who had visited earlier crossing the street and heading straight toward his shop. If Angelique had actually done something, her presence in his shop might encourage the police to delve into his own personal affairs.

Turning toward the woman, Charlie said, "If your name is Angelique, you might be interested to know there are a couple of officers, one from Interpol, coming this way."

"What?" She turned around and looked toward the window next to which Charlie was standing. "Is there a back door?"

"Go in there," he replied, motioning with his head toward the storeroom. "Close the door behind you. Be quick."

The door snapped shut just as Nesbit and Thwait entered the shop, setting off the tinkle of the door chime.

"Howdy, Charlie," Nesbit intoned, speaking as if he had just heard a joke.

"Hello, Mr. Saunders," Thwait added, trying to appear as amused as Nesbit but failing to pull it off. There was nothing mean or cynical in either his looks or his tone of voice.

"Well, if it isn't Laurel and Hardy," Charlie replied, smiling in a way that made it clear that he wasn't pleased to see them.

"Who?" Thwait looked at Nesbit.

"Before your time, my friend. I'll explain it later." Nesbit turned to Charlie. "You're not surprised to see us, are you?"

"No, but I'm not thrilled, either. Is there something I can do for you?"

"I don't know," said Nesbit. "That depends on you." He cleared his throat. "We, my colleague and I, had a report of a woman coming into your shop a little while ago. I believe she was dressed in white…"

"She was wearing an evening gown."

"Thanks, Tom. Yes, she was wearing a white, evening gown."

"This early in the morning? If that's all you're looking for, you'll find a number of ladies like that in the store next door. Lots of dresses, lots of ladies, and I'm sure you can find an evening gown or two, if you know what I mean."

"Funny. Someone noticed her coming in to your shop, although she seems to have slipped out…unless, of course, she is behind door number one." Nesbit gestured to the door behind the register with a movement of his head.

Charlie walked over to Nesbit and stood directly in front of him. It was surprising that he didn't seem to bear any of the shocks of middle age that crossed his own face, none of the lines or the heavy pores or the scars. Nesbit was close to Charlie's age, and yet he seemed relatively untouched by the years, except for the faint lines around his eyes. Maybe it was his suit, which didn't betray a hint of city grime. Thwait, on the other hand, was simply an overgrown child in an ill-fitting suit with a constricting collar.

"If she's behind door number one, as you say, you'll never know unless you can pull something legal out of your…pocket, shall we say." Charlie didn't attempt to smile this time.

"Fair enough, Charlie boy. But let me tell you something," Nesbit began while pointing his index finger at Charlie's nose, "If you're in bed with her, and I'm only speaking figuratively, you're going to find yourself in big trouble."

"Get your finger out of my face."

Nesbit slowly nodded and took a step back.

"What do you want from me?"

"Only the truth, Charlie boy. Is Angelique here?"

"Excuse me?"

"Perhaps I didn't make myself clear. Is Angelique somewhere in your shop?"

"What's the matter with your eyes?"

Nesbit glanced at Thwait. "This doesn't seem to be going well, Tom. I'll ask him another way." Turning back to Charlie, Nesbit glowered at him and said, "I don't think you realize what you're doing. I was willing to give you the benefit of the doubt – maybe you're only a dupe – but now I'm beginning to think you're in on it with her. So let me ask you one last time. Is Angelique here, possibly in that backroom of yours?"

"You want the truth from me? Why don't you tell me the truth first, and maybe – maybe – I'll answer your questions."

Thwait took a step in Charlie's direction, but Nesbit motioned him to stop with a gentle, backward movement of his right hand.

"Fair enough. We want to talk to her about some unfortunate activities she may be involved in. One of our men spotted her in this area, and we came over to see if she had come into your shop. Now, two questions: Did she come in here and, if she did, is she in your back room?"

Charlie was quiet for a moment. Shaking his head and glancing at his feet, he told Nesbit that she hadn't come into the shop and, to deflect questions as to whether he was certain, added that no one had been here today. "Except you two. You're the first."

"No one else?"

"Not even the postman. However, you're welcome to hang around here as long as you want. I'm sure he'll be here later in the afternoon. But you'll have to get your own chairs, because I certainly don't have any for you. Maybe you have some in your car?"

Nesbit slowly nodded his head and rubbed his chin. "Okay, I'll bite. The shop does seem empty." Turning to Thwait, Nesbit winked as if that was their signal to leave, but instead of leaving he turned back to Charlie. "Charlie, you wouldn't mind if we had a little peek behind the door, would you? I mean, if you're telling the truth, you certainly have nothing to worry about."

Thwait didn't say anything, although the puzzled look on his florid face suggested that he, too, had something on his mind.

Charlie shrugged his shoulders and started to walk over to the door. Stopping suddenly, he turned around and looked at Nesbit. "You know, I don't care whether you look in the room or not, but I don't think I'm going to open it now. There's something here you're not telling me, and so I think I'll wait for a warrant, if you don't mind."

"Are you sure?"

"What would you advise?" he asked, looking directly at Thwait.

38

"I…I…I think it's better to cooperate," the younger officer stammered, surprised that anyone would ask him such a question.

"All right," Charlie said. Glancing at Nesbit, he walked confidently toward the register, but when he came close to his stool, he slipped and got entangled in the stool's legs, bringing the stool, himself, and nearly the register to the floor with a loud crash. "Damn," he groaned, as he slowly rose from the floor and held his side.

Nesbit and Thwait, not quite believing what they were witnessing, remained where they were and watched Charlie as he stood up somewhat unsteadily.

"You okay?" Nesbit finally asked, trying to mask his irritation over one more thing that prevented them from checking out the room.

"Would you like a hand?" Thwait asked, taking a step toward the register.

Charlie shook his head and gripped the top of the stool to steady himself. Taking a deep breath, he carefully eased himself onto the seat while he held his left side and grimaced.

"Would you like us to take you somewhere?" Thwait asked, starting to think that Charlie could actually be injured.

"No, I need to rest for a few minutes."

"Perhaps while you're resting, my colleague and I could take a quick look in your room," Nesbit proffered while Charlie bent over and quietly groaned.

Without looking up, Charlie shouted hoarsely for the two men to leave. "If you come back, bring a warrant," he gasped.

Once outside of the shop and heading toward the car, Nesbit smiled and said, "Quite a performance."

"He seemed to have hurt himself."

"Accidents happen even during the best performances."

"So you think she's in the shop? Maybe we should have stayed."

"No," he replied, shaking his head. They got into the car and, after Nesbit buckled in on the passenger side, he leaned his shoulder against the door.

"Please be careful, sir. The door sometimes…"

"No, there was no reason to stay, my friend. She wasn't there."

Thwait jerked the car into traffic. "I'm sorry, sir," he began hesitantly after a few moments, "But I don't understand. Didn't you notice…"

"If she were truly in the back room, it would have been folly on Charlie's part to let us come so close. We might have heard something from inside – a sniffle, the rustle of an expensive fabric, the tinkle of something accidently knocked aside – and once that happened, Charlie knew that there was no force in the world that could have prevented us from opening the door and investigating further. No, I'm convinced she wasn't there."

"I don't get it, sir. Why the act? You still think it was an act, right?"

"Yes, of course. Charlie can't fool me. He was just calling our bluff."

"Calling our bluff? I'm afraid I don't understand."

"He was trying to find out if we knew anything. Had we stayed, it would have been a clear indication that we knew something and hence were willing to put up with his second-rate performance to get what we came after. Since we didn't stay, he's pretty confident that we don't have a thing on him and couldn't get a warrant even if we wanted to."

"We don't, really, know anything, at least not about him."

"But he doesn't know that."

"Excuse me? I'm afraid I still don't understand, sir."

Nesbit glanced at Thwait and then turned his eyes back to the busy streets, where Thwait was moving quickly around slower vehicles. "Since we didn't stay, Charlie is convinced that we don't know what he and Angelique are up to, right? Does this make sense so far? Watch out for that... Okay, this is exactly what we want him to think. If he's convinced that we don't know anything, there's a good chance that he's going to act a little more freely, more brazenly (and, why not, since we're apparently clueless?). Ultimately, this will increase the likelihood that he'll figuratively trip up somewhere and, when that happens, you and I will be there to catch him. Now do you understand?"

"Sort of. But there's one more thing, sir."

"Yes, I know. We need to speak to your man who spotted Angelique. Did he say he saw her near Charlie's shop or going into it?"

"I don't remember. Sir, did you happen to notice the perfume smell in the shop? It seemed rather strong and fresh. Is it possible that..."

"Yes, I noticed it, but it was nothing. It probably blew in from the outside. Let's not get sidetracked by unimportant details. Watch out for that..."

Chapter 8

Once Nesbit and Thwait were gone, Charlie slowly walked to the outside door and, after taking a quick peek through the window, locked the door. Rubbing his side, he went to the storeroom and tapped lightly on it, telling Angelique at the same time that the coast was clear. "They're gone," he said in a normal voice. The door receded into the darkened storeroom and Angelique appeared.

"Are you okay?" she asked him, after she glanced around the shop. "I heard some commotion, and I was afraid that they'd done something to you, you know. Some of them are brutes." There was a look of genuine concern on her lovely face.

"No...well, yes. No commotion, I just...I just stumbled, that's all."

"That's nice. I mean, I'm glad you're not hurt. Are you sure?" She stood looking at Charlie as if she wanted to say more but couldn't quite make up her mind.

He smiled and, for a few moments, silently looked at her face and eyes. "So tell me, Angie," he began, finally breaking the increasingly uncomfortable silence. "Yes, Angelique. Tell me, Angelique, why are they looking for you?"

"Do you need to ask?" She smiled as if she were flirting with him and walked (in Charlie's eyes, floated) over to a shelf of books that appeared to be 19th century editions, at least according to their titles.

"Aren't you Charles Sanders, the antiquarian bookseller?"

"Saunders. If you're not sure, you can have one of my business cards."

Angelique turned and walked slowly around the room, pausing now and then to examine the spine of some book but not touching it. "Do you have a license or identification?" she asked as she looked at one particular spine.

"Do I have a driver's license or identification? Of course, but I'll only show it to you if you're going to buy something. Say, how about a nice poem instead? 'Ah, broken is the golden bowl! The spirit is flown forever!'"

She suddenly stopped and slowly walked back to Charlie. With the index finger of her left hand, she traced a line from the top of his upper lip to his chin. "Let's start with a driver's license," she practically purred.

Charlie fished his wallet out of his back pocket and pulled out the license. "Satisfied?" After placing it back in his wallet, he looked at her eyes intently for several moments while she returned his stare. "All right, it's your turn," he said. "Tell me what you're up to and why you're in my shop."

She hesitated. "I heard you're very good."

"What?"

"I also heard you're discrete."

"Where did you hear that?"

Angelique tried to touch Charlie's cheek with the tips of her fingers, but this time he grabbed her wrist and held it tightly. "Start talking or get out of here. And don't try to snow me. I know those clowns are following you, and I don't like them hanging around my shop. It's bad for business."

She yanked herself from his grasp and her soft, smooth features momentarily became hard and serious. "All right, Charlie, have it your way. I represent a very important client who's looking for a very special book."

"I got all kinds of books."

"No, he wants a specific book. The book is unique, one of a kind, and I'm told that you alone have the kind of talent needed to acquire this particular item." She smiled briefly while rubbing her wrist and then adjusted her necklace.

"Lady, you're telling me nothing. Who's been talking about me?"

"I have my sources. But if I'm wrong about you, if you're not up to the job, I'll go somewhere else to get what my client needs."

Angelique glanced at the door as if she were about to leave. Charlie's interest, however, was piqued, and despite his usual wariness, he was loathe to let her go until he found out the whole story, especially if there was something in it that he could exploit for a few pounds. "Wait a minute. I'm looking for information, that's all. Who's this client of yours?"

"That's confidential. You know how it is."

"Yeah, I know how it is." He paused and looked at her, observing the manner in which she adjusted her shoulders and moved her head, and, when she glanced over her left shoulder, he noticed a small mole near her right earlobe. That little blemish made her seem less perfect, more attractive. "Okay, so you have this unnamed client that may or may not have recommended me. Can you at least tell me what he's looking for or is that confidential, too?"

"Don't be silly." Smiling, she leaned forward, offering a better view of her mole, and whispered, "He's looking for a whale of a book."

"A whale of a book?" He observed her eyes as she leaned back. "Do you mean a book about whales? Does he need a field guide for whale watchers? Come to think about it, I know a great book on killer whales. Did you know they're not actually whales?"

"You're getting warmer, Charlie, but what I'm really interested in is a very special book on whales. It's an American book that's unlike any other in existence."

"I see. Since in you're in my shop, I suppose it wouldn't be a stretch to assume the book's in the UK, maybe even in London, as we speak."

Angelique adjusted the gold earring in her right ear and then lightly tapped the mole with her index finger. Looking intently at him, she lowered her voice and said, "I've said too much already. Is it safe to talk here?"

Charlie went to the outside door and turned the OPEN sign over. "Come with me," he said as he walked to the storeroom. He turned the light on and motioned her to a chair next to the table, after which he closed the door. Taking the chair opposite her, he said, "So tell me what you want and without all the subterfuge crap."

Angelique glanced around the room. "It's different with the light on. Okay, no subterfuge. There's an exhibition called *Melville and His British Contemporaries* at the Wakefield Library. The centerpiece is a first edition of Hermann Melville's *Moby Dick*. A first edition of the book is generally worth a hundred thousand pounds. But this one is different. It's the very first book of the first edition that was published in England in 1851. Melville gave it to his friend Nathaniel Hawthorne, but the book disappeared after Hawthorne's death in 1864. It resurfaced a few decades later in a castle in Wales, but it was stolen and not seen again until it came to light among Herman Goering's looted treasures. Shortly after the war, the book was returned to its owner, an English gentleman whose name escapes me for the moment, but after he died it changed hands several times, eventually ending up in the possession of an anonymous conglomerate, which loaned the book to the Wakefield for the exhibit. My client is passionate about this particular book, and he feels that it should have been his instead of the conglomerate's. Now, do you see why this is not just another first edition of the great American novel? Do you understand why you were recommended? You're in the business of procuring these kinds of items, and I have it from an unimpeachable source that you're the best in the business." She smiled as if she expected Charlie to agree that he was the best.

The storeroom was beginning to feel closed in and stale. For a few moments, he was speechless. Indeed, he was in the business of procuring unique or at least important books. But he had never acquired something quite as important as she was describing, and all of his acquisitions without exception were handled using a middleman, generally one who was fairly legit. Charlie was a businessman, or at least he was trying to be a businessman, and so it didn't make sense that anyone could have pegged him for being anything other than a businessman, albeit one whose income derived from retailing book plates. For a few seconds as he looked at her, it occurred to Charlie that she might be playing a practical joke on him. This whole thing was so preposterous that he wouldn't have been surprised if twenty or thirty friends suddenly burst into his shop and began slapping him on the back, congratulating him for being such a good sport while razzing him for being so gullible. But this didn't make sense, either, because he didn't have any friends and didn't like cultivating joking relationships with anyone.

Once again observing the tiny mole on her ear, it occurred to him that her proposal might be a setup arranged by those two dunderheads to trap him in something. And yet it was hard to understand why they would go to such trouble over someone like him, and it was even harder to fathom how Angelique could be part and parcel of such a fantastic scheme underwritten by government funds. He wasn't big time, and the only thing that anyone could reasonably tag him with would at most cost him his business license and maybe six months to a year, if that. No, they were only interested in Angelique, although this did nothing to explain the woman's confidence in a complete stranger. Still, even if things didn't add up – even if it turned out that Angelique had mistaken him for somebody else – he wasn't the kind of businessman to let such an opportunity (assuming it was a real opportunity) slip through his fingers, especially if there were a few pounds in it for him and if the risks were manageable. Naturally, he would need a little more information from her, since he wasn't interested in another forced vacation.

"Do you know what you're asking?" he practically whispered, trying to demonstrate how serious he was taking her offer. "It takes time, and it's not simple. Have you or your people considered the risks?"

"Of course, and that's why I'm coming to you. You're the expert. You know how to accomplish these sorts of things. But let's be clear – the risks are all yours, and for that you'll be amply compensated."

Charlie was unable to resist what interested him most, what interested him even more than her lovely little mole. "How much? It won't be cheap. This is a complex job, and the risks are significant."

"I understand, and so does my client. That's why we're prepared to pay you fifteen thousand pounds up front and 100,000 upon delivery –

provided the delivery is made within ten days. Please note that if you fail to deliver on time – fail to deliver for any reason at all – you will have to return the money immediately, plus a 100% penalty. And, once again, all the risks are yours."

If Charlie was speechless before, he was practically stunned now. He didn't know that much money actually existed. Over the years, he had met a few colleagues who claimed to have completed jobs for a half-million or more, but it was hard to give the claims much credence, given what these colleagues were. Most were simply telling tales to justify their existence while they counted off the days, months, and years. "Fifteen thousand now?" he gasped.

"Yes, and the rest upon delivery within the specified timeframe. Remember, failure…"

"I know, is not an option. But something like this isn't easy. Ten days is hardly enough…"

"Take it or leave it."

"Why ten days?"

"The exhibition is ending soon. No extensions."

"Okay, but can you at least tell me anything about the exhibition? I haven't seen it, and so I can't tell you if what you're asking is feasible. It may cost more upfront to accomplish."

"There isn't anything more upfront or in back. It's a flat-rate deal, no negotiation."

Charlie paused and nodded with feigned confidence. "Fine. What about the exhibition?"

"I saw it a few days ago. The book is in a special gallery. There are large paintings of seascapes on the walls, and there are a number display cases with other books in them. I don't want these books. The Melville is all by itself in the center of the gallery. You can't miss it, because it's enclosed in a glass case and has a series of small lights shining down on it. I didn't notice any security cameras around the case or even in the room. There're security guards in the library, but in the twenty or so minutes I was in the gallery, there wasn't a single one there. There were a handful of visitors, but that's it. Should be an easy job for someone like you."

"It's never as easy as you think. Just because you don't see security doesn't mean it's not there. How much is the book worth? It's got to be worth more than you're paying me, and so there'll be a security system somewhere to prevent exactly what you're proposing."

"The value of the book is irrelevant. As for its acquisition, you're being paid to understand the security and everything else."

Charlie grimaced as if something were troubling him. "Look, this sounds more complex than you think. I don't know if it can be done for under a half million."

Angelique smiled coolly. "Like I said, the rate is non-negotiable. If you can't do it with fifteen, I'll get someone who can. I am surprised you can't see the bigger picture – the losses you incur now will be made up on delivery."

Charlie looked thoughtful, as if he were churning the job and all its complications over in his mind. In truth, he was merely thinking about the hundred thousand and wondering how he could eventually get more out of her. "All, right," he said reluctantly. "You have the down payment with you?"

"Of course."

Charlie acted cool and calm, the attitude of a true professional, although the thought of so much money within reach made him involuntarily smile. Shaking his head slowly to compensate for the smile, he said, "Lady, you're something else. We're in this room and no one can see us. What makes you think I won't take the money from you, if you actually have it, and skip town?"

Angelique pulled a neat stack of bills out of the large purse she was carrying and, placing it on the table, pushed it toward him. "Because I have a gun," she added, retrieving the black weapon from her purse and aiming it at his nose as he reached for the money. "Count it if you like, but I was hoping we could conduct business on trust."

Charlie's smile immediately disappeared when he saw the barrel and noticed the manner in which she held the gun, which suggested that she knew how to use it. "Looks like a .380," he said somewhat nervously.

"It shoots like a .357."

Charlie hesitated and then slowly retrieved the money, keeping his eyes on Angelique as she pushed the gun back into her purse. It was no use rushing her at this point, because like a true professional she kept her hand on the gun while it was in her purse. "Don't think it, Charlie," she said after he finally collected the money. "You're not fast enough."

"Okay, we have a deal. So how will I contact you when I have the book?"

"Just come to your shop like normal. I'll contact you."

Chapter 9

Only a handful of officers showed up this time to get an update from Nesbit and Thwait on Angelique and Charlie, who throughout the week had become as central to the investigation as Angelique herself. The Chief had to bow out of this meeting like he did the other meetings due to a prior engagement or a personal matter of some sort. The officers who did attend this day's meeting were sitting comfortably around the table, sipping drinks and avoiding the papers stacked neatly in front of them. Unlike Thwait and the others, Nesbit was on his feet and pacing from one end of the conference room to the other. His calm, self-satisfied expression at the earlier meetings was gone, and he seemed on edge.

"I don't understand. And, for God's sake, I don't understand why no one here knows the exact date of Shakespeare's First Folio. Fine, but the confidential source that started this investigation – you're saying it was actually an anonymous tip on a suicide hot line? You couldn't tell me this earlier?"

"We just got it from HQ," one of officers said. "They seemed awfully interested, since it coincided with Angelique Dubois' arrival."

Nesbit paused momentarily and looked at the officer and then continued his pacing. "Okay, I can live with that. Sources come in all shapes and sizes, and in this instance your HQ was obviously right. Was the source a man or a woman? Okay, you don't know. But the passport photo...where is it? Would somebody please pass it back to me?"

There was a shuffle of chairs, and Thwait walked up to Nesbit and handed him a printed copy of the image in question.

Nesbit held it at arm's length and then turned to someone a few chairs away. "I don't understand. So the picture isn't the clearest, but Thwait and I met the man – more than once – and this is him. The same hair, the same face, even the same hangdog expression. What makes you think this isn't our Charlie. Look, it has the right name, Charlie Saunders. Are you telling me it's a forgery?"

One of the officers in the back raised his hand. "No," he said, "It's genuine..."

"Then what's the problem? Why isn't this our Charlie?"

"Check the name carefully...," the officer began.

"I'm not blind. I can read the name. Charles Saunders. Are you trying to tell me his name isn't Charles Saunders?"

The other nodded his head and raised his eyebrows. "I'm afraid so. The name on the passport is actually Charles Sanders, not Saunders. You and Constable Thwait met Charles Saunders, not Charles Sanders."

"I don't understand. I don't understand any of this." Nesbit brought the image closer to his face and scanned it carefully. "This is him, I'm positive. Thwait?"

"I'm afraid the name is actually different, sir," Thwait replied. "I'm as surprised as you are."

Nesbit practically put his nose against the image. Looking back at the other officers, he said, "Maybe the passport's wrong. The picture's our man. Can anyone explain this?"

"It's actually not, sir," Thwait continued. "Inspector Sedgwick," he added, alluding to the officer standing at the back of the room with her arms crossed, "Inspector Sedgwick went to Mr. Sander's..."

"Saunders?"

"Sander's, sir, Mr. Sander's residence and spoke to him. Mr. Sanders made his passport available, and it matched our photo in all particulars. Inspector Sedgwick also says that Sanders is a dead ringer for Charlie Saunders, hence part of the reason for the mistake."

"Did anyone contact the Canadians about this? Surely, they can straighten out this mess."

"Yes, Inspector Sedgwick contacted..."

"Anyone else check this out?"

"The Canadians," Thwait continued as if he hadn't been interrupted, "confirmed our mistake. They didn't have a Charles Saunders, but they sent another example of Sanders' passport – which you have in your hand, sir – and it matches the..."

"Damn," Nesbit shouted and wadded up the paper and threw it across the room, where it bounced off the wall just above Sedgwick's shoulder. Sedgwick's left lip drooped slightly, but she didn't flinch. "I don't understand how this could have happened. What went wrong? And this Shakespeare book..."

"I'm afraid we misread it, sir," Thwait said.

"Misread it? I can't believe it. Okay, okay, let me think," Nesbit muttered as he continued to pace back and forth across the room, rubbing his hands together. He stopped and looked at Thwait and then the rest of the officers. "Okay, the passport doesn't matter. Angelique and Charlie are connected because she was spotted entering his shop. Simple. The passport never really mattered. We have the right Charlie."

"Well," another one of the officers began, "We're not sure that she actually entered his shop. She was spotted in the vicinity, really, but she could have been going to…" He stopped when Nesbit glowered at him.

"Don't tell me you're backtracking on this, too," he demanded. "You informed me that your men had identified Angelique as the person entering Charlie's – our Charlie's – shop. This is a critical connection."

"Not exactly. No one to my knowledge said that. What was said was that she was spotted in the vicinity. Anyone have different information?" The officer looked at the others around the table.

"All right," Nesbit said when no one contradicted the officer's statement. "Tom and I can verify she was there and hence make the connection. She was in the storeroom when we were there earlier today."

"You saw her?" the officer at the opposite end of the table lifted his head off his arms to ask.

"No, we didn't need to. I could smell her perfume. It was fresh and strong. It was obvious to us that she ducked into the storeroom when she saw us coming. We weren't trying to hide our presence. Gentlemen, I believe this is conclusive proof of the connection."

"Excuse me?" one of the other officers asked, "But couldn't the scent have originated from outside the shop? Are you sure it was perfume you smelled?"

"How do you know it was her scent?" asked the first. "A lot of women wear the same…"

"There's no doubt that it was her scent," Nesbit interrupted, tapping the side of his nose lightly. "I've come across it before, and never from any of the women you mentioned. As for coming in from outside, as you say," he added, looking at the same officer, "The scent was too fresh and strong to have originated from anywhere but inside the shop. Besides, the street door was closed, and nothing fair or foul was coming into the place. And here's something else," he continued, this time speaking to everyone, "Remember that fall we described? Charlie was doing his best to prevent us from gaining access to the storeroom. What do you think that was all about? How could that fool trip over the same chair he had been sitting in day after day after day? Tom, do you remember the way he held his side after the fall? It was slapstick, it was vaudeville, it wasn't an accident. There was someone in the room that he didn't want us to see, and that someone was Angelique. If our hands hadn't been legally tied, we'd have Angelique behind bars as we speak."

"Behind bars? What for...," someone began, but when Nesbit glanced around the room, everyone was silent.

"Okay, I don't know why I need to do this every time, but let's go back to the basics," Nesbit began, looking around the room for the officer who had groaned. "Angelique is up to something big, something that concerns a national treasure. Is everyone in agreement so far?"

"Yes, sir, I believe we all are," Thwait said when no one else responded.

"Are we also in agreement that our Charlie is connected in some fashion to Angelique? Before you answer, keep in mind that Thwait and I are confident that she was in the storeroom the second time we spoke to Charlie. Not only that, I am equally confident that other witnesses to their interactions eventually surface. Now, are we in agreement?" The room was quiet, and officers were motionless. "Good. It therefore stands to reason Charlie is up to something with Angelique."

"Sir," Thwait began cautiously. It was clear that something was troubling him, perhaps about the evidence or Nesbit's line of reasoning, or both. "While I agree with..."

"Excellent, Tom. Now, let's put aside all the other nonsense and focus our combined energies on Angelique and Charlie – Charlie Saunders. Tom and I will intercept Charlie tonight and see if we can scare some information out of him. Is anyone [Nesbit gestured vaguely to the officers around the table] able to put in some of their time to help locating Angelique? I can't do it all by myself." There was more silence around the table. "Need I remind you all that we're running out of time and, if we don't act quickly, the Gutenberg, Beowulf, that God damned Shakespeare, or some other artifact of British heritage and character could be lost forever." Sensing an end to the meeting, the remaining officers got out of their chairs (the hard, rasping sounds the chairs made as they scraped against the floor resonated throughout the room) and left before Nesbit could reiterate his call for volunteers.

Nesbit and Thwait watched the officers leave the room, noticing some chuckles and small talk as they passed into the hallway. Turning to the younger man, his face cold and his eyes narrowed, Nesbit said, "You're with me on this, aren't you, Tom?"

"Yes, sir."

"Do you have any doubts about the path we're on?"

"Sir?"

"Do you think we're after the wrong man, or that Charlie's not the one we should be focusing on?"

"No, sir."

"Good. Let's go back and pick up Charlie before he gets scared and attempts to leave the country."

"Yes, sir, but what grounds do we have…"

"What grounds?" Nesbit practically shouted.

Thwait's heavy eyes opened widely. "I'm sorry, sir. Maybe…well, are you sure we should put so much emphasis on Mr. Saunders when Ms. Dubois appears to be the one in charge, or at least the pivotal figure? I suspect she's been in touch with others we might locate, and since she's probably traveling on an EU passport, there's bound to be a trail of some sort that we could follow. Maybe we can find her hotel. Surely, the establishment would have collected her information, and in that case…"

"Yes, yes, we can do all that when there's time. I am still hopeful that one of your men will follow up on these details. But as I stand here, I am certain our Charlie holds the key to everything, even if he isn't the person in charge. Once we speak to him, and we'll find her and everyone associated with her. Speak to him, and we'll save a monument to British character."

"What if Ms. Dubois is already gone?"

"Tom, you're putting up roadblocks before you've laid down the road. Everything I know about Angelique tells me that she's contracted with Charlie to get the monument, and as long as Charlie is here and accessible, she hasn't yet secured it. Now, I want you to reconsider his background, look at the manner in which he operates his shop, and compare that to how Angelique works. Can you honestly tell me that once he passes her the…the monument or whatever the damned thing is, he's going to stick around and continue with that phony shop of his? Nothing about the man or his shop suggests that he has roots here, or even that he's trying to put down roots anywhere. He's as free as a bird, my friend, and once he hands her the heritage and gets his cut, he's out to the Riviera, where he'll be getting the tan he's needed all his life. No, Tom, as long as he's still in London, she doesn't have a thing, not a blessed thing. Sooner or later the two will have to connect, and we'll get that information when we speak to him."

"I see, sir. But what if he won't speak to us? Remember last time…"

"Forget about the last time. He'll talk to me, trust me. He's the weak link in the chain, and as soon as we break him we'll be able to break Angelique."

"Yes, sir."

There was a brief pause while both men appeared to be thinking of something related to the case.

"I'm just surprised that some of your men don't understand how important this case is to the country, to the Queen, and to their careers." Nesbit tightened his lips and shook his head knowledgeably. "It's their loss, I suppose. You and I will get the job done, and we'll earn the country's eternal thanks."

"Yes, sir."

Nesbit hesitated. "Tom, do we actually know where our Charlie lives? I mean, in case he runs before we have a chance to intercept him."

"I'm afraid not, sir."

"Not a minute to lose, then."

Chapter 10

Charlie followed Angelique to the door and watched her through the widow as she walked across the street and disappeared around the corner. He was tempted to follow her, but he quickly realized that there was no point in following her unless he wanted to absorb more of her slender figure as it progressed up one street and down the next. Smiling warmly at the thought, he locked the door, flipped the sign to CLOSED, and pulled down the blind.

Back in the storeroom, Charlie locked the door behind him and reached for the money that Angelique had left on the table. He nearly fell over when it wasn't there – 'had she taken it with her, had someone else been in here?' he asked himself over and over – but after a few frantic searches on the floor and in the shelves, he spotted it resting neatly on the chair on the other side of the table. He couldn't recall how it got from table to chair, but he supposed that it didn't matter as long as he had the money, every single bill. Money in hand, he pulled a screwdriver from a shelf, kneeled down, and unscrewed the vent on the floor, after which he lifted out a flat piece of metal and placed the money at the solid bottom of the vent. Carefully placing the metal on top of the money (which because of its thickness required some fairly heavy downward pressure), he secured the vent back onto the floor and pocketed the screwdriver. Just before closing up, he made a quick phone call.

The sun was glowing faintly behind a thick bank of gray clouds as he locked the door of his shop. Smiling once again at the thought of Angelique, he walked toward the Underground with a light step and a feeling that this was one of the best days of his life. For a brief moment, he wanted to walk back to his shop to reassure himself that he really did have all that money and that there was even more money coming if he pulled off the job. But he didn't, of course, and as he continued on his way another thought occurred to him. Angelique had put a lot of trust and confidence in a complete stranger. While he was confident that he could pull off the job (assuming it was as simple as she made it seem), there was no way that she could have gathered enough information about him to make the same assessment. Why was she so certain of her judgment? And how could she be so certain he wouldn't renege on the agreement and either skip town with the money or grab the book and sell it himself, realizing far more than she was planning to pay? Perhaps she had a backup plan in case he tried to pull something.

Charlie tried to sidestep something on the sidewalk and stepped on a piece of blackened chewing gum. Scraping it off on the edge of the curb, he started to think that the job might not be quite as easy as she claimed. Since she wasn't an expert, she could have missed a lot of things that might make the job an unpleasant fiasco. On the other hand, maybe she wasn't interested in the book and had something else on her mind. He didn't know what, but at least he knew enough not to trust her as completely as she apparently trusted him. As he mulled things over, Charlie began to think that it was a mistake to take chances based solely on her word. He'd experienced his share of confined quarters, and he wasn't anxious to see her gun again, and so he decided that the smartest thing to do under the circumstances – perhaps the only thing to do under the circumstances – was to forget the hundred thousand and to skip town with the proverbial bird in hand. What could be less complicated? He would abandon his shop (which, as those stupid cops said, wasn't worth much) and take only his bookplates (which were worth something) and the cash from the register. And, equally important, he'd have no regrets leaving this bloody island and going back to where the air was warm and one could actually see the sun setting on the horizon. Sure, the extra money would have been nice, but he had more than enough to tide him over for quite some time and maybe even enough to travel out west. In fact, he had enough money to do what most of the others only dreamed of doing.

Charlie hesitated as he walked along a bank of tall, glossy windows. Noticing his reflection, he was shocked at what he saw. Instead of looking like he felt – youthful, alive, and free – he appeared old and drab, and the color and fit of his clothes suggested an undertaker with too much business on his hands. Rubbing his thin chin, he wondered if a change of clothes would help or if he needed a couple of those women whose services made their clients feel and look years younger. No, he told himself, he didn't want to waste his money on such women, and in fact at his age he wasn't even interested in them. He wasn't interested in women in particular except for one. Was it possible that her trust in him was a sign that she might have a thing for an old gravedigger like him? Despite her gun, he was beginning to have second thoughts about absconding and hanging her pretty neck out to dry.

Telling himself that he was getting soft in his old age, Charlie started to walk away from the windows when Nesbit and Thwait loomed behind him in the reflection. Their images were so clear and precise that he if he hadn't known better, he would have sworn that they were walking out of the window.

Turning around, he noticed the two men not more than twenty feet away and approaching. He didn't move and, when they reached him, Nesbit said, "Hi, Charlie-boy. You look surprised. We're kind of surprised we spotted you, too. I'll bet you were hoping you wouldn't see us again, am I right?"

"You guys are like bad fish."

"What?" Thwait whispered to Nesbit, speaking out the side of his mouth.

"I'm afraid my colleague doesn't get the allusion. The smell doesn't seem to go away, does it, Charlie?"

"How about Mr. Saunders?" Charlie growled, suddenly nervous because of the money in his shop. "My first name is reserved for friends."

"Aren't we your friends, Charlie?"

Thwait looked at one man and then the other, never fully comprehending the banter.

"No. What do you want?"

"How about that? He doesn't want to be our friends. That's too bad. But tell me, even if we can't be friends, do you mind if we have a little chat? We can do it someplace a little more discrete than here. What do you think, Charlie?"

Charlie started to reply, but he changed his mind and started to walk away. Grimacing, Nesbit reached out to grab Charlie's arm, but Charlie was too quick and swung around. "Don't touch me," he said and walked up to Nesbit and stood practically nose to nose with the other man. "If you have a question, ask it, and then bugger off."

Thwait took a step toward Charlie. His thick shoulders and barrel chest offered a formidable contrast to Charlie's thin frame, but as usual Nesbit waved him back. "Okay, Charlie, we can do this the easy way or the hard way. I'd prefer the easy way, though I'm not so sure my friend does." He motioned his head toward Thwait. "There's a nice quiet restaurant in this place (he motioned again with his head, this time to the building next to them), and I'd suggest we grab a bite and have a nice little chat before it gets too late. If everything is pleasant enough, you've only lost an hour of your precious time. What do you say?"

Charlie glanced at Thwait. "All right," he replied cautiously, "one hour and then I'm out and you can go to…"

"We can do that anytime," Nesbit responded just as Thwait stepped closer.

The restaurant was dark and practically deserted. They took a table near the blind-covered windows, which were illuminated by a weak overhead light and by a garish blue glow emanating from a large fish tank a few feet away. With Nesbit and Thwait sitting on one side and Charlie sitting on the opposite, there was a moment of silence while the three settled in and Thwait distributed the clothbound silverware. Charlie was the first to speak.

"You better be paying," he said, looking first at Thwait, who raised his eyebrows, and then at Nesbit, who smiled and nodded his head. "Good. Looking at you two makes me hungry."

A middle-aged woman wearing black slacks came over. Her tall bun of white hair nodded as she distributed the menus and took their drink orders (Nesbit requested water, Thwait a soda, and Charlie an expensive 18-year-old single-malt scotch, neat). With an accent that had a southern U.S. edge to it, she read off the daily specials and then pulled a notebook out of the back of her slacks when Charlie indicated that he was ready to order dinner. Nesbit and Thwait both declined to order (the former was too disgusted to eat while the latter was too worried about expenses), but Charlie told the friendly waitress that he was especially hungry and proceeded to order the most expensive item off the menu (steak and lobster with a side of French truffles). Once he was done, the waitress winked at Charlie and said, "Honey, I knew you was going to eat like a real man the minute I seen you."

Charlie smiled at the waitress, and after she left he turned back to Nesbit and Thwait. "I've never been here before, but I can already tell that this is a mighty fine establishment. I'm glad you boys are footing the bill, because I'm starving."

"Okay, Charlie, but since we're paying, we expect you to clean your plate."

"Oh, I see, India and all that."

"No, Charlie, and you know what I mean."

The waitress came back with the drinks and carefully placed them on the table. Just as she was about to leave for a second time, Charlie lightly touched the top of her wrist and told her to keep them coming. "I sure will, honey," she replied, smiling broadly at Charlie. "You sure your friends don't want something a little stronger than water and soda?" she asked without looking at Nesbit and Thwait.

"No, you don't have to worry about them. Their goal in life in to make sure I'm well fed and my whistle is thoroughly wetted." Charlie whistled three short high notes followed by one long low one, which made the waitress laugh as she was leaving.

Once she was gone, Charlie picked up his drink and, winking at Thwait, took a slow sip. Placing his glass on the edge of the table, he turned to the men and smiled broadly. "Are you sure you got the money for this?" he asked Nesbit.

"Charlie, my friend," Nesbit began, "I'm puzzled. Excuse me, but are you offended that I called you my friend? Please don't be. Now, do you know why I'm puzzled? No? No guesses?"

Charlie stared at Nesbit and took another long sip.

"Charlie," Nesbit continued, after glancing over his shoulder to make sure the waitress wasn't listening, "Charlie, you're not at all what you seem. I initially thought you were Canadian, but I was recently and rudely informed that this isn't so and that... I guess you're something else entirely. Care to elaborate? No matter. Mistakes happen, and I don't mean to insult your heritage either way. But this mistake brings up an interesting question. Charlie, if you're not the Canadian I was looking for, who are you and why are you mixed up with Angelique?"

Thwait didn't say anything and kept his eyes glued on Charlie.

"Angelique?"

"Charlie, if you want me to pay, this isn't the time to play games. We asked you about Angelique before, and now it's time to start leveling with me."

"Oh, yeah, I seem to recall you mentioning someone by that name the last time we spoke. Angelique, right?'

Nesbit smiled as if he already had the goods on Charlie. "Yes, Angelique, and she was in your shop the other day. Oh, by the way, how's your side? Not a bad injury, I hope. You should be more careful around stool legs and sharp angles. It's kind of amusing – you got all tangled up and crashed to the ground just after we asked to see your storeroom. Quite a coincidence, don't you think?" Nesbit chuckled to himself and shook his head. "Charlie, did you really think you were fooling anyone? You're fine actor, but you're certainly no Lawrence Olivier or George C. Scott. Did you think we couldn't see through your little stunt? Did you think we're that stupid? Wait, don't answer that yet." Nesbit continued to smile, although this time he nodded slightly as if to show that he and Charlie were thinking the same thing. "Angelique was in your storeroom, right? Come on, Charlie Chaplin, it was obvious. We knew she was there the moment we came in. We didn't have to

57

see her, and you didn't have to... do you know what gave it away? Her perfume. Can you believe it? Her perfume told me you were lying. It was the first thing we noticed when we came in. You probably weren't aware of it then because you were already acclimated to it. Ten more minutes and it would have been the same with us. But it was Angelique's scent, all right, and it was too strong and fresh to have come in from the outside." Nesbit stared intensely at Charlie, hoping for a sign that he was right about the perfume.

Charlie was taken aback by Nesbit's insights. If the fool could deduce so much from so little, then the man might already have substantial insights into his business, not to mention the plans he had made with Angelique. But this also created another problem. If Nesbit were to say something about Charlie's small-time criminal history, she might get wind of it and come back with her gun to cancel the deal. Sensing that he now had few good options at his disposal to turn the tables (and it was pointless to attempt a stunt in a public place where the restaurant personnel and the police would be all over him in seconds), he decided to take a chance and call Nesbit's bluff and return the man's cold, knowing look with one of his own, which he had perfected over the course of a multi-year stretch.

"No use clamming up, Charlie," Nesbit continued, breaking the increasingly uncomfortable silence. "We know what's going on. Angelique was at your place at least two times, and she isn't in the country to buy souvenirs or visit small shops, especially unprofitable ones like yours."

"The people who come into my shop," Charlie finally responded, "are interested in only one thing, buying my books. If Angela was in my shop, as you insist, then she was there to buy a book. You know, if I remember right, she might have been the person who bought a first quarto edition of Webster's wonderful play, *The Devil's Law Case*, which came out in 1623. I'll bet you didn't know that was the same year as Shakespeare's First Folio."

When Nesbit failed to respond quickly enough, Thwait cleared his throat and said, "If it's true about the sale, you must have a receipt or a sales record of some kind. Since this is a valuable book, you could get into serious trouble if you tried to hide your income."

"Exactly," Nesbit finally said. "And you shouldn't have any trouble finding the receipt in your otherwise empty coffers."

Fearing he might get trapped, Charlie calmly admitted that he hadn't sold her anything. "No, I only said 'might.' If I remember correctly, there was a woman in the shop about a week ago, but she didn't buy anything and I didn't ask her name. Angela, right? Do you have a picture of her, so I can compare the two women to see if there's any relationship?"

"Charlie, we've already played this game. But just to prove I'm a good sport, I'll let my colleague here show you a recent picture of Angelique to keep in mind. And, as you know, her name is Angelique. Tom, if you please."

Thwait pulled a mug shot out of his breast pocket and slid it across the table to Charlie.

Picking up the picture, Charlie made a pretense of carefully examining the image, which he could tell from a single glance was her, even if she wasn't made up or smiling like she did in his shop. He wasn't surprised that she had a mug shot, but it saddened him that she was still exquisite in such a cold, ugly circumstance. "Hard to tell," he said quietly, slowly shaking his head while examining the picture. "What's this strange script at the bottom of the picture? Anyway, the woman who came into my shop was more attractive, I think, and possibly better dressed."

Charlie put the picture down and reached for the soup that the waitress had just placed on the table in front of him.

"Careful, honey," she said as she was about to leave, "It's hot. You might blow it."

"Okay, Charlie, so you agree there was a woman. Now, it's time to tell me a couple things. I want to know what you two talked about and where I can find her."

After winking at the waitress, Charlie blew on the soup to cool it and then proceeded to eat as if Nesbit and Thwait were involved with their own meals. "If it's the person I'm thinking of, we didn't talk about much," he said between blows and loud slurps. "Hey, she didn't want to buy anything, and so there's no way I could have got her contact information. Not really my type. Maybe if I see her again, I can ask her for her address and number. Would you like me to get anything else?"

Nesbit's smile began to fade and he shook his head. "Charlie, Charlie, Charlie, I'll give you one last chance. Tell me what you two are up to and where she is. In fact, I'll make it easier. Just tell me where we can find her. She's not wanted for anything right now. We just want to speak to her."

Charlie continued to slurp noisily one spoonful of soup after another. "If you got something, lay it on the table," he replied when he was nearly done. "I'd like to finish my soup while it's still hot."

"You're only making things harder on yourself," Thwait chimed in.

"My impatient colleague is right, Charlie."

Charlie finished his soup and carefully wiped his mouth and chin.

"Charlie, don't make it harder…," Nesbit began to say but stopped. He watched silently as Charlie pushed his bowl to one side and signaled to the waitress, using his right index finger, for a refill of his scotch. Nesbit glanced at the waitress and, when he noticed her friendly smile and knowing nod, he turned back to Charlie, who was smiling.

"I know all about your bloody shop," Nesbit snapped, unable to countenance Charlie's insolence any longer. "I know how you get the money to keep it running. And I know all about Angelique. I know all about her clients, and I know how she dupes fools like you into doing her dirty business. I know everything, my friend, everything." Not wanting to make an ass of himself, and realizing that if Charlie challenged him he couldn't begin to say how Charlie's shop made money, Nesbit stopped, took a deep breath, and resumed speaking after he felt a little calmer. "It's not hard to put two and two together. We're going to take Angelique down, and you're going with her unless you cooperate now."

Charlie didn't respond. Nesbit's statements (as well as what he didn't say) told him that he was in the clear, at least for the time being, and so he wasn't going to say anything that might incriminate either himself or Angelique. When the waitress stopped by with his drink, he smiled and gave her another wink, and then instructed Thwait to give her a good tip.

Thwait immediately waved the waitress away from the table with his ham-like hand. Fearing another outburst from his colleague, he loosened his tie and squared his shoulders toward Charlie. "We can help you, Mr. Saunders, but you'll have to level with us. If you're not involved with Ms. Dubois, tell us where we can find her."

Charlie picked up his drink and, while he sipped it, he looked hard at Thwait and then at Nesbit. "Who's this Dubois?" he asked as he examined the contents of his glass in the overhead light.

"You bloody…," Nesbit began but stopped when Thwait interrupted him.

"Angelique Dubois, that's her name," Thwait said calmly, sincerely. "Just tell us where we can find her. We only want to ask her some questions."

"About what?"

"Get out of here," Nesbit stammered, gritting his teeth and standing up.

Charlie gulped the rest of his drink and got up from the table. Walking toward the door (he felt a little unsteady because of the drinks), he stopped in front of the waitress and, after exchanging a couple of words, gave her a tip. As he left the restaurant, he waved goodbye to Nesbit and Thwait, who were watching him leave.

Nesbit turned away and stared across the table to where Charlie had been sitting. "He had his chance," he mumbled.

The waitress came back with Charlie's order and carefully placed it in the center of the table. "Who's eating this?" she asked.

Chapter 11

Neither Nesbit nor Thwait said anything on the way back to the hotel. The following afternoon, Thwait found Nesbit sitting gloomily at the table in his room. Thwait had just come back from the station, where he had picked up some papers related to the investigation that Sedgwick had pulled for him. Yanking them out of a manila folder and stacking them on the table, Thwait sat down opposite Nesbit but decided to wait before explaining the papers. Nesbit, pencil in one hand and vodka tonic in the other, was ruminating over something, and Thwait was reluctant to interrupt the man's thoughts.

"Sorry," Nesbit began when he noticed Thwait sitting across from him. "I let Charlie get to me. I don't normally go off on someone like that, even creeps like Charlie."

"There's nothing to be sorry about, sir. I was pretty mad at him myself."

"I don't know, Tom. I've been in this business for over thirty years, and I still haven't completely succeeded in separating my personal feelings from my professional ones." Finishing his drink and dropping his pencil, he laughed half-heartedly at himself and shook his head. "I get mad at these worthless... these useless, pointless individuals as if their actions and attitudes were directed at me personally, which of course is not the case. No, Tom, they're mad at the system, at their families, at themselves, not at me or you. Someday, maybe after I've captured Charlie and Angelique, I'll be able to relax, retire, and rest on my laurels. But I have to hand it to you, my friend, you kept your cool."

"I understand your feelings, sir. There are times when I, too..."

Nesbit abruptly sat up and held up a report that he had been looking at earlier. Keeping it at arm's length, he shook his head and began speaking to Thwait without looking at him. "You know, Tom, something's not right here. Charlie's our guy, and yet we can't seem to find a damn thing on him. There's no doubt he's connected with Angelique, and yet you'd think there would be something on him somewhere, because she doesn't work with novices. He has to have been in the business for years, he has to have been into something, anything, for decades, and yet we have nothing. How can we have nothing on that old guy? Not even his nationality. Can you explain it, Tom?" He looked up at Thwait, who was carefully observing him.

"Perhaps Charlie goes by a different name."

"Then what is it? According to your boys, he checks outs for a nearly a year, but there's nothing before that. I ran him through Interpol's database, and there's nothing on him there, either. Surely, there has to be some to be some history, school, flats, operator's licenses, and the like somewhere, but there's nothing, zero, zip, nada. Of course, we have his business license and registration, thanks to what's-her-name, and a tax return, but since these didn't require in-depth information or a background check, they are practically useless."

"Useful to him, certainly."

"Then there's that shop of his. It boggles the mind that he can continue to operate it without an income. Where's he getting the money for the inventory, the overhead, the space, and his personal living expenses? Has anyone found out where he lives?"

"Officer Sed..."

"Yes, I know. What's-her-name couldn't find him at the address listed on the official forms. Is that even legal here?"

"He could have changed his address. It happens all the time. People change their addresses and neglect to notify the authorities. I'm sure all legal forms are sent to his shop, and as far as he's concerned..."

"You don't need to defend him. Are we the only ones looking at this stuff? Hasn't anyone else noticed the anomalies?"

Nesbit glanced at the copy of the passport photo of Charles Sanders, which was on the table to his left. "A dead ringer," he mumbled as he pushed his chair back and stood up. Placing his hands on his back, he stretched and, after grunting, began pacing the room. "I wish your boys could give us better information. This stuff they gave us is crap, pure crap. Sometimes, I think they're sleeping on the job."

Thwait reached for the papers he had placed on the table, but Nesbit waved him off as if there was nothing there he didn't already know.

"I'm sorry, I know they're not," Nesbit said without looking at Thwait. "The Chief has them doing other things, and they're giving us what they can. But I wish they would put a little more time and effort into what they are giving us."

"Sir..."

"I know, I know, the case is getting to me. Maybe it is. Maybe it's just Charlie. He's so damned inscrutable. He's got cheek, too, I'll give him that."

"Sir…"

"But, I agree, we don't have time to sit back and admire his baser qualities." Nesbit glanced at Thwait, who was anxious to say something.

"What is it, Tom? You got something?"

"Sir, I brought…"

"Come on, Tom, spit it out. You're stuttering again."

Thwait was going to present the new information, but a thought occurred to him that sidetracked his original intention. "Sir, just how confident are you that Mr. Saunders is our man? I mean, we don't have…"

"One hundred percent, my friend. Remember, he has a connection to Angelique, he has a bookshop with the right sort of books for cover, he doesn't have a background – all blank – and, of course, he's an impudent devil. If he didn't have anything to hide, he'd be bending over backward to cooperate. And while we're at it, I think we should keep an eye on the waitress. She was awfully friendly to him – too friendly, if you ask me – and she has that accent. Where in the world did she come from?"

"Possibly from the southern region of the States."

"What? I've been in the South more times than I can count, and I've never heard anything like it."

"Sir, your points are all well taken with respect to Mr. Saunders, but I think there's something else you should…"

"What? Something else I should…what are you saying? What is it, Tom? Don't hold your tongue now. Are you having trouble controlling it?" Nesbit was now standing on the other side of the table looking at Thwait.

"Well, sir, there may be something about Mr. Sanders."

"Charlie is connected to Sanders?"

"No, I mean, not exactly…"

"Yes, yes, come out with it, man."

Thwait pulled out the papers he brought from the station. "Inspector Sedgwick did some research, and she found some odd coincidences between Mr. Saunders and Mr. Sanders. Apart from the physical similarities between the two men, Mr. Charles Sanders is a dealer of antiquaries. His shop is only a couple of blocks from Mr. Saunders' shop, on the other side of the Ravenswood Museum."

"Antiquaries?"

"Old and rare objects."

"Not books?"

"A few. But there's more, sir. Mr. Sanders is reputed to have connections to an international cartel trafficking in stolen artifacts, including rare manuscripts. He's also been implicated, but... well, here, look at this." He held out one of his papers, which Nesbit didn't seem to notice.

"Implicated? What do you mean?"

"The Ravenswood Museum accused him of trying to sell them certain stolen items, but the charges were for some reason dismissed. We don't have all the details, I'm afraid. He's been living in this country on and off for several years, but he's still a Canadian citizen. Unfortunately, we don't yet have a lot of information on him, and the Canadians haven't been able to provide much due to a computer glitch or something. Nonetheless, I wonder if we..."

"What are you telling me? You don't think we're barking up the wrong trail, do you?"

"No, sir. I just wonder if we should speak to Inspector Sedgwick..."

"Sedwurk? Why should we care about what Sedwonk thinks? This doesn't make any sense. Charlie's hiding something and...and Angelique was spotted near his shop not once but twice. And then there's the perfume – you smelled it as well as I did." Nesbit dropped into his chair and looked at Thwait.

"Yes, sir, but I'm not sure a scent would qualify as evidence in court. We also lack proof they've been in communication..."

"Damn it all, Tom! We could have had all the evidence we needed if only one of your boys had the gumption to stake out his shop and tap Charlie's lines. It's not my fault."

"It's no one's fault, sir. I'm only...Inspector Sedgwick is only suggesting that there might be something to the similarities, coincidences, if you will. If you look at this..." Thwait started to hand Nesbit a paper from the folder but hesitated when Nesbit abruptly sat up.

Nesbit rubbed the back of his neck with his right hand. Noticing the hopeful look on the younger man's heavy face, he said, "Okay, Tom, if you honestly believe that we've made a mistake..."

"No, sir, it's not that. I just think it's important to the investigation that we look into Mr. Sanders. If the Chief asks about him, we'll need to say that we checked him out as well as every other lead. Perhaps if you looked at this..."

"Good point, my friend, good point. What's the name of Sanders' shop?"

Thwait again proffered the paper to Nesbit. "World Antiquaries. I have the information here. Inspector Sedgwick thinks the shop has decent foot traffic, but she also said that more people are bringing objects into the shop than carrying them out. It should be the opposite in a retail outfit."

"World Antiquaries, did you say? How do you get antiquarian books from that?"

"I believe he carries all kinds of things, sir. According to…"

"I know, I know."

"Yes, well, Inspector Sedgwick confirmed that his shop has a handful of old books in it."

"Did your Inspector find any connection between Sanders – Sanders, right? – Sanders or his shop and Angelique?"

"No, sir, I don't believe she has. Her time was limited, as you know, and now she's being pulled from her current duties to work another case…"

"Yes, yes, enough of Inspector what's-her-name."

"There's one more thing, sir." Thwait finally placed the paper on the table in front of Nesbit. "While she was researching Mr. Sanders, Inspector Sedgwick found a possible connection between Mr. Sanders and a foreign-government official who is rumored to be a buyer of stolen artifacts from the cartel."

"Name?"

"Sir?"

"This foreign official."

"Oh, yes. Mr. J. B. Tonson. Several persons from the shops in the area have sighted him, which is easy to do because he has at least two body guards with him at all times. You know how some of these foreign dignitaries act. Anyway, check this out, sir." He picked up another sheet of paper from his papers and placed it in front of Nesbit.

"Any convictions, warrants on Tonson?" Nesbit didn't seem to notice this paper, either.

"No, sir, and it's unlikely that we'll be able to get such information from his government. But there's more."

"You don't have to say from whom."

"Inspector Sedgwick thinks that she may have located one of Mr. Tonson's homes. It appears to be located in the same resort town where Ms. Dubois reportedly lives or spends her winters." He reached for his folder and began looking through the last of his papers. Finding the right one, which he confirmed by a careful perusal, he placed this one, too, in front of Nesbit. "Inspector Sedgwick found two or three additional locations where Ms. Dubois and Tonson have both frequented. We don't yet know if they were ever at these locations at the same time. A lot of the information comes from Interpol, of course."

"Of course. What else did she come up with?"

"I'm not certain. I was only able to speak to Inspector Sedgwick briefly, so I don't really know where she was headed. There may have been something else, though." Thwait paused, moistened his lower lip with the tip of his red tongue, and began sorting through his papers. After a few minutes of fruitless searching, he looked at Nesbit and shook his head. "I'm afraid there's no direct link between Ms. Dubois, Mr. Tonson, or World Antiquaries."

"I wish you'd said something earlier."

"I'm sorry, sir. No one's had time to follow up on the information."

"Okay, fine. World Antiquaries, you say?"

"Yes, sir, it's Mr. Sanders' store."

Nesbit started to stand up but then immediately sat back down. Scratching his chin for a moment, he stared at Thwait and said, "It sounds pretty farfetched to me. There're a lot of people in this town, and the odds of running into someone who looks and acts like somebody else are pretty good. Furthermore, there's got to be more than one crooked bookseller in this town, and I wouldn't be surprised if more than a few are named Charles. Still, you have something that bears checking out. Maybe we have another one of Angelique's minions. Good work, Tom. HQ could use others like you."

"Sir, thanks really should be given to…"

"Yes, indeed, but right now we need to consider our next steps with respect to both men. I understand your concerns, and so if we're wrong about Sanders, we'll have to pivot back to Charlie tout de suite."

"Sir, I think thanks should be given…"

Nesbit got up and began pacing back and forth. "Yes, we have to cover both, but your boys aren't going to give us the resources we need, are they? No need to answer that. Tom," Nesbit began but stopped and looked at Thwait. "Since we don't know where our Charlie is at this moment, let's pay a visit to Sanders and find out what he's been up to lately." He was about to resume pacing but again turned to Thwait. "Do you think you could get your boys to pressure immigration to put out bulletins on Angelique and both men? If they're still in the country, we may have the upper hand."

"Yes, sir. I'll ask."

"With a little luck, we may be able to get Charles Sanders before he closes shop. Any idea what his address is?"

Thwait pulled a sheet out from the papers in front of Nesbit. "I think we're in luck, sir. Inspector Sedgwick…"

"Don't tell me. It's time to put this stuff away and start paying calls."

Chapter 12

Thwait stood up and began to stack up the papers on the table. As he did so, he uncovered the morning newspaper, which happened to be lying open at his elbow. Nesbit, too, was picking up (neither wanted the maid or anyone else to enter casually and see such sensitive papers) when he noticed the newspaper. Glancing briefly at it, he held it by one corner as if it were a foul rag and handed it over to Thwait. "Some days these things don't interest me in the least," he said.

Thwait took the paper and was about to toss it in the trash can when he spotted the cultural section, which had nearly slipped out as Nesbit handed it to him. On the front page of the section, there was an article and picture on an exhibition called *Melville and His British Contemporaries*, which was being held at the Wakefield Library across the street from the Ravenswood Museum.

"Sir," Thwait uttered, barely looking up from the page. "Sir, I have something that might be of interest."

Nesbit stopped and looked at younger colleague.

"Sir, we know Ms. Dubois is in London for something big. It's something that can only be found here but may not be here forever, hence the timing of her visit. This being the case, why don't we try to find what this something is?"

"I'm not following you."

"Sir, there are some major exhibitions going on now that are attracting international attention. If we check them out, we might find one that has the culturally significant book she's after. Finding that, we could stake out the event and either protect the book or catch her associate in the act. I know it's a longshot…"

Nesbit stared hard at Thwait. "What exactly are you getting at?"

Thwait held up the cultural page. "Take a look at this."

Nesbit took the paper and began reading the article. Thwait stood directly across from him, eagerly watching his eyes as they moved from one side of the page to the other and back again. While Nesbit read, Thwait had trouble standing still, for he was nearly certain that his esteemed colleague would arrive at the same conclusion he did.

When he was done, Nesbit looked at the younger man. "Interesting, I suppose. What are you proposing, Tom?"

"The Melville at the Wakefield, sir. There's a book by Melville there that, according to the article, is extremely rare and valuable. Anyway, the book is still on display, though the exhibition is going to end fairly soon. If you're right that Ms. Dubois's tenure here is also coming to an end, perhaps the reason for her eminent departure is this very book."

Nesbit thought for a moment. "Close, my friend, but I don't think it makes sense. The Melville is certainly interesting, but it doesn't stand to reason that Angelique would come to England to steal an American book. No, she's after a piece of British heritage, which can only be found on this 'sceptered isle,' or however the saying goes. Realistically, if she wanted something American, she would have gone to the States and found it there. Good try, though."

"I don't know, sir. With all due respect, the book is one of a kind, and it's here and not in the States. The article says that the owners paid the highest price ever paid for a…"

"No, Tom, Angelique is after something that has real, lasting value, like Beowulf or Gutenberg or Shakespeare. Did you know there's only a few Beowulf manuscripts left? Do you have any idea what they're worth? Imagine some criminal type, his pockets bulging with ill-gotten gain, offering a seemingly endless pile of money simply to be the one person on the planet to possess one or all of them? Or imagine someone else ransoming it to Her Majesty's government or using it to make demands of the government? Not Melville, my friend, not Melville. Who would care?"

"I suppose you're right, sir," Thwait said, shaking his head.

Nesbit handed the paper back to Thwait and watched as he folded it up. Just as he was about to toss it in the trash, Nesbit put his hand on Thwait's arm and asked him to hold still. Nesbit took the paper from him, shook it out, and looked at the article again. When he was finished, he turned to Thwait and with a wry smile on his face, said, "My friend, I owe you an apology. Melville holds the key. Look at this." He pointed to an article on an exhibition of the Royal Sapphires.

Thwait read the article. He blinked a couple of times to make sure he read the correct article and reread it. Looking over to Nesbit, he had a questioning expression on his face. "Is this what you mean? I don't understand."

Nesbit couldn't help smiling broadly. "Look again."

Thwait reread the article. "I'm afraid I still don't understand."

70

"Come now, Tom, observe the address of the exhibition." Nesbit began pacing.

"Yes, sir?"

"Now compare that to the address of the Wakefield."

Thwait did as instructed but still had a bewildered expression on his face.

Nesbit walked over and put his finger on one address and then on the other. "Here it is. The exhibitions are across the street from one another. Now do you get it? No? Okay, listen carefully. Let's suppose that Angelique isn't interested in an old book, after all. Let's suppose, instead, that she's actually interested in the Royal Sapphires. Okay, how's she going to get her clean, soft hands on them without having her delicate wrists bound by commonplace steel bracelets?"

Thwait continued to stare at Nesbit.

"Okay, let me put it another way. Her connection with the antique books dealer is either a ruse to throw us off the scent or, more likely, a priceless act of subterfuge – she's going to cause a ruckus at the Melville exhibition to focus attention there while she's across the street pilfering the sapphires. Or something like that. Maybe she's going to put the sapphires in an old book to ferret them out of the country, I don't know, but it's clear that she's after the sapphires – a true monument of British heritage."

"Are you sure it isn't..."

"Positive."

"Sir, with all due respect, a ruckus at a book exhibition to distract from the..."

"No, she's interested in something far more important than an insignificant American book. If she wanted something from the States, why in the world would she go anywhere but there to acquire it?"

"But the book is the only one of its kind. It's the first..."

"So are the sapphires, and there's nothing more valuable than a symbol of country and queen."

"Well, okay, but do you actually think she's going to do the heist herself? I thought her MO was to get others to take on the risk."

"She does whatever she has to do to keep her hands clean. But that doesn't mean she won't scope out the place or be on hand when the job goes down. Since this is a public venue, she'll probably relish the opportunity of watching a consummate professional like Charlie purloining the sapphires."

"Sir..."

Nesbit held up his hand so that he could roll something quietly around in his mind. "Good thinking, Tom," he mumbled as he glanced again at the article. Nesbit suddenly stopped and looked at Thwait. "Why didn't you tell me? The article states that tomorrow is the last day of the sapphire exhibition."

"You think it might go down during the exhibition?"

"No, no, you're right. It's too dangerous even for Charlie. But I wouldn't be surprised if the heist were planned for tonight, after the exhibition closes. If that's the case, she might want to take one last gander before it closes just to be sure everything is as she expects it to be."

"Sir?"

"Think, Tom. If there's only a one-in-a-million chance that she or Charlie will be at the exhibition today, don't you think we should take those odds and scope out the place?"

"What if they went earlier in the day?"

"It's possible. But you know what I'm thinking? I'm thinking that the sapphires are their most vulnerable not when the museum opens in the morning but just before it closes. The guards are tired, they're concentrating on shooing all the visitors out, and at the very same time they're planning their own evenings."

"It's fifteen after five, sir, and I believe the exhibition will only be open for another..."

"No time to explain. Grab your coat and let's go see the Royal Sapphires. I'll fill you in on the way."

Chapter 13

Nesbit and Thwait ran up the stone steps of the Ravenswood Museum. Flashing their badges at the guard, they quickly walked into the building, worked their way down the long central hall, and entered the rotunda, which functioned as the exhibition space. The space was huge and elegantly decorated, with long, white sheers draping the small and elaborately framed windows along two-thirds of the walls. On the far side of the entrance, tables had been set out for drinks and refreshments, and a little to the right of the tables a chamber orchestra (about eight or nine musicians in all) played quietly (actually, the din of people conversing echoed throughout the round hall and severely limited what one could hear from the orchestra). And in the very center of the rotunda were glass display cases housing the Royal Sapphires, each case glowing in the light and separated from the crowd by a soft, purple rope about an inch in diameter. Guards stood outside the ropes occasionally speaking to one another and frequently asking the guests to step away from the ropes. Hundreds of guests were milling about, all in formal attire and all decked with their own glistening jewels. Naturally, the thickest part of the crowd surrounded the display cases, but there were quite a few people standing near the food tables and wandering around the circular hall, connecting with persons of importance or merely exchanging pleasantries with business acquaintances.

Nesbit and Thwait stationed themselves so that they could see the guests entering and leaving the rotunda or milling about the display cases. Scanning the glittering crowd in front of them, Nesbit seemed slightly on edge, as if Angelique or Charlie were somewhere in the crowd and now practically within his grasp. In fact, he was convinced that everything before him – the people, the jewels, and the music – had been the backdrop to a dream he once had in which this very night witnessed the culmination of years of hard work and keen analytical insight. Thwait, on the other hand, was merely nervous. He still wasn't entirely convinced that Nesbit was on the right track, and he worried that if Nesbit were mistaken, Ms. Dubois would be long gone before the event closed for the evening. But assuming that Nesbit was indeed right and that Ms. Dubois was somewhere in the crowd, Thwait was also concerned that it would take a miracle to find her in this faceless mass of nearly identical black suits and long, formal evening dresses. And there was something else: While he and his esteemed colleague were well-positioned to observe the mass of people in this room, this same mass of people was equally well-positioned to observe them – and, assuming that Ms. Dubois knew that they were on her trail, she was as well-positioned as anyone else to spot the officers and flee before they even had a chance to know she had been there. At least, the sapphires were still in sight.

Nesbit suddenly turned from the crowd to Thwait. "Tom, what's the point of standing here like a couple of idiots," he said, offering Thwait a fleeting hope that he had finally seen the folly of trying to identify anyone from where they were positioned. "We need to get closer to the sapphires. If Angelique and Charlie are here, they're going to be as close as possible to the prize, not hanging around conversing with a bunch of stuffed shirts."

"What if they try to leave, sir?" Thwait asked, a little reluctant to charge into the crowd without a definite plan of something. "I mean, do we know how we're going to handle their flight, if it comes to that?"

Nesbit thought for a moment. "You're right as usual," he replied. "You have two jobs, Tom. One is to stay put and keep an eye on everyone entering and leaving the rotunda. The other is to keep an eye on me. If I find either one of them, I'll need you to make the formal arrest."

"Sir, I'm not sure that we have enough to detain either one of them at this juncture."

Nesbit smiled. "If they're here, we will. If nothing else, we can haul them into the station for questioning – and save the country's heritage."

Without another word, Nesbit hustled toward the display cases, pushing between people, going around others. When he finally arrived in front of the sapphires, he turned toward Thwait and waved to make sure his colleague was watching. But just as Thwait waved back, he noticed that Nesbit had turned and was walking (practically running) through the crowd toward the chamber orchestra. He could see Nesbit fairly clearly, but he couldn't figure out where he was going or why he decided to leave the vicinity of the jewel cases. Watching Nesbit, he began to regret that he hadn't supported Nesbit more forcefully when he asked the Chief for additional resources, for it would have been useful to have some officers among the crowd, particularly if they had the fancy earphones that he had seen so many times in the movies.

Nesbit managed to break free of a small knot of people and approached a woman from behind. Dressed in a sparking red, floor-length gown, her bright hair glistening like a knob of gold on the top of her slender cane-like form, the woman was standing by herself with a cocktail glass in one hand. Nesbit grasped the back of her arm and, leaning over her shoulder, appeared to be saying something in her ear.

Thwait couldn't believe Nesbit's luck, and he began to feel a slight pang of guilt for having doubted his older colleague. Whatever his mistakes or errors in judgment, it was now clear that Nesbit was a discerning, skillful detective, and that the older man had lots to teach him. Indeed, Thwait was a mere infant compared to his experienced Interpol colleague, friend, and mentor. Thwait started to move forward to help Nesbit when his phone rang.

One minute later, heart palpitating, Thwait rushed into the crowd, nudging people aside (at the same time, knocking at least two drinks out of the hands of impeccably dressed ladies – one drink doused the front of a beautiful pastel-colored dress – and eliciting a number of groans and recriminations, particularly from a protective, male companion) and arrived, out of breath, his side painfully throbbing, just in time to hear his colleague's incoherent explanation for why he had "manhandled" a strange woman who was the wife of Lord so-and-so and who, because of her husband's position of importance both with the government and the museum, could ensure that he, Nesbit, never again worked for any law-enforcement agency. Thwait interrupted the charming tête-à-tête and informed Nesbit that Angelique had been detained at Heathrow.

"Why she chose Heathrow instead of crossing through the Chunnel is anyone's guess, but the most important thing is that an old book was found in her possession," Thwait gasped while the woman, now behind Nesbit, was wailing that she would not be ignored by the likes of a "mere" policeman.

"Did they give you any more details?" Nesbit demanded as they left the howling woman and charged back through the crowd toward the entrance.

"Yes, it appears to be an old edition of something, maybe Melville. They haven't been able to reach anyone at the Wakefield…"

"It's closed."

"…and so the Chief has arranged for an expert to authenticate the book."

Outside and running toward the car, Nesbit hollered to Thwait over his shoulder, "We don't have a second to lose."

"It's our first chance to question Ms. Dubois…"

"I want you to contact HQ and inform them that we're going to question Sanders and bring him in if he doesn't have the right answers."

"Saunders?"

"Sanders. Charlie is bad, and I know he's up to something no good. But I have a gut feeling he's not our man for this caper."

"But shouldn't we speak to Ms. Dubois first? Surely, she can make the case against him."

"We have plenty of time to speak to her. Right now, before it's too late, we need to..."

Thwait yanked the car away from the curb with a squeal of its tires and began passing cars on both sides of the street.

"Shouldn't you use a siren or emergency light?" Nesbit asked as he struggled to buckle his seatbelt while the car jolted violently back and forth as Thwait maneuvered through traffic.

Momentarily taking his eyes off the road, Thwait reached for something under the dash.

"My God, man...," Nesbit gasped as the car arced abruptly to the right, flinging open the passenger door. Despite his bulk, Thwait had surprising reflexes, and just as he looked over at Nesbit to inform him that the car didn't have a light, he spotted the door and immediately lunged across his colleague and yanked the door closed.

Thwait managed to regain control of the car after it started to drift into oncoming traffic in the opposite lane. But as Nesbit pulled himself upright, there was another hard corner, this time not only pushing him against the door but also forcing his face against the door's window.

"Perhaps we could slow down a little," Nesbit said as he got himself settled in the seat and the car began traveling in a relatively straight line.

"Sir?"

"Never mind. Please keep your eyes on the road. As I was trying to say, we need to stop Sanders before he slips out of the country. Remember...Tom, do watch out for that...yes, fine. Remember, remember, remember nobody hangs around after a crime like this. Oh, for God's sake..."

Chapter 14

A few days after his deal with Angelique, Charlie arrived at his shop while it was still dark. He couldn't sleep and, instead of lying awake and counting off the minutes and seconds until his alarm started to wail, he decided to go into the shop and straighten up things before Angelique's arrival.

Naturally, he had no reason to believe that she would show up this day as opposed to any other day, and yet he couldn't shake the feeling that today was going to be special, that this was going to be the big day. Ever since Charlie decided not to leave Angelique holding the bag, the extra money began to loom larger and larger in his imagination. At first, the idea of having so much money was more fantasy than reality. People like him never got rich. People like him never got enough of anything that enabled them to stick it to the man and spend the rest of their lives time smelling the roses. But as each day passed and he undertook certain preliminaries, the money began to seem real and tangible. There were even moments when he could practically feel it weighing down his pockets or sense the tight strips of duct tape pulling the skin and hair on his chest as he strolled through customs with it secured under his shirt. On the other hand, he couldn't quite calculate the physical space that so much money occupied, and he was becoming slightly concerned regarding next steps if it were too massive to be conveniently strapped to his chest and hidden in his carry-on. But how could it be so unwieldy, he asked himself, if Angelique herself was going to bring it into his shop?

Once the lights were on and he was seated comfortably on his stool, Charlie began to dream about what he would do once he was out of the country with the money safely in his hands. Unfortunately, there were so many possibilities that it was a little hard to decide. But after weighing a number of these possibilities, he finally decided that he would first change his wardrobe – Hawaiian shirts, blue jeans, and boat shoes – and then bundle up his gray suits and hand them to the first beggar on the street he encountered. Next, he would buy a briefcase, a nice leather job with a shoulder strap, which would show everyone how important he was and, at the same time, hold most of the money in the form of cashier checks (he wasn't going to trust the thieves at the banks). Pulling a tabloid from his desk, Charlie noticed a photograph of a movie star surrounded by a phalanx of reporters, and it suddenly occurred to him that he would like to see Hollywood one day.

Mindlessly thumbing through the newspaper, Charlie wondered if Angelique would be interested in joining him. It wasn't hard to imagine lying next to her on a warm, sunny beach, the waves rushing over their feet and around their sides, or watching her dance through the streets, the shouts and laughter reverberating throughout the twilight-enveloped buildings. But when he considered spending a quiet evening with her, both of them curled up in a thick blanket and staring out the window at the evening sky, he began to suspect that he was deluding himself. Why would she be interesting is settling down with him, an old man probably twice her age? Why would she even consider retiring from her line of work, when it was clear that she was still happily obtaining illicit items for her fancy clients and making so much money that she apparently wasn't interested in absconding with his paltry hundred thousand? Smiling wanly at his foolishness, he placed his magazine down on the desk and, glancing absently at the door, noticed that he hadn't turned the sign over.

Charlie shrugged his shoulders and walked over to the door and turned over the CLOSED sign. Returning to his stool, Nesbit and Thwait unexpectedly came to mind, and he began to wonder if he was missing something. He didn't consider either officer particularly astute, although they obviously had something on Angelique even if it wasn't enough to arrest her. While their presence hadn't forced him to alter his business model, he began to entertain the possibility that they could show up unexpectedly and wreck his plans and everything else. Could they be standing outside in the dark watching his shop, waiting for Angelique to appear? If this were the case, there would be no way to prevent them from apprehending her, and if they got her, they got his money and everything that he had worked a lifetime to achieve. Turning around, he stepped back to the window and practically pressed his face to the glass to see if he recognized anything in the dark shadows, but the only thing he could see with any clarity was his own tired, ludicrous face. Stepping back, he reassured himself that they were idiots, and there wasn't any conceivable way they could catch Angelique and stumble on his money – his money! She wouldn't let it happen.

Angelique didn't come to the shop that day. On his way home that evening, Charlie chided himself for having expected her so soon. While superficially it was a simple job, she was certainly smart enough to know that it would take a little time to pull off successfully. It was odd, though, that she planned to find him when the time was right even though she had no way of knowing when the time was right, if by that she meant that the job was complete. Charlie half expected her the next day, too, and when she didn't appear by the time he closed the shop, he told himself that she would appear the following day, and if not that day, then the day after that.

During this time, the money she promised was never far from his thoughts, although its appeal gradually began to fade with each passing day, because it was now increasingly hard to believe that anyone would give him so much for so little in return. Why would anyone pay so much for a book that any number of competent thieves could acquire for less than the money she provided as a down payment? 'What was the hitch?' he couldn't help wondering whenever he thought too long and hard about the money. Was he dreaming or merely being conned? Was he deluding himself? Could he trust Angelique? Even though he knew how easily a beautiful woman could manipulate almost any man, he couldn't quite make himself believe that Angelique was like these women, especially when he recalled her smooth skin, the delicate lines on either side of her mouth, her large, dark eyes, and her mole, all of which seemed to reach inside of him whenever he thought of her. Was it possible, he would ask himself just before ruminating on the duplicity of certain beautiful women he knew in the past, was it possible that she felt something for him and that when she looked at him she was trying to communicate this feeling?

The idea that Angelique might actually desire him momentarily erased all the other thoughts floating around in his head, and he imagined how they might get together and share the flat he owned. It was a small flat, of course, but it was several floors above a busy street where in the warm summer nights music from one of the nightclubs below floated gently into the open windows. He dreamed of how they would take walks, hand in hand, passing by the clubs as they headed to a nearby river, where they would stroll in silence enjoying one another's company. Such thoughts started to become more elaborate until he noticed the pain in his shoulder and felt with his tongue the recession of his back gums, which reminded him of the absurdity of thinking that a beautiful young woman would want to tie herself down with a ridiculous old man.

When Angelique failed to arrive on a day that seemed reasonable, he told himself that if he ever saw her again, he would make her a proposition: Stay with him for six months or six years, depending on how she felt, and there would be no legal ties that could complicate matters. It had been an easy decision to make, because he was beginning to think that she wouldn't return and that he could console himself with the money if she did and rebuffed his offer. Just before Charlie was ready to close shop for the weekend, he made a reservation at an upscale restaurant (he had extra money and no longer felt the need to scrimp and save) and tucked a couple of tabloids under his arm to pass the time while he ate. As he reached for the doorknob to leave, the phone in the storeroom began to ring incessantly. It was Angelique.

"Did you miss me?"

"Where the hell have you been? I was beginning to think you were dead."

"I am very much alive, and it's none of your business where I've been. Do you have the package?"

"Package?"

"Don't joke with me. Do you have the book? You said it would be ready when I called."

"I have it. There were a couple technical difficulties…"

"Really? Something about that doesn't sound right."

"Sorry, everything is okay. I was just was tired of waiting, that's all."

"But you have the book?"

"I said I have it."

"And you've been waiting with the book?"

"I've been waiting with it."

"That's almost funny, don't you think?"

"Why?"

"You've had the book long enough to get tired of waiting for me."

"I didn't say that. I said I have it and have been waiting with it. What's funny about that?"

"How long have you had the book, exactly?"

Charlie knew something was wrong by the tone of her voice – it was firm and penetrating, as if she were a parent who knew something and was waiting for the child to confess – and by her curiosity over how long he had been waiting with the book. Because a slip of the tongue could blow the whole deal apart, he decided to tread as lightly and vaguely as he could, at least until he understood what was behind her questions. "Not long. Like I said, there was a slight complication, but that's over and I have it."

"The book?"

"Yeah, the book."

80

"You do?" she said as if she were giving him one last chance to confess.

"Yeah, I do."

"Are you really sure you have the book I asked for?"

"What's with all the questions? Did you change your mind? If you're not certain, why don't you come and see for yourself? You have the money, don't you?"

There was a long pause on the other end. "May I tell you a funny story?" Angelique finally began, her voice now sounding dull and flat.

"Sure, go ahead, I could use a laugh."

"I think you'll appreciate it. I went to the exhibition every day this week, including today. In fact, I just got back from the exhibition."

"Did you like it?" By this time, Charlie knew what she was going to say.

"Very much. Do you know the moral of the story or, perhaps I should say, the punch line?"

"No."

"It's simple. I didn't come to your shop earlier, because I saw the book at the exhibition. As long as it was there, I knew you didn't have it – the book, I mean – and so why come and give you more money for something you didn't have?"

"Seems reasonable."

"You're funny. So, as I said, I just got back from the exhibition…"

"And was it as good as the first time, or did you see something else that piqued your interest?"

"Now, Charlie, didn't you suggest that you would have the book by now? In fact, didn't you just tell me you had the book?"

"The answer to both is yeah."

"But how can that be? I just saw the book at the exhibition."

Charlie paused this time. "Were you able to examine the book? I mean, are you sure that was the book?"

"What are you saying?"

"Did you want a scandal on your hands? Look, let's not talk like this. Meet me at" – he named the restaurant where he had a reservation – "and I guarantee that within five minutes you'll be smiling. You're hungry, aren't you?"

One hour later they were sitting across from one another in a discrete corner of the restaurant where they could talk privately and see anyone entering or leaving the establishment. Charlie changed the reservation to get this particular table, because he didn't entirely trust Angelique and wondered if she had friends who might be on the lookout for him. The conversation, however, was pleasant, more or less. There were smiles, nods, and the occasional pat on the forearm. They were interrupted a few times by the waiter, who took their orders and made sure that everything else was exactly to their liking. After perhaps ten minutes, the friendliness seemed to fade (at least on Angelique's part) and, at one point, she stood up evidently prepared to leave. Charlie, however, reached over to her and gently guided her back to her seat, after which he leaned toward her and said something that appeared to change her mind about leaving, although her expression seemed to hover between anger and coldness.

Charlie continued talking while Angelique remained silent, and occasionally he interrupted his own words with a quick glance around the restaurant or at the waiter, who insisted on providing service even though Charlie kept waving him off. Whatever Charlie said, it must have been persuasive, for the coldness soon left Angelique's face and body, and she resumed her pleasant, charming, and even flirtatious manner. When the conversation was over, having apparently ended on a positive note, he pulled something out from under his shirt and handed it to her under the table, which she quickly deposited in the large purse she brought with her (it was difficult to see precisely what was going on because of the tablecloth and constant flow of people and staff in front of the table). She immediately got up, leaned over and kissed him on the cheek, and left the restaurant with a confident stride.

Interestingly, Angelique didn't give him anything in return, not even a business card. Charlie remained seated for a few more minutes and, after paying the bill, left the restaurant, walking in the opposite direction.

One hour later, Charlie was seated comfortably on the evening train, the pallid overhead light casting dark shadows throughout the practically empty car, which jerked back and forth whenever it changed tracks.

Chapter 15

No sooner had Charlie opened his front door than he was met with an insistent phone call. The conversation lasted no more than a minute, if that, but it was long enough to sour his relatively positive frame of mind (that is, if Charlie could ever be said to have a positive frame of mind). On his way back to the city, he stopped at the news stand at the entrance of the Underground and picked up a couple of tabloids. The proprietor of the stand, Mr. Jenkins, liked Charlie and always tried to exchange a few words with him when he had the chance.

"Charlie, are you sure those are going to be enough for you?" The unshaven Mr. Jenkins was heavyset and dressed rather shabbily, today wearing gloves without fingertips. "You still got room in your backpack. Okay, but here's what I don't understand. You have that fancy bookstore, and yet you seem to be more interested in this trash. You're a curiosity."

Charlie smiled and, after pocketing his wallet, patted Mr. Jenkins firmly on the shoulder. "Nothing curious about it. I can appreciate Shakespeare, Webster, Milton, and the rest, but there are times when I prefer to be entertained by the trash, as you call it. In fact, I find some of this more interesting than *Hamlet*, especially when it concerns the common man, like you and me. What happens to kings and queens may be the stuff of grand tragedy, but it will never be as compelling as what happens to ordinary people."

"I'm with you, my man. I never cared for any of that fancy stuff they rammed down our throats at school."

Charlie smiled again and then walked quickly into the Underground. That was the last time Mr. Jenkins saw Charlie.

Chapter 16

Sedgwick had only been able to pull up a few more things about Sanders after Thwait called and requested more background on Charles Sanders and his shop. Sanders was either divorced or separated and was living alone or with a grown son in the flat above the shop. The shop had been operational for nearly a year and, although it didn't do a landmark business (compared to the surrounding shops and business), it nevertheless saw a steady stream of customers going in and out of its front door. The shop should have been closed (according to its business hours) when Nesbit and Thwait arrived, but the front door was unlocked and Sanders was inside helping a white-haired woman settle on a plain, black vase.

Sanders looked at the door when the men entered. Smiling, he greeted them and promised to help them as soon as he was finished with the woman and her vase.

Nesbit nodded pleasantly in return and, after wandering around the small shop while Sanders disputed with the woman, he positioned himself in front of the door in case Sanders got nervous and tried to flee. Thwait, at Nesbit's instruction, placed himself a few feet away, in sight of Sanders but far enough away to prevent Sanders from being spooked at their presence. While they waited, both men glanced at Sanders from time to time, and both were surprised by Sanders' close resemblance to Charlie, despite the former's blue leisure suit and open collar.

When the woman finally left, vase in hand, Nesbit walked over to Sanders, flashed his credentials, and immediately began questioning him about his business, his whereabouts during the past week, his travel plans, and his relationship with Angelique, whom Sanders denied knowing. Since Nesbit had neglected to bring a photo of Angelique, he was forced to describe her from head to foot, but Sanders continued to deny any knowledge of her, just as he obstinately refused to confirm that he had ever been involved in any criminal enterprise.

"So you deny that you were ever at the Ravenswood Museum?" Nesbit demanded at one point.

"Ravenswood? No, I don't deny that. What made you think…"

"Then what were you doing there?"

"Seeing the antiquities, what do you think? I'm in the business. What else do you do there?"

84

Nesbit glowered at him. Before he was about to answer Sanders' question, Sanders told him that he wanted to close his shop so that customers, if they came in, wouldn't be privy to their conversation. Nesbit was hesitant to allow him so close to the door, but when Thwait positioned himself practically in front of it, he relented and allowed Sanders to lock the door and flip over the OPEN sign. When Sanders returned, this time with Thwait directly behind him, Nesbit peppered him with several more questions about the museum.

Scratching his chin, he stared at Sanders as if he had something on his mind. "Tell me again when you were there last?"

"What? I don't know. A week ago, I suppose."

"You suppose? Aren't you sure?"

"Why should I be? I don't keep a diary. If I go there, it's usually Sunday when my shop is closed."

"And what were you doing there?"

"What? When?"

"Okay, my friend, you're only making it harder on yourself. What were you doing there the last time you were there?"

"Last Sunday? I don't know. I looked at the Richardson Stones, and I tried to see the Royal Sapphires, but the line was too long."

Nesbit eyed Sanders carefully, as if the latter had said something that opened up a new line of questions. He was about to follow up on this line when Thwait lightly touched his sleeve and quietly asked if he could speak to him privately.

Observing Sanders warily in case he tried to slip away, Nesbit whispered quickly to Thwait that he had Sanders where he wanted him. It was only a matter of minutes before he incriminated himself.

"That's just it, sir," Thwait whispered back, watching both Sanders and Nesbit.

"What is? I don't understand. Do we have to discuss this now?"

"Well, sir, Angelique doesn't have the sapphires, and so our questions to Mr. Sanders…"

"Of course, she doesn't. But that doesn't mean he isn't plotting to get them."

"That's correct, sir. But my point is that if the sapphires are safe, which we know to be the case, then I'm not sure we have any cause to question him about the sapphires. Ms. Dubois, after all, was apprehended with a significant-looking book…"

"Melville?"

"I don't know, sir. But if that's the case, we might get something by asking him about the book and his relationship with Ms. Dubois from that angle."

"Tom, there's something wrong about this character. He looks too much like Charlie, he could even be his younger brother, and his hesitations and inconsistencies tell me that he's hiding something about the sapphires. I can smell it."

"Yes, sir, I noticed the resemblance, but right now we only have the book. I fear that if we continue pushing him on the sapphires, we may inadvertently give his representation something that will blow the case out of the water. That's only my opinion."

Nesbit was silent for a few moments. Glancing at Sanders and then at his colleague, he appeared to churning something around in his mind. "Are you sure about this book?"

"It hasn't been authenticated, but she's got a book."

"And the sapphires?"

"Right now, they're safe and..."

"All right," Nesbit replied, interrupting Thwait. Although he was whispering, his voice sounded strained and his jaw muscles twitched. "Fine, you got this from Sandwich, right? I hope she's right, because if she's the least bit off, this case might be blown sky high."

"Sir?"

Nesbit turned toward Sanders, his jaw muscles continuing to twitch, and glowered at him silently for a few seconds. When Sanders returned his stare, he turned back to Thwait, observing the young man's earnest, heavy features, and he felt sorry that his collar appeared tight and threatening to strangle him. Nesbit's features softened and once again became the Nesbit that Thwait admired and respected. "I'm sorry, Tom, you're right," he conceded. "I just don't know what I was thinking. Everything you said was right, and I owe you my sincere thanks for putting us back on track."

"Sir, I'm sure you would do the same in my shoes. We can rest assured that if anything changes, Inspector Sedgwick..."

"Tom, you and I need to be calling the audibles here. When the time is right, we'll reach out to...to whatever her name is."

"Audibles? Her name is Inspector Sed..."

"Right. Now, let's get back to Sanders here. Something about the man doesn't sit right with me." He glanced at Sanders, who was now tapping his right shoe impatiently.

"Sir?"

Nesbit hesitated for a moment and straightened his back. Still facing Thwait, he motioned to Sanders with a backward movement of his head. "Take a good look at him. It's obvious he's involved in something. Notice the guilty look, and remember how he evaded my questions regarding his activities? He's not acting like an innocent man."

"I don't understand, sir. We weren't questioning him about the book…"

"No," Nesbit snapped but immediately changed his tone. "That's correct. But there's something bigger here. There's something wrong with his confidence, his calmness, his shifty eyes and…and all the rest. Normal people, people who have nothing to hide, don't…they don't respond to questions like he's doing. They get nervous, they hem and haw, and they agree to almost anything if you push them hard enough. I don't think we could beat the truth out of him."

"Sir?"

"Don't forget the contradictions. He can't get the times straight when he visited the museum. It's smells bad, Tom."

Thwait looked at Sanders and then turned back to Nesbit.

"Sir, we are speaking about the book now, correct?"

"The book, the sapphires, they're all related. But, yes, I am referring obliquely to the book."

"Sir, may I ask one more question."

Nesbit smiled. "Of course, my friend, only make it quick. I have a feeling that we're going to be putting that character on ice in a few minutes."

"Well, sir, you rightly noted that he'd run once the goods were delivered. If, as it appears to be the case, Ms. Dubois has the book, then it stands to reason that if he were associated with that crime, he would at least be making preparations to get out of Dodge. Is that the correct phrase? Anyway, his shop looks full and tidy, and he was clearly taking his time with a customer when we arrived. He doesn't look like he's in a hurry to go anywhere."

"He doesn't know we've apprehended Angelique. As far as he's concerned, he can make a leisurely exit from the country."

"Yes, sir. One more question please, because I am only trying to understand."

"Quickly, my friend, before our iceberg over there starts getting suspicious." He shot a quick smile to Sanders, who glanced at his watch.

"Officers," Sanders said before Thwait had a chance to ask his question. "Do you mind if I close out my register?"

"Sure, do what you have to do," Nesbit replied, glancing over his shoulder at Sanders. But no sooner had he concurred than he began to have second thoughts and walked over to the register and demanded to see inside the drawer. Once he was confident that there wasn't a weapon inside, he stepped back to Thwait and turned his full attention to the younger man.

While Sanders was carefully counting out the contents of the drawer, Thwait continued speaking, albeit with a troubling look on his round face. "Sir, would it matter very much if he didn't know? I mean, concerning Ms. Dubois. With all due respect, once he's handed over the book, his part of the job is finished and there's no reason for him to stick around. He doesn't have a solid long-term business here, and so he doesn't appear to have anything that would encourage him to stay, especially if there's any possibility of Ms. Dubois implicating him in return for a reduced sentence."

Nesbit thought for a moment and took another hard look at Sanders, who was busy noting the contents of the drawer on a slip of paper and didn't see Nesbit staring at him. "Maybe you have a point," he said turning back to Thwait. "But how would you explain my sense that something's not right in the state of Denmark, as Othello once said? I don't need to tell you that my sense has been honed through years of solid criminal investigations."

Thwait looked at Nesbit, knowing that he was on shaky ground. "Ah, well, sir, I…that is…"

"Come on, man, you're stuttering and we're running out of time."

"I would never doubt your sense, sir. Perhaps if he allowed us to check his flat, we could make a final determination as to whether he's really trying to leave. If nothing's out of place, we may have the wrong man."

"Allow us to check his flat? Good thinking. But why don't we just demand it?"

"I'm not sure we have cause, at least not yet…"

"No worries, Tom, he'll let us in. If I'm right, the place will be in disarray, and we'll have everything we need to take this one step further."

Nesbit smiled on one side of his mouth and, mumbling to himself, said, "They're peas in a pod."

Thwait nodded vaguely. They walked to Sanders, who, having finished counting the till, was increasingly anxious for the officers to leave.

Nesbit smiled knowingly. "Okay, are you ready, Chuck?"

"I suppose it depends on you gentlemen."

"Perhaps you'd like to tell us about other institutions you may or may not have visited recently."

"I told you what I did at the Ravenswood Museum. What do you mean by other institutions?"

"Are you planning any travel in the near term?"

"What? No."

"And yet you've cleaned out the register. If I'm not mistaken, the money is in the paper bag you're holding."

"I close out the register every evening. If you care to check, there's two hundred and thirty-five pounds in the bag [he held it out for Nesbit to inspect], which I'd like to drop off at the bank. There's another fifty in the till to start tomorrow's business."

Nesbit inspected the bag, which was exactly as he said, and handed it back to Sanders. Staring at him for a moment and tugging at his left earlobe as if something suddenly came to mind, Nesbit said, "I suppose you wouldn't mind showing us your flat, would you?"

"What? Why do you want to see my flat?"

"No reason. I'm just wondering if you have any immediate travel plans."

"I said I didn't. You can check the airlines and trains, if you don't believe me."

"Do you own a car?"

"No, why should I?"

"Why, indeed."

"Look, I live right upstairs." He motioned upward with his thumb. "I don't need a car. But if it will get you two out of here, then, please, by all means, check out my flat."

Nesbit smiled, while Thwait looked at one man and then the other.

Sanders led them to a staircase at the opposite end of the shop. Once inside the flat, he sat down on a chair in the kitchen and let the men inspect the place from one end to the other. Besides the kitchen, there were two small bedrooms, a tiny living room, a bathroom and three closets. There was also an assortment of furniture and wall decorations, none of which seemed rare or expensive. Nesbit and Thwait inspected the closets and drawers, which were filled with clothes and sundry items, and then checked the refrigerator and kitchen cabinets, which were both packed with a variety of food items. Nothing was out of the ordinary. Nothing suggested to either man that Sanders was going anywhere anytime soon. Since they had no reason to detain him, Nesbit gave him a stern warning not to leave town, and he and Thwait left the flat and shop.

Back inside the car, Nesbit sat sullenly, at first wondering if and when Sanders would bolt. Sanders' resemblance to Charlie – both his physical appearance and his attitude – angered him, but what bothered him even more was the fact that since they couldn't charge the man, they couldn't put out an alert at the borders in case he tried to leave the country. He held Sedgwick at least partly responsible for this, although he couldn't have said why Sedgwick was responsible for this or anything else. Thwait, in passing, noted that they could question Ms. Dubois tomorrow morning. "It's too late to see her now," he stated and then expressed his confidence that Nesbit would get her to finger her accomplices.

"Wait a minute," Nesbit said, sitting up in his seat and looking at Thwait. "There's still Charlie. Let's check on him one more time just to be sure."

Narrowly avoiding an oncoming vehicle, Thwait turned the car around and, squealing the tires briefly, headed directly to Charlie's shop, which was only a couple blocks away.

"I hope it's not closed," Thwait said.

Nesbit held onto the dash and silently looked down at his shoes.

Chapter 17

Nesbit refused to relinquish the idea that Charlie was at the heart of whatever was going down – the book, the sapphires, it didn't matter. Since it was getting late, most of the shops on the street were closed or closing, including Charlie's. Noticing that the shop's lights were out and a CLOSED sign was hanging in the door window, Nesbit nodded to himself, as if this were all the evidence he needed to demonstrate Charlie's involvement in Angelique's criminal enterprise. Both men were surprised when they noticed in the pale overhead light that Charlie's door wasn't completely closed, an indication that someone had closed it but hadn't taken care to see if it was secure. Nesbit reached out and gave the doorknob a slight twist.

"Funny," he whispered, as if he didn't want anyone to hear them talking, "The door is locked."

"Locked?" Thwait responded, also whispering.

"Yes. What do you make of it?"

"I don't know, sir. Perhaps Mr. Saunders didn't carefully close the door when he left for the day? I think we might be advised to call in before we proceed further. I mean, even though the door is clearly open a little, it's nevertheless locked, which could be legally construed to mean that Mr. Saunders had intended the door to be inaccessible regardless of its actual condition. If we enter now, without a warrant, knowing it's locked, we are essentially entering without his permission. What I meant to say, sir, that entering now could constitute unlawful entry…"

Nesbit paused and looked at his younger colleague. "You could be a solicitor, my friend," he said and, keeping his eyes on his younger colleague, pushed the door completely open with the side of his shoe. "But as you can see, the door is clearly open, and neither one of us applied any undue pressure to open it. Do you know what I think? I think the knob was accidently locked or jammed – it happens all the time – and therefore Charlie's intent was not to keep us out of his shop. If this were indeed his intent, Tom, how do you explain the fact that the door is now open?"

Thwait looked at him with a puzzled expression on his heavy face.

Nesbit shrugged his narrow shoulders as if to suggest that his logic was airtight. Turning toward the door and crouching slightly, he took a step into the dark shop and whispered loudly, "Charlie, old boy, are you there? Charlie? Charlie, do you mind if we come in a look around a bit? If you object, please let us know now." Nesbit turned back to Thwait. "See," he said, still whispering, "He didn't object, so it appears that we are well within our purview to enter and look around as we see fit."

Thwait smiled faintly. "I guess so, sir."

Nesbit switched on the glaring, overhead light. "Charlie?" he said again, this time in a normal voice. "Is anyone here?"

When no one answered, Nesbit quietly closed the door behind them and pulled down the blind over the door. Confident that they could work in private, he and Thwait took a look around the shop. At first glance, nothing appeared amiss or out of the ordinary. Walking toward the back of the shop, Nesbit noticed with distaste the volume that Charlie had tried to sell him. It was sticking out of the shelf where Charlie had reinserted it, and Nesbit, gritting his teeth, shoved it back into the shelf, knocking over a couple of other books in the process.

Thwait was on the other side of the shop while this was happening, and, as he strolled behind the table where Charlie normally sat, glancing at the floor and shelves as he moved, he practically ran into the register drawer, which was hanging open like the tongue of a panting dog. It surprised him that, unlike Sanders' drawer, it was completely empty. Turning around, he noticed that the storeroom door, which was always closed when Charlie was in the shop, was half open. Thwait was about to call for his colleague when he noticed that he was already at his shoulder. Nesbit nodded silently in recognition of his colleague's discoveries, and motioned for Thwait to 'cover him' while he cautiously entered the storeroom.

"Tom," he called out from inside a few seconds later, "Come look at this." When Thwait entered, Nesbit was on his knees in front of a hole in the floor, the floorboards having been pushed aside. "Looks suspiciously like a place to hide a strong box. What do you make of this? Is there any money in the register?"

"No, sir. If there was ever any money in it, it's been cleaned out."

"Strange, Sanders left a few pounds in his." Nesbit stood up and pointed out an overturned bookcase, the contents of which were on the floor. The table in the center of the room had been cleared, too, and there were some books on the floor, quite possibly having once been on the table.

"A robbery, sir?"

"Or the result of someone leaving quickly...before the authorities caught up with him."

"What about the toppled shelf?"

"Not our concern."

"Where do you think Mr. Saunders is?"

"My guess is on his way out of the country."

"Do you think he was actually involved with Ms. Dubois, then?"

"I don't think it, my friend; I know it. If we hadn't wasted our time with that Sanders fellow, we might have caught Charlie on his way out the door."

"What should we do now, sir?"

Nesbit tugged lightly at his left earlobe. "That's a good question. Since we don't know where he lives – I suppose I should say lived – we might as well look around a bit for something that might help us find out where he is now."

"Yes, sir, that makes sense. We'll have to write this up, so it would also be useful to get a better sense of what happened here."

Nesbit nodded absently.

Thwait went back to the main entry and inspected the handle, latch, and keyhole. "No signs of forcible entry, sir."

Nesbit walked over to the door and, after giving it a cursory inspection, agreed. "No signs that anyone tried to get in. Our boy must have been in a hurry. He didn't care whether the door was locked or not as he left."

"I'll call it in, sir," Thwait began to say when he noticed Nesbit on his knees, fumbling with something on the floor at the base of one of the book cases, the one which held pre-1800s books. "Sir?"

"Look at this, Tom. What do you make of it?" Nesbit held up a small card with Charlie's name on it.

"A business card?"

"Yes, but look at this. The address…it doesn't match the address of the shop." He stood up and, after brushing the dust from his slacks, handed the card to Thwait. "What do you think?"

"A home address? Seems rather strange to put a home address on a card."

"I agree. But maybe this is old, or at least older than the shop. Maybe he was working out of his flat at the time he had it printed. Take a quick look around. Do you see anything else of interest?"

"Not immediately. I'll call it in, sir."

"No, if I'm right about what I'm thinking, we don't have time. We can call it in on our way."

"Way, sir?"

"To Charlie's flat." Nesbit began walking toward the outside door.

"What if this is an old address?" Thwait asked as he struggled to keep up with his colleague.

"It could be, Tom, but right now we don't have anything else to go on. Hurry, he could be leaving this very second."

Nesbit stopped abruptly when they reached the car. Turning to Thwait, he held out his hand. "Give me the keys, my friend."

"Sir?"

"I'll drive this time. You navigate."

Chapter 18

It should have been a relatively straightforward trip. Indeed, it was practically a straight shot (except for a few curves and a great number of roundabouts), but it quickly became complicated when Nesbit disregarded Thwait's direction and made a wrong turn not more than fifteen minutes from their destination. Trying to correct his mistake, Nesbit compounded the problem by getting lost in a maze of narrow, one-way streets that seemed invariably to direct them to the outskirts of the village. At one point, they could actually see the road they needed to take, but since there was no way to enter it (all the connections to it allowed traffic to exit the road but not enter it, at least not from this part of town), they were forced to run parallel with it as it led them to the outskirts. By sheer luck, and a well-timed suggestion from Thwait, they managed to find the one connection that took them back into the village and, with a minor detour along the way, to the building where Charlie lived.

The building was a square, brick edifice that looked exactly like all the other buildings in the neighborhood. Nesbit and Thwait entered the main door, which was next to an open vegetable shop, and climbed the four flights to the address (the elevator was out of order). Standing on either side of the dark, wooden door, Nesbit knocked three times and then craned his head toward the door to listen for signs of life on the other side.

There was no answer. Thwait took his turn and pounded on the door five times, each one louder and more forceful than Nesbit's solid knocks. When there wasn't a response after thirty seconds, Thwait turned around and stood with his back against the door. Nesbit shook his head and, tapping the younger man gently on his large, perspiring chest, led him by his sleeve away from the door. With both men now positioned on either side of the door, Nesbit carefully leaned forward and placed his ear to the door, slightly above the doorknob, and listened intently as if he were examining the heart of a dying patient. For a second or two, he heard the faint whoosh of an ocean-like sound, but it quickly faded and nothing else filtered through the door, not even a creak from the building.

Nesbit straightened up and looked at Thwait. "No one's inside," he said quietly. "Or else they're listening for us." Stepping around the door and pulling Thwait by the sleeve, Nesbit led him a few feet away so that they could talk a little more freely. "What do you say?" he whispered in Thwait's left ear.

"Should we give him a couple of minutes to think we left, or kick the door open now and catch him in the act?"

"The act?"

"Of escaping."

"What? No, sir, we can't do that. We don't have authorization. What if it's the wrong address?"

"My friend, I can do that. You can follow me in, and you've done nothing wrong."

Thwait hesitated. "I don't know, sir."

Nesbit looked at him and, without saying another word, went over to the door and tested the handle. It opened. Quietly opening the door an inch, Nesbit glanced at Thwait, smiled, and then entered. Thwait quickly followed.

The lights were on but no one was in the flat. Nesbit checked both rooms while Thwait checked the bathroom. When they were done, they returned to the living room and stood on either side of the small table next to the wall. The table was empty save for an old book without its cover. Nesbit picked it up and examined it, after which he handed it to Thwait.

"It's pretty ragged," said Thwait, handing it back to his colleague.

"It's an old book, Tom, the kind our friend purveys," Nesbit added and tossed it back on the table. "I think we should look around a little more carefully."

Thwait immediately went into the bedroom, where he examined an old dresser against the wall and the closet, one of the doors of which was out of alignment and wouldn't open or close. Satisfied that there was nothing of particular interest in the room, Thwait went into the lavatory where he examined the medicine cabinet and picked up a couple bottles of something from the edge of the tub (a half-empty bottle of shampoo and a full bottle of conditioner). When he returned to the main room, Nesbit was again standing by the side of the table and staring at the coverless book.

"Sir," Thwait began cautiously, as if he were hesitant to disturb Nesbit's concentration. "His stuff appears to be here, but the contents in the drawers are messy and unfolded. It looks a little like someone was in a hurry and grabbed some stuff on the way out."

Nesbit turned to the younger man and eyed him as he churned something around in his mind.

"Yes, and take a look at this," Thwait continued, holding out a slip of paper. "I found it in the top drawer. It's a credit-card receipt from a restaurant, and it has Mr. Saunders' name on it. What do you make of it?"

"It reinforces what we already know – that we have the right place," Nesbit replied, looking at the paper without reaching for it. Rubbing the back of his neck with his left hand, he glanced around the room for something and then turned back to Thwait. "Let me take another look at this," he said reaching for the paper. He silently studied it, looking at the front and back and then holding it up to the light. "Find anything else?" he asked when he completed his examination.

"Nothing much, just some clothes...."

"Did you check under the bed?"

"Yes."

"Did you happen to notice that the address of the establishment and the time out friend visited it are both on the receipt?"

"Yes, sir."

Nesbit was silent for a moment. "Tom, don't you find it curious that Charlie would leave something like this behind? It places him in London at a specific location and time. We might be able to use this to get more information and track his movements."

"I suppose it could have fallen out of his pocket."

"Possibly, but I'm in no mood for suppositions. You know what I think, my friend? I think it wasn't a mistake. I think he's playing with us, and when someone's playing with me, I know I have our man."

"You're certain this is the right man, not Mr. Sanders."

"Charlie's our man, all right." Nesbit pocketed the receipt and they walked silently out of the flat.

When they were on the ground floor, Nesbit told Thwait to check the street and then the area behind the building.

"Sir?"

"Now's not the time for questions, Tom. Charlie might be hiding somewhere or he might have dropped something else incriminating. A cursory look, that's all. I'll go around from the other side."

When they were both back in front of the building, Thwait said deferentially, "Should we contact the landlord to see if he moved out or provided forwarding information?"

Nesbit considered his question for a moment. The phone in his pocket began to ring.

"Aren't you going to answer it, sir? It could be important."

"I'll check the message later."

"There's also the grocer downstairs who might have seen or heard something. Maybe he knows Mr. Saunders."

Nesbit smiled vaguely and nodded, and together they visited the landlord and the grocer. Neither person had information that was useful to the case. The landlord, a sickly individual who spoke to them through a half-closed door, didn't care whether Charlie was gone or not because he was paid up to the end of the month. The grocer was a large, sweaty man with a thick black mustache, and he seemed happy to speak to Nesbit and Thwait while he straightened the large vegetable bin in the front of his store and then washed the floors down with a garden hose. At first, he denied knowing Charlie (he even demanded a photo because, he claimed, he remembered faces better than names), but after he wiped the sweat from his forehead with a stiff, red handkerchief retrieved from his back pocket, his memory gradually returned and he admitted that he saw Charlie from time to time, adding that Charlie often purchased the beets (he pointed to a small wicker basket on the floor), which were better than any found in London. However, he insisted that he didn't know where Charlie was and, blowing his bulbous nose into the same handkerchief, he stated that he wouldn't say even if he knew, not even if he were strung up by his weak, inflamed ankles (he pulled up his trousers to emphasize their precarious state). "But let me say this," he said, glancing from Nesbit to Thwait, small crystalline droplets hanging onto the edge of his mustache, "He's a gentlemen, that's what he is, and a gentlemen won't have nothing to do with what you're claiming. I hope he calls Scotland Yard, that's what I hope."

Three hours later, they were finally at the station. The trip back might have been quicker, but Nesbit, who was again driving, complained about his night blindness which, he emphasized, had caused him to miss their exit three times and forced them to travel through city streets instead of using the expressway when they could. Once inside the building, they had to meander through the darkened hallways (some of the lights had been turned off to conserve energy) until they finally reached Thwait's desk. Sedgwick was still in the office when they arrived, and she came over to them as they were going through some papers.

"Seggi," Nesbit uttered, smiling and trying to be friendly. "I'm glad to see you. Tom and I were just talking about all your good work."

"Inspector Sedgwick," Thwait gently interrupted, "We just got back from Mr. Saunders' shop and flat, and it seems he skipped. We don't know his location at the moment, but judging from the disarray of both places, he left in a hurry."

Sedgwick was dressed in a plain, dark suit, although she appeared fresh and alert as if she had just arrived at the station. She had, in fact, been at the station since early morning. "After your call," she began in a slightly monotonous tone, the left side of her mouth drooping noticeably, "A couple of our officers were dispatched to the shop. They scoured the place but couldn't determine whether it had been robbed or Saunders had been abducted. We aren't ruling out either at the moment."

"What?" Nesbit cried out, his nerves strained by the day's events and the fact that, for some reason, he didn't like Sedgwick. "Abduction? What are you talking about? He wasn't abducted. He's a grown man, for crying out loud. He skipped, and it was probably because he heard that Angelique was apprehended. And the only way he could have known that was through a leak in your department. You should do some checking, Ms. Sedg, before things get ugly."

Sedgwick looked at Nesbit for a moment before turning to Thwait. "Constable Thwait, I'm not sure what Agent Nesbit is speaking about. Angelique Dubois has been released. I thought you knew."

Nesbit nearly fell down. When he got himself back under control, he glowered at Sedgwick as if this were her fault. Taking a step forward to tell her what he thought of her work, he immediately took a step back when Sedgwick stepped forward and challenged him to say what was on his mind. Thwait immediately intervened and, standing next to Nesbit, respectfully asked Sedgwick why Angelique had been released. "She was apprehended with the stolen book," he added. "She was attempting to leave the country. How could she be released?"

Inspector Sedgwick sighed. "Come with me to the Chief's office. He's still in. We'll fill you in there."

Chapter 19

The Chief's office was a large, practically empty room. There was a tall bookcase against one wall – and besides a few books on law enforcement, the shelves contained a silver trophy with a tennis player on top, a framed service award (face down), and a framed photograph (face up) of his wife and twenty-two year old son – a small, round table in the center of the room, and at one end an undistinguished desk with a worn, black executive chair behind it and three plain, black chairs in front. Sedgwick knocked quietly at the closed door and the three entered when Chief grunted a barely audible "enter"

"Inspector Sedgwick, I'm glad to see you," the Chief said when he saw Sedgwick. "And I see you've brought Constable Thwait and Agent Nesbit." Without getting out of his chair, he motioned for the three of them to come into his office, meaning in front of his desk. "Your timing is impeccable, Inspector Sedgwick. Do you know what time it is, by the way? I was expected home hours ago."

Ignoring both the others and the small talk, Nesbit demanded an explanation for the situation regarding Angelique. "She's been released, is that correct? I thought there was enough to put her away for life." He was angry and ready to lash out at anyone who provided the wrong answer.

"Sit down," the Chief said, pointing to the chair directly behind Nesbit. "Constable Thwait, would you kindly take a seat, too?" The Chief motioned to a chair on his other side. Sedgwick started to leave, but the Chief asked her to stay. "We'll need you, too."

The Chief pulled a pencil from his top drawer and began tapping the sharpened end on the surface of his desk. After squinting first at Thwait, who recoiled slightly from his gaze, and then at Nesbit, who returned his gaze defiantly, he informed the officers that Angelique had been officially released.

"By whose stupid orders?"

The Chief momentarily stopped tapping his pencil. Sitting up rigidly, his military bearing clearly evident, he squinted at Nesbit and said, "Agent Nesbit, you will speak to me with a civil tongue. Do I make myself clear?"

Thwait involuntarily leaned back in his chair, his sagging eyes wide open.

"Yes," Nesbit grumbled.

"Sir."

"What?"

"Sir."

"Yes, sir."

"Now, Agent Nesbit, what was your question?"

Gritting his teeth, he asked, "Who gave the order to release Angelique, and why was she released…sir?"

The Chief looked at Thwait for a moment and then at both officers. Tapping his pencil, he replied, "I was the one who gave the stupid order, as you kindly termed it, Agent Nesbit, to release Angelique. We didn't have anything on her, and so we couldn't hold her without raising a host of legal issues that I didn't want to deal with. In fact, her legal representation said the very same thing."

"What? Who cares about solicitors? She was apprehended with a stolen book, the Melville first edition, if I'm not mistaken. Since the book is priceless, you could have kept her on ice for some time, especially given the fact that she is, or was, a flight risk…sir."

The Chief's pencil suddenly fell from his hand and landed on his desk, where it rolled noisily to one side and rested against a stack of folders. Squinting at Nesbit, he said, "We don't operate that way in this country, Agent Nesbit, and, for your information, I care about solicitors and barristers. Dubois was hardly a flight risk, since we didn't have any basis to detain her, and neither the EU nor Interpol has issued any warrants on her. If you have a problem with Interpol, that's your business."

"She isn't a British subject, and you didn't need a red warrant. All you needed was the book – a priceless, irreplaceable object of British heritage."

The Chief glanced briefly at Sedgwick. Turning back to Nesbit, he replied, "Her citizenship and the book aren't relevant, Agent Nesbit."

"What are you talking about…sir?"

"I'm not quite sure what you're talking about. She was detained because of the book. We rushed a book expert to take a look at it, and it didn't take thirty seconds before he burst out laughing."

"Laughing, sir?" Thwait interjected.

"Agent Nesbit, Constable Thwait, the book she was carrying was a fake. Well, maybe that's giving the forger too much credit for his efforts."

"I still don't understand," Nesbit stammered.

"I can't say I'm surprised." The Chief paused and picked up his pencil. Tapping it against his desk, he continued, "Officers, whoever made the fake, if we can call it that, took a commercial reproduction of the book –

probably obtained from the exhibition – and replaced its cover with a 19th century cover. The book looks old on the outside, but isn't on the inside." The Chief smiled briefly, squinting at the same time. "The upshot is that we didn't have anything to hold her on – and no one has yet reported a missing book cover – and so we had to let her go. Are there any questions?"

"Sir, there was a book at Mr. Saunders' flat..."

"The cover," Nesbit gasped. "It's the cover that's valuable," he said out loud, speaking to no one in particular. "I'll bet that fool didn't examine the book very carefully. But if the cover itself isn't valuable, then there's something hidden inside of it. That's it. That's the key. Where's the cover now...sir?"

"I believe she took it with her when she left," interjected Inspector Sedgwick. "It was her book, cover and all."

"Damn it all!" Nesbit shouted and stood up.

"Sit down, Nesbit," the Chief said calmly and yet forcibly.

Nesbit complied. "With all due respect...sir," he said, barely able to control his emotions, "With all due respect, how long ago was she released?" He appeared to have trouble swallowing as he uttered the word 'released.'

"About four hours ago," noted Sedgwick.

"Four hours?" Nesbit stammered, looking at the Chief and ignoring Sedgwick. "She could be out of the country by now. This is outrageous...sir. How come we weren't informed earlier?"

"We tried calling you," Sedgwick said. "I left you a message. I left one on Constable Thwait's phone, too."

Nesbit looked down for a moment at the pocket holding his phone and then took a deep breath. "Okay, did anyone speak to her while we were gone?"

"I did," said Sedgwick. "But she refused to say anything until her representation arrived. Later on, after the book was examined, she stated that it was hers but refused to provide any additional details."

"That's all?"

"I'm afraid so."

Nesbit glanced briefly at Thwait. "If only we had a chance to speak to her..."

The Chief pulled an old briefcase from the floor next to his desk and placed it on top. "If only, but I don't think it would have changed anything."

Nesbit looked up and once again a determined look came across his face. "What about Charlie Saunders? Where is he?"

"We don't know," said the Chief, leaning back in his chair after having put some folders into his briefcase. "We'll look into it as a possible disappearance."

"Charles Sanders?"

"He's not wanted in this case. And right now, we don't have anything outstanding on him."

Nesbit nodded quietly. "...sir, Tom and I would still like to pursue this case."

"What case? There's no case now."

"There are a couple things we'd like to clear up regarding Charlie."

"Saunders?"

"Yes. We'd like to find out where he's at. Something doesn't add up."

The Chief thought for a moment and then squinted at Thwait, as if he were trying to gauge his young officer's interest. "All right," he replied, squinting at Nesbit. "You have three days, no more. Is that satisfactory?"

Nesbit nodded.

"But no extra resources, and you're responsible for the bar tabs at the hotel."

Chapter 20

The following day, Nesbit and Thwait checked with immigration to see if there was information on Charlie. They were almost certain that he left the EU, or at least the UK. But when that effort proved fruitless, they returned to the HQ and began paging through civil and criminal databases for something that might help them locate the man or at least understand his background. By the end of the evening, they had managed to uncover a few more details about him, but for the most part these merely confirmed what they already knew about him. Charlie had been renting a flat for about a year, and during the same period he had leased a small commercial space for his bookshop. There was nothing on him prior to renting the flat and taking out a proper business license. Unfortunately, no one seemed to have verified any of the statements he made or even if his name was actually Charlie Saunders. His name might have been Charles Saunders, or some variation on the names, but then again it could just as easily have been Harrison Bottoms, Bud Ox, or a host of other names attached to men approximately the same age and appearance as Charlie. No one checked. Nesbit and Thwait pulled together a thick portfolio of mug shots of persons who might be Charlie Saunders, but it was difficult, if not impossible, to make a firm connection because they didn't have anything else to confirm the connection.

Nesbit reluctantly concluded that their man might not be called Charlie Saunders. But since they didn't have enough objective information or evidence on which to make this claim, they were still no closer to apprehending the man than they were at the outset of the investigation. Perhaps it wasn't exactly surprising that there was no shortage of derogatory information on a certain Charles Sanders, who didn't appear to be the same individual as their Charlie. Once its network was back online, the Canadian embassy, however, provided a wealth of information on Charles Sanders and, in addition to a range of petty crimes and suspicions, he was a convicted thief, extortionist, forger, black-marketer, dealer in stolen antiquaries – and this information pretty much confirmed what at least Thwait was beginning to suspect – that is, that Angelique, like Nesbit and Thwait themselves, had mistaken Charlie for Charles, and this mistaken identity had apparently (luckily?) put the kibosh on the heist (both the sapphires and the Melville were safe and sound). Nevertheless, mistaken or not, it was abundantly clear to Nesbit that Charlie was up to something. How else could someone explain his blank background, the absence of business revenue, or his abrupt departure from both his business and his flat – not to mention the mysterious, butchered book left in his flat, which may have provided the cover for the book that was in Angelique's possession? Could Charlie have duped Angelique and serendipitously foiled what could have been a monumental theft of British (or American) heritage? To Nesbit, it was beginning to seem that way.

"So were they working together all along or not?" Thwait asked Nesbit once they were back at the hotel and sitting across from one another with a new stack of papers spread out in front of them. A bucket holding an expensive bottle of French wine was next to the papers.

Drink in hand, Nesbit paused and considered the question. "Fifteen minutes ago, I would have said no, and fifteen minutes before that I would have said yes – and thirty minutes prior to either one, I would have said it's a fifty-fifty chance." Nesbit was much calmer now. He accepted the fact that the case – this case – was coming to an end and that he lacked enough information to continue his pursuit of Angelique (and now Charlie) to another country or continent, which would likely be the case. Breathing deeply, meditatively, he continued, "The problem, of course, is that he's gone, Angelique's gone, and we've only got their theoretical fingerprints on the book Angelique took with her out of the country. We can't even be sure if he was the Charlie who Angelique originally pegged for the heist. But, if you ask me, I'd say that he was in it for himself and duped the pretty thief. He probably got payment in advance and, when he realized that the job wasn't going to be easy, he jimmied up a quick fake and galloped off into the sunset."

"Then that's the end of it?"

"No, my friend, that's not the end of anything. In some ways, it's just the beginning. Sooner or later he's bound to stumble, and we or someone else will be there to catch him."

"Ms. Dubois?"

Nesbit leaned back in his chair and glanced at the ceiling. "Angelique, my friend, is a careerist. It's only a matter of time before we catch her. She's addicted to crime, especially big-time crime, and so even though this one might have been a learning lesson for her, she'll be back – and sooner than you think."

"But, sir, if, as you say, she paid something to Mr. Saunders, that money has to come from somewhere, and she's going to be responsible."

Nesbit sat up and smiled. "You're right about that, Tom." He chuckled a couple of times. "Our Charlie boy may have done us a favor if she doesn't have the money to pay for the item. This is probably going to cost her dearly. If we're lucky, Angelique's business dealings could be seriously curtailed. It's a wonderful thought."

"You're not suggesting that someone will kill her for what happened?"

Nesbit hesitated and smiled again. "I don't know. But would that be such a bad thing?"

Thwait shook his heavy head, his jowls moving in the opposite direction. "So unless we come up with something by the Chief's deadline, where does that leave us? We don't have Ms. Dubois, we don't have Mr. Saunders, and we don't know what exactly was going on between them. And Mr. Sanders...what about him?"

"Guilty of something, I'm sure, but definitely not related to our case." Nesbit stood up and stretched his back and neck. Facing the papers on the table, he shook his head and looked at Thwait. "It's eleven in the PM, my friend, and I can't think straight. Maybe it's the drink, but I needed it this night. Let's hit the sack and pick up again in the morning."

Thwait went back to his room. Early the following morning, he was awakened by pounding on the connecting door.

"Tom, wake up and come in here," Nesbit practically shouted.

Putting in his robe, Thwait came into Nesbit's room where he found him fully dressed and standing in front of the TV, watching a news bulletin.

"Can you believe it? Can you believe it?"

Thwait stood openmouthed in front of the TV as a news reporter announced that the Ravenswood Museum had been the victim of a daring midnight robbery. The reporter stated that while museum officials were preparing the Royal Sapphires for transport back to Buckingham Palace, they discovered that one of the display cases had been compromised and that its contents, some of the most valuable pieces of exhibition, were nowhere to be found. The image on the TV suddenly shifted away from the reporter to the museum, and while the camera gradually explored the museum and its various exhibits, the reporter added details about the museum, the history of the stones, the differences between sapphires and other precious jewels, and the exhibition itself, showing footage of the exhibition prior to its closure. When the cameras switched back to the reporter, he noted that even though the missing stones were priceless and their loss a tremendous blow to British heritage, museum officials had assured him that both the museum and the British public came out comparatively lucky. The thieves had been able to disable the exhibition's alarm system, and they could have made off with the entire collection had the other display cases not proved to be "unassailable." Smiling wistfully, the reporter promised to update the public as soon as Scotland Yard released additional information on the robbery.

"I can't believe it," Thwait said, finally closing his jaw. He was every bit as surprised as Nesbit, although his feeling of surprise lacked the element of joy in Nesbit's.

"My friend, time to get dressed and hit the road. We have some errands."

"Do you think it was Mr. Saunders? It seems strange that he would take the sapphires, since he seemed to be solely focused on the book. Maybe it was Mr. Sanders. After all, he is or was a retailer of antiquities."

"It doesn't matter either way. What's important is that we're back in business."

"Do you really think the Chief will extend your service and keep me on the case?"

Nesbit laughed. "Of course. Look, Tom, we're the only ones intimate with both the case and the suspects, metaphorically speaking. You know, I'd bet a pound against a good, old American dollar that the gentlemen and ladies at the top are holding the Chief's uncomfortably tight wingtips to the fire to solve this case quickly. By God, it's a national emergency, and we're the only ones positioned to take his smoldering toes out of the flames. Will the Chief keep us on the case? Can there be any doubt? He'd be a fool not to. Now, let's get moving."

Thwait ran back into his room, dressed in minutes, and then came back into Nesbit's room, where the TV was still blasting the news. But this time, his colleague wasn't quite as ebullient as before.

"I'm ready. What's the matter?"

"Take a look at this," Nesbit replied and motioned toward the TV. The news was still going on about the sensational robbery, but one of the TV reporters managed to get a spokesman from the department to say something about the situation. It was Sedgwick.

"We are working the case right now," Sedgwick was saying, the left side of her mouth drooping and her voice sounding slightly monotonous as she stood behind a makeshift podium in front of the station's main doors. "We have several substantive leads, but we are unable to provide additional details at this time because of the sensitivity of the sources. We are, however, at liberty to note that we have apprehended at least one possible suspect, a local dealer of antiquaries, who was caught on the museum's security cameras in and around the exhibition space near the Royal Sapphires. The subject in question has denied any knowledge of the theft, although a subsequent search of the subject's premises revealed several unrelated stolen items. We are also looking into the possibility that others aided the subject in the heist, quite possibly an international cartel that stretches halfway around the world. The subject denies being connected with this chain or any other criminal elements. We will provide more details as the investigation unfolds. Thank you."

Sedgwick was immediately deluged with shouts and demands for answers from a mass of reporters, many of whom were angling a smartphone, camera, or microphone toward her attractive but dour face. Unfazed, Sedgwick left the podium and, without looking back, quickly made her way into the building.

"We will continue to bring you the news you want to hear," a smiling, attractive female reporter said once Sedgwick was gone.

Nesbit shut off the set with the tip of his patent-leather shoe and tossed the remote on the bed.

"So it's Mr. Sanders, after all," Thwait gasped. "I wonder what information the station has. But it's strange, sir, that Inspector Sedgwick didn't mention Ms. Dubois. Maybe she's not involved. Maybe Ms. Dubois was only after the book…"

"No, it was Charlie," Nesbit insisted. "My gut, which is never wrong, tells me that he was the one who pulled off the heist, he and Angelique. Tom, he tricked us into believing that he and Angelique were only after a book. An American book, for God's sake, and who in their right mind would come to England to purloin something like that? Especially some book about sharks or dolphins…yes, whatever. I know a thing or two as well, and I can assure you that we're not going to be fooled by Charlie, Angelique, or anyone else. The sapphires were a priceless piece of British heritage, and by God we're going to get them back."

"But when Ms. Dubois was arrested…"

"Pure subterfuge, Tom. Charlie was always the main culprit, but we didn't see it at the time. Angelique, I'm afraid to say, may be a small fry and quite probably working for Charlie."

"Yes, sir, but…"

"More importantly, my friend," Nesbit said, his face suddenly stern, his body erect, "Why didn't the Chief call us? We were the ones working the case. We were the ones who visited the museum to prevent this crime. We were the ones who discovered and fingered Charlie."

Thwait hesitated. "I don't know. Maybe he's waiting until we come into the office. Maybe he thinks we're already on it. Maybe Inspector Sedgwick is working things until we…I guess I don't know."

"I don't know either, but it's time we found out. It's time we took control of this case."

Once back in the office, Nesbit with Thwait in tow charged through the main area where most of the officers had desks, stormed past Sedgwick, who vainly tried to get Nesbit's attention, and barged in to the Chief's office, where he was meeting with two other officers.

"You're supposed to knock," the Chief said to Nesbit and Thwait, who was standing in the doorway. He turned to the other officers and asked them to leave for a few minutes. When they were gone and the door was shut, the Chief, ignoring Thwait who was still standing near the door, turned to Nesbit and squinted at him as if he were an enemy invading the homeland.

"I did knock, but perhaps you didn't hear me."

"What do you want, Nesbit?"

"This…"

"Sir."

"Sir…why weren't Tom and I informed about the robbery and Charlie's arrest? We had to hear it on the news this morning. And, if anyone should have spoken to the reporters, it should have been me… and Tom, too. It's still my case… I mean, it's still our case…"

"What do you mean 'our case'?"

Nesbit stared at him. "What do you mean 'our case'…sir? Thwait and I have been working this case from the very beginning. We identified Charlie. I was charged from the outset with pursuing Charlie and Angelique."

"You were working on the stolen book case."

"The two cases are the same. I located Charlie, not…not what's-her-name, and I…"

"Who's 'what's-her-name'?"

"Smithereens, whatever."

"Inspector Sedgwick, sir," Thwait meekly interjected

The Chief's eyes narrowed. Staring at Nesbit, he reached inside one of his desk drawers and retrieved a pencil.

Thwait pressed his back to the door to keep a decent distance from Nesbit.

"She wouldn't have known about the man if it weren't for me," Nesbit continued once it seemed appropriate to speak, "...and of course Tom."

The Chief seemed on the verge of saying something to Nesbit but then looked over his shoulder at Thwait.

"Is that true, Constable Thwait?"

Thwait involuntarily pressed closer to the door. He couldn't recall how they got Charlie's name, although he was fairly certain that he and Nesbit were the first and only ones to question him. "Sir, I...," he stammered, his fat arms dangling limply at his sides.

"It doesn't really matter," the Chief interposed, turning back to Nesbit. "Inspector Sedgwick has been gathering a lot of good information, some of which she shared with you. You both had a chance to crack your case, and since Dubois is apparently out of the country..."

"Angelique Dubois...sir," Nesbit interjected angrily, as if the Chief's omission of her given name was meant to belittle both her significance as a criminal and Nesbit's stature as investigator of such criminal luminaries as Angelique Dubois.

The Chief paused and continued. "Dubois is out of the country, and we have nothing to suggest that she's involved in the theft. If Inspector Sedgwick finds evidence of her involvement or her connection with the thief or thieves, we will notify you."

"By thief, you mean Charlie Saunders," Nesbit added as if another slight had been proffered.

"What? What are you talking about?" The Chief eyed both men as if they were speaking a strange language.

"You apprehended Charlie Saunders. We saw the news reports."

"Nobody arrested Saunders."

"Then I respectfully suggest that you review a transcript of what Sedg-whatever told the press...sir." He glanced at Thwait, who appeared to be trying to sneak out of the room, and then turned back to the Chief. "It was all over the news. And I predicted it – this was the monument to British heritage that Charlie was after from the start."

Squinting at Nesbit, the Chief ordered Thwait to stay and then began tapping the tip of his pencil on the top surface of his desk. "In the first place, nobody arrested Charlie Saunders. I don't know how you made that connection. Inspector Sedgwick certainly didn't say that. If you review the transcript, you'll see that she mentioned a scumbag named Terrance Nottingham (alias Nick Nickelby, alias Gerald Cruncher, alias Johnny Chester, and so on). We identified him from the museum's security video and picked him up a few hours after the crime. He has a history of this kind of stuff. We haven't seen anything to suggest that Charlie Saunders was involved."

"What? I can't believe..."

"Right now, I'm afraid you'll have to believe. You'll also have to understand why I'm giving this case to Inspector Sedgwick. She was the one who identified Nottingham and led our men to his hideout, if you could call it that, and arrested him. If it turns out that Charlie Saunders is even remotely involved, Inspector Sedgwick will still be in charge of the case. Am I clear, gentlemen?"

Thwait nodded quickly from his perch next to the door and then glanced nervously at Nesbit, who was dumbfounded that the Chief couldn't recognize Charlie's connection with the heist and, more troubling, that he had essentially given his case – the case that he alone had brought to light – to Sedgwick. As Nesbit's mind regained some of its equilibrium, he felt almost sick over the idea that he would have to work with Sedgwick, which also meant that he would have to spend his valuable time rectifying her stupid blunders.

"One more thing," the Chief said, stunning an already shell-shocked Nesbit, "Constable Thwait has been reassigned to help Inspector Sedgwick to work the jewel heist. Agent Nesbit, since your services are no longer needed, I'm going to request..."

Nesbit stared wide-eyed at the Chief and fell into one of the chairs near the Chief's desk. Dazed, not quite believing the extraordinary turn of events, he tried to fathom the injustice of handing over his case to someone else to solve, someone who would reap the glory from all his years of hard work. How would he explain this to his superiors back in New York, who had expected him to lead the charge against Angelique and put her away once and for all? Nesbit started to rise when it occurred to him that if he were to leave now, one of the best chances to understand and eventually capture Angelique and Charlie could be lost forever, especially since Sedgwick and the others were going to be preoccupied with jousting at windmills over this Nottingham character. Nesbit hesitated and looked at the Chief.

"…sir," Nesbit began calmly and almost sounded contrite, "I know this is the end, but may I respectfully ask you for a favor. If Charlie Saunders isn't involved in the jewels heist, he's involved in something else. I can practically taste it. What I mean, sir, is that Inspector Sedgwick uncovered some tantalizing information on the man, and I would like a chance to follow up on this information to find out what if anything he's up to. If necessary, I'll defer most matters to Inspector Sedgwick." Nesbit cleared his throat, and his eyes appeared to be pleading for understanding. "I'm just asking for a little more time. I just want to accomplish something before…before I leave."

The Chief leaned back in his chair and crossed his arms. Although he didn't have a warm feeling for Nesbit and didn't entirely believe his obvious sincerity, he was nevertheless inclined to be a little sympathetic, since the case had just blown up in the man's face. "All right," he said after a moment's reflection. "You can have to the end of the week. After that…"

"One more thing, I would appreciate it if Constable Thwait could help me. He's been instrumental…"

"I won't give you that. But I'll give you a desk, and during this time you are free to look through our files to your heart's content."

Chapter 21

Thwait arranged for a small party at his desk in Nesbit's honor. A couple of the officers attended (not the Chief, and not Sedgwick, because she had been out of the station at the time), and they toasted Nesbit and wished him well in all his future endeavors. At the end of the party, just before Thwait had to report for work on the Royal Sapphires' investigation, Nesbit grasped his younger colleague's hand and thanked him for his hard work and pleasant company (Nesbit was moved by his own sentiment and doubtless by a few sodas too many). "You are," he said, holding Thwait's fat hand, "almost like a son to me." Releasing his hand, he sat down in one of the two chairs placed at the disposal of the party, while the other officers left. Thwait alone remained, glancing nervously from time to time at his watch, because he didn't want to be late.

"I know I'll see you again before I leave, so if you have to go, please do."

Thwait turned to leave but was stopped when Nesbit, who was facing the opposite direction, began to say something else to him. "I don't mean to be sentimental, my friend, but I have enjoyed our time together. And I meant what I said when I mentioned a certain filial instinct toward you. You'll be a fine officer someday."

Thwait again was about to leave when Nesbit added one more comment, although this time he turned to look up at his younger colleague. "But speaking of filial, I suppose you've been curious about my only child, who deserted me after the divorce. I suppose it was only right. I was too involved with work, too involved in hunting Angelique...but maybe I already told you that. Do you have to leave now? Let me tell you one thing before you go off to your case. I looked him up a couple of years ago, my son, that is – and, believe me, it wasn't easy, the way that boy changed addresses and didn't make anything public – I looked him up and called him. For a moment, I thought we might have a nice conversation, but the second he heard it was me, he hung up. Just like that. Not another word since."

"Sir, I'm sorry to hear that, but I have to go..."

"Can you believe it, Ben...I mean Tom. Ben is my boy's name – or he was my boy, although he's nothing to me now."

"Sir, I need..."

Nesbit stood up and, again grasping Thwait's large paw, gave it another strong shake. "But don't let me keep you. Our Inspector Sedgwick – is that right? – has big plans for you. My God, she reminds me of my ex-wife..."

"Thank you, sir, I really must..."

"I mean she looks and acts and speaks..."

"Sir, they are waiting..."

"Yes, yes, I don't mean to keep you, Ben, I mean Tom. Remember me well. Hey, I'll clean up the mess on your desk after you leave. These paper cups sure leak..." Nesbit couldn't finish, and waved at Thwait as he lumbered out of the room and down the hall to where others working on the case were waiting for him.

Working alone, Nesbit spent the rest of the week going through boxes of paper files stored in a long, narrow storeroom. Once he had gone through these, he searched old immigration files and a couple of other databases that weren't normally available to the station's officers (Sedgwick gave him access to these resources). But by the end of the week, Nesbit wasn't any closer to identifying Charlie and understanding his movements than he had been when he and Thwait went through the station's criminal and civil records. Yes, he could trace the man who opened the shop and filled out his tax forms, but as before this man didn't exist beyond these paltry records. It was infuriating, it was disappointing, and it meant that Charlie and, once again, Angelique had slipped through his fingers. On his last day, Nesbit handed Sedgwick all the material he had gone through, most of which was carefully stacked in manila folders, and left the station, the hotel, and the country. He returned to New York, where he went back to work on a number of cases that had waited for his return.

The case against Nottingham was progressing quickly. While all but one of the stolen sapphires had been recovered, there was ample evidence to keep the man safely behind bars for the duration of the trial and for years to come. One evening about three weeks after Nesbit departed, Sedgwick took a well-deserved break from the case, went over to the desk where Nesbit had been sitting, and began sorting through the material that he had left behind. Given the volume of material that Nesbit had either collected or generated, she was thankful that he had placed everything in carefully-labelled manila folders, which would reduce the number of evenings that she needed for sorting and organizing. But as she was going through one of the boxes, she discovered a small stack of photographs and papers in the bottom that had apparently escaped Nesbit's attention.

As she gathered the materials, she noticed a group of four photographs apparently taken of one man, a dour-looking individual who bore an uncanny resemblance to Charlie. The resemblance was even more striking when she flipped back and forth through the images and compared them to one another and to the mental image she had of Charlie, whom she had seen at his shop. The men were about the same age, and they had the same gaunt, haunted face that Charlie had, with identical lines beneath the eyes and alone the nose. But when she glanced at the information clipped to the backs of the photographs, Sedgwick realized that these were unrelated individuals with vastly different names. Pausing to rub her tired eyes, she laughingly told herself that she must be going blind from overwork. She placed the pictures into a folder and labelled it "miscellaneous photographs." Sedgwick was about to file the folder with the others in a gunmetal-gray filing cabinet in the corner (organizing and sorting the additional folder could wait for another day) when a strange, unsettling feeling came over her.

She didn't exactly know what was bothering her and, as she stared blankly at the stack of folders in front of her, she absently traced the downward slope of her lips with a slender index finder. Suddenly reaching for the additional folder, she opened it and spread the photographs out on the desk in front of her. For several minutes, she carefully examined each photograph, searching for commonalities and disparities, after which she studied the accompanying information on the individuals (mainly biographical material, including vital statistics such as arrest and incarceration dates). But when she failed to uncover anything new or particularly interesting about the photographs, she reluctantly gathered them up again and stacked them neatly together. But just as she was about to place the stack back into the folder, she spotted another photograph in the folder, this one all but obscured by a sheet of notebook paper half-covered with Nesbit's gobbledygook scrawls.

Sedgwick extracted the photograph and examined it carefully. Once again retrieving the other photographs, she spread them out on either side and compared the men in the photographs. The man in the recently-discovered photograph bore a passing resemblance to the others, although he seemed much younger and, contrary to what she understood about Charlie, he was smiling. Actually, it was more smirk than smile, and yet there was something about the young man's cold eyes and almost defiant posture that piqued her curiosity and likely Nesbit's interest (she had to assume that Nesbit had been interested, because she couldn't decipher anything in his notes that referenced the man). The man was leaning against what appeared to be a school wall (in the upper left-hand corner of the picture, partially obscured by a shadow, were the letters "chool") and, although he was shaped more or less like Charlie, he was wearing a hot-pink polo shirt, green plaid pants, and what appeared to be a mortarboard (the angle of the hat made identification difficult). Sedgwick continued to study the young man, but neither she nor apparently Nesbit could detect anything that definitively connected the image with what was known about Charlie.

According to the information clipped to this image, the individual, a Mr. Lavender, had at one time been an English teacher at a high school in the States. He had received a number of awards for his classes on Shakespeare, but the awards and commendations ceased after he claimed to be tired of Shakespeare and insisted on covering other, less illustrious writers of the same period. ("He's a cheeky devil," Sedgwick muttered to herself.) Later, there were complications of a vague sort, several reprimands, and everything came to a head when the school authorities suspected him of having a criminal record that they claimed he had failed to disclose. Even though the authorities didn't provide proof of the record, he was nevertheless fired. Following his termination, he was implicated in a string of second-story jobs (the evidence was too flimsy for an arrest), and later accused of stealing several valuable books from a noted library. According to the complaint, Mr. Lavender had absconded with the library's priceless Italian incunable that had been on display in a special room, somehow replacing it with a crude reproduction and selling the genuine article to a criminal syndicate operating throughout the States and Europe. The theft and substitution came to light a month later when he was caught milling about in the same room after hours. The smirking individual in the bright clothing was fined and served two-and-a-half years in a state lockup. The book was never recovered, and Mr. Lavender disappeared immediately after he was released. There was nothing in the folder to indicate how the individual's bio was uncovered in London.

There were, however, a couple of additional pieces of information that made this individual stand out, at least in terms of what Sedgwick knew about Charlie. First, the individual (Mr. Lavender or whatever his name actually was) was something of a chameleon. He was thought to have assumed other names and identities, especially when he was setting up "business ventures" (never clearly defined in the records) that appeared to leech off of other, unrelated and successful business ventures (once again, never clearly defined or illustrated in the records). When Sedgwick looked at the names with which this individual was thought to attire himself from time to time, Charles came up in numerous variations, including Charlie. By itself, this was fairly interesting, but it also meant that the actual identity of the individual in question might never be known, since the prison's biometric records had been destroyed in a recent fire, and there were no other known biometrics on the individual. The other piece of information was certainly intriguing, at least in terms of its implications. It was reported that the individual, while behind bars, had managed to upset a fellow inmate (for reasons unknown) and in the ensuing scuffle was badly injured. The information clipped to the photograph stated that as a result there was a scar on the individual's right hand without, however, providing visual evidence.

Sedgwick again closely examined the image, and this time studied the individual's right hand, which was spread across his left bicep. Sure enough, there was the scar – and the scar, she realized, looked exactly like the scar on Charlie's right hand. Both Nesbit and Thwait had mentioned the mark, though neither one thought much about it except to note it briefly for the record, and here it was on the hand of a man who was beginning to look more and more like their suspect – a suspect whose behavior and activities mirrored what Nesbit and Thwait had reported about Charlie's actions. Maybe these were coincidences, and there certainly was no definitive information available, but taken with everything else, it was difficult to dismiss everything out of hand.

Sedgwick went to the computer and pulled up Charlie's business records and, quite by chance, located a photograph of him (a three-quarter view standing with his arms crossed) attached to one of the electronic forms. She didn't know why this image hadn't been included with the other images, but maybe it had something to do with the image quality (it was blurred) and the subject's facial features – he looked older than Charlie and, in some ways, it was difficult to say with any certainty that it was the same man in one or any of the other pictures. But when Sedgwick spotted the scar on the man's hand, and compared it with the scar on the school teacher's hand, she knew that it was one and the same man.

Sedgwick also realized that the information wasn't enough to implicate Charlie in anything except perhaps fraud and maybe forgery (he had entered the country on a false passport). But the more she thought about Charlie, the more she considered everything she recalled from discussions with Nesbit and Thwait, the greater her confidence that this was indeed their man and that their man couldn't be trusted to be on the straight and narrow. It was too great a stretch to connect him with the Royal Sapphires case, and yet she wouldn't have been surprised if Charlie were associated with individuals connected with this crime and maybe others as well. In fact, Nottingham himself hinted darkly that an "event" of a similar nature occurred more or less around the time of the sapphires heist, the details of which he might disclose only if given complete immunity from both crimes ("assuming," he added, "I did something wrong."). According to the sources he claimed to have, the second event involved a sleight of hand which, like a magician's trick, could only be exposed by a fellow conjurer (not him, an innocent source).

Sedgwick leaned back in her chair and stared blankly at the image on the computer. It was now nearly midnight and she was exhausted. Perhaps she was too tired to think straight (she was so tired, in fact, that she had difficulty extracting herself from the chair), but it certainly seemed as if she had uncovered provocative information about Charlie, and it appeared reasonable that someone should at least keep an eye on the man wherever he was. She told herself that she would put Thwait on it to see what he made of the information, although if Charlie had actually left the country the results might not matter much to the station. Pulling her flat hair behind her ears, Sedgwick wrote a couple of quick emails that outlined the information that Nesbit had pulled up. She also added another piece of information that until this moment seemed of little importance. On a small strip of yellowed newsprint innocuously stuck to the back of a school playbill, there was the New Orleans address of the former school teacher who directed the Ben Jonson's play *Volpone*.

Chapter 22

The grayish glow of the rising sun could be seen just above the buildings across the street. Although the city hadn't completely settled down, most of the ardent revelers were going away and the noise level was significantly less than it had been only an hour ago. Despite the sudden bursts of firecrackers down the street, most of the people who lived in this section were respectable and generally settled down when the sky began getting brighter.

The woman still looked fresh and unruffled as she practically danced into the dusky living room. Although she had been out among the revelers for several hours, she had avoided the unruly crowds and had been careful not to drink excessively. Still dressed in dark silk slacks and a loose blouse, she slid into one of the two loungers positioned in front of the open patio doors, she stretched out, slipped her shoes off with her toes, and inhaled the early morning air, which had a sour, alcohol-like edge to it.

Shortly after she made herself comfortable, an older man came into the room from the kitchen with a book under his armpit and a cup of coffee in each hand. "Here," he said, offering one of the cups of coffee, "You probably need it."

"Thanks, I'd like one, but I don't need it. I didn't drink that much, just a couple short ones earlier in the evening."

"So, how did you like it? Was it as much fun as you thought?"

"I don't know. I certainly enjoyed the street bands, but I wouldn't want to do this every night. Maybe once a year. It would have been so much better had you come with me."

"It doesn't appeal to me anymore. I'm glad you had fun, though."

"How about you? Did you have a pleasant evening?"

"It was all right. I certainly didn't show anyone my Tupperware."

"I'm too old for that. So what did you do?"

"Oh, I started re-reading *Moby Dick*. Can you believe it? I haven't read it in years."

"Is it any good? Is it the same as you remember?"

"Yes, it's a wonderful book. Exciting, informative, and I'm enjoying rereading some of the passages that made a great impression on me when I was much younger. The book holds up extraordinarily well, although maybe not in this light."

The man was wearing a light-colored bathrobe. He stretched out in the other lounger and, after placing his coffee on a side table and the unopened book on his stomach, he put his hands behind his head and watched the sun coming up on the buildings across the street. After a while, he could hear the distant sounds of street sweepers and garbage trucks.

"Darling," the woman began, her voice hesitant while her heart was filled with the freedom that only darkness and dim light allow. "I think this is the point at which you tell me how you accomplished everything. I still can't believe I contacted the wrong person. You had the right name, more or less, your shop was where I expected to find it, and you knew the right code – the 'golden bowl.' Incredible...you either planned it, or fate or something else took charge of the events. Don't get me wrong: Nothing could have turned out better. Do you believe in fate, or was it the most amazing coincidence in all of history?"

"I don't know," he replied without looking at her. "The 'golden bowl' came from *Lenore*. I had a modern edition of Poe that I thought might interest you."

"But how were you able to switch the books? I'm talking about *Moby Dick*. I don't think anyone has a clue what happened, or if anything happened at all. If they do, they certainly haven't said anything to the press. Do you think they'll notice it? What do you think will happen when they do? They will notice it sooner or later, I presume."

He placed his book on the table next to his coffee and nestled deeper into the seat. Crossing his arms across his chest, he turned to the woman and observed her ghost-like profile in the still dark room. "I don't think they're going to find it for quite some time. Look, if the book isn't falling apart, and they have no reason to be concerned about its authenticity, then they're not going to examine it or touch it more than absolutely necessary. If for some reason they do check it out, so what? Sure, they'll see it's a fake, but there's nothing they can do about it. They'll never connect it to me; and, even if they did, they couldn't touch me or your client. We're too far away, and it would take years before their extradition requests were finally rebuffed. I'll tell you a dirty little secret about museums and libraries and all those august places. They don't like admitting that they have fakes, because fakes hurt the credibility of the organization and cut down on the traffic coming through their doors. Of course, I'm not going to risk going back, but right now I'm not in the least bit worried by what they find or what they might try to do."

"That makes sense. But tell me how you did it. It must have been difficult."

"Actually, it was fairly simple. The hardest part, I suppose, was convincing myself that it was as easy as it looked. I visited the exhibition and bought two of the reproductions from the gift shop. I also reached out to one of my contacts and got a couple of appropriately-sized old books. The books were worthless (nothing texts that had been badly damaged by bookworms), but the covers were in good condition and very close to the Melville cover. They weren't exact, of course, but it didn't take much to make them look like the real thing – a few well-placed abrasions, shoe polish to get the color right, and a little eyeliner for the lettering on the spines. I replaced the original texts with the texts from the gift-shop books to give the fakes a little more authenticity, thereby giving the world two more priceless works by the American master. The public won't know the difference."

"I know what I told you about the job, but it really couldn't have that easy."

The man chuckled lightly and picked his coffee and took a long drink. "It was," he said as he placed the cup carefully back on the small table, "just exactly as you said it would be. I scoped out the security the day before I planned to make the exchange. The security was a joke. No one batted an eye when I came back the next day wearing a heavy coat and carrying an empty bag (the fake book was hidden in my coat), and no one even noticed when I pulled a stocking cap over my head and strolled into the exhibition room with the bag. You were right, it was empty, and there were no electronic devices on the case. I thought I might have trouble with the screws holding the case to the wooden pedestal, but the wood was so soft that I was able to pop them out with my thumbnail. After that, the switch was a piece of cake. When I readjusted the case, I simply pushed the screws back in place."

"It's unfathomable why they didn't try to protect the book better. They're responsible for its loss."

"Here's the funny part. As I was leaving the library, there was a guard at the front door (he must have taken a potty break before), and he wanted to know what I had in the bag. I don't know why I was still carrying the bag, since I had already pocketed the book, but I showed him and told him that I was taking the bag home as a souvenir. He smiled as if he understood, but didn't ask a single question or demand to see the inside of my coat – and who wears a heavy coat on a warm day even in London? He waved me though the door and that was it. I don't know what I would have done if he had asked to see my coat."

"We're both lucky," she said and reached out in the dark for the man's hand, which he gave her. They were both silent for a few minutes before she turned to him. "Darling, please tell me again why it was necessary for me to carry the other fake through customs. If I had gone through empty handed, they wouldn't have stopped me and I wouldn't have spent any time with London's finest citizens in that foul-smelling pig sty."

He turned slightly toward her. "It was a tough call. I knew the police were convinced that you and I were working together, and so I figured that if they detained you with what appeared to be the book, they would concentrate on you and leave me alone – long enough, that is, to slip out of the country with the real McCoy."

"So they judged the book by its cover."

"I guess so. But I was also certain that as soon as they realized the book was fake, they would release you, and by that time I'd be long gone. Seemed to work pretty good, don't you think?"

"I suppose, but I sure wish you could have come up with something that wouldn't have kept me there even for a few minutes."

"If there's ever a next time, we'll do things differently. The good thing is that we have the money, your cut and mine, and we can do anything we want."

"Start another book store?"

"Why not? I've always wanted to do that. I had every intention of running a legitimate shop, but people just weren't buying, and I didn't have enough money set aside to wait. It's not the same now."

"We have enough money to keep you going for a quite a while."

"Maybe. Right now, though, I'm only interested in doing some reading and looking at your beautiful face. Have you read *Volpone?*"

"You'll have to turn on a light or wait until the sun is up." The woman turned to the man and adjusted herself to see the shadow that was still holding her hand. "Are you sure my client has the real book? I wouldn't want to be looking over our shoulders for the rest of our lives if there was a mistake."

He looked at the woman, whose features were becoming clearer and more becoming as the room became lighter. "We have nothing to worry about, unless of course the Wakefield was exhibiting a fake. It looked right to me, through I'm no expert."

"I have to say it again, darling, you're amazing. I felt comfortable with you from the first moment I set eyes on you."

The man's expression softened for a moment, and he looked much younger than his years. "Are you saying that because you're here with me?"

"Of course. And you're happy, too?"

"For now."

They were both quiet for a few minutes, and as if their movements were synchronized, they leaned back in their chairs and closed their eyes.

"Darling," she began, once again breaking the silence. Her voice was soft, and there was a slightly-troubled edge to it. "Darling, the other thing..."

"Nothing to worry about. I can't believe that fool – what was his name, Nottingham? – pulled the heist and thought I was Sanders. I don't know how he got my number, but he was gracious enough to bring the sapphires into the shop and lay them out as if I knew what to do. Can you believe it? He thought I was that stupid fence. I put him off about the payment, and then I put on a disguise and unloaded all but one of the sapphires on Sanders, who was so anxious to get them that he didn't notice one was missing. I kept it just in case."

"In case we need the money?"

"Maybe."

"But what if Nottingham and Sanders find out?"

"Nottingham will accuse Sanders of cheating him out of the money, and Sanders will deny it and accuse him of holding one of the stones back."

"And the authorities? Nottingham will tell them your address."

"So? We're out of the country, and it will ultimately be his word against mine – and everybody knows that he and Sanders were in cahoots."

"I see."

They turned back and relaxed in their chairs. Once more, they were silent, enmeshed in their own thoughts for a few more minutes. "Sweetheart," she said at last, staring out the window at the buildings across the street. "I'm serious about the retirement. I didn't like my previous life. We can do this together, as long as we go straight, at least for a while. That means..."

"I know, be kind to books." They leaned toward one another and pecked each other lightly on the lips.

"One more thing," he began with a smile. "Since I'm older, there may come a time when you're going to have to cut me free."

She turned back to the window. "I know," she said. A few minutes later, she turned to him and observed the shadows on his face and shoulders. "I never asked you. Did you try to copy Sanders' name or was it a coincidence?"

"No, it was just a coincidence. I didn't know Sanders existed until a few months ago."

"I'm sorry for asking so many questions. I just think it's better to ask them now, so we don't have to interrupt things later on. Since we're going to be here for a while, maybe you can tell me what your real name is."

He dropped her hand and they both turned toward the door.

"Saved by the bell," he said.

The Gray Ladies

Chapter 1

"It's going to rock this bloody town, I promise you. Once we get the Gray Ladies, I'll let our favorite constable in on the big secret. He's always mouthing off about big cases, but he's never seen one as big as this. The government will fall – 'We trusted 'em to protect our country's treasures!" – and Scotland Yard, Interpol, and all the rest of them buggers will be scurrying around like roosters with their heads bit off. Know what? He'd never figure it out on his own. Even if he did, it'd be too late."

"I'm afraid that's all we have right now. The Chief said HQ will send the rest as soon as possible. I really don't know any more about it. By the way, sir, I'm glad you're coming back for this case. Everyone at the station is looking forward to seeing you, too, including the Chief and Inspector Sedgwick. Did you know your success in New Orleans was the talk of the station for quite some time? I suppose you couldn't have known that. But I can tell you HQ was so impressed that they requested your help for this case. Well, I'm really looking forward to working with you again, Agent Nesbit. It's been quite a long time." Thwait sniffed and cleared his throat, and with his free hand rummaged about in his top drawer for another piece of candy.

Nesbit chuckled slightly when Thwait suggested that the Chief and Sedgwick were looking forward to seeing him. More likely, they were jealous of his success and, if they truly wanted to see him again, it was only because they needed him for something or wanted to profit from his success. Still, Agent Nesbit of Interpol was glad to be back in the UK, and he was pleased to be working again with his good friend, Constable Thomas Thwait of the Metropolitan Police Service. Nesbit was also eager to solve the case quickly so that anyone who thought New Orleans was a fluke would have to think again.

"My friend," Nesbit began, smiling to himself, "I look forward to seeing you, too, and I know we're going to have a grand time together on this case. Since I checked into my hotel less than an hour ago, I won't be coming into the station until later this evening. You'll still be there, right? Good. I need a shower, a few winks, and a good dinner before I..." He paused briefly. "Say, Tom, why don't you join me for dinner? How about 7:00 at the Gray Friar?"

"I'd certainly like to," Thwait replied somewhat hesitantly.

"You know where it's located? You like that kind of food, right?"

"Yes, sir, but..."

"Well, what is it, man? It's been a long time. What – three years, or nearly so? I'd think you'd jump at the chance of having dinner with me, especially at that place. Are you sure you're familiar with it?"

"I've heard of it, certainly, but...what I mean to say...that is..."

"Come on, spit it out. Good God, are you still stuttering? I thought our time together cured you of that once and for all."

"It's not that, sir. I'd like to meet you anywhere, but the Chief won't pay the expenses. I'm afraid he's still upset about the money we spent the last time you were here."

"What? I can't believe he's still angry after all this time. Nothing we did was out of line, my friend. The Chief didn't have to shell out a penny if he had any reservations about the expense reports."

Thwait cleared his throat again and continued searching his drawer for the candy that he was almost certain was in there somewhere. "Maybe we shouldn't have had so much wine, sir, or all the other drinks, the cocktails, and the..."

"Nonsense! It was part of the job. If they wanted us to function optimally, then a few libations to grease the squeaky wheels were just what the doctor ordered. But no matter, my friend, this one is on Interpol, which knows a thing or two about reasonable expenses. So you'll join me, right?"

"Well...yes, sir, absolutely, sir."

"Fine, fine, that's a good fellow. Can you bring the wiretap with you? Oh, I mentioned 7:00 at the Gray Friar, right? I guess I'm a little groggy from the lack of sleep. The flight left after midnight New Orleans time, and there was a screaming baby behind me that didn't shut up until we landed. Not until we landed! It doesn't matter now, although I sure could use a little shuteye before dinner. Okay, don't forget." Nesbit hesitated. "On second thought, Tom, let's postpone our meeting until tomorrow evening. Will the same time and place be good for you? I'm not entirely sure I can wake up in five hours (nine, is it?) and make it to the restaurant on time. I also need to keep my strength up because of something important I need to do in a couple of days.

I'll fill you in over dinner. Are you sure tomorrow evening works for you? Good, then tomorrow it is."

"If it's good for Interpol, it's good for me." Thwait tried to sound funny but, like every other time he attempted a joke, it fell flat. Nesbit didn't react.

"Excellent. Don't be late, and don't forget the wiretap. We'll have this case wrapped up in a jiffy, as we say in the States."

Thwait was still smiling when Nesbit hung up, but within seconds a look of concern swept across his fleshy features. He had forgotten to tell Nesbit that although the Chief allowed him to read the wiretap over the phone, he didn't want anyone to take a copy from the station. The Chief mentioned something about its sensitivity but refused to provide any other details. Well, maybe he could ask the Chief tomorrow to see if an exception was warranted, since he and Nesbit were the leads on the case. Grimacing briefly over his forgetfulness, Thwait rolled his thick shoulders to ease the discomfort caused by the seams of his shirt and then tugged at his collar to allow the blood to flow more freely to his head. He also adjusted his bulk in his increasingly confined chair before returning to the notes he was writing for a case he had just finished supporting. The crime wasn't particularly unusual (just another instance of shoplifting at a small department store), but he was confident that he had carried out his part of the investigation effectively, efficiently, and, most importantly, by the numbers. The Chief wanted the case done by the numbers. Once the notes were complete and filed, he was free to dedicate his time and energy to supporting Agent Nesbit. It was going to be like old times, when he and Nesbit worked day and night to expose an international syndicate trafficking in rare books and foreign antiquities, except that this case promised to be more challenging and exciting.

Okay, so maybe the Chief was right to object to some of Nesbit's "business" expenses (dinners at upscale restaurants, cases of vintage wines, the long-term rental of an expensive hotel suite), and maybe he had a point that Nesbit wouldn't have succeeded in New Orleans without the station's help and the intervention of the New Orleans police department. But it had been Nesbit's keen investigative insights and his relentless pursuit of the couple that led to their discovery and arrest in an upscale New Orleans hotel – and if Nesbit hadn't succeeded, the station would have been left with egg on its face for letting the criminals slip through its collective fingers in the first place. It only seemed right, therefore, that since the station had been remiss in giving

Nesbit his full due, HQ would make amends by requiring the Chief to bring the Interpol agent on board for a case that would doubtless make national and international headlines and once again thrust Nesbit back into the limelight. Yes, indeed, working with his great friend and mentor augured good days, exciting days, in the coming months.

It was nearly midnight by the time Thwait finished his notes, which still left him plenty of time to rest and to prepare for his new adventures with Agent Nesbit.

Chapter 2

The following morning was one of the most beautiful that Thwait had ever seen. An unusually heavy fog had settled in sometime before sunrise and, according to most reports, it wasn't supposed to lift until late in the afternoon. In some places, the fog was so dense that it was practically impossible to see more than five or six feet away, and even then most of what could be seen were vague shapes dancing from one side of the sidewalk to the other. There were quite a few people out that morning, judging from the shuffling sounds their shoes made against the pavement and their almost universal condemnation of the weather and the amount of time it was expected to remain in place. Cars and trucks made their appearances now and then, but these, too, were vague, dark shapes that whooshed by as quickly as they appeared. Although Thwait was as sensitive to the fog as the next person, he hadn't given the weather much thought, because he had other things, more important things, on his mind.

Indeed, as soon as he arrived, he immediately went to his desk. But instead of handling some of his usual duties (annotating and archiving case files, inventorying the supply closet, and helping where he could on some of the more mundane cases), Thwait started cleaning up the disorder on his desk and in its drawers, tossing away great wads of candy wrappers, straightening up his papers and pencils, and finally taking a wet paper towel across its scratched, metal surface. When all this was satisfactorily accomplished, he turned on his computer and, after a quick check of his email, pulled up the weather forecast for the rest of the week, read some of the daily news, and then paged through some old case files he knew to be relatively interesting. Thwait struggled out of his chair around noon and headed directly to the cafeteria, where he spend the next couple of hours, eating two cheese pizzas and reading the paper. Under normal circumstances, Thwait would have helped some of the officers who were behind in their work, but he didn't want to get involved with anything now that might spill over into the following day and interfere with his important work with Nesbit – and Thwait was prepared to dedicate himself body and soul to Agent Nesbit.

Shortly after his last pizza, Thwait returned to his desk and squeezed into his chair. Leaning back and resting his hands comfortably on his ample chest, he closed his eyes and ignored the hubbub of people swirling around him. Half asleep, he began to imagine the kind of work that he and Nesbit would be doing – the strange and exotic places they would visit, the beautiful people they would interview, and the mountains of evidence they would sift through – and the unexpected conclusion they would present, which would be based on a single, coruscating filament of irrefutable evidence that everyone else had missed. Without opening his eyes, he reached down with his left hand and unfastened the top button of his slacks to give himself a little breathing room, after which he brought his hand back to his chest and envisioned the camera lights flashing as he and Nesbit stood in front of a makeshift podium and explained to the media how they did it. Thwait might have envisioned other cases and even wilder adventures, but Sedgwick unexpectedly arrived and tapped him pleasantly on one of his beefy shoulders.

"Constable Thwait, I'm glad I caught you," said Grace Sedgwick, the Chief's second in command. "The Chief wants you to archive these files," she added, holding a stack of papers and folders nearly a foot thick.

Sedgwick – and no one ever called her by her first name, not even the Chief – was in her mid-thirties, five years older than Thwait, and one of the youngest officers ever to hold such a position. It was, however, a distinction that she acquired honestly – her work was by all accounts outstanding and, in her spare time, she had completed an advanced degree at Oxford (Thwait was never clear in what field). And unlike colleagues who acted as though their position or rank was proof of their innate superiority over others below them, she treated everyone as equals, including her superiors, and demanded only that they accord her the same level of respect. Sedgwick, though, was puzzling to Thwait. While he respected her and admired her accomplishments, he couldn't understand why such an attractive woman wore nothing but dark or gray business suits, why she never donned jewelry of any kind, why she never did anything with her straight, slightly ragged shoulder-length hair, or why she never wore makeup, not even to mask the slight droop of the left side of her mouth. But what baffled him even more was Nesbit's reaction to her, unless of course his friend's attitude had changed since the last time he had been at the station.

Thwait glanced at the folders in Sedgwick's hands and then at Sedgwick herself, after which he rolled his shoulders as if he were preparing to free himself from his chair. Once Sedgwick placed the folders on his desk, Thwait calculated that each case file was over an inch thick. "This could take hours," he mumbled, noticing one folder that was at least three times the size of the others, "especially if the staples haven't been removed." It was obvious that there were staples on some of the papers, as well as paperclips, fasteners, and even rubber bands, all of which would have to be removed before scanning and archiving. Thwait contemplated the nightmare that now awaited him.

"I expect some will. But you needn't to finish them today. It'll be fine if you get them done by the end of the week." Sedgwick spoke in a slightly monotonous tone, which Thwait sometimes thought might be due to the left side of her mouth. She turned to leave but immediately turned back as if she had just remembered something. "You met with Agent Nesbit last night, right? How did it go? Where is he, by the way?"

"He got in late, so we decided to postpone the meeting until dinner this evening."

Sedgwick eyed Thwait when he mentioned dinner, recalling the extravagant meals that Nesbit charged to the station the last time he was here. "I see, dinner this evening. A word to the wise, Constable Thwait – it would behoove you to be a little more circumspect regarding expense reports this time, if you know what I mean."

"Yes, ma'am," Thwait nodded, and he knew that sooner or later the Chief would give him the same admonition.

Sedgwick was again about to leave when another thought came to mind. "I'm sorry, Constable Thwait. I forgot to tell you that the Chief wanted to see you as soon as possible. I don't think anyone's in his office at the moment." She smiled becomingly and left the area.

As he struggled to extricate himself from his chair, Thwait couldn't help thinking that some of the other officers were playing a practical joke on him by giving him the smallest chair in the office. When he was finally free, a feat he achieved by pushing upward with his heavy legs and downward on the chair's arms with his thick forearms, he stepped to one side, smoothed the front of his black uniform, and, exiting the large office space that he and several other officers shared, walked down the hallway to the Chief's office.

The Chief's office was a large, practically empty room. There was a tall bookcase against one wall – and besides a few books on law enforcement, the shelves contained a silver trophy with a tennis player on top, a framed service award (face down), and a framed photograph (face up) of his wife and twenty-two year old son – a small, round table in the center of the room, and at one end an undistinguished desk with a worn, black executive chair behind it and three plain, black chairs in front. Thwait knocked quietly at the closed door and entered only after the Chief grunted a barely audible "enter."

The Chief was seated behind his desk and writing something on a notepad when Thwait quietly walked over and stood in front of his desk, silently waiting for permission to sit down. Without looking up, the Chief waved his left hand for Thwait to take a seat in one of the chairs in front of his desk. The Chief was an imposing man. Unlike Thwait, who was average in height, overweight, and never seemed to have a suit or uniform that wasn't straining at the seams, the Chief was a little over six feet tall and, because of his closely-cropped hair and his trim, muscular physique, he had the look and bearing of a military officer. If the Chief had one quirk, it was his tendency to squint (usually with his left eye) as if he was having trouble seeing or was a heavy smoker, neither being the case.

Since the chairs in front of the chief's desk were much larger than his own desk chair, Thwait was able to slip into one and immediately make himself comfortable. While he waited for the Chief to finish writing, he glanced around the office and then fixed his gaze on the stacks of case folders on the corner of the desk to his left. They looked exactly like the ones that Sedgwick had handed to him, and, for a few minutes while the Chief was occupied, Thwait had a sickening feeling that the Chief was going to assign him all the other cases to archive, which would probably take him the rest of the week to complete and would delay his important work with Nesbit. Even under the best of circumstances, Thwait would have dreaded the Chief's assignment – it was pure drudgery, hardly the kind of police work that he aspired to do, and, more than anything else, he hated the smell of the scanner as it got hot from all the pages fed into it. Thwait was silently praying that the files would be handed off to someone else when the Chief stopped writing and placed the notepad in one of the side drawers of his desk. Turning to Thwait, the Chief squinted at him as if he were waiting for Thwait to confess something.

Thwait immediately sat up straight and, staring at the Chief's hard, military face, swallowed with difficulty.

"Constable Thwait," the Chief said, breaking the uncomfortable silence, but then silently glanced around the office. "Excuse me, Constable Thwait, but where is Agent Nesbit?"

Thwait tugged at his collar and stated that Nesbit wouldn't be in today as planned. "He got in late last night, sir, and he...I mean, we, sir, decided to meet up this evening after he had a chance to rest."

Without taking his eyes off Thwait, the Chief reached into the top drawer of his desk and pulled out a pencil. "I see," he replied, and began tapping the eraser end of his pencil on the surface of the desk.

"Yes, sir, I…we are meeting at a restaurant at seven…"

The Chief stopped tapping and let the pencil fall from his hand onto the desk, where it rolled noisily across the slick surface and stopped against the case folders.

Thwait held his breath as he watched the object come to an unpleasant stop. "It won't be charged to the office, sir," he said nervously.

"No, I expect not."

Squinting at the junior officer, who practically quailed beneath his gaze, the Chief got up from behind his desk and walked around to the other side where he sat on the corner directly opposite Thwait. With the toe of his black shoe practically touching Thwait's knee, he looked at him for a few more seconds before speaking.

"Constable Thwait," the Chief began, speaking with his usual quasi-military tone of voice. "I don't know what's going on here. We're supposed to investigate something based on a few, ambiguous sentences from a wiretap. HQ, which bequeathed these sentences to us, has for some reason not seen fit to provide us with any explanatory details – not the context in which the line was tapped, not the time and location of the tap, not the names or genders of the speakers, not even the definition of a Gray Lady. Sure, Scotland Yard was mentioned, but given everything we have so far, we can't be certain that the government mentioned in the wiretap is Her Majesty's government and not some other government. Constable Thwait, I truly don't know what we're supposed to do with what little we have. Maybe Agent Nesbit will enlighten us, but I wouldn't be surprised if he has even less information about this than we have. Regardless, I have to say that I am not especially pleased by this arrangement with Agent Nesbit." The Chief paused and appeared to have something particular on his mind.

Thwait wanted to assure the Chief that things would be different this time, but before he could open his mouth the Chief silenced him with a squint.

"Constable Thwait, let me assure you that I don't dislike Agent Nesbit. I have no doubt he's a decent bloke within certain, controlled situations. I'll also give him his due as a law-enforcement official. While he could benefit from a little guidance, he paid his dues with the New Orleans case, even though you and Inspector Sedgwick made significant contributions to it. As for the stunts he pulled the last time he was here…okay, that was three years ago, and I guess a lot has changed since then. But do you know what's really bothering me, Constable Thwait? No, of course you don't. It's HQ telling me how to run my business. I'm not pleased that I have to use Agent Nesbit on this case, nor am I thrilled that I have to relinquish you for an indefinite period simply because he requested your assistance. We have more pressing issues on our plates." The Chief stood up and went back to his chair. Picking up his pencil, he began tapping it nervously on the desk's surface. "Okay, Constable Thwait, I'm willing to play along for the time being," he said squinting at Thwait, "but the minute that things get out of control…"

"No, sir, they won't," Thwait interjected.

The Chief continued squinting at him as if he expected something more, perhaps a plan illustrating how Thwait would prevent the problems that arose the last time Nesbit was at the station. But when Thwait failed to follow up on his words (nothing came to mind, although he desperately wanted to assuage the Chief), the Chief continued speaking in his firm, military tone. "All right, I'm going to give you the rules of engagement. If you fail to comply with any of them, I'll have you back here before you can blink an eye – and I won't care what HQ says or does as a result. Maybe I can't touch Agent Nesbit, but I can certainly make your life uncomfortable. Do you understand me, Constable Thwait?"

Thwait nodded quickly.

"First, all expenses incurred by Agent Nesbit will be paid either by Interpol or by Nesbit himself. I expect you to keep a close accounting of your own expenses. I also expect you to adhere to station regulations regarding out-of-pocket expenses. And you will be responsible for everything that falls outside of these regulations. Are we clear?"

Thwait nodded quickly.

"Second, you will keep me apprised of the case at all times. I am told that this is a sensitive case, whatever that means in this context, but since I am at least nominally in charge, you will not hold anything back from me or from the officers I designate. In this regard, you should inform Agent Nesbit that you will be reporting to me and certain station officers on a regular basis. Are we clear?"

Once again, Thwait nodded quickly.

"Third, since you are assigned to work with Agent Nesbit full time, the station will not supply any additional resources to this investigation. You may use one of our computers, but if you need research, analysis, or whatever, you will have to do that yourselves, or else Agent Nesbit can ask Interpol to lend a hand. Should the inconceivable happen and something interesting develops in this case, I may allow one or more of my officers to volunteer to help, but they will do so on their own time and at their own expense. Are we clear?"

Again, Thwait nodded quickly.

"Finally," the Chief paused and placed his pencil carefully on his desk, where it paused for a moment before again rolling across the surface and landing next to the folders. "Finally, if Agent Nesbit objects to any of this, he is free to bring his objections to the attention of HQ, Interpol, or anyone else, but not to me. I'm not interested, and I don't have the time to waste on his nonsense. Are we clear?"

"Yes, sir."

Turning away from Thwait, the Chief retrieved his notepad and took up where he left off. This was the signal for Thwait to leave.

Standing up, Thwait thanked the Chief, who acknowledged neither his words nor his presence, and then silently left his office, closing the door carefully behind him.

Thwait hadn't taken more than three steps when Sedgwick suddenly appeared and handed him a sheet of paper. Taking the sheet without looking at it, Thwait couldn't help thinking that Sedgwick knew more about the case and the situation with Nesbit than he did (which wasn't very much), and he felt certain that Sedgwick had in some way been privy to what had just transpired in the Chief's office. But then, as the Chief's second, she would have been in on practically everything happening at the station.

Divining some of the younger officer's thoughts, Sedgwick smiled pleasantly and nodded knowingly. "Yes, I know all about it. The Chief briefed me a little while ago. I think he's entirely right about the resources, but that's his call to make. I really don't think he'll object if I do a little research for you and Agent Nesbit, but there'll be limits on how much I can do and when I can do it. If something big comes up, I'm sure things will change. Anyway, he said that you could have a copy of the wiretap," she continued, pointing to the paper Thwait was holding at his side, "as long as you didn't misplace it or share it with anyone other than Agent Nesbit. Now, I've done some research on the Gray Ladies, but I'm afraid I couldn't find anything relevant. I'll try to do some more searches later on, and I'll let you know if I come up with anything."

"Is this some kind of ongoing case and they're still tapping the line or some other phone?"

"I don't know. We're all in the dark on this one. HQ did say that something else could be coming down the pike, but they didn't elaborate and, whatever it is, we don't know when we'll get it. If we're lucky, we'll get more of the wiretap. Incidentally, the Chief told me that before HQ sent us the wiretap, they had already engaged Agent Nesbit's services. They're certainly keen to have his expertise on this one." Sedgwick again smiled pleasantly, this time to suggest that she understood his predicament.

Thwait hesitated and eyed Sedgwick cautiously. "What do you think of him – Agent Nesbit, I mean – if you don't mind my asking?"

Sedgwick knew and understood Thwait's admiration of the man. "I think he's a fine agent, and I think he certainly burnished his credentials with the New Orleans case."

"That's what I think, too, ma'am."

Thwait adjusted his shoulders in his ill-fitting, black uniform and absently watched Sedgwick walk down the long, poorly lit hallway to her office.

Thwait arrived at Nesbit's hotel a few hours later. Despite the Chief's obvious disdain for the man, Thwait was eager to work with him again, and he had little doubt that Nesbit would be able to solve the case before anyone else fully understood the facts. Thwait, though, had other reasons for wanting to see the Interpol agent. Naturally, he liked Nesbit and considered him a friend. But he also admired the man, and he couldn't help being impressed by the way Nesbit kept his shoulders back and commanded attention and respect (though not always from the Chief) no matter where he was. Thwait briefly recalled his father, who toiled away year after year in the family's East End butcher shop, smiling at everyone and never taking offense at anything customers said to him. But as much as he loved his father, who retired some years back and was now living in Middlesmoor tending sheep, Thwait never aspired to the sort of life that gradually forced one's shoulders forward and one's head down. He dreamed of living like Nesbit, traveling around the world, dining with exotic people and heads of state, and doing such amazing things that, well, made him famous. In a sense, Thwait hoped that Nesbit would be his ticket to this other, more glamorous world, although he was realistic enough to recognize that people like Nesbit are rarities and that it would be easier to train a pig to be a butcher than a butcher's son to be a great officer like Nesbit. For now, though, it was enough just to be near him and to hope that he, Thwait, could gain something by hovering in the great man's shadow.

Chapter 3

Thwait didn't hesitate and immediately pounded on the door (several times, in fact) until Nesbit slowly opened it as if he weren't expecting anyone this time of day. Nesbit was a good head taller than Thwait and, although he was well past the half-century mark, he was amazingly thin (not the slightest bulge above his belt) and still retained a full head of dark, albeit slightly graying, hair. Immaculately dressed as always, he wore a dark, pinstriped suit with a matching vest, and there was a white silk handkerchief protruding from his coat pocket. Before Nesbit could utter a word, Thwait proffered his plump paw, which Nesbit eagerly gave several solid shakes.

"My God, it's good to see you again, Tom," Nesbit said, smiling and ushering Thwait into his room. "You're looking as...as well as ever. How have you been doing since the last time?"

Thwait was about to express his joy in seeing his old friend and mentor again when Nesbit noticed the paper in Thwait's paw (he didn't think to bring a briefcase) and immediately reached for it, telling Thwait that he had been anxious to see it for himself.

"I knew you'd bring it," he added, holding it in both hands as he walked over to a round table in the center of the room, "and, by God, you did. You certainly did, my friend." Nesbit sat down on one of the two chairs at the table and absently motioned for Thwait to do the same.

"Yes, of course...," Thwait replied, as he took a seat on the opposite side of the table and watched Nesbit read the paper. He was a little disappointed that business came front and center so quickly, but his disappointment quickly gave way to a slight embarrassment when he noticed how wrinkled and smudged the paper was. The smudges (how did it get so dirty?), especially, made him feel unprofessional. Any other officer, he was certain, would have secured the precious page in a briefcase or even in a breast pocket and presented it at exactly the right time – that is, after they had a chance to speak freely and privately as old friends do when catching up. Well, he and Nesbit would have this talk sooner or later, although Thwait was increasingly concerned that he wouldn't have anything to tell Nesbit. While Nesbit had been out making the world a safer place, he hadn't advanced a single grade and was doing more or less the same thing he had been doing three years ago, the last time he saw Nesbit.

Nesbit placed the paper near the edge of the table and smoothed out the wrinkles with the side of his right hand. Flicking off a speck of something from its surface, he continued reading and rereading the page, mouthing each word as if he were sounding it out for hidden meanings, anagrams, or whatever that might shed a light on the crime, including the time, the place, and the perpetrators who were plotting to bring down the government.

Thwait, however, hadn't been able to make a lot of sense out of the wiretap. Sure, there was a definite threat of some kind, and it was clear that it was aimed at changing the present administration, but beyond that little else was said, at least to his mind, and he certainly couldn't find anything in the words to tell him what he and Nesbit needed to do in response (you can't lock down the country on the basis of some vague statements by unknown persons). As he glanced at the paper and then at his friend, who was underlining some of the words with the clean, manicured nail of his index finger, Thwait couldn't help smiling in admiration at the man who could solve anything given enough time.

Nesbit finally looked up from the page and at Thwait, who was still smiling. "There's more coming, right? Good. So, what you make of what we have so far, my friend?"

Thwait hesitated but couldn't hold back. "Sir, let me just say that it's good to see you again."

"I feel the same way, Tom," he said as he briefly smiled and nodded. "We'll make time to chat later. Right now, tell me what you think of the tap. I'd like to see how well your impressions accord with mine. I presume the Chief has seen it, too...well, of course, he has, and I have little doubt that he's expressed his disdain regarding the value of the wiretap and the significance of the case as a whole. No matter," he added, raising his right palm to stop Thwait from defending the Chief (something that hadn't crossed the younger man's mind), "he'll understand everything in due time, in due time. Now, back to your valuable thoughts, my friend. I want to hear from you, because you're the only one at the station who has a head on his shoulders."

Pleased that Nesbit wanted his thoughts, and proud that this amazing man thought that he, Thwait, had his head on his shoulders – and the only officer at the station who did – Thwait cleared his throat a couple of times and tried to articulate something (perhaps something he heard from Sedgwick) that would help him live up to Nesbit's expectations. "Well, sir," he began, once again clearing his throat to buy some time while he searched for an intelligent statement to make, "I'm inclined to think it's like this. A criminal action is going down – maybe, maybe not right now, but soon, very soon – and if the perpetrators aren't stopped – and, of course, it's our job to see that they are – then I'd say the government (and, although we can't be sure which government, my sense is Her Majesty's government because of Scotland Yard) could…"

"Right you are, my friend, right you are," Nesbit said, interrupting him. "Go on, Tom, I'm all ears."

"Thank you, sir. Well, what I mean to say is that the masterminds of whatever this is – and I have genuine concerns about what this really is – this…these masterminds, these perpetrators, these…they intend to taunt someone at the station, if not HQ, over what this really is, if you know what I mean. They could even have you, sir, in their crosshairs, even though you're not a constable…"

"Yes, I see where you're going with this. Quite right, quite right, but I have to disagree on the latter part of your argument. 'Constable' cannot refer to me for the very reason you cited – I am neither part of Scotland Yard nor of such a lowly rank. Small issue, but good work overall. Keep going, my friend."

"Well, sir, they – and I guess we're certain there are at least two individuals involved, since the wiretap is a dialog of sorts – they, they, they, they are after a cultural artifact of some sort." His voice rose slightly as if he were unsure about the validity of his suggestion. He was almost positive that someone at the station said something about an artifact (or had he imagined it?), and he was fairly certain that someone searched for it but couldn't find it (yes, yes, it was Inspector Sedgwick). "Unfortunately, so far we haven't identified the Gray Ladies. It could be a 'gray' herring. Inspector Sedgwick has already…"

"Sandwich? She's an Inspector now? Well, don't listen to her, Tom. You're spot on about the artifact reference. 'We trusted them to protect our country's…treasures,' right? And, as you suggested, it is an artifact of the highest order, which we know for two reasons."

"Two, sir?"

"Yes, two. One, its loss (meaning either lost to England or to the world, which is tantamount to the same thing) is so significant that the government will crumble as a result." He paused for a moment to let the import of what he said sink in. "And, two, HQ is decidedly on edge, so much

140

so that they felt compelled to call in reinforcements (me, my friend) to ensure that the worst of all possible scenarios does not come to fruition and scuttle this government. Correction – future governments as well, for if my guess is right, the outcome of this case could reverberate for generations to come. Do you understand where I'm going with this?"

"You mean it's big, sir?"

"Precisely." Nesbit got up from behind the table. Staring meditatively at the floor, he clasped his hands behind his back and began walking around the table, trying to visualize the Gray Ladies while squeezing between Thwait and the wall. As soon as he returned to his side of the table, he stopped and looked at Thwait. "How do you propose to begin, my friend?" But before Thwait could answer, Nesbit started another circuit, once again struggling to get around Thwait even though the junior officer had pulled himself as close to the table as he could. "Say," Nesbit said as he again stopped on his side of the table and stared at Thwait, "what about your colleague, Sandpitch?"

"Inspector Sedgwick?"

"Yes, whatever. She's a fairly good egg, isn't she? Do you think she might do a little research for us? Maybe for references to all the artifacts termed Gray Ladies (which, presumably, refers to upstanding ladies) who, for some god-awful reason, were probably robbed of their color..."

"I'm afraid she's checked already and didn't find anything relevant."

Nesbit narrowed his eyes and, leaning forward, placed both fists on the table. "Couldn't find anything relevant? Who is she to determine relevancy?"

"I only mean, sir, she couldn't find any specific references to the Gray Ladies – people or artifacts."

Nesbit stood back and crossed his arms across his chest. Once again pacing, this time back and forth along his side of the table, he began speaking as much to himself as to Thwait. "I should have known as much. Probably didn't have her heart in it. Gray Ladies, Gray Ladies, Gray Ladies, this one puzzles me."

"Sir," Thwait said hesitantly, "sir..." When Nesbit didn't respond, he repeated the word more loudly, "sir, I believe this is important."

Nesbit stopped, rubbed his chin, and looked at him. "Go ahead, Tom. I'm listening. You don't need to yell."

"I'm sorry, sir. I only mean...well...it seems, although it's not up to me..."

"Get on with it, man."

"What I mean to say, sir, is that we can't count on Inspector Sedgwick or any other officer to help us. They might lend a hand if they have the time, but the Chief said he doesn't have the resources to expend on this case. He said if we needed something, we should go through Interpol. More importantly..." Thwait hesitated, cleared his throat, and practically burst out, "more importantly, I'm required to give the Chief a daily update on the investigation. I'm sorry, sir, but the Chief made it very clear that I can't be part of the investigation unless I report regularly to him or his designee, which I presume will be Inspector Sedgwick."

Nesbit stared at Thwait for a moment. His face was tense and unyielding, almost like the Chief's. Thwait was trying to come up with something that he hoped would mollify the man when Nesbit suddenly clapped his hands loudly several times and burst out laughing. "My friend," he began, as he leaned across the table and patted Thwait fraternally on his thick, ham-like shoulder, "don't look so hurt. It was to be expected. Your Chief has his priorities, and I have mine. Apart from your presence, I can do without his help, and my people are fully prepared to foot the bill wherever it takes us. That is, they are ready to pay our expenses no matter where the case takes us. Is that okay with you? We'll do just fine without the Chief's aid, and you can report to him all you want. In fact, that's a good idea. It won't be long before he's begging to be involved in the case and doling out resources like there's no tomorrow." Nesbit gave a few more hearty laughs and sat back at the table.

"Here's what I think, Tom. The Gray Ladies – and note the initial letters, my friend, which are not capriciously capitalized (you can sense their denominative presence by the manner in which the words are stressed) – the Gray Ladies, as I was saying, refer to a series of sculptures, not to a painting or paintings. Setting aside the number for a moment, do you know why I think the Gray Ladies are sculptures and not paintings or fine works in some other glorious media?

Thwait shook his head. He wasn't certain why they should be artworks as opposed to anything else, but he was confident that Nesbit wouldn't have taken such a leap without figuring out things beforehand.

"It's rather simple. If they were paintings, Sandpit would have located them in minutes, and you would have handed me a picture of them along with the hardcopy of the wiretap. Okay, let me put it you in another way. Paintings are never gray. They can be dark, they can be dull, they can even lack luminosity, but they are always colorful. And do you know why? Well, unlike

142

a sculptor's stone block, an artist's pigments are inherently colorful (they're called colors for a reason), and therefore not even a blind artist could fail to leverage a quality as fundamental to the craft as a monochrome block of stone is to sculptor's profession, and certainly no maestro of…of…of the Mannerists would arbitrarily brush aside the very characteristic that drew him to the profession in the first place. Does that make sense? If such an anomaly did exist, it wouldn't have been hard to separate it from all the billions of colorful paintings currently weighing down this city, especially if it were important enough to bring the government to its collective knees. Tom, it would have stood out like the proverbial sore thumb. No, Sickwick's failure was predictable."

"I don't know if she actually looked for…"

Nesbit shook his head and looked at Thwait as if the latter were about to raise a significant objection.

"Yes, yes, you are right, my friend," he continued. "I can see where you're going with this. There are indeed a few modern daubs that violate this important quality, but I challenge you to name a single one important enough to pull down the Queen's knickers. You can't, and Sedgy couldn't do it, either. Now, as I was saying, sculpture is a different beast altogether. Sculpture often lacks color because of the nature of the materials the sculptor uses to accomplish his task. Marble is white, my friend, and mud is, well, mud. In fact, the degree to which this rule is followed can be seen at a glance in any museum worth its artistic salt. If it's lucky enough to house grand works of any kind, the works will all have a single, uniform tonality. Now, do you see why the Gray Ladies have to be sculptures and not something else?"

"I think so, sir."

"Fine, and since we agree that we are dealing with sculptures, I think we can safely say that we are also dealing with several sculptures, wouldn't you say? Yes, the perpetrators clearly referred to the objects of their heinous exercise in the plural, ergo more than one. But, if there's more than one, is it possible to say how many more than a single instance we might be dealing with? My friend, I'm going to scurry out on a very strong limb and suggest that the wiretap actually refers to three Gray Ladies, not to two or multiples of that number. How can I be so confident? It's obvious – there isn't a single reference in the wiretap to the concept of 'both.' If there were only two works, the speakers at some juncture would have noted 'both' ladies, or indicated by some other non-numerical designator the fact that there were two old gals, not more, not less. It's completely natural. We commonly refer to two of anything as 'both,' or 'dual,' or a 'couple,' or 'something and something.' Now, if there were more than three, it would be equally common for us to indicate that number in some fashion. One wouldn't spot a herd of razorbacks (what do you call a grouping of those animals? Your father's still in the business, isn't he?) – anyway, one couldn't look at a mass of those things without indicating their number either by generalizing (lots of pigs) or by grouping them (assuming you don't know the exact number, you might say a hundred of them, or fifty, or some other numerical designation). Do you see what I'm getting at? With three, though, it's natural to use the plural without specifying the actual number. Suppose I were to tell you that I ate all my meals in the room today. Unless I qualified my meals by the term 'both' or specified the exact number, you would correctly assume that I had three. We naturally think of three, but not two or a hundred and two. Is this also making sense? Speak up if you disagree."

"Now, my friend," Nesbit continued, "let's put our heads together on this. Here's what I'm thinking about the kind of sculptures mentioned in the tap. Are you ready? Okay, since we are dealing with 'three Gray Ladies,' it stands to reason that we aren't dealing with this modern stuff where you can't tell a lady from a cement mixer. That being said, I would also suggest that we are dealing with pieces of ancient origin. If they were pieces by a famous sculptor of the near past (say, anywhere from the 1400s to the late 1800s), we would expect the individuals in the wiretap to mention the name of the artist, wouldn't we? Would they actually mention the Three Gray Ladies and fail to note that the ladies in question were sculpted by Mike Angelo, Rodin, Rembrandt, or some other grand old master? Of course, they'd make these connections – the artists would be integral to understanding the pieces – but in our case they didn't, which leads us to believe the pieces are anonymous and hence of more ancient origin, say, of the Greek or Chinese era, where one can't tell who did what. Now, being of ancient origin, they are almost certainly clothed. If they were in the nude, like the works those old Italian boys tended to carve, the wiretap would certainly have intimated as much. How could one discuss three gray ladies dispassionately if they were all naked? Some mention of the state of their attire or lack thereof would have to have been made. Do you see what I'm getting at here?"

Thwait nodded his head.

"Good, good, I knew you could follow a chain of tight reasoning. One last point, then. I am also convinced the Three Gray Ladies were hewn out of precious marble, the ultimate medium for the great sculptor. Why? This, too, is simple – with one or two exceptions, all of the ancients' great sculptures are bound by this medium, and, as any historian worth his salt will tell you, almost all of these magnificent creations have discolored, often becoming black, because of the pollutants in our modern air. Are we on the same page now?"

Thwait followed most of Nesbit's arguments, but when he caught sight of the wiretap resting comfortably in front of Nesbit (and from Thwait's point of view, the wiretap was upside down), he couldn't help wondering how Nesbit actually got from Point A (the note) to Point B (the discolored Greek or Chinese sculptures). He was hesitant to disagree primarily because he didn't know what he disagreed with or at what point Nesbit's logic might have failed. To ease his mind, he decided to ask for clarification on something Nesbit said about Michelangelo, but before he could open his mouth Nesbit smiled and slapped the surface of the table.

"Excellent, my friend, excellent! You're a heck of a lot sharper than Sinkfish or whatever her name is."

"Inspector Sedg…"

"Yes, yes, it doesn't matter. But what does matter is that we are on the same page. Of course, this does bring up a conundrum, Tom. Where in this country do you find the greatest number of gray sculptures? Let me put it another way – here in this country (and we are in agreement that this country is the location of the crime, are we not? Yes, good, good.)…at any rate…where was I? No, I don't need to be reminded. Where in this country are we most likely to find ancient, gray sculptures?"

"I'm afraid, I…"

"On a cathedral, perhaps? But all the wonderful sculptures on the ancient cathedrals in this country (and, remember, we are only concerned about this country) are practically black. Here's something else – the wiretap said nothing about a religious institution, and any thief worthy of the name would have mentioned a church if it were relevant. If you're going to pry something off the face of church, you better well say so or else your blokes are going to be doing a lot of driving around to find the right location. No, there was no mention of either a church or building of any kind. So, what's the most likely spot to find such a work of art?"

"Well, I suppose there are several museums that might…"

"Once again, spot on, my friend. The problem here, as you rightly hesitated to affirm, is that there are a number of possible candidates. But we need to narrow down the search before the deed is done. Let's cut to the chase. By the way, are you hungry? Yes? There are really only two museums in this country that could conceivably house something so important that it could bring down the government – the National, of course, and the Ravenswood Museum. The former houses sculpture from around the world, while the latter cradles the notorious Richardson Stones. So, how do we choose, or do we divide our time between them? And let me also note that time is of the essence here, since the wiretap is in the present tense, which indicates that the bad guys are pushing their plans forward, not waiting until some vague point in the future. Where was I? Yes, yes, I remember. How do we choose which august institution to concentrate most of our energies on? No idea? How about this – only the Richardson Stones are surrounded by the kind of controversy that could bring the government down. Steal a Michael Angelo from the National, and all you have is a controversy at the National. But purloin three Richardson Stones, and you not only have a controversy at the Ravenswood, you've also got Mesopotamia, the rest of the EU, and everyone else and his brother at the Queen's doorstep." Nesbit stretched his neck slightly and smiled, his angular face softly defined and pleasant. "Yes, Tom, it's the Richardson Stones, and it's now time for us to find out which Stones and put a stop to the madness. However, I would suggest there's a more pressing concern right now. Your expression tells me that something's on your mind. Are you hungry? No worries, my friend, this is on Interpol."

146

Chapter 4

They walked to an upscale restaurant around the corner from Nesbit's hotel. Once they were seated, Nesbit ordered an expensive bottle of wine and, after blessing it with a long and meticulous tasting, he leaned back in his chair and, glass in hand, smiled benignly at Thwait. Thwait, however, didn't quite understand his friend's strange attitude (Nesbit was rarely so openly happy), and when he gingerly inquired about it, Nesbit nodded is if he had already mentioned the reason, or as if Thwait had only asked a rhetorical question.

Nesbit finished his glass and poured another, after which he carefully, pleasantly, and silently topped off Thwait's glass. Taking another long, thoughtful sip of his own glass, he smiled once again at the younger man.

"I suppose," he began, staring absently at the faint, diamond-shaped shadows that the chandelier overhead cast across the table and Thwait's shoulders, "I suppose you're wondering about my reticence this evening, which I presume is somewhat different than my normal, outgoing self. No, no," he added and waved one hand up to silence Thwait's potential protest, "there's no reason to think I might be offended by your inquiry – and really, my friend, after all our time and work together, how could you possibly think I could be offended by anything your said? You are right to inquire, because our emotional state could have an impact on the quality of our important work. Well, let me assure you that I am happier now than I've been in, if not years, then decades. Yes, it's absolutely true." Nesbit leaned forward and, while still holding his glass, placed his elbows on the table. Looking directly into Thwait's eyes, he said, "I'm happy to be working with you again, my friend, and, well, my ex-wife recently passed away."

Thwait sat up and, fishing around for the appropriate words, mumbled something slightly incoherent about Nesbit's loss.

"No, no need to be sorry, Tom, if that's what you meant. I, too, felt something resembling a slight pang when I heard the news, but I have to admit that it was difficult to feel more than that. We had been estranged for more than decade and...my God, she had such a troublesome personality." Nesbit took another drink and then held the glass up toward the light to admire the liquid's color and clarity. "In fact," he said after placing his glass carefully back onto the white, double damask tablecloth, "our estrangement was quite bitter, owing mainly to her desire to punish me for some imagined wrong. She also wanted to rob me of my son, who is now in his early twenties (not quite your age), fresh from college, and finally his own man. Did I tell you he's an engineer? I suppose I hadn't. He recently landed an important job with a firm based in Oxford. If I understand correctly, the firm specializes in the destruction of buildings, and they're able to take down the tallest building without putting a speck of dust on the surrounding landscape. Amazing, but I digress." Nesbit finished off his glass and poured himself another.

"At any rate, my former spouse stood between me and my son for years, filling his imagination with all sorts of lies, innuendoes, and half-truths such that during the proceedings – divorce, my friend, and he was only twelve or thirteen at the time – he felt compelled to take her side against me, even though I had never done anything except love the boy. Have I told you this before? Well, given the circumstances and everything else, I suppose his position was understandable, and his refusal to speak to me after the divorce was…I suppose I can understand that, too. But, I'm happy to say, things began to thaw between us after her death."

Nesbit finished the remnants of the bottle and motioned to the waiter to bring another of the same.

"Less than a year ago, she was diagnosed with a rare form of something or other and, lickety-split, she's resting comfortably in the morgue (the news came by registered letter from the hospital). I suppose I was sorry for her and all that, but since I lost most of my feelings for her years ago, her untimely demise seemed to me like any other. The really positive aspect to her death was that my son – did I tell you his name is Ben? – my one and only child, reached out to me shortly after the funeral and wanted 'to put things straight.' By God, those were his exact words – he wanted 'to set the record right.'"

"That's wonderful," interjected Thwait, reaching across the table for the bottle and spilling on the pristine tablecloth as he tried to top off his glass. Spotting his mistake, he wiped the dark liquid off the tablecloth with his left coat sleeve and somehow managed to bump his glass, spilling more of the wine onto the tablecloth. Thwait wiped this up in the same manner and then carefully resupplied his glass. Nesbit had been eyeing this strange pantomime, noticing as well the younger man's round, flushed face, when Thwait caught sight of his observant gaze and motioned with his clean sleeve for him to continue.

"Yes, of course…well, by the grace of God Almighty, it certainly was a most wondrous thing. We were on the phone the first time for a couple of hours at least. He told me about his life, his work, and even confessed – confessed, mind you – that he should have been more critical of some of the crap his mother told him about me. I told him – truthfully, and with all my heart – I told him that I understood and I explained that his past behavior was unsurprising given the circumstances. By the way, did I tell you that my Ben has been following my cases over the years, particularly the New Orleans case, and he said he admired my skill and my ability to cut to the heart of the most intractable issues. Boy, that young man certainly has a head on his shoulders. But to make a short story even longer, we didn't leave it at one measly phone call. We spoke three more times, each call a conversation like the first, albeit with more comfort and familiarity, and the upshot was that we agreed to meet the next time I had a chance to get to London. I gave him my word. He couldn't come to see me because of work-related difficulties. Well, here it is – four or five or six months, six days, a smattering of hours, and I don't know how many minutes since her timely demise, and, in a day or two more, I will finally be reunited with my son. Tom, old boy, do you know what?"

Thwait looked up abruptly as if he had dozed off. "No, sir. Should I?"

Nesbit motioned to the waiter for another bottle, although they hadn't finished the second bottle. "No, I suppose there's no reason you should. My beloved son Ben (I told you his name, right?), my beloved son offered to meet me in Oxford when I had a few minutes to spare. Isn't that something? More wine, my admirable friend?"

Thwait eagerly nodded affirmatively.

"I'll give you more details when I get them, but...my God, isn't it a wondrous thing? He actually wanted to put something in its place or straighten out something or other. Say, Tom, I want you to meet him, too. He's a handsome lad, a real blick off the old chop, and I know he's got everything together, as far as his life goes, which is extraordinary after what that woman...here, take a look at this." Nesbit pulled a worn photo of a toddler out of his wallet and handed it to Thwait, who had been holding up his sagging head with one hand while resting his elbow on the table.

Thwait looked at the picture and then at Nesbit three or four times before handing the picture back to his friend.

"Sorry, I don't have anything more recent, but I'm sure you can still see why I'm so proud." Nesbit smiled as he put the picture back into his wallet. "Tom, he reminds me of myself in so many ways it's almost uncanny.

But enough of this. Let's get back to the case. What? My goodness, we forgot to order."

Dinner and another bottle of wine were served a half hour later. While they ate and drank, they went over the evidence (which was little more than the tap) and studied the Richardson Stones, images of which Thwait brought up on his phone. Since Thwait knew very little about the sculptures, he relied on Nesbit's vague knowledge not only to determine which pieces were the most likely candidates, but also to map out the most effective means of staking out the museum gallery where the pieces were displayed. "I've been thinking about this from the second you read me the wiretap. It'll be a piece of cake. We'll catch them with their hands on the goods," Nesbit practically crooned.

Thwait, though, wasn't certain that it would be as simple as Nesbit implied. For one thing, they didn't have permission from the museum authorities to conduct police business on museum premises; and, while he wasn't certain how to get permission, he was fairly confident that it wouldn't be easy given the scant evidence they possessed. For another, he knew that the Chief wasn't going to lift a finger to help them, at least not this early in the case or with the wiretap as their only piece of evidence. Of course, Nesbit might have special connections with HQ, he might even have a relationship with the museum authorities, but Thwait didn't feel that this was the right time to express his concerns or ask Nesbit what he could bring to the table to get the two officers past the authorities, especially not while his, Thwait's, eyesight was slightly cloudy.

When dinner was over and the last bottle was empty (Nesbit doled out the dregs evenly between himself and Thwait), Nesbit insisted that they go to the Ravenswood Museum and have a look. "Nothing official, mind you, just to get the lay of the land, if you will," he said while signing the bill. Standing up, he put on his coat (which had been draped over the chair next to him) and proceeded directly to the door. Thwait, who struggled to get out of his chair and was fumbling with the buttons of his coat while trying to keep up with his friend, didn't understand Nesbit's need to see the museum at this juncture, since they had seen the museum many times while working on a case three years ago, and, as far as he could tell, the museum was closed at this hour (he couldn't focus his eyes enough to see his watch).

"We should check the entrances and exits, as well as the placement of the security cameras, if there are any," Nesbit was saying as he stopped on the sidewalk in front of the restaurant and waited for Thwait to catch up, "and then spend some quality time with the pieces themselves. I don't think it would hurt to acquaint ourselves with the objects of the crime, do you? The images on your phone weren't exactly first rate." Nesbit put his hands in his jacket pockets and looked absently up and down the dark street. The street lights were casting pale lights across the road and illuminating portions of the buildings, except for the area directly across from them, which seemed engulfed in a deep gloom. Smiling warmly, he turned to Thwait, who had just walked up, and asked, "Tom, you wouldn't happen to have a car, would you?"

Thwait was about to explain that he brought his own car. He had requested an official vehicle, but the Chief for some angry reason had refused to let him have one while on the case. Thwait would have emphasized, though, that he would be happy (he would be proud) to let Nesbit use his personal vehicle, but he was interrupted before he could even say that he had a car.

"Not a problem. I took the liberty of renting one, at Interpol's expense, of course. It's parked in the garage over there." Nesbit pointed vaguely into the darkness across the street, where there were at least three garages.

As they sauntered across the street in search of Nesbit's car, Thwait hung back a couple of steps to observe his great friend. Nesbit walked briskly and confidently, and, as Thwait noticed, he kept his shoulders back and his chin level, as if he had once been a tightrope walker. Nesbit, however, had never been in the circus, and it was doubtful that he had ever been to one, either. He had joined the Buffalo police force directly out of college and, after serving with distinction for nearly ten years, was promoted and asked to serve as the force's representative at international law-enforcement conferences. It should be noted that it was in Oxford at one of these conferences (which focused on the rehabilitation of incorrigible prisoners) that he met his future wife, who was one of the event's organizers. Smitten, he resigned his position and joined Interpol to be near her. Throughout the twenty-five years or so that he had been with Interpol (and several of those years were spent stationed in the States), Nesbit had built a stellar reputation, punctuated by famous cases, high-profile bad guys, and lots of media attention, or so it seemed to Thwait. Indeed, Thwait looked forward to the day when he could sit down with Nesbit and listen to the man discussing some of his most intractable cases and the high-profile bad guys that he had personally escorted to the 'slammer.' But as he watched the older man, admiring the proud, unflinching manner in which he seemed to approach everything, even searching for his car, he began to wonder if he should say anything about the usefulness of visiting the museum at this particular hour. "Sir," Thwait said, breaking the silence that had lasted until they walked into the garage where Nesbit expected to find his car, "do you think the museum is still open? I mean, it is rather late. Maybe it would be better if we go tomorrow. We could be there when the doors open."

"Nonsense, my friend," Nesbit replied as he stood looking up and down the parking aisles and squinting at the numbers painted on the spaces. "It will be open. If it's not, we can have a jolly time just the same walking about the building and checking the entrances and...do you know what floor we're on?" Squatting down, his slender knees splayed, Nesbit looked under a row of cars to see if he recognized something. "My God, somebody must have moved..."

They followed the ramp up to the next floor and the floor after that, and then down to the lowest level in the basement. At one point, Nesbit stood in the middle of an aisle and scratched his head while glancing around the garage. "I could have sworn..."

"Did you note the space number on your ticket, sir?"

Nesbit stopped and turned to his friend. Without moving a muscle in his face, he reached into his coat pocket and retrieved the parking ticket. "Good thinking," he replied as he carefully observed the ticket. "No, unfortunately, I didn't. But what I think we can gather from this ticket is that we're in the wrong garage. The name on the ticket doesn't match the name on that wall over there." He motioned with his head to the wall in question. Forty-five minutes later they located the car, a nondescript black sedan parked across the street in the garage connected to the hotel. The car was squeezed in between two other cars, and on a different floor than he remembered, both of which he attributed to one of the attendants having moved the car without his permission. Thwait laughed because he thought that Nesbit was joking, but he immediately ceased when Nesbit mumbled something about speaking to the hotel manager if such a thing were to happen again.

Chapter 5

It took no more than thirty minutes to reach the museum but nearly twice as much to find a parking place (despite the late hour, the few spaces open for public parking were almost all taken). By the time they reached the top of the elegant stone stairway which ended at the museum entrance, a bearded guard with a hat slightly askew was holding the door open and waving the last of the visitors out of the museum. Noticing Nesbit and Thwait approaching, he stepped out of the doorway and, shaking his shaggy head, told them that the museum was closed and that they would have to go back down the stairs. (He made an emphatic gesture with his index and middle fingers toward the stairs as if the officers might have trouble finding their way back.) Thwait, the fog in his head now clear, walked over to the guard and flashed his badge. The two conversed quietly for a moment, after which the guard stepped aside and waved them inside, much to the consternation of an elderly man who had just been ushered out of the building. The guard agreed, as one officer to another, to let them wander around the main floor for twenty minutes while the upper and lower floors were being inspected and cleared. But, he added, "if you're still inside after the door is closed, you'll be shot as intruders." He winked at Thwait, who asked him how to find the Richardson Stones.

Nesbit and Thwait reached the gallery in seconds. But when they were about to pass under a wide, rococo archway at the gallery's entrance, another guard suddenly appeared and refused to allow them inside. Thwait squinted at the man, who was even taller than the Chief, and tried to explain that he and Nesbit had been given permission to look at the Stones while the other floors were being cleared, but the man wouldn't have anything of it. "I don't care what Archie said," he replied, cutting off Thwait in midsentence. "The gallery is closed, gents. Now, if you don't mind going back to where you came from...," he was saying as he positioned himself in the middle of the archway, directly in front of the officers. They turned to leave, but as if on cue they both glanced over their shoulders to see the sculptures that were visible from outside the gallery. "Hey, hey, none of that," the guard called out and took a couple, menacing steps toward them but didn't go any farther. As they silently made their way back to the entrance, Nesbit and Thwait were surprised that the pieces were gleaming white and didn't appear to have the slightest hint of gray (at best a tooth-like tonality, but definitely not gray).

On their way out of the main lobby, Thwait grabbed a museum brochure on the Richardson Stones, which he and Nesbit studied in the overhead light inside Nesbit's quietly purring car.

"I don't get it," Thwait uttered after they had thoroughly exhausted the meager brochure. "I can't find anything that might pass for three gray ladies."

Nesbit was about to agree when something in the brochure caught his eye. He stared closely at it for a moment and then turned to Thwait with a wide smile on his narrow face. "This is it. Since we didn't have these same images earlier, it was hard to visualize what exactly we were looking for. Look closely at this picture." He held the brochure up so Thwait could see it and pointed to the sculpture. "Do you see this? Three figures – clothed, as I suspected – and all them are snuggled next to one another like dogs in a bed. Don't be put off by the missing heads and arms; that's just the way they carved things back then. Look instead at the title of the work – the three something or other, which, if I may be so bold, roughly translated means the three ladies. Yes, of course, those are names, but nobody can pronounce them and, besides, it still means the same thing. If you look at the coloration, my friend, you'll also see that the marble of these headless lovelies has a grayish cast to it."

Thwait nodded, although to him the gray appeared to be a slight shadow caused by the angle of the lighting.

"That does it, the three Gray Ladies. You can report that to the Chief." Nesbit paused and, scratching his chin, appeared to be thinking of something. "Yes, yes, report that to the Chief. But explain that I have a plan to capture the thief before he takes that flawed, fatal step. You know, Tom, it isn't just law and order with me. I believe in compassion, forgiveness. While I'm not willing to let the bugger off the hook, I would like to prevent him from throwing his entire life away. Yes, there will be jail time, quite a lot of it, I would hope, but that doesn't mean I would oppose someone helping him get back on his feet during the later decades of his term." Nesbit absently turned the ignition key again and the engine screeched painfully in response. Without another word, he pressed the accelerator and angled the car away from the curb.

"But there are two, aren't there, sir? I mean, the conversation in the wiretap suggests…"

"Yes, yes, quite so. We'll put both of the buggers securely behind bars for a good, long time."

The car lurched once and continued smoothly and quickly.

"Where are we going, sir?" Thwait asked, looking at the street in front of him after having exhausted the brochure. Nesbit's logic seemed sound enough, Thwait told himself, even though some of the details were a little fuzzy (were the Stones truly gray, were the speakers actually referring to three works, and were the Gray Ladies really among the Richardson Stones?), and yet there was something else that didn't quite sit well with him. For a few moments, he didn't know what that something was, and it troubled him that he could have reservations about what was obvious to his great friend. But a bump in the road loosened whatever it was that was stuck, and he realized what was bothering him – it was the logistics. If Nesbit were right about the Richardson Stones, then how were the thieves going to get such large works out of the museum without being seen or arousing suspicion? A single glance into the gallery told him that each of the Stones had to weigh as much as their car, if not more. Of course, if Nesbit were wrong about the sculptures, then some of the other suppositions upon which he built his case were probably wrong, too.

Shortly after Nesbit veered out of the right-hand lane to avoid a head-on collision, Thwait noticed some familiar buildings and, a few minutes later, the garages where he and Nesbit had searched for the car. Glancing across the street, he spotted Nesbit's hotel and, just when he expected Nesbit to slow down and veer toward the building, the car's speed increased and they passed the entrance as if Nesbit hadn't seen it. Thwait couldn't tell if Nesbit was lost or if he was taking him some place else. "Sir," he asked cautiously, "did you miss the hotel entrance?"

"By a good mile, my friend, but that's not where we're going." Nesbit pulled up in front of a nondescript building and immediately got out of the car. Thwait had to scurry as Nesbit headed for the entrance of a pub and then disappeared inside. Thwait went inside as well, and in the dimly lit establishment he thought that Nesbit might be meeting with an undercover operative who had a line on their case. For a moment or two, it all seemed very exciting and Thwait was thankful as always for the opportunity of working with Nesbit. But as his eyes and other senses adjusted to the environment, he could see that the place looked nothing like the kind of establishment that would be home to such intrigue. This impression was reinforced when he noticed Nesbit being escorted to a nearby table. While Thwait hesitated and tried to make sense of what was happening, Nesbit motioned to him to come over and take a seat.

"I don't understand," he started to say as he sat down opposite Nesbit, but Nesbit interrupted him in a voice filled with the certainty that he was on the verge of solving another important case.

"Yes, of course, we had dinner not so long ago. But it's time to call it an early evening. There'll be no shortage of late nights later on. You need to loosen up a bit, my friend. A quick one now and you'll be raring to go. Sorry, I mean ready to work tomorrow."

Thwait looked anxiously around as if the Chief might be lurking around the corner or seated at the next table over. That was absurd, of course, but he couldn't help feeling that he needed to show anyone who might be interested that he wasn't even thinking of charging the station for a drink.

"What's the matter, Tom? You look like a goat got your something or other. That's wrong." He leaned forward a little and scratched his chin. "No, it's the cat that's got something of yours. By God, that doesn't sound right, either. Say, what's the problem, Tom? Aren't you thirsty?"

"Yes, sir, but..."

"No buts, my friend. Whatever the sheep's got, Interpol's got this one. So what else is on your mind?"

Somewhat assured about the costs, Thwait's mind immediately went back to the Richardson Stones, because there were so many aspects of the sculptures, including their individual sizes, shapes, and weights, that were troubling if one assumed that the thieves were going to steal them. While he was confident that Nesbit would clarify everything sooner or later, Thwait was eager to begin the clarification process sooner rather than later so that he could explain things to the Chief and, maybe if he was on the same page as Nesbit, contribute in some fashion to solving the case. "Sir," he began, speaking cautiously to avoid sounding stupid or making Nesbit think he was questioning his judgment, "well, sir, the thing is...shouldn't we be watching the museum now. I mean, if you are right (and I have no reason to doubt), couldn't the thieves be moving the pieces now while we're relaxing? By the way, sir, this is a lovely place. I don't think I've ever seen it before. Are you sure it's okay?"

"Absolutely, my friend, you are right to be concerned, but let me assure you that Interpol's got this one covered and that we aren't relaxing in the least. Excuse me, but I believe this kind gentleman would like to know what you want to drink." With Nesbit gently guiding Thwait's choices, they ordered drinks and instructed the waiter to bring several appetizers.

Moments later, after the first round was delivered, Nesbit smiled at his young friend and said, "I think you'll appreciate this. Smooth, isn't it? Now, as I was saying, I have a puzzle for you, which, as you'll quickly see, isn't quite as puzzling as it initially appears."

Nesbit leaned back in his chair and took a long, appreciative sip of his drink. "Tom, as you aptly noted earlier, the Richardson Stones are remarkable in terms of their proportions and their notoriety, and if you and I wanted to steal them (hypothetically, of course), we would have to do something to disguise these two essential qualities – for if we didn't, then I can assure you that before we took a half-dozen steps out the back door, the police (us) would arrive and hand us (them) first-class tickets to the slammer. Yes, yes, of course, we would need a forklift to move the blocks, but that's really beside the point at this juncture. Concentrate, my friend. As I was attempting to articulate, we wouldn't try to move one of these things, with or without a forklift, without first finding the kind of cover that would prevent the harsh light of reality from revealing the inherent qualities of these pieces and, at the same time, highlighting our perverse activities. Now, what kind of cover would serve this very specific need of ours? No, a tarp would be too conspicuous, my friend. But how about darkness? If you think about it, darkness is quite possibly the only cover sufficient enough to hide both the sculptures and our activities from prying eyes as we attempt to secrete the gigantic things out of the museum. Given enough time and the right kind of thinking, you and I and all the other common criminals would come up with exactly the same conclusion."

Nesbit hesitated briefly and smiled as if something else had just come to mind. "But upon further reflection, I wonder if we should pause a moment before acting on what we know common criminals like ourselves would do under the same circumstances. My friend, I know what you're thinking, and your instincts are good ones. Why should we wait even for a single second when we now have within our grasp the means to foil the crime of the century? Yes, we can turn on the lights and expose this caper, this corpus delicti, this...this whatever. The answer to the latter question isn't, I'm afraid, as simple as it appears to be, and the reason for this is that we aren't dealing with common criminals. This crime is too audacious for common criminal mindsets like ours, and the objects of their crime are too...are too...too big for the run-of-the-mill bad guy to handle without some uncommon means to achieve the desired ends. What am I saying here? But first, have another sip of this. Well, a gulp is fine, too. It never ceases to amaze, my friend, or warm the cold heart. At any rate, this crime is too complicated, too uncommon, too audacious, and therefore darkness as cover simply won't cut it. Let me rephrase this – darkness, in this instance, would become light, and what should be a successful criminal enterprise would be exposed before our unfortunate but thieving friends made it to the front door."

Thwait leaned forward on his elbow slightly, but he was too close to the edge of the table and his elbow slipped off and his chin nearly landed on his glass. Quickly recovering, he acted as if he were still concentrating and nothing unusual had happened. Nesbit, however, had been looking off in the distance and hadn't noticed.

"How is that?" he continued, "why would the best cover in the world be useless for this particular crime? It's complicated, but I believe there are essentially three reasons for this. First, let us assume that the only cover of darkness suitable for this crime is the night. Night alone is capable of concealing both the museum and the surrounding grounds – and, yes, the area surrounding the museum must be covered, too, for the perps (perpetrators, my good friend) will need to get the blocks out of the museum unseen and into an awaiting truck, which will wait patiently idling while the blocks are being moved from their resting places. Tarps would be too obvious. But while night is eminently achievable, there are far too many problems awaiting the unsuspecting criminal when the evening is quiet, and quaint canoes prow the motionless tributaries of the Thames under a moon-lit black sky. In fact, this leads us directly to the second reason. Second, while darkness obviously provides a certain level of comfort for thieves, nighttime activities at the museum would be a dead giveaway that something untoward is up. Remember, we said that for a crime to be successful, the varlets need sufficient cover to prevent curious eyes and minds from observing and eventually reporting them to the authorities. Nighttime, in this case, becomes daytime, for anything happening at the museum after hours in the dark is bound to attract undue attention (and it wouldn't take much, a solitary gleam from a flashlight, the soft purr of a truck engine, or a fleeting shadow across the sidewalk). Neither this nor any other museum operates in darkness in the middle of the night. When those grand blocks of stone were ferried into their current positions, the museum officials did so during the day and with all the lights in the galleries blaring down on the workers like miniature suns floating above them. No one was taking any chances with such precious objects. In fact, had the workers undertaken such efforts without sufficient light, a simple slip, a stumble over an uneven tile, and the block would plummet to the floor where it would be vacuumed up the following morning by the cleaning crew. And, as if that weren't enough, darkness, nighttime, after normal hours, whatever, adds any number of additional complications to such a despicable undertaking, for the knaves would have to disable alarms, disconnect trip wires, poison the dogs, and all the rest that a fine institution like the Ravenswood implements to protect its crown jewels while everyone else is comfortably sleeping in their warm beds. Nod your heavy head if you're still with me."

Thwait moved his head vaguely. He tried to narrow his eyes on Nesbit to make it appear as though he was carefully following his friend's logic. But while he had little trouble comprehending most of his words and phrases, he was finding it increasingly difficult to remember them and to connect them in a way that made sense and conveyed whatever it was that Nesbit was trying to convey. The drinks, of course, were part of the problem (and this includes the drinks during dinner, which were now conspiring to affect his mind, too), but the more he narrowed his eyes, the less distinct the man became. Nesbit's head and shoulders were suddenly becoming soft and fuzzy, and his eyes, nose, and lips were blending into his forehead, cheeks, and chin – as well as into each other. Shaking his head to clear his senses, Thwait yanked his tie to one side and tugged at his collar, after which he leaned against the table and tried once again to focus on what Nesbit was saying.

"Good. Now, listen closely; this is important." Nesbit paused and stared at Thwait meaningfully. "I am convinced that our remarkable criminals are planning to take the grand old dames, our Gray Ladies, out of the museum in complete daylight – the most remarkable cover of all – and, equally remarkable, they are going to take them out the very same front door that lets in all the tourists with their screaming children, bouncing strollers, and tottering grandparents. No one could possibly anticipate such a thing, and no one would think anything amiss as the sculpture is carefully forklifted (yes, a forklift) to an awaiting, official-looking truck. This audacious action also eliminates a host of minor difficulties that would certainly bedevil a nighttime burglary. The cover is perfect – light becomes dark, and deception becomes routine. Pretty slick, don't you think? We are dealing with criminal geniuses, if you want my considered opinion."

Nesbit leaned back in his chair and put his hands behind his head. Looking up at the dark, wooden ceiling, he was reminded of a certain bar in the French Quarter where he often went after a long, satisfying day at work.

Something Nesbit said unexpectedly came through the fog in Thwait's mind. Taking a big swallow of his drink and then emptying it for good measure, he tightened his lips and tried to squint at his friend, although one of his eyes didn't seem to be working properly. "Tell me, shir, why wouldn't the guards try to stop them? Sirly, they would know if the Stones were to be moved, given all the logistics and security arrangements needing to be made before touching one of the ieces...pieces. I'm just sassing." Thwait tried unsuccessfully to get the waiter's attention.

Nesbit sat back upright and stared at Thwait for a moment. "That's a good question, Tom, a very good question." Nesbit lapsed into a studied silence until the waiter brought the bill a few minutes later (the waiter had come by earlier to see if Nesbit needed anything else). Signing his name with a flourish, he stood up and looked down at Thwait. "Tom," he said, tossing his napkin on the table and then brushing off the front of his pants, "the answer to your question is simple. Some of the guards are in on it. Say, did anyone, maybe that Sandkook of yours, happen to discover the location of our thieves' call? I wouldn't be surprised if it originated from the museum itself, maybe even from the director's office."

"Inspector Sedwidge-wick, sir. I'm afraid I don't know. I'll ask the Chief tomorrow. It's a little late to call now."

"Good, good." Nesbit charged out the pub and headed for the car, with Thwait behind and struggling to keep up. Once back in the car, Nesbit turned to the out-of-breath younger officer and said, "yes, ask the Chief about the origin of the call. But if you can, let's keep some of this other stuff quiet for the time being, at least until we have more information. I wouldn't relish seeing the Chief or that Sandale of yours running off prematurely and blowing the case out of the water before we've had a chance to dip our toes. I'm sure you understand."

When they were back at the entrance of the hotel, Nesbit took the shoulders of his slightly tipsy companion and, angling him toward the garage where his car was parked, told him to come back to the hotel at 7:00 AM sharp. "We have business tomorrow, my friend" was the last thing that Thwait could recall Nesbit saying that evening.

Chapter 6

The Chief was leaning back in his chair with his hands clasped behind his head and staring at the ceiling. "The morning has barely begun...," he began as Sedgwick seated herself in one of the chairs in front of his desk.

Sedgwick remained silent while she waited for the Chief to continue his thought.

"...and they're already a nuisance," he continued after a short pause. Sitting up, he turned to Sedgwick, who appeared neat and tidy in her gray business suit, even though she had been working for several hours already.

"I presume you're referring to Constable Thwait and Agent Nesbit."

"Who else?"

"Constable Thwait has reported then?"

"In a manner of speaking. He sent me an email, explaining that he and Nesbit didn't have anything yet, which is understandable, and asked me if I wouldn't mind stepping back for a few days. They needed time to get some information and, once they had it, they might have something interesting to report. Can you believe it, asking me to step back? I called Thwait a short while ago and, after I set him straight about our relative responsibilities, he came clean."

"What did he say?"

The Chief picked up his pencil and began tapping it on the top of his desk, at the same time squinting at Sedgwick. "It seems that he and Nesbit have determined that the individuals in the wiretap are part of a gang of thieves out to steal the Richardson Stones from the Ravenswood Museum. They are convinced the gang is going to use a forklift to pick up the pieces and drive them out of the museum – and in broad daylight, of all things. It's so preposterous that I had to pinch myself to keep from laughing. What's almost as funny is that they're now staking out the museum entrance, hoping to catch the thieves driving the pieces out with a forklift. They've apparently snagged a good parking space in front of the museum, so I'll give them that."

"Perhaps the bad guys aren't the only ones who are losing their marbles."

"Quite. It gets better. When I asked him how the forklift could hoist the block and drive it out of the museum without alerting anyone – say, the guards, the museum staff, or even the visitors – he hemmed and hawed a bit and admitted that it would be a 'little difficult.' When pressed, he confessed that Nesbit thought there might collusion among the staff, but they didn't have enough information to be more specific. He was going to get more information from Nesbit and let me know the next time he reported."

"What?" Sedgwick leaned forward, as if she had to be closer to the Chief to make sure she was hearing everything correctly.

"That's only half of it. When I instructed him not to approach the museum staff, particularly the director, without my express approval, he was silent for a moment before agreeing to speak to me prior to approaching the officials. I took his statement at face value, but I'm starting to wonder if his statement will restrain Nesbit. What do you think? I think his influence over Nesbit is limited at best. Am I concerned over nothing? So far, I haven't got any angry calls from the museum."

Sedgwick thought for a moment and then shook her head. "I'm sure Constable Thwait will follow the rules, although like you I'm not entirely sure about Agent Nesbit. He can get a little carried away at times. Are you contemplating something, I don't know, to keep them out of trouble?"

"That's just what I've been puzzling over." The Chief dropped his pencil, which sought its usual place against the stack of case folders. "I'm inclined to leave them alone for a while. Should Nesbit cause any problems, I think we can let Interpol handle the fallout. Maybe that would get the noted Interpol agent out of our hair."

"Are you sure that's the right course? It could come back to bite us."

"I don't think anyone will lay blame at the feet of a junior officer, especially when it's clear he's only following the lead of a seasoned Interpol agent."

"I suppose, as long as we're certain he won't be left holding the bag if something does happen."

"Look," the Chief again squinted at Sedgwick, "have you ever seen me do that to any of my officers? I'll protect him unless he's gone over the edge. Despite Nesbit's presence, I don't think Thwait is the kind to step too far out of bounds."

"It sounds like this is more about Agent Nesbit. You really don't like him, do you?"

"My feelings are immaterial. Okay, if you want to know the truth, I think he's an insufferable bore who acts like he's the American Sherlock Holmes. He's either watching too much TV or completely off...but, no, that's not why I wanted to see you."

"Would you like me to do some research to help keep them on the straight and narrow?"

The Chief loosened his tie and undid his collar button. "Maybe, we'll see. I reached out to HQ about the rest of the wiretap, and they made it very clear that it will be available when it's available."

"That's rather peculiar."

"That's a polite way of phrasing it."

"Didn't they give you any indication why it's not available now? Are they still collecting on the line?"

"I think they were being straight when they said the line's been cut. They also said that the whole wiretap amounts to little more than a minute of conversation. But they wouldn't tell me why they were holding the rest, and I certainly don't like their silence about when it will be available."

"It doesn't make sense, Chief. How do they expect us to conduct a thorough and timely investigation if they're holding some of the evidence? Given everything we have so far, which isn't much, it could be crucial to the case."

"You're speaking to the choir." The Chief frowned, although there was apparently something else on his mind.

"Did they at least give you a sense of what else might be on the wiretap? Is there anything they can give us to work with?"

The Chief picked up his pencil but this time didn't immediately begin tapping it. "In a manner of speaking, I suppose. My contact at HQ suggested that something at a high-profile institution could be at risk, but he was quick to insist that he didn't have any additional information."

"What? Wait a minute. Do you mean Constable Thwait and Agent Nesbit are on the right track?"

"Come on, how can anyone make off with one of the Richardson Stones? Does that make any sense to you? If an art work's at risk, it's likely a painting, a jewel, a manuscript, or anything else that can be taken and easily disposed of. For crying out loud, I'd be more confident of what Nesbit and Thwait were doing if they had singled out a stuffed porcupine from the natural history collection instead the Richardson Stones. You can sell a porcupine, but who's going to buy one of the world's most famous sculptures, especially if it can't be extracted from the museum? Or the city, for that matter."

"I see what you're saying, Chief."

"More to the point, I don't know what we're supposed to do with this choice tidbit. An institution? Fine, which one? And this stuff about treasures – are we talking about a work of art or something else? We need details, or else this thing, if this is a thing, could blow up in everyone's face. But you don't need to say it. I tried to get some more information, I spoke to a couple of other people, and all I got was the runaround. Nobody was saying anything, especially when I pressed them about this constable business. With what we have now, we can't even be sure that the rest of the wiretap won't contradict it. It's like having a white puzzle piece and being expected to construct the entire image from it."

"Good point."

"It's all so…," the Chief began and then gritted his teeth. "Okay, when we get more of the wiretap, or anything else, for that matter, maybe we'll have something to go on. In the meantime, let's keep an eye on Nesbit and Thwait to make sure they don't get in over their heads."

"Why not pull them from the case? Surely…"

"I can't right now. This is my other problem. HQ requested Nesbit, and Nesbit requested Thwait, and so my hands are pretty much tied at the moment. If something in the wiretap pans out, or if the extraordinary should happen and Nesbit and Constable Thwait come across something useful, I'll put more officers on the case – none of whom will answer to Nesbit."

"What do we do until then?"

"That's the $64,000 question."

"The what, Chief?"

"Never mind. HQ just requested my presence for a meeting later today. I don't know what they want, but I'm supposed to bring a case file from something we handled several years ago." He named the case and added a couple of details. "The timing, though, isn't ideal. I was planning to pay a field visit to Nesbit and Thwait today, but there's little chance of this if I have to waste my time at this meeting. Now, since I'm not comfortable postponing the visit (and who knows what might come up tomorrow?), I want you to visit them in my stead. Nothing special, just see what's going on, lend a hand if you feel like it, and report to me if anything's amiss." The Chief paused and tapped his index finger on the desk several times. "Come to think of it, why don't you have Thwait copy you on everything he sends to me? It would make me a little more comfortable to have two sets of eyes on those gentlemen. If anything pressing comes up, you reach me on my cell."

"This sounds like a bigger commitment than a simple field visit. How long do you expect to be out of pocket?"

"You never know with HQ. I'm just a little concerned that Nesbit and Thwait lack adult supervision. But, don't worry, it's only temporary."

"I don't mind, Chief. I was just curious."

The Chief hesitated. "One more thing – you and Thwait are my officers. I know I can count on you, but I need you to make sure that Thwait doesn't lose his senses while Nesbit has him chasing after shadows."

Sedgwick nodded. "Will do, Chief."

The Chief retrieved a notepad from his top drawer and positioned it on his desk directly in front of him. Retrieving his pencil, he started to write what appeared to be a rather long note about something, a clear indication the conversation was over.

As soon as Sedgwick closed the door, the Chief put the notepad back into the drawer and, leaning back in his chair, once again clasped his hands behind his head.

Chapter 7

The sky was more or less a dull, heavy gray, even directly overhead where the sun was supposed to be. The air, though, was warm and comfortable, and in the distance one could hear the sounds of children shouting and laughing. The surveillance vehicle (actually Nesbit's car) was positioned at an angle to the museum entrance, making it fairly inconspicuous to people streaming in and out of the museum's main doors while affording the two gentlemen inside the vehicle a fairly unobstructed view of the front and one corner of the museum.

Several evenings ago at a nearby pub, Nesbit and Thwait had discussed how best to position the car so that they could discretely observe the entrance doors for anything suspicious. Initially, they had been positive that the thieves would abscond with the sculptures through the main doors – the combined opening, after all, was bigger than any two sculptures put together, and there was no other location in the building better situated for hiding in plain sight. But last night, after a spirited discussion at another pub that was followed by a late-night stroll around the perimeter of the building, Nesbit and Thwait realized that there were other entrances the thieves could use to commit their unconscionable crime – specifically, any one of the four gigantic loading doors in the dock at back of the building. Each of the loading doors seemed nearly large enough to handle Big Ben (on its side, of course) and still have extra room on the top and sides. While Nesbit and Thwait were still confident that the thieves planned to use the main doors, they couldn't entirely discount the possibility that the thieves would resort to one of the loading doors if something went wrong or if the main doors weren't available at the time of the robbery. As luck would have it, there was a single cobblestone service road that connected the loading dock, with the four loading doors, to the street running in front of the building, and it began practically at the base of the museum's front stairs. Nesbit and Thwait quickly realized that they could park their car in one of the museum's front parking spaces and easily spot any unusual activity occurring either at the main doors or entering and exiting the cobblestone road leading to the loading dock at the back of the museum.

But, despite the clarity with which he could see the museum doors and the service road, Nesbit seemed distracted and he appeared to be having trouble concentrating on the museum, the road, and practically everything else. In fact, two or three times his body stiffened and his head jerked upward as if he had been awoken from a short nap. The source of his inattention was the dry tome (according to him) that he had acquired from the museum to familiarize himself with the sculptures and the motives of the would-be robbers. He had been up later than normal the prior two evenings poring over its contents, which not only shed light on the cultural context in which the works were created, but which also detailed Sir Richardson's early 20th century discovery of them in Asia, the august gentleman's financial agreement with the local government for the right to bring them to English shores, the local government's later repudiation of the agreement (though not of the payment) after it understood the monetary value of the sculptures, the local government's incessant demands for the return of these irreplaceable objects of its cultural heritage, and finally England's invocation of its inalienable right to keep them. Admittedly, most of the material bored him (reading generally bored him), but he couldn't quite put the book down at night as it detailed the implications to international relations should anything happen to the sculptures while in England's care.

Shortly after lunch, which they bought from one of the street vendors near the museum, Nesbit asked Thwait to "spell" him for fifteen minutes so that he could rest his eyes. Thwait cheerfully agreed, knowing that when his turn came Nesbit would do the same for him (actually, he would have agreed even if Nesbit weren't accommodating, since he felt lucky to be working with the great man and considered it a privilege to be able to make any number of sacrifices for him). Three hours after his request, Nesbit's head was leaning back against the headrest, his mouth open, his eyes closed, and deep, chortling sounds were emanating from his nose and throat.

Thwait would have gladly let him sleep until the end of their shift, but shortly after granting Nesbit's request he, too, succumbed, perhaps lulled by Nesbit's incessant snoring. And he might have remained in that state for the rest of the day and most of the evening had his slumber not been disturbed later in the afternoon by a series of deep-throated growls accompanied by the monotonous pinging of a tiny bell. Glancing groggily at his sleeping friend, Thwait turned to go back to his own slumbers when a series of sharp popping sounds erupted next to his left ear. For a second, Thwait thought he had heard gunshots, but then a large man in workman's overalls with a metal construction hat on his head unexpectedly loomed into the side window and was tapping on it to get Thwait's attention. Startled upright, Thwait immediately rolled down the window and peered at the man, who had a protruding belly and a long, dust-covered gray beard.

167

"Sorry to bother you gents," the man began and then waved at something near the museum, "but would you mind moving your car back a few feet, just beyond the hydrant? I got a forklift and a lorry waiting to come through here, and I'd hate to see your vehicle get nicked in the process. What are you guys doing here, anyway, staking out the place?" The man smiled in a good natured way and then abruptly leaned away from the car and hollered something to another worker who was flailing his arms in the air.

Leaning out the window and angling his head toward the gesticulating worker, Thwait eyed the cobblestone service road and then spotted several other men in overalls and hardhats either standing on the road itself or off to one side, on the grass lining it. Some of the men on the road were carrying or pulling noisy machines, while others were hauling large barrels and bloated, black plastic bags. "What? I mean, yes, we'll move," he mumbled somewhat incoherently.

After giving the roof a couple of friendly pats, the man hollered "thanks, mate," and walked quickly toward the service road. Before he reached the road, he began shouting directions to all the workmen in sight.

Curious, but thinking nothing amiss, Thwait turned to Nesbit, who was in the driver's seat, and nudged him lightly on the shoulder. "Wake up, sir," he said, "we have to move the car. There's some work going on around the museum." Nesbit grumbled something but didn't budge. Thwait nudged him several more times, each time with as little success as the last. "Sir," he said, much louder this time, "we need to move the car. Workmen are waiting to get past us. There's a lorry, a forklift…" He hesitated and, turning his attention to the service road, stared open-mouthed at the men and machines coming and going around the building. Turning back to Nesbit, he nudged him several more times. "Sir, you need to wake up. There's something you have to see." While Nesbit fought to remain asleep, Thwait was beginning to suspect that the activity on or around the service road – the movement of vehicles, the activities of the workers, and especially the forklift – might be the very signs that he and his esteemed colleague were waiting for. "Sir, sir," Thwait shouted and shoved Nesbit against the door.

Nesbit woke up with a loud snort and cautiously glanced around to get his bearings. Noticing Thwait's strange gesticulations, he said with both surprise and amusement, "what is it man? Can't I have a couple winks? You're acting like a…"

"Do you see what's happening over there?"

Nesbit looked in the direction into which Thwait was now frantically pointing. For a few seconds, he couldn't see anything amiss apart from Thwait's peculiar antics. He was about to tell Thwait to stop jitterbugging and to say what was on his mind when he, too, noticed the incongruous activities that appeared to be heading down the cobblestone road to the service entrance out of sight at the back of the museum. "My God, man," he shouted as he struggled to undo his seatbelt. "Why didn't you tell me earlier?"

"Sir, I only just..."

Finally released from his seatbelt, Nesbit lurched across Thwait to have a look outside Thwait's window. "The trucks, the men, the...I was right, I was right!" Without looking at Thwait, he added, "they've been at it for some time. My friend, you must have been sleeping on the job to have missed all this." He sat back into his own seat and smiled at his friend. "No matter, we're onto them now. Let's go!"

Nesbit leaped out of the car and charged toward the service road. Most of the men and their machines were heading toward the dock and disappearing around the corner of the building, and Nesbit followed them until he, too, was out of sight behind the museum. Thwait, who lacked his friend's speed and agility, lumbered toward the road and then followed it as it paralleled the building and angled around behind. Pushing himself as hard as he could, especially after Nesbit was no longer in sight, Thwait nevertheless began to slow long before he reached the turn, and, as soon as he rounded the corner, he was forced to stop to replenish his lungs and ease the terrible pain in his right side, which he did by grasping it with his right hand while using the other to keep himself upright against the building. Once the pain subsided somewhat and he could finally focus his senses on something other than the limitations of his own body, Thwait glanced around and spotted among the museum's gray shadows a group of men not more than twenty yards away. Some of the men were moving toward the center of the group, while others were either stepping back toward the periphery or simply standing motionless, staring at other individuals in the group. A few seconds later, Thwait heard shouting and grumbling coming from the men, and, as he tried to understand what they were saying, he spotted Nesbit, who, judging by his movements, was arguing with one of the men. Taking a deep breath, Thwait pushed off from the building and walked over to Nesbit and the men.

"I told you I want to see your orders," Nesbit said to the man, speaking with an authoritative, uncompromising tone.

"Like I keep telling you, mate, I don't got the kind of orders you're asking for. We come here once a week to empty the containers, sweep off the docks, and do some yard work. That's our job. Nobody's got to give us special orders to do that. Do you see the name on the lorries?" His face increasingly dark, he motioned behind him without turning around. "They're the ones that tell us what we got to do. But you can tell us what we got to do if you pay us more."

Nesbit was just about to respond when Thwait, having pushed his way through the crowd, finally reached them and flashed his badge at the man, who turned out to be the foreman of the crew.

"Sorry, sir," Thwait said breathlessly to Nesbit, "but I got here as quickly as I could."

Nesbit smiled and nodded and was once again about to assume command of the situation when the workers stepped aside to let two museum guards, who came out of one of the building's back doors, jog up to where Nesbit, Thwait, and the foreman were all standing.

The guards were dressed in black uniforms, each one with a large, silver badge prominently affixed to the left pocket. Neither guard was armed, but both men (one about Nesbit's age, with graying hair, and the other about Thwait's age, albeit taller, slimmer, and with a slight dusting of dark whiskers on his chin) were carrying large, steel-cased flashlights. Nesbit didn't understand the purpose of the flashlights, since the sun was still overhead (though obscured by clouds of varying thicknesses) and the shadows cast by the large building were light and transparent. Nesbit turned to the older guard, who was the first to reach him and who appeared to be in charge, and demanded to know his name and what he was doing outside of the building (and out back, of all places) where there was ostensibly little or nothing to guard.

"I'm the head of physical security for the museum," the man said, and then he and the other guard, who was now standing at his side, showed Nesbit and Thwait their official identifications.

Thwait immediately reciprocated, after which Nesbit casually flashed his Interpol credentials.

"So why are you gentlemen here, and why are you interrupting the crew? Is Interpol taking an official interest in our trash, or has the Ravenswood Museum contracted with Interpol to take over the sanitation crew's duties?"

"So you think this is funny," Nesbit responded, his eyes narrowed and the muscles in his thin jaws throbbing. "Our job requires us to look at many things, and, yes, sometimes we look at people's trash. But, right now, I'm not interested in anybody's trash. Right now, I'm interested in what these gentlemen are doing out here at this particular time of day." Without turning away from the guard, he motioned with his right hand toward the men standing around and watching this peculiar scene.

The older man smiled slightly. "Fair enough, officer. They're emptying the trash…"

"Agent – but I'm not here for fun and games, my friend. I'm protecting this museum."

Thwait elbowed his great bulk between two men and positioned himself next to Nesbit. "Do you know these gentlemen?" he asked the guard. Thwait's breathing was still slightly labored, but this time it was due to his anger over the man's obvious lack of respect for Nesbit and for what Nesbit had accomplished throughout his storied career.

The guard nodded. "This gentleman here," he said, pointing to a man standing immediately behind Nesbit, "is the foreman of the crew. He comes here every week. I've known him for years. I know some of the others, too." He leaned toward the foreman and winked at him. "And how are you doing today, Teddy?"

The foreman smiled broadly, and then looked back at his men to let them know that he was on a first-name basis with the head guard.

"Fine, Jim, just fine. Maybe you can speak to these here gents for a while, so we can go back to our business. We need to get loading them pallets of refuse into the lorry."

The guard smiled and, completely ignoring Nesbit and Thwait, nodded for the man to leave, adding, "sorry for the bother."

"No bother," the other replied as he went back to his men. After giving them a few quick words of instruction, they all went back to work, some disappearing around the corner, others moving about in the slight shadows near the bay doors.

Nesbit stared at the guard for a moment. "You realize," he finally said, "that you are interfering with official police business." Thwait once again flashed his badge at the guard.

"And you're interfering with the city's official sanitation policies," the guard replied. "So, what can we do for you and your colleague? I'm afraid I didn't catch your name."

"Constable Thwait, and this is Agent Nesbit," Thwait said heatedly.

"I'm not very good with names, I'm afraid. So, what do you want with these men? And why couldn't you come to the front office to let us know what you wanted?"

Nesbit eyed the man for a few moments before sketching out his reasons for having stopped the men from doing their work. Since it was too early to place a lot of trust in the guard, Nesbit was careful not to reveal too much, and most of what he did say was whispered to prevent the workers from overhearing the conversation.

"There's going to be a robbery. We've identified the pieces but not the robbers. We also have an idea of how it's going to be done, albeit not the exact time. These men out here could be doing something more than just...did you say they were emptying the trash? Yes, well, more than that. Now, tell me, how well you know these individuals, especially this...what was his name?"

"Do you mean Chatsworth?"

"Who?"

"Teddy. His last name's Chatsworth."

"Yes, yes, this Chatsworth fellow. How well do you know him?"

The guard craned his head slightly. "I've known him for years, like I said. If you want to know how long he's been with the company servicing our museum, you'll have to ask his employer. But I have to say that it's a little amusing that Interpol thinks it knows more about the security of this museum than our guards, of which there are more than me and Flannery." He nodded to the other guard. "Even if you had information we don't, it might have been helpful if you'd spoken to us first. Have you relayed any of your concerns to the director?"

"I'm speaking to you now, and if you've let the thieves off because of your interference..."

"What interference? I'm in charge of the guards, and everything that happens inside or on these premises is my business. I know most of these people, and I'm fully aware of the details of their contract to come here and clean the outside of the building." He paused briefly and squinted as if he had just discovered something. "Say, you two look familiar. Are you the blokes that come out here every day to sleep in your car?"

172

Gritting his teeth, Nesbit stepped closer to the guard until he was practically nose-to-nose with the man. The other guard took a step closer to Nesbit, forcing Thwait to take a step closer to all three of the men.

Chapter 8

"Excuse me, Chief," Sedgwick began, having quietly opened the Chief's door and poked her head inside. "I'm sorry to bother you, but I need to speak to you and I couldn't reach you on your cell."

The Chief was standing behind his desk and pulling a thin folder from his briefcase. After dropping the folder to his desk, he leaned down and placed the briefcase on the floor next to his chair. Standing back up, he motioned Sedgwick in with a sideways movement of his head. Although he was frowning, he didn't mind Sedgwick's intrusion, because she was the closest thing to a friend he had at the station. "You don't have to stand on ceremony. You won't believe this. I just got back from HQ, and...," he began but noticed the concerned look on Sedgwick's clear face. "What's the matter? Do we have a problem?"

Sedgwick positioned herself in front of the Chief's desk and absently brushed a few errant stands of hair from her forehead with the back of her hand. "I'm afraid there's a spot of trouble..."

"Did HQ contact you?" He squinted at Sedgwick.

"No, Chief, it's not that..."

"Then it's got to be Nesbit and Thwait."

"I'm afraid so, and it appears rather urgent."

The Chief sat down behind his desk and motioned for Sedgwick to take a seat across from him. "I'm all ears," he replied.

"I was just in touch with Constable Thwait. I wanted to speak to him to find out where he and Agent Nesbit were, but before I could even begin he informed me that they were at the Ravenswood Museum. He seemed a bit frazzled. Anyway, the problem appears to have started when Agent Nesbit threatened to arrest the museum's sanitation crew. If I understand correctly, he's already arrested two of the museum's guards."

"What? I don't understand. This is a joke, right? Agent Nesbit can't arrest anybody." The Chief reached for his pencil, but for some reason it wasn't where he expected it to be.

"True, but Constable Thwait can. He seems to have provided the official wherewithal to make the arrests."

"You're serious? They arrested the guards and are threatening to arrest a sanitation crew? Tell me again who told you this."

"Constable Thwait, Chief."

174

"I guess I shouldn't be surprised. Well, give me the details."

"Constable Thwait informed me that he and Agent Nesbit had gone around to the back of the museum to investigate some suspicions activity by the sanitation crew. After speaking to them, they were about to arrest one or some of them (I'm not exactly clear on this) when the museum guards showed up and interfered with their lawful activities. I mean the lawful activities of Constable Thwait and Agent Nesbit. Constable Thwait said that he and Agent Nesbit suspected the sanitation crew of trying to steal the Richardson Stones. I'm afraid there's more."

"Excuse me? The sanitation crew was trying to steal the Richardson Stones?"

"I believe that's what he said, Chief."

"So, they arrested the guards but not the thieves."

"It seems so, but I admit he wasn't entirely clear. He was, as I said, a little frazzled. Anyway, Agent Nesbit and Constable Thwait could have made what they deemed to be appropriate arrests had the guards not intervened and tried to control the situation. There is more."

The Chief turned away from Sedgwick. He tugged at his top drawer for a few moments until it finally yielded, after which he reached inside and fumbled around for his pencil. Having retrieved it, he slammed the drawer closed and began tapping the eraser end of the pencil against the top of his desk. After taking a deep breath to calm his nerves, he said, "those two are supposed to be solving the wiretap case, not chasing down sanitation workers."

Sedgwick shrugged her trim shoulders while the side of her mouth drooped slightly. "I believe they were trying to do that. Constable Thwait said they were monitoring the sanitation crew when…"

"How many people are in this crew?"

"I don't know, Chief. But from what I can make of what Constable Thwait said, I'd say seven to ten, maybe more."

"Ten or more? All right, so what happened next?"

"The situation seems to be rather fluid at the moment. I don't believe either Agent Nesbit or Constable Thwait is in imminent danger, but they might need some backup. However, like I said, there is more."

The Chief looked at Sedgwick for a few seconds before starting to squint. "By control, do you mean make the arrests?"

"I suppose that's a possibility. Once again, Constable Thwait wasn't very clear, and I didn't hear from Agent Nesbit. He – I mean Constable Thwait

– was a little rushed. It appears that some of the workers have left the immediate vicinity, though it's possible they're still somewhere on the museum grounds. Constable Thwait indicated something about rounding them up. But Chief..."

The Chief's pencil fell from his hand onto the desk, where it rolled partway across the desk and landed against the folder he had retrieved from his briefcase.

"Chief..."

The Chief held up his hand to stop Sedgwick from speaking. Closing his eyes momentarily and taking a deep breath, he picked up his pencil and, once again tapping the top of his desk, told Sedgwick to continue.

"Chief, you're not going to like this. I should have noted at the outset that the museum director, Sir Ronald, came outside when he heard the ruckus and is now in the thick of things, as it were."

"Put me out of my misery right now. Don't tell me they've arrested him, too." He squeezed one end of his pencil so tightly that it snapped in half.

"No, I don't think it's anything like that. Constable Thwait said he wasn't under suspicion. He had only come out of the building to see what was causing all the commotion. Anyway, I insisted that Constable Thwait and Agent Nesbit stand down on anything to do with Sir Ronald without your express permission, although I don't think my word will have any force on Agent Nesbit. Once again, I thought you'd want to hear about this immediately."

"Yes, that's fine." The Chief looked down at his desk and again closed his eyes for a few moments, giving one the impression that he was praying for guidance. Indeed, he would have prayed for guidance had he thought it would help. Awakening from his apparent reverie, he turned to Sedgwick and said, "I'll ring Sir Ronald, but I want you to speak to Nesbit and Constable Thwait. Tell them to stand down on all arrests until they have definitive proof of something specific."

"Yes, Chief."

"If Nesbit gives you any pushback, kindly remind him that the station is in charge of the investigation, not Interpol or HQ. We therefore have a say in what he does for the station."

"Right, Chief." Sedgwick was about to leave when the Chief motioned for her to remain seated.

Chapter 9

The Chief was silent for a moment. "Tell me, Inspector Sedgwick," he began as if he had something on his mind, "from what you know of the case so far, do you think there's any merit to Nesbit's Gray Ladies theory? I'm not talking about stealing the Richardson Stones. But I'm curious to know if you've seen anything in the last twenty-four hours that might lead you to believe that they're at least headed in the right direction."

"By right direction, do you mean the Ravenswood Museum? I really don't know, Chief. If the speakers in the wiretap are referring to an artwork, I suppose the Ravenswood is as good as any museum, assuming that the work is in a building and not on the front of a church or the top of a cathedral. But you've got something else on your mind."

"As I said, I met with HQ. I handed over the old case file – I think I told you that it concerned busting the Sanders' family for trafficking in stolen antiquities – and then we had a nice, long, pointless discussion about station operations. When I mentioned the case file and asked why they were interested in it, they changed the subject and demanded details about the current investigation, or whatever Nesbit and Thwait are doing. I insisted that in the absence of any evidence, it was going about as well as could be expected; I also asked to see the rest of the wiretap which, I assured them, could be helpful in moving the 'investigation' further along. No one batted an eye, no one offered additional details about the wiretap, and, what practically floored me, they assured me that Nesbit was on the right track. But when I demanded to know how they could be so confident, given some of the rather large gaps in his reasoning, they essentially patted me on the head and told me to soldier on. They did, however, give me some letters, which I'll show you in a minute. So, what do you think? Am I missing something? Does this even make sense to you?"

"It certainly doesn't make any sense to me. Maybe, as you suggested, there's something else in the wiretap they're not sharing."

"Maybe." The Chief paused for a moment.

"Chief, shouldn't you ring Sir Ronald? HQ is likely to go ballistic if our people ruffle his feathers."

"I wonder if the capitalization of the Gray Ladies in the wiretap is a mistake. If it's not a proper noun, then Nesbit and Thwait might be on the wrong trail despite what HQ insists. On the other hand, if it is a proper noun, we're back to square one and possibly looking for something by that name."

"Chief, it may be rather urgent to reach out to Sir Ronald. I don't really think that Agent Nesbit and Constable Thwait are in serious trouble, but it could only be a matter of time before they wear out their welcome with him."

"I suppose you're right," the Chief replied after another short reverie. Squinting, he reached across the desk and retrieved the black receiver from the official phone. He began dialing the number but stopped halfway through and replaced the receiver. Briefly pinching his chin, he looked down and yanked open his top drawer. Once again, he fumbled around for a pencil (pieces of the broken pencil were still on his desk) and, after finding a suitable one, began tapping it against the surface of his desk.

"Did you forget the number, Chief?"

"No, I have it." He glanced at the small trophy on his bookshelf, which was visible above Sedgwick's left shoulder, and then turned back to her.

"You're not thinking of throwing Agent Nesbit to the wolves, are you? And Constable Thwait?"

"No," he shook his head. "No, that's not it. As tempting as it is, I'm not going to let HQ have either one of them."

"I don't understand, Chief. Shouldn't you at least…"

"There's time." The Chief opened the folder on his desk and carefully pulled out three sheets of paper and handed them to Sedgwick. "Here, take a look at these. These are the letters HQ gave me which, they insist, are related to the investigation."

The pages were photocopies of three typed letters. Sedgwick read the pages carefully before looking back at the Chief. "I don't understand," she said. "They all say more or less the same thing – send 10 million pounds or else – but they don't provide any details. Why should anyone give somebody all that money? And if they wanted to, how would they go about it? There aren't any delivery instructions. Who received them? They weren't sent to HQ, were they?"

"The letters came from the Ravenswood, of all places. They were apparently sent to Sir Ronald. According to Sir Ronald's secretary, Miss Flora Montague, Sir Ronald read them but apparently didn't take them seriously, at least not seriously enough for her. She contacted HQ and faxed them the letters. HQ was gracious enough to share the information with me."

"I still don't understand. Is someone threatening the museum or Sir Ronald?"

"Good question. I don't know. HQ told me that the letters and the wiretap are connected."

"They are?"

"I guess, although they didn't give me a single reason why they think there's a connection. They did give me to understand that this is one of the reasons why Nesbit is at least pointed in the right direction."

"No explanation at all? Well, do they think the author of the letters is one of the speakers in the wiretap? I'm prepared to believe the letters are serious, but at the same time I need more than this to understand what they have in common with the wiretap. Maybe if there's something in the museum called the Gray Ladies, we might be able to connect the wiretap to the museum, but we certainly need a lot more than this to connect the letters to the wiretap."

"My thoughts exactly. I called Miss Montague while I was at HQ and asked her about the Gray Ladies. She searched the museum's catalogue and didn't come up with anything. But, like she said, she's not an expert."

Sedgwick shook her head. "I can't help thinking that someone is playing a joke…"

"I think the whole thing is a joke, one big, monstrous joke. But, right now, unless we have something that proves there's no connection between the letters and the wiretap, or something else that shows just how loony Agent Nesbit and Constable Thwait are, we have to accept HQ's official wisdom, as it were."

"Wait a minute. Did Miss Montague provide any context for the letters? Is there a reason why the director might be threatened? Have there been layoffs at the museum? Are there any disgruntled employees? Are the working conditions lowering morale?"

"Funny, I asked her the same questions, and she very kindly informed me that the museum was a great place to work, that Sir Ronald was a dear, and that if there was anything in the air that might cause such letters, she wasn't aware of it. She stated that the first letter arrived a couple of weeks ago, the last one a few days ago, and couldn't recall when the middle one showed up. For some reason, the envelopes were tossed, and there's no way of retrieving them. She did state that as far as she knew, no one apart from her and Sir Ronald knew of the letters and their contents."

"I presume there's a mailroom with one or two attendants."

"Yes, indeed. I spoke to her about this as well. All the mail coming into the museum is routed through the mailroom. There is a single attendant responsible. He's a young man in his mid-twenties, and he's evidently undergone a background check of some kind. Although Miss Montague says that he's been on the job for less than a year, she vouches for him. She doesn't believe he paid much attention to the letters – they were part of everyday mail – but he's the one who delivered them to her, that is, to Sir Ronald's office. If Agent Nesbit and Constable Thwait want to be useful while they're out there, they could interview the attendant and find out if anyone else knows something about the letters."

"I'll tell them."

The Chief shook his head slightly. "Maybe once we have a chance to see the rest of the wiretap, everything will be a little clearer." He put the copies back into the folder and slid it to the side of his desk.

"Chief, I'm sorry to harp on this, but what about Sir Ronald?"

The Chief looked down at his desk for a moment. "Yes," he replied finally, as if he had more important things on his mind. "I'll reach out to Sir Ronald."

"Chief," Sedgwick began as she stood up, "I'm happy to deal with Constable Thwait and Agent Nesbit, unless you'd prefer to handle things since Sir Ronald is involved."

He squinted at Sedgwick for a moment. "No, you look in on our men, and see how things are going. Let me know if there's a problem with Sir Ronald, and I'll reach out to him immediately."

"You know him personally?"

"I know him. Maybe not personally, but I know him."

"Chief," Sedgwick began as if something had just occurred to her but then changed her mind. "I'll give you an update."

Chapter 10

Sedgwick arrived at the museum thirty minutes after having spoken to the Chief. She drove to the back of the building where she expected to find Nesbit, Thwait, and the others Thwait described in his call, but no one was there, and there weren't any obvious signs (refuse, scuff marks) either on the pavement or along the base of the building to suggest the sort of commotion that Thwait had described. Naturally, this made Sedgwick wonder if she had driven to the wrong part of the building or maybe even to the wrong building. But she couldn't verify this because Thwait wasn't answering his phone. In fact, Thwait hadn't called or texted her since the last time they spoke (which was less than an hour ago), and she was beginning to wonder if the situation might be more serious than Thwait's failure to follow the proper protocols of answering the station's calls and informing the station of one's whereabouts.

Sedgwick called the station and described the situation to the desk officer, adding that she would reach out to the Chief as soon as she found something. Pulling over to the first of the four unoccupied loading bays, she got out of her car and proceeded to look around the area. Since she didn't know what she was looking for, she began by scanning the back wall of the museum, which blankly towered over her some four or five stories in height (there were no windows that she could see), and then peered at each of the loading bays, and examined from a short distance what appeared to be the only human-sized door in the back of the building. Located next to the first loading bay, it was windowless and, judging from its gray color and the occasional glint off its surface, it appeared to be constructed out of metal, just like the loading bay doors.

As she gradually moved closer to the building, Sedgwick couldn't help being impressed by the cleanliness of the area and, when she looked closer (she thought she saw something on the pavement, which only proved to be a darkened, flattened piece of gum), she could see that it had recently been swept. Sedgwick stepped over the base of the stone building and noticed that this area, too, had recently been swept, as had the steps leading to the back door. The door, not surprisingly, was locked, and as she headed back to her car, she spotted a black, cylindrical object on the ground. It was a ballpoint pen. Picking it up to see if it had any relevance, she discovered the station's lettering on one side, a sure sign that one of the station's officers had been there (who else but Thwait?) and had dropped his pen. Pocketing the item,

Sedgwick got into the car and drove around to the front of the building where she parked in a space reserved for police vehicles. Once again, she tried to reach Thwait, and once again there was no answer. And once again she informed the dispatcher of her whereabouts and what she was going to do – that is, go inside the museum and make inquiries. Had Thwait succeeded in arresting the museum guards, someone in the museum would have some information, and someone would have known about the commotion in the back, although it was strange that, to her knowledge, no one from the museum had called the station to report a disturbance.

Stepping briskly up the stone steps leading to the main entrance, Sedgwick strode through the grand doorway (bound on either side by a faceless, yard-thick black door) into a marble-covered rotunda. The lobby, which felt more like a domed stadium than a passage to the galleries, offered tickets on one side, gifts on the other, and lines for the galleries at the back. Whatever she might have expected before entering the building, she was slightly disappointed. Nothing appeared out of the ordinary – people, tourists mainly, were coming and going, laughing and chatting, as if this day was just like any other day. Walking up to the line waiting to enter the galleries, she flashed her credentials to an attendant and then proceeded toward a series of hallways leading to different sections of the building. But instead of immediately searching out the guards' station or the director's office to find out what happened to Nesbit and Thwait, she felt compelled to take a minute to check out the Richardson Stones first (the gallery housing them was immediately to her left). Sedgwick's sudden interest wasn't aesthetic; she was looking for clues not only for the whereabouts of the men, but also for the reasons behind their obsession with these particular works.

The sculptures were displayed in a large, barn-like gallery. Indeed, wheat threshers could easily have been accommodated in the center of the room had someone moved the sculptures to one side. But there was little else in the gallery except for some small, standing placards placed next to each sculpture that either provided general information (no smoking, no gum chewing, no loitering, no anything else) or details about the creation of the work (the artist or artists were unknown), its meaning, and the location of the piece when first excavated. To aid the viewer's experience and understanding, there was also a long, continuous painting (fresco?) along all four walls which depicted life-size versions of the sculptures as they might have looked over a thousand years ago in their original setting (most likely an ancient temple).

Sedgwick glanced around the gallery and then walked through the exhibit, briefly noting each piece. They were all interesting to some degree, but she like the Chief couldn't understand why anyone would try to make off with one of them. Logically, it was impractical, since some of the works were over ten feet tall and each one had to weigh at least a ton. There was also a good chance that they were bolted or fastened to the floor to prevent some idiot from moving them either accidentally or on purpose. But even if thieves were to make off with one of the pieces, what could they do with it afterwards? Where could they hide it? How could they get it out of the country? You certainly couldn't check it or hide it in your carry-on luggage. She paused and, looking at one of the pieces (an armless, headless soldier astride what appeared to be a decapitated, three-legged cow), it occurred to her that if someone were really interested in using these pieces for political gain (and the wiretap did say something about bringing down Her Majesty's government), then why wouldn't they just destroy the works in place? Terrorists have been doing this for years, and in the 1970s an international furor arose when some clown took a hammer to Michelangelo's Pietà. Shaking her head and deciding that it was time to leave, she turned and nearly stumbled on a large, metal stand practically in the center of the gallery that provided some additional prohibitions with respect to this particular gallery. Using both hands to stop the stand's movement, she naturally glanced at some of the words and then noticed a rather incongruent statement in small letters at the bottom of the plaque.

"I wonder," she muttered to herself and quickly fished her phone out of her pocket. Keeping her eyes on the stand as if it offered directions for what she needed to do next, Sedgwick dialed Thwait's number. And, like every other time she tried to reach the officer during the last hour or so, there wasn't an answer – there wasn't even a ring. Just to be certain, she tried the number again, and again there wasn't an answer or a ring. Realizing that there was no service in the gallery, she ran into the hallway and once again tried to reach her colleague. This time, however, the absence of a response didn't trouble her. In fact, it buoyed her spirits, because it suggested that Nesbit and Thwait weren't necessarily in trouble, simply in a part of the building that didn't have connectivity, or at least that's what she earnestly hoped. Glancing around to get her bearings, she went in search of a docent or a museum guard who could direct her to the director's office, which she reasoned was the most likely place where they could be (unless, of course, they were locked up in the guard's quarters). Once she had the office number, which had been given to her by the ticket-taker who allowed her into the gallery, she charged up a deserted stairwell and practically burst onto the second floor. Looking back and forth and deciding that she needed to go to the right, she walked down a short hallway lined with darkened, life-sized portraits of museum trustees and past directors until she came to the end. She was facing Sir Ronald's office.

The office appeared to have a single entry, an oversized, black wooden door vaguely resembling one of the museum's front doors. Sedgwick was about to knock but noticed that the door was slightly ajar and releasing a sliver of feeble light into the dusky, gray hallway. Instead of pushing the door open, she paused and then leaned forward slightly and listened for signs that someone was in the office (and she hoped that this someone was Nesbit or Thwait). For a minute or so, there were some faint, nonhuman sounds – a slight hush resembling the sound that came from a large seashell she had as child – but this died out and afterwards there was total silence broken only by the sounds of her own breathing. Glancing around and then turning back to the door, she began to feel slightly uncomfortable standing so close to the door; if someone spotted her, they might think that she was eavesdropping or doing something illicit, which of course was ridiculous because she was a law-enforcement officer and pursuing official police business. Sedgwick was just about to push open the door when she noticed a faint chirping sound emanating from within the office, a sound that quickly changed to a buzzing and just as quickly changed back into a chirping.

Craning her head, she began to recognize faint snatches of speech, although she couldn't quite understand what was being said, how many persons were conversing, or who the speakers were. Since the conversation didn't appear to be flagging (and therefore it was pointless to wait for someone to come to the door), Sedgwick decided to venture in and inquire about the whereabouts of Thwait and Nesbit.

Chapter 11

The office was almost as big as the gallery downstairs. A curved, off-white ceiling hovered a good twenty feet above the gray-marble floor of the office, probably the same distance between floor and ceiling as in the gallery. But unlike the gallery, the wall opposite the door was punctuated by several skyscraper-like windows stretching practically from floor to ceiling, each one flanked by dull sheers that were the same color as the indifferently-colored walls. Sedgwick stretched her neck forward and noticed, to her left, a series of long, dark bookshelves that were packed with ancient, leather-bound books of all sizes, some small enough to fit in the palm of her hand and others nearly as big as her own front door. The far wall also to her left was covered by a single, massive painting, a dark, shadowy affair portraying two men cudgeling one another as both were sinking up to their waists in quicksand. She paused, thinking that she had seen the painting before, but shrugged her shoulders when she recalled that this was the first time she had ever been in this room.

Taking a couple of steps deeper into this apparently unoccupied room, Sedgwick caught sight of a large secretarial desk a few yards away, which from the looks of it appeared to have been abandoned only minutes earlier (gray steam was still rising from a coffee cup placed less than an inch from the desk's edge). Behind the desk and its chair, which was angled a short distance from the desk, was another door, this one closer to human proportions and, like the other she had just stepped through, slightly open. The opening was more of a crack and hence not wide enough to peer inside; but since she could hear the unmistakable sounds of human voices emanating from the other side of the door, she ventured quietly behind the desk (in the process nearly knocking the cup of coffee to the floor) and sidled close enough to the door to catch snatches of real conversations.

"The first arrived two or three weeks ago...," a man's voice was saying. He had a deep baritone, and his voice sounded firm, decisive, educated. "Not clear on the exact timing...I read it quite by chance, but my lovely Flora...Miss Montague, I mean, my secretary, that is, insisted... Dreadful business this...but I suppose one is now duty-bound to take it seriously...though, I suppose these sorts of things happen from time...but certainly not here during my... You can therefore understand why I wasn't concerned even...the second and third...each saying more or less the same thing. A little absurd, don't you think? Well...incomprehensible, to be sure…but the letters threatened…and Flora, Miss Montague, felt that… Even so, we are simply not equipped…either way, the numbers don't allow us…"

"All the more reason, Sir Ronald," another voice said, interrupting the first. Sedgwick craned her ear to hear more, because it resembled Nesbit's haughty tenor. "Given what we knew coming in," the voice continued, "it is beginning to make sense. What do you think, Constable Thwait?" There was a short period of silence following this question, after which the mumbling began again, suggesting that all three individuals (if not more) were talking at the same time. As if on cue, they all stopped and a series a different, unconnected sounds rose in the air – a long screech, a short poof, a fluttering of something, another screech, and finally the heavy thuds of footsteps heading toward the door. Realizing that a decision had to be made immediately, Sedgwick stepped quickly to the door and pulled it open. She was immediately confronted by a well-dressed gentleman in his early sixties whose carefully trimmed gray hair was slightly ruffled on one side as if he had just mussed it up with his fingers.

"Well, hello, there," the man uttered slowly upon seeing Sedgwick. Unconsciously, he took a half step back and eyed Sedgwick from head to foot. "May I have the honor?"

"She's from the station, Sir Ronald," Thwait said nervously, jumping up from a large, ornate black-leather chair that was positioned at a slight angle from the much larger and certainly more ornate desk in the center of the reasonably-sized business office. Nesbit remained seated in an identical chair on the opposite side of the desk. With his legs crossed and one arm draped over the back of the chair, he coolly stared at Sedgwick.

Thwait hurried over to introduce Sedgwick but, before he could say a word, Sir Ronald reached for her right hand and said, "I can promise you that the pleasure is most assuredly mine. But don't tell me you're Inspector Dimwet…"

"Sedgwick, Sir Ronald, she is Inspector Sedgwick," Thwait desperately interjected, "my superior at the station."

"Sedgwick?" Sir Ronald asked and, although he was smiling pleasantly, there was some confusion evident on his aging, sagging, face, particularly around the edges of his large, watery eyes. "My apologies, my dear, Officer…Sedgwick is it? I was afraid you might be that peculiar individual Officer Nesbit mentioned. I believe the name was Inspector Dimwet, Dumwit, Dimwit, or something like that. I don't recall – a man or a woman? Well, no matter. A curious name, to be sure, but I suppose its origins are to be found in the increasing cultural diversity of the country. I'm sure he or she is a fine officer, regardless. Once again, I am delighted to meet you, Inspector Sedgwick. I am the director of the Ravenswood Museum – but where are my manners?" He delicately kissed the top of Sedgwick's slender hand and then directed her into the room, one hand gently touching the back of her left shoulder and the other, open palmed, motioning toward an ornate chair directly in front of his desk. While Thwait sheepishly returned to his chair, Sir Ronald waited for Sedgwick to be seated, all the while observing her graceful backside, before returning to his own luxurious chair behind the equally luxurious and oversized Louis XIV desk.

"I hope I'm not intruding, Sir Ronald," Sedgwick said, observing the director's flaccid, smiling face before glancing at Nesbit and Thwait. Thwait looked down and away from her gaze, while Nesbit stared unflinchingly at her with a slight, insolent smile. "No one was at the door…"

"Quite so," replied Sir Ronald. "I'm glad you came, my dear, very glad. Unfortunately, my secretary seems to be out at the moment." He craned his head to look into the other room, but quickly turned back to the officers. "Yes, otherwise I would offer you some tea or another beverage. Perhaps I can offer you something from the café downstairs or the one across the street."

Sedgwick noticed that Nesbit and Thwait were holding tea cups and saucers. "No, I'm fine, really." She glanced around the room, which, though large, was still a fraction of the size of the outer office. It was furnished more or less like the outer room (and there were towering windows on the same wall or side of the building), except that in one corner (to Sir Ronald's left shoulder) there was a tall glass-covered case housing several small figurines. Before Sedgwick could say anything else, Sir Ronald quickly picked up the thread of the interrupted conversation.

"Actually, I was going to ask my secretary to…but you didn't by chance see her leave when you came in, did you, Inspector Dim…I'm sorry, I mean Inspector Sedgwick, yes? Quite a lovely name, I must say. But you didn't see her? Well, I suppose it doesn't matter for now. At any rate…" He paused, reached over to a large metal basket near the corner of his desk, and retrieved several papers that had been folded and refolded by unknown hands. As he held them out for Sedgwick, Nesbit reached over and took them out of Sir Ronald's hand. "Yes, well, at any rate," Sir Ronald continued, "here are the three letters I mentioned earlier. They are recent arrivals, over the past few weeks, as I noted."

When he had seen enough, Nesbit handed them to Thwait, who immediately passed them to Sedgwick without looking at them. Sedgwick quietly studied the letters for a few moments. She was about to return the letters to Sir Ronald but hesitated. "Do you mind if we keep the letters, Sir Ronald," she said, smiling pleasantly at the older gentleman. "I'd like our forensics lab to have a go at them. They might be able to glean something useful." Sir Ronald not only agreed with her request, but also offered to lend her his briefcase if she needed something in which to transport them. "It's not necessary," she replied and slipped them into her bag before Nesbit could touch them.

Sir Ronald smiled at Sedgwick and for a few moments appeared to be lost in thought. "Yes, well," he said, coming out of his reverie, "first, the author doesn't detail the consequences for not complying with the demands. 'Or else'...what? Second – and I must say that this is rather amusing – second, there are no directions for paying the ransom should the museum agree to the author's demands. Perhaps I am old fashioned, but if our Trustees decide to pay all or some of the money, I shall insist upon a traditional (old fashioned, if you will) address and a secure method of delivering said funds." Sir Ronald again smiled at Sedgwick and tugged gently on one of his hairy earlobes. "My dear Miss Sedgwick (it is Miss, is it not? No, of course, it doesn't matter)... well, there may be additional letters of this ilk, but these are the only ones that made it to my desk. Now, I suppose you found it a tad peculiar, maybe even incomprehensible, that I didn't take the letters more seriously. After all, they appear to be threatening our great institution. Perhaps, but let me assure all of you that we are not in the habit of receiving threats of any kind, and so we may not be as versed in responding as certain commercial institutions are. Our troubles, if I may say so, generally run the gamut of unruly visitors and, on rare occasions, vandalism...but wait, is that my lovely Miss Montague?" He cupped a hand around one ear. "No? I'm afraid I must be hearing things." Sir Ronald stood up, and Sedgwick, Thwait, and Nesbit immediately followed suit. Shaking his head and apologizing, he said that he needed to locate Miss Montague and that he would return in a few minutes.

Once Sir Ronald was out of the room and the officers were back in their chairs, Sedgwick turned to Nesbit and Thwait and inquired about the incident behind the building. "Constable Thwait reported that you, Agent Nesbit, wanted to arrest the museum's sanitation crew. He also reported that there was some other trouble with the museum's guards and that one or more had been arrested. Can either one of you fill me in on the details before Sir Ronald returns?" She glanced at Thwait, who seemed increasingly uncomfortable in his tight clothes and his noose-like collar, and then at Nesbit, who smiled insolently again but didn't appear inclined to provide the information.

"Ma'am," Thwait responded, sensing that Nesbit was going to take his time before responding, "Agent Nesbit was surrounded by the workmen – he was questioning them because…"

"I already know that much, Constable Thwait."

"Well, ma'am, one of the guards, I think, went to fetch…"

"Fetch?"

"To get Sir Ronald, who came out and defused…what I mean to say is that he took control of the situation. This is not to say things were out of control. In fact, well, what I should have said…"

Nesbit refused to enter into the debriefing and, leaning back in the chair and observing the interactions between Sedgwick and Thwait, quietly sipped his tea, holding his cup in one hand and the saucer in the other.

"…well, sir, I mean ma'am, it's kind of like this…"

"No luck, I'm afraid," Sir Ronald said as he walked back into the room and returned to his chair behind the large desk. Sedgwick, Thwait, and Nesbit immediately stood up and then sat back down in their chairs. "I caught a whiff of your conversation, and I must say that Constable Thwait is spot on. Our Deputy Chief Guard Landrum called to apprise me of something going down (I believe that was the phrase he used) on the loading dock. I informed our Chief Guard, Officer Terrance, and he and Officer Landrum repaired to the scene, as it were. I followed shortly after when I didn't immediately hear back from them. However, I must say that based on what we now know regarding the case (courtesy of Officer Nesbit), everyone's response was reasonable and, if I may also add, professional. Since I've known the guards and the sanitation crew for years, I was happy to vouch for them and assure the officers that they were above reproach."

Nesbit took another sip of tea and smiled again at Sedgwick, this time with less subtlety.

"Ma'am," added Thwait, looking directly at Sedgwick, "we had no reason to detain the workers or the guards once Sir Ronald arrived. During the ensuing conversation with Sir Ronald, he mentioned the letters and we thought it best to investigate and determine their relevancy to this case."

"Exactly," added Nesbit, looking first at Thwait and then at Sir Ronald. "I could sense their significance the instant they were mentioned. The letters are consistent with the other evidence we have, and they confirm our analysis of the case – the bad guys are not undertaking a random crime, but are seeking to prove a point of some kind and reap a windfall if they succeed. My gut feeling tells me that it won't be long before we get to the heart of the matter and solve the case to everyone's satisfaction." Nesbit leaned back and winked confidently at Thwait.

"Quite so, quite so…," Sir Ronald added but immediately trailed off.

A rather portly, middle-aged woman suddenly appeared in the doorway. Sir Ronald immediately jumped up and, gesturing as if he were urging her to come on stage, introduced her. "Officers, may I finally present to you my secretary, the efficient Miss Montague."

Sedgwick, Nesbit, and Thwait quickly stood up and smiled at the woman, who nodded and smiled at each one in turn.

"Sir Ronald," she said in a tone that was pleasant though firm, "I was only around the corner. Your appointment is ready. Shall I say you're running late?"

"No, no, my dear, I'll be right there."

He turned to the officers. "I'm sorry, officers, madam. This will only take a few minutes. Madam Sedgwick, you should know that I'm making arrangements to give your officers unfettered access to the museum, at Officer Nesbit's suggestion. Madam, and gentlemen, I will be gone five minutes at most." Once again, Sir Ronald bolted for the door.

Sedgwick, Nesbit, and Thwait were all silent as they sat down. While Sedgwick calmly waited for Sir Ronald's return, Nesbit nonchalantly slouched in his chair and with his right hand fidgeted with a small object on Sir Ronald's desk. Thwait, however, appeared uncomfortable, both from his collar and from Sedgwick's silence. Finally, when the silence was too much to bear, he turned to Sedgwick.

"Ma'am," he said with a slight tremor in his voice, "I will of course detail all this in the report to the Chief."

"Yes, please do. I believe the Chief will be keenly interested in what you have to say. Would you also copy me on the note?"

"Yes, ma'am. Not a problem, ma'am."

After some additional moments of uncomfortable silence (to Thwait), Sedgwick adjusted herself in her chair and turned to Thwait (her back now facing Nesbit). "You know, I must say that I'm not entirely comfortable with your assumptions regarding this case," she began, speaking quietly to Thwait. "I've seen the sculptures, and I can't quite envision anyone taking a big chunk of rock out the front door, especially under the cover of darkness – no, during the day, right? I have to admit that it seems impractical and fraught with endless difficulties, to say the least. But I will also admit that having walked through some of the galleries here, I can't help thinking that I'm missing something. Perhaps you could enlighten me, especially if it concerns evidence or information you haven't yet conveyed to the Chief." Sedgwick uttered the last sentence loud enough for Nesbit to hear.

Nesbit sat up and turned toward Sedgwick. Still at Sedgwick's back, he remained silent, angling his head this way and that to pick up everything that was being said.

"Nothing? That's good for a start. But tell me, what makes you so certain that the letters and the wiretap are connected? You're not completely certain? Okay, but you should know that HQ believes there is a connection, though neither the Chief nor I are privy to their rationale. I suppose it's possible, given the timing of the letters and appearance of the wiretap, but I don't think we have enough information to completely discount the possibility of both coming to light serendipitously."

Thwait didn't immediately respond and glanced at Nesbit for help. Nesbit, for his part, remained silent and glowered at Sedgwick behind her back.

"Maybe we should talk about this at another time. Once again, I want to be neutral but I cannot fathom why anyone would try to slip the Richardson Stones out the front door in broad daylight."

"Excuse me," Nesbit interjected, unable to contain himself. His voice was loud and forceful, and Sedgwick immediately turned her head and shoulders toward him. "Before you criticize the facts..." Nesbit's train of thought, however, was interrupted when Sir Ronald burst back into the room. All three immediately stood up.

"Please, please, madam and gentlemen," Sir Ronald said, motioning with his palms down for them to take their seats. "It's all settled. Officers – and I included you, Madam Sedgwick – you will have unfettered access to the museum at all times. I hope you can wrap this up as quickly as possible. And, since this concerns our inestimable institution, I would expect you to keep me advised on every aspect of the case."

"Sir Ronald, we will do our...," Sedgwick started to say but Nesbit interrupted.

"Our first goal, Sir Ronald, is to apprehend the culprits before they do their dirty work. Our second goal is to undertake our work as efficiently as we can with as little interruption of the museum's normal operations as possible. We will do our work, we will catch the bad guys, and we will keep you informed, Sir Ronald."

"Thank you, madam and gentlemen." Sir Ronald reached across his desk and extended his broad hand to Sedgwick, but Nesbit thrust his hand in front of hers and shook the museum director's hand first. When Sedgwick, Nesbit, and Thwait reached the door, Sir Ronald called out, "please see the attentive Miss Montague on your way out to get the requisite identification cards."

Once they were in the hallway outside of the offices, Sedgwick turned to Nesbit and Thwait. Glancing back and forth at both men, she said calmly, "Constable Thwait's phone call led me to believe that you officers were having some trouble with the museum guards, and so the Chief asked me to look in on you to see if there was anything I could do to help. The Chief was also concerned about Sir Ronald. The director, as you know, has a great deal of political pull, and the last thing the Chief wants is for him to be inconvenienced and hence complaining to HQ. I can assure you, though, that if at any time it becomes necessary to involve Sir Ronald in this investigation, the Chief will not hesitate to do the right thing. But I am relieved to see that things are on track and that you are both fine after the earlier events."

She turned to Thwait, who practically cringed before her gaze. "Constable Thwait, I am a little puzzled. Can you tell me what happened between the time we spoke and my arrival at Sir Ronald's office?"

Thwait rattled on about their activities for a couple of minutes, noting among other things the pleasant way in which Sir Ronald ended the confrontation and brought them into his office for a "chat," as he termed it. When Thwait was done and practically breathless from his efforts to explain everything, Sedgwick nodded to affirm that she understood. Turning to Nesbit, she asked him if he had anything to add, but Nesbit remained silent and looked away at something down the gray hallway. "Constable Thwait," Sedgwick said, once again looking directly at Thwait, "the Chief expects a detailed report on today's activities by the close of business today. Please make sure that you leave nothing out with respect to your interactions with Sir Ronald."

Sedgwick stepped away from Thwait and again turned to Nesbit, who again refused to look at her. "Agent Nesbit, the Chief cannot fully evaluate today's encounter until he's had a chance to read Constable Thwait's report, but I would advise both of you to respect the laws, limitations, and procedures governing our ability to arrest and detain people. I would also add that Interpol has no authority in such matters."

Sedgwick pulled the pen from her pocket and handed it to Thwait. Smiling feebly as he took it, he watched her walk down the hallway to the elevators.

Chapter 12

Once Sedgwick disappeared into the elevator, the doors closing after her with a soft, muffled thud, Nesbit turned to Thwait and smiled indulgently. "My God, she reminds me of my ex-wife. She looks and sounds like...and every time I see her, I can't help...," he began but paused and changed the subject as if speaking about his ex-wife was an unpleasant topic. "But enough of that. Let's get going, my friend. We need to plot our next moves, which we can do over an early dinner at Interpol's expense. I know just the place."

Thwait nodded, although the heavy folds between his eyes and on either side of his mouth betrayed concern. "I'm sorry, sir," he practically burst out, "but shouldn't we stay here in case something happens. I mean, don't the letters suggest some urgency?"

Nesbit stopped at the front of the elevator. Before pushing the down button, he smiled and shook his head in a friendly, indulgent manner. "No, my friend, we don't need to starve. The malefactors are still awaiting a response from the museum, and they aren't going to jeopardize their position until one of two things happen – the museum either refuses to negotiate or the negotiations (which haven't started) break down. Look, in addition to everything else on their pathetic, little minds, these characters are seeking easy money – if they weren't, they wouldn't have sent the letters in the first place. No, my friend, there's still time, especially since it's rather late in the day to be waltzing the sculptures out the door."

Thwait's face softened, showing signs of weakening. "But if they only want to embarrass Her Majesty's government..."

"Tom, if they only wanted to embarrass the government, they could have done so a long time ago. They could have stolen the Gray Ladies and skipped town before I was brought on board to solve this case. No, the extortion letters only postpone their satisfaction. Of course, the money may be part of the embarrassment they're seeking to achieve, but here again the museum hasn't responded, and until they do...well, do you see what I'm getting at?"

Nesbit pushed the elevator button and turned back to his friend.

"Kind of, I guess," Thwait responded. "But there weren't any directions for delivering the money. Surely, if the money is so important..."

"Tom, you're getting too far down into the weeds when you should be looking at the field. Even the smartest bad guys blunder sometimes. When our friends are ready, or when they discover their error, they'll give the museum all the information it needs to make a delivery." Entering the elevator, they both faced the doors and waited silently as the ponderous and squeaky cage slowly inched down to the main level. When the doors finally, reluctantly opened, they stepped into the hallway and Thwait immediately turned to Nesbit. "Sir," he began somewhat hesitantly, "I am not questioning your analysis. I only wanted..."

Nesbit patted the younger man gently on the shoulder. "No need to apologize, my friend," he said sincerely. "I depend on you to keep me from veering off true north. But in this instance, I have a gut feeling, which is both hungry and rarely wrong. Let's revisit these issues over food, okay?"

"Yes, sir." The thick folds between Thwait's eyes disappeared the moment Nesbit mentioned his dependence on the younger man. It was amazing that the great man should look to him for anything. But the wrinkles immediately returned when he recalled Sedgwick's admonition about reporting the day's activities. "Sir, perhaps I should go to the station first and write up everything. You heard what Inspector Sedgwick said..."

"Don't be so serious, my friend. I heard her loud and clear. But if you must, why don't you meet me back at my hotel, say, around eight? In the meantime, write up whatever you need to write up, while I conduct some private business in the interim. How does that sound?"

"Fine, sir, I guess. What do you have planned, if I may ask?"

"You may. But for now, let's just say a little night work."

Chapter 13

The Chief was gone by the time Sedgwick returned to the station. She went to her office and, after plopping down on the chair behind her desk, she slipped off her left shoe and began massaging her toes. Reaching out to the phone with her other hand, she was going to call the Chief when the phone suddenly came to life. It was the Chief.

"I'm not coming back to the office today," he began without any preliminaries. "And I'll probably be at HQ for most of the day tomorrow. As always, contact my cell if you need me. So what's the upshot of the riot at the museum?"

Sedgwick detailed the meeting with Sir Ronald. She also added the details that Thwait provided, but omitted mentioning Nesbit's insolent behavior. "I hate to admit it," she said at one point, "but the wiretap and the letters could be related. There's the timing issue, and then they're all making similar threats. If the speakers in the wiretap are looking to set off a political firestorm, why not do something at the Ravenswood. After all, the Richardson Stones are certainly controversial."

"You're kidding me, right?"

"I'm no more convinced than you that someone's going to steal them, but you have to admit that they offer an interesting target for someone seeking adverse publicity."

"You mean destroy them?"

"If it comes to that. But what if their goal is only to extort money out of the museum, and by extension Her Majesty's government?"

"I must be going out of my mind. You saw the letters before you went out there, and now you're suddenly convinced they're related to the wiretap, the Richardson Stones, and I don't know what else. You're not really listening to Nesbit, are you?"

"I don't know how to explain it. The best I can say is that it's one thing to read them, and quite another to be there and visualize what can actually happen. By the way, I brought the originals back with me, and I'll send them to forensics…"

"Okay, let's put aside the metaphysical crap for a moment. Assuming for the sake of argument you have a point, what makes you think someone's targeting the sculptures as opposed to any number of other pieces in the museum's collection? Did you see something in the letters that I didn't?"

"No, but any damage to them would certainly create an international outcry. There are several countries that would like Her Majesty's government to return them to the country of origin."

"But what's in the wiretap or the letters that suggests the Ravenswood is the target? Why not the Edmonds? Don't they have a couple of pieces that might draw international fire if something were to happen to them? And let's not lose sight of the fact that it was Nesbit who pulled the Ravenswood out of his..."

"Yes, Chief, it bothers me, too. I don't want to think about how or why Agent Nesbit chose the Ravenswood, but it is rather curious that the wiretap came to our attention around the same time that the letters were delivered to the museum. I don't know, Chief. I'm not a hundred percent confident, but until something else turns up – say, another institution gets a similar letter or the rest of the wiretap contradicts everything we now have, which I admit is next to nothing – I think we should at least keep an eye on the Ravenswood. What else can we do?"

The Chief was silent for what seemed to be an inordinate amount of time. "All right, Inspector Sedgwick," he said finally, "I get where you're coming from, but I'm not buying into any of it without something more concrete. Still, I'm willing to keep an open mind, since, as you pointed out, we don't have much else to work with. However, in return for my open-mindedness, I want you to make sure that everything Nesbit and Thwait do is fleshed out properly and by the book. I don't want any wild-goose chases, and I don't want HQ coming down on me because Nesbit got the city wrong or Thwait arrested the Prime Minister. And I definitely don't want HQ charging in and taking control of our business because one of these men screwed up something."

"Are you asking me to be part of their team, Chief?"

"No, I have far too much respect for you to do something like that. Instead, I want you to take charge of the investigation. You don't need to micromanage them, but they should report directly to you and, if there are any issues you'd prefer not to handle, I'll deal with them. I do not, however, want you to work with HQ. If they reach out, you send them directly to me. Are we clear?"

"Let me see. You want me to oversee the investigation, make sure that Nesbit and Thwait don't go off half-cocked, and keep HQ off your back. Do you need anything else?"

"Don't get cute. Look, I'm due at a meeting in a few minutes. We can talk more about this later on." The Chief hesitated. "There's one more thing. I've talked to a few people here, and I'm getting some strange vibes. I can't put my finger on anything, and naturally everyone who's possibly in the know is keeping mum."

"Maybe they're just concerned about threats to Her Majesty's government."

"Maybe, but I'm not sure whatever is bugging them relates solely to Her Majesty and Her government."

"What do you mean, Chief?"

The Chief was again silent for a few seconds.

"Chief?"

"I'm sorry. I'm being called. There's also some buzz here about Nesbit. I don't know what it is, and I don't know if it's connected to the investigation, but I sincerely doubt that it has anything to do with his crime-fighting prowess."

Sedgwick adjusted her phone to ease the slight discomfort caused by its hard, unyielding surface. "He's involved in something there?"

"No, I'm not getting that impression. I've heard his name mentioned a couple of times, but whenever I've asked anyone about him, I get a cold stare or shrugged shoulders. You know, I have a sneaking suspicion he doesn't know any more than I do."

"Anyone you can speak to on the q.t.?"

"No one here is willing to speak to me on that level. Well, I'll be in touch if I hear anything more. Good luck with those two, and keep me apprised of what's going on."

After hanging up, Sedgwick took off her other shoe and gently massaged the soles of both feet.

Chapter 14

After leaving Nesbit, Thwait went directly to the station and set to work writing his report, which included details about their attempted arrest of the sanitation crew, their arrest of the museum guards, their release of the crew and the guards, and of course their conversations with Sir Ronald. Normally, such a report might be a page in length, two if there were a lot of facets to the case, but since Thwait took Sedgwick's admonition to heart, he filled ten full pages of details and remarks, none of which were repetitive or trivial. Thwait was midway into his sixth page when Sedgwick stopped by and asked him how things were going and whether or not he needed any assistance.

Sedgwick had just come inside the building and was walking past the large office room where Thwait and others had desks when she noticed Thwait at his desk, the junior officer's large shoulders hunched over his computer and his thick fingers (mainly his two index fingers) furiously pounding on the keyboard. Upon receiving a pleasant, respectful "no, ma'am, not at this time" to her request, Sedgwick started to leave when Thwait added that he was meeting Nesbit later in the evening and that they were planning their next moves in the case. She nodded, bade him a good evening, and once again headed toward her office. Sedgwick hadn't pressed Thwait on the details of his get-together with Nesbit, because she hadn't yet received the previously noted call from the Chief and at that point didn't feel it necessary to demand details when she trusted Thwait and knew everything would be in his report.

And Thwait didn't volunteer any extra information. Indeed, it would all be in the report, excepting perhaps observations on Nesbit's behavior, and he was pressed to finish his report as quickly as possible in order to get to Nesbit's hotel at the agreed-upon time. As soon as Thwait finished the report, he briefly proofread it, saved and sent it, and then made a hard copy for the Chief's desk (the Chief and many others at the station still preferred hard copies of important documents). By the time he was ready to leave, he was famished and looking forward to something special at Interpol's expense.

He arrived at the hotel a few minutes before eight. The hallway was bright and congenial, but Nesbit's door was suspiciously open (it was obvious from down the hall). When Thwait entered (no sense knocking), he spotted Nesbit comfortably slouched in a black, leather chair, while a white-aproned waiter was cleaning off a portable dinner table in preparation for its removal. The table held significant remnants from Nesbit's dinner – most of the plates and bowls still held their original contents, while there was a large wicker basket filled with dinner rolls and a silver ice bucket cradling a slightly askew, unopened bottle of champagne – which in all likelihood could have supplied a small party, although it was obvious, judging by a napkin and the single setting of silverware, that Nesbit had ordered it for himself. But, as he informed the waiter as the gentleman slipped the tip into a large pocket in his apron, he hadn't been as hungry as he thought. "However, what little I did manage to eat was quite tasty and worth every penny." The waiter silently nodded and pulled the rumbling table out of the room into the hallway, quietly shutting the door behind him.

"I don't know why I ordered so much," he mumbled to Thwait when he noticed him standing to one side, making room for the waiter to exit. "I wasn't very hungry, and yet I couldn't help ordering things that even with your generous help couldn't have been entirely consumed in a single setting."

Thwait smiled vaguely. Now that his stomach was growling and aching for sustenance, the idea of having missed so much food temporarily sapped some of usual pleasantness from his heavy, glowing cheeks.

Appearing to awaken from a reverie, Nesbit looked at Thwait as if he hadn't been aware of his presence until now. "Oh, there you are, Tom," he bellowed. "Don't stand on ceremony, man, take a seat over there." Nesbit motioned to a chair on the other side of a coffee table almost direct across from him.

They had been unaccountably silent for a few moments when Nesbit suddenly stood up, took off his dark, pinstriped dressing gown and, walking to the other side of the room, hung it neatly in the closet. During these few seconds, Thwait tried to assuage the gnawing and growling of his large stomach by looking around the room and observing the things he either hadn't observed or thought to observe previously. Next to the closet where Nesbit had been fumbling with his dressing gown were two framed lithographs featuring different views of the same still life, a basket of shiny apples, pears, and a lobster. Directly across from where he was seated were two king-sized beds and to the right, just out of reach, was a large, dark cabinet, the top of which held some obvious remnants of prior snacks (wrappers, an empty box of something, an open, nondescript bottle) while the double doors obviously concealed a sizeable and presumably well-stocked refrigerator.

Nesbit returned and sat down opposite Thwait. Reaching over the table and tapping the younger man on his ham-like knee with the tip of his forefinger, Nesbit smiled warmly and then leaned back and eyed his friend. "So, how did the report go? Did you finish it? More importantly, will Wedgesick approve?" He laughed at his play on Sedgwick's name, but when Thwait didn't respond and seemed to be staring at the dark cabinet to the left and behind Nesbit, he became concerned. Glancing back at the cabinet and then again at Thwait, Nesbit leaned forward and again tapped his friend on the knee.

"What's on your mind, my fulsome friend?" he asked in a father-like tone. "Dinner? No, I didn't forget. I decided to eat without you – if you can call that eating, as I wasn't particularly hungry – I decided to continue without you because I didn't know when you would arrive. I was famished by six, or at least I thought I was, and so I ordered with the strong supposition that you wouldn't arrive until much later and that, because of your late arrival, you would have already eaten – how many hours can one go without a decent amount of food? But you finished the report, am I right? Ah, I can see hunger in your bloodshot eyes. If only I had known that you'd be here about now, I could have ordered for two, although I still don't think I could have eaten much. I'd order again, but it would take at least an hour, and Interpol would likely baulk at two consecutive dinners of this size." Nesbit was quiet for a moment while he, too, quickly glanced around his room. "Say, how about this, my friend, how about something from the bar behind me? Not much there, but there's a few soft drinks, candy bars, and I think a bag of nuts. Sound good?"

Thwait needed no prodding. He jumped up and scoured through the bar, stuffing candy bars and other items in his mouth and, eventually, downing two cans of soda. After he had consumed enough to get through the next hour, he sat back down in the chair and, the bag of nuts in one hand and another can of something in the other, ready to give his full attention to Nesbit and the case.

Nesbit was a little surprised by his friend's voracity. But instead of mentioning it, he smiled pleasantly and asked him, when he seemed to be momentarily full, if he wanted anything else. "Help yourself, if anything's left."

Thwait nodded and took a big gulp of the liquid. His mouth full of peanuts, he slouched down in his chair and waited for Nesbit to begin their evening session. Nesbit, observing his friend finally relaxing, leaned back in his chair and, cupping his hands behind his head, glanced at the ceiling and then at Thwait. "Well, my well-fed friend, we might be in for a long night. Yes, yes, get something else if you need it, if it helps you settle your nerves."

Taking another huge mouthful of the soda, Thwait waited for Nesbit to follow up his statement, but when he didn't (or when it seemed as if he was going to keep it a secret), he asked, "are we going to spend the night at the museum? If so, I think I'd like to pick something up along the way. Maybe fast food – there're a couple places not too far from here."

Nesbit silently eyed Thwait for a few moments as if he were giving Thwait's statement about spending the night at the museum serious consideration. "Spending the evening at the museum? A novel idea, my friend, but I'm afraid there's no need. I only meant that we may have an anxious night waiting for the start of our business in the morning. Sure, we could go to the museum tonight and, in our spare time (which would be significant), soak up a Greek vase or two. But what would that accomplish, unless our goal was to avoid the jostling crowds eager to take a peek at the same vases? No, I've seen nothing to change my mind about the manner and timing of the malefactors' heist."

Thwait shrugged his shoulders and opened his fourth can of soda. The nuts and almost everything else were now gone.

Nesbit again eyed Thwait, but this time it was because he still couldn't believe that anyone could eat so much in such a short span of time. After raising his eyebrows and clearing his throat, he continued his previous line of thought. "At any rate, I've been thinking that we might need a new calculus if Sir Ronald and the Trustees fail to negotiate or pay the ransom. Everything changes at that point."

"I suppose you're right, sir," Thwait replied and sat up slightly. The pain in his stomach had finally subsided, although he was now feeling a little lightheaded from the soda. "But when do you think we'll see any kind of movement from the bad guys?"

"Certainly not until Sir Roger…"

"Sir Ronald, sir."

"Whatever. They're not going to do anything until Sir Ronald replies. Remember, they're after the money, too, and they won't attempt anything until they're absolutely certain of the museum's position."

"The museum's position, sir? I mean, I don't understand how Sir Ronald can reply without an address or contact information."

"Not to worry, my friend. When our criminals are ready, they'll forward the details. At that point, Sir Ronald (with my consultation) will make a counteroffer, which naturally will buy us additional time to track down said criminals before they act."

"I see. I guess it makes sense."

"Yes, of course it does."

"But, sir, counteroffer? Are they planning to negotiate with the criminals?"

Nesbit smiled and gently stroked his narrow chin. "My personal plans for this evening fell through unexpectedly, and so while you were at the station I contacted Sir Rog...Sir Ronald and discussed the matter with him. He agreed with my proposal that when the time came, he would respond to our bad guys by offering a much lower figure and, if that failed to interest them, demand clarification of some kind. The purpose, as I just suggested, is to keep them engaged but not active until we can locate them and bring them down."

"What if it upsets them, and they take action without the money?"

"No, the money is too appealing. They won't act until it's delivered or it's clear that it won't be forthcoming. My friend, I've considered your earlier objections from every possible angle, and I'm afraid I can only conclude that these are indeed patient characters. The very fact that they've sent multiple letters without providing all the details for payment reinforces this."

Thwait nodded and then hesitated. "With all due respect, sir, but couldn't the same thing suggest impatience? I mean, they sent at least two additional letters without waiting for a response from the first."

"Tom, an impatient individual would have acted quickly and, after acting, would have sent a letter demanding more money to prevent a reoccurrence."

"But why wouldn't the individual do that anyway, patient or impatient?"

"Let's not jump too far down into the philosophical rabbit hole just yet, my friend. If we're not careful, we could parse this to kingdom come."

Thwait nodded absently while he scanned the surface of the table as if he were looking for something else to eat. "I'm sorry to question you, sir. I know you're right," he said, looking back at Nesbit and unconsciously showing his admiration for the older man. "Sir," he began with some slight hesitation, "I have one more question."

"That's what I'm here for."

"Do you really think this could be an inside job? I'm only asking because I'd hate to see Sir Ronald involved in anything like that."

"That's a fine question, Tom, and I too would be troubled to find out that Sir Ronald is involved in such unpleasantness. In fact, I am almost certain that he isn't and that the insiders...well, let's just hold off on the insiders until we get closer to the end game with the criminals." He hesitated for a moment and glanced around as if someone could be standing in the shadows listening to their conversation. "You haven't mentioned the insider angle of this case to the Chief or Sinkbutt, have you?"

Thwait looked at him with wide eyes. "No, sir, I wouldn't..."

"I'm sorry, Tom. I don't mean to doubt you. You agreed to hold off until the time was right, and I know you're a man of your word. I apologize for suggesting otherwise. It's just that this case is so...so sensitive."

"I understand, sir. So what is our next step?"

"For me, as I think I intimated, it is to get a good night's sleep. You should do the same, although I suspect your stomach may have other ideas. How about this? Go to the restaurant in the lobby (I believe it's still open). Order anything you like and put it on this room. Somehow or other, I'll get Interpol to cover it. Sound good? Yes, and after that go straight home and get that sleep you need. Tomorrow, we meet at the museum's doors at eight, two hours before opening."

"Are we are going to position ourselves on the inside?"

Nesbit smiled. "I'll give you all the details tomorrow after I've worked them out. Prepare yourself for an interesting day."

Chapter 15

Instead of going to the elegant restaurant that Nesbit suggested, Thwait immediately headed toward a couple of fast food restaurants that were almost within walking distance of the hotel. He felt a little guilty foregoing Nesbit's recommendation, but he didn't feel right asking Interpol or anyone else to pay for what his own station wouldn't cover. Of course, he didn't mind letting Interpol foot the bill whenever he and Nesbit were together, because that somehow seemed different, even if he couldn't have articulated why.

Once he was back on the road, Thwait started toward his flat but then had second thoughts and, reversing directions, headed for the museum to make sure that everything was safe and sound. Without Nesbit at hand to interpret the facts, Thwait for some reason couldn't entirely agree with his friend that the bad guys were patient, and he also wasn't comfortable with the notion that they wouldn't act while the museum was closed. In fact, because the latter point began to gnaw on him as much as his stomach did earlier, he pushed down the accelerator a little so that he could assure himself that he was doing everything he possibly could do to guarantee that the institution and its contents were safe and that Her Majesty's government wasn't in any immediate danger.

Six blocks from the museum, Thwait was forced to yield to an emergency vehicle, its wailing siren echoing among the outside walls of the buildings. Two blocks later, he again pulled to the side when another emergency vehicle shot past, its siren screaming and echoing like the previous one albeit with a slightly deeper pitch. He was about to pull away from the curb when a third vehicle, this time a command truck, shot past, its blinking lights flashing frenetically as the truck headed in the same direction as the others. Surprised by the commotion, Thwait was nevertheless disinclined to follow the vehicles, because he felt that he needed to check out the museum before he did anything else. A few minutes later when he was practically within walking distance from the museum, he noticed bright, pulsating flashes of light illuminating the sides and upper edges of the surrounding buildings. Turning onto the street that ran in front of the building, the same street that he and Nesbit took every morning to get to the museum, Thwait came to an abrupt halt because the street was barricaded and policemen in luminescent vests and carrying flashlights were angrily directing him out of the area.

Thwait drove around the corner and found a parking space about three blocks away. He walked quickly toward the museum and, when he reached the barricade, he waved his badge (without asking questions) and continued toward the museum, the façade of which was aglow from the pulsating lights of the emergency vehicles and from the broad, sun-like beams of the spotlights near the base of the building. Dozens of firemen and policemen were scurrying back and forth between the emergency vehicles and the building, and he noticed in the street to the left of the building a glowing tent under which several officers were conferring. Looking up at the front of the museum, he watched smoke billowing out of several second-story windows, some of which appeared to be those of Sir Ronald's office. Seconds later, he detected a strange acrid smell permeating the air, no doubt emanating from the very same windows.

He continued toward the entrance, which was still some three hundred feet away, but suddenly veered to the right and walked over to a policeman, who was occasionally directing police and other officials to the entrance and stations around the building. Hoping that the officer could tell him what happened and give him the status of what was still going on, Thwait presented his credentials to the man and demanded information.

"Well, sir, I'm glad you asked," the officer replied, clearly pleased to impart something other than the same set of instructions he had been giving to everyone. "There's been an explosion in the office area on the second floor, if I understand correctly." The officer appeared to be older than most of his rank, and in the dim light the heavy lines and shadows across his face gave him the appearance of someone who had seen just about everything throughout his long career. "See the area beneath the windows?" he said in a voice that sounded firmer than his meager appearance. Angling a hairy index finger at the building, he said, "Do you see any signs of an impact? I don't either, which strongly suggests to my mind that the explosion originated from within the building. Just to be certain, a couple of our men scoured the area for signs that something was launched, possibly from a handheld rocket launcher. Well, sir, they didn't turn up anything that would explain what we're seeing on the outside of the building. You know what I think? It was a bomb, pure and simple, and it was detonated from somewhere inside. And it was a big one, too, not the kind of chicken scratch you see every day in some parts of this bloody town. Notice the windows? Practically every one of them shattered, which wouldn't happen if a space heater or can of lacquer went off. No, sir," he continued, taking off his hat to run his ragged fingers through his gray hair, "this was prime time. We'll have to wait for the bomb boys, but I'll bet they'll say pretty much the same thing. Say, what station did you say you're from?"

"When did it happen?" Thwait asked as he absently watched several firemen with masks and helmets enter the building.

"Don't have a clue. I've been out here a while, but it was going full guns when I arrived. See that officer over there? No, the one standing next to the barricade. Not that barricade, the one to the right. No, my right. Yes, well, that's a good mate of mine. We went to the same school, and if you want someone to talk your ear off about fishing, he's your man." He tugged at his left nostril and then swiped it a couple of times with his index finger. "Not much interested in it personally. But, as I was saying, he's been here twice as long as I have, and he tells me there were already lots of folks here when he arrived. Now, take a look past him to your left. Yes, that's right, I mean my left. Do you see the officer holding his cap and wiping the sweat off his forehead? The bald one. His hat's back on now. If you think my friend Harry is a talker, you should hear good old Sean…"

Thwait turned around and walked to a secluded area forty or fifty feet away. Glancing back at the officer, who was now directing others to the building, he pulled out his phone and quickly dialed Nesbit's number. Thwait wanted to inform him that the museum had been attacked, but at the same time he hoped that the great man would hurry to the museum and make an assessment for himself. Unfortunately, he didn't pick up. Thwait redialed the number (Nesbit probably didn't hear the first call), and again he didn't pick up. He tried it one more time just to be certain, but the result didn't change. Reaching around to his back pocket, he fumbled in it for nearly a minute before painfully retrieving a rumpled scrap of paper with a number in Nesbit's hand scrawled across it. When the clerk at the front desk answered, Thwait asked to be connected to Nesbit's room. The phone rang several times without an answer. He called the hotel again and demanded to know if the clerk had connected him to the right room. After the clerk assured him that neither she nor any other staff member was in the habit of making such mistakes, Thwait was again connected to Nesbit's room – and the result was the same. He left a message on both lines and then called Sedgwick, who informed him that officers from the other stations were already on the scene. She added, without being prompted, that it was too soon to tell if the event was connected to the Gray Ladies' case. But since it was late, Sedgwick suggested that Thwait go home and get some rest. "You can't do anything now. Tomorrow may be the start of some long days for you and Agent Nesbit."

Once the conversation was over, Thwait again tried Nesbit on both phones (by this time, the clerk was answering the desk phone with a snide "Hello, Constable Thwait. What can we do for you now?"), and each time with no more luck than the first. Since Thwait was certain that Nesbit would want some firsthand information, especially this early in the case, he decided to stay a little longer and do some investigating on his own. Quickly passing the officer he had spoken to earlier (who now appeared to be trying to keep a small, nondescript group of people, reporters likely, from crossing police lines), he jogged up the steps and immediately fell in with a line of firemen lugging a long, flattened hose into the building. Despite his misgivings about entering a burning building – and, in the process, ignoring the warnings of another officer and at least two firemen – Thwait felt rather pleased with himself for having traveled a fair distance (and up some of the steepest stairs anywhere!) without breaking a sweat. Now practically in the center of the rotunda, Thwait looked around through the gray haze that filled the room, stepped quickly aside to make room for a set of grunting and shouting firemen lugging their snake-like equipment, and then stepped to the nearest wall where he leaned heavily against it and held his side to ease the discomfort.

Chapter 16

"My God, the stench is horrible," Nesbit said, having entered the museum twelve hours later and spotted Thwait sitting next to the wall on one of the museum's marble benches. The smell, which called to mind a combination of burning wire and smoldering rubber, was still strong even though the fires had been out for several hours. There was a handful of people still in the rotunda (a couple of them were adjusting the controls on two large generators placed in the center that were keeping the lights on throughout the building), but they were moving calmly and at a snail's pace compared to the flurry of activity that filled the area barely an hour ago. Standing directly in front of Thwait, Nesbit observed the soot and grime that covered his listless friend, whose meaty body leaned forward and slightly to one side while his chin rested on his barrel-like chest and his slab-like arms dangled at his sides, allowing the knuckles of his swollen paws to rest on the hard, stone floor.

"Why didn't you call me?" Nesbit demanded, looking at the top of Thwait's head. The younger man's wet, greasy hair was plastered to his scalp, revealing little clumps of debris scattered in his hair and across his skin.

Thwait slowly raised his heavy head and attempted to stand up.

"No, no, stay seated, my friend. You look terrible." Nesbit pulled out a white silk handkerchief from his pocket and dusted off a section of the bench next to Thwait. Placing his left shoe on that section and leaning on that leg, Nesbit paused for a couple of minutes before demanding to know what had happened. "I'm going to inspect the damage site in a few minutes, but I'd like to know what to expect. Have you seen it yet? What do you think? Is there any word on the cause?"

Thwait shook his heavy head. "Not a lot of details," he said, barely able to raise his head toward Nesbit. "An explosion…happened shortly after closing…there's…there's…" Coughing, trying to spit out the soot lodged in his lungs, Thwait couldn't finish.

Nesbit stepped back and began pacing. "I knew it, I knew it," he said, repeating the words as though they had a pleasant, invigorating effect. "It shouldn't have been a surprise to anyone – not to anyone, my friend." Sensing a strange crackle emanating from the floor, Nesbit abruptly stopped and looked down at his shoes. The black patent-leather was dusted around the edges by the same gray dirt that covered the floor and the bench he had just wiped off. He reached for his handkerchief to wipe his shoes, but changed his mind and went back to Thwait, and stood directly in front of him. "Is anything left of our Gray Ladies?" he asked the top of Thwait's head. "My God, the ramifications of this are incalculable."

"No..."

Nesbit slammed his right fist into the palm of his left hand. "They're not going to get away with this. They can't destroy a...a...and create all this commotion and get away with it, not on my watch." Grimacing angrily, he turned, took a couple of steps to the left, but then returned to where he had been standing. "Tom, I had it pegged all along, and the only reason I couldn't have anticipated the exact timing was because they must have changed their minds at the very last second. Something must have spooked them to make them take such a risk after hours and at night – I wonder if one of your officers accidently let the word out that I was on the case. You know what loose lips can do. Well, we're not going to let the bad guys get away with this. No one is going to destroy valuable art and create an international stir if I have anything to say...wait, have we heard anything from Asia or the EU? They've got to be buzzing like fireflies right now." Thwait started to answer, but Nesbit didn't give him the opportunity. "By the way, have you told anyone back at the station about this? The Chief? Sedneck?"

"...Sedgwick, sir."

"Whatever."

"Yes, sir. I'm afraid they all knew before I did. But the sculptures weren't..."

"There were more? No, you mean they missed one or more of the Gray ladies? Well, we can be thankful for small favors, I suppose." Nesbit stepped back and glanced around the lobby. Shaking his head in disgust, he turned back to Thwait, who seemed only marginally more alive than before. "But what about the culprits, man? Who are they? Where are they? Were they caught?"

"They weren't touched." Thwait momentarily closed his exhausted eyes.

"What? Identified but ignored? My God, what kind of outfit is the Chief running?"

Thwait didn't immediately respond. He started to stand but changed his mind and slowly brushed off his clothes. When he came to his right sleeve, he noted with some distress that there was a small tear across the edge.

"No, I can't say I'm entirely surprised. But what's wrong, Tom? Do you need a hand? Are you hurt in any way? What exactly have you been doing here?"

When Thwait again failed to respond (he continued to puzzle over his injured coat), Nesbit took him by his thick shoulders and shook him as if he were trying to wake the younger man. "For God's sake, man, get ahold of yourself. We'll get through this together. Now, give me the details unless you're hurt. And if you're hurt, we'll rush you to the hospital and talk along the way."

Thwait suddenly came to his senses. "What?" he asked just as Nesbit released him. "I'm sorry, sir. I guess, I guess, I guess I'm just a little tired. I'm much better now. I was helping the firemen and the stations. The sculptures are fine, as far as I know. There were other things, though, mainly small pieces...they were destroyed when Sir Ronald's office was hit. I don't think any of them are left."

There was a heavy, metallic clang reverberating from some distant, undefinable place in the building. Both men glanced toward the sound, and seconds later they noticed the grayish haze of smoke floating out from the elevator shaft (the door, for some reason, was partly open, although the car was on another floor) and a few seconds later the smoldering-rubber smell intensified. Nesbit shook the dust out of his silk handkerchief and pressed it against his nose and mouth, while Thwait merely crinkled his nose a little, coughed a couple times more, and seemed otherwise oblivious to the odor.

"Go on," Nesbit insisted through his handkerchief.

"The bomb squad...and the forensics team...look, sir, there's one of them now." He motioned weakly to a man in a white jumpsuit and white mask dragging a large canvas bag across the rotunda. Thwait stretched his shoulders and shook his head slowly to convey the sadness of what he had to relate. "It seems to have gone off somewhere near Sir Ronald's office."

"My God, Sir Ronald? Why didn't you tell me this earlier? Is he okay? Was anyone else hurt?"

"Someone from the station – the Chief, I think – spoke to him a little while ago. He's fine, maybe a little shaken. He wasn't in the museum. It was closed. The security guards were in another wing." He tried to catch his breath and coughed slightly. "Inspector Sedgwick said an explosive charge was placed near the office and went off just after the museum closed. Everything is pretty sketchy now."

"Stinkbug is here?"

"Inspector Sedgwick, sir. No, she's been here, but I think she's meeting with the bomb people or the forensics team, or somebody else. She told me, I think. I don't recall."

Nesbit reached down and helped Thwait to his feet. Once Thwait steadied himself and appeared ready to move, Nesbit smiled and patted him on the shoulder, producing a puff of gray dust. "Well, my dusty friend," Nesbit said as he brushed the grime from his hands, "let's roll up our sleeves and lend a hand." He hesitated. "Did you say if anyone was hurt?"

"Undetermined, sir."

Nesbit paused and stroked his chin thoughtfully. Suddenly breaking his stillness, he looked intently at Thwait. "On second thought, I have a theory. Come with me. There's no time to lose."

"Where are we going, sir?" Thwait called after Nesbit, who was now hustling down the hall toward the sculpture room.

Nesbit called to his colleague from over his shoulder. "The explosion may have been a diversion. But we won't know until we check."

Chapter 17

The following afternoon, the Chief, Sedgwick, and several officers were crowded into the Chief's office. Sedgwick and three other officers were sitting in the chairs surrounding the Chief's desk, while the others were standing or leaning against the walls. The Chief was sitting down behind his desk and, pencil in hand, squinting at each officer in turn. "It's amazing that no one was seriously hurt," he began as if the conversation had been going on for some time. "A couple firemen suffered minor injuries from smoke inhalation, but they've been treated and are back on the job. Unfortunately, we can't say as much for the building or some of the museum's collection. Sir Ronald stated that several priceless antiquities were lost, as well as everything else in his office, which turned out to be the epicenter of the blast." The Chief dropped the eraser end of his pencil to the desk and began tapping it. "The disposal unit informed us that there were two bombs. One obviously went off, while the other for some reason failed to detonate. The unit was able to disarm the device, and they took it to forensics where it is currently being…"

"Excuse me, Chief," interjected a grayish officer wearing what appeared to be a gray lab coat, "but the bomb needn't have been disarmed. The timer failed, and so there was no chance of it going off under normal circumstances. In fact, you could have dropped it from a ten-story building and nothing would have happened, unless of course you were standing directly underneath it."

"Thank you, for your insights, Dr. Fellows," the Chief replied and squinted at him. "Since the bomb is now safely in one of your labs, perhaps you could tell us what you're doing with it in terms of collecting evidence."

"Yes, certainly. We are currently examining the device for fingerprints, after which we plan to subject the outside shell to chemical analysis in order to identify any bodily effluents that might still be there. While it appears to be intact – it was hidden behind a pillar and escaped most of the impact from the other bomb – we are not entirely sure that there will be enough effluents left to make a meaningful collection. We are also planning to deconstruct the unit to see if we can match its components and construction to any of the devices that we may have on file. But if I may add, Chief, we should be thankful the bomb had not gone off as planned, because it could have undermined the structural integrity of the floor beneath the office. I believe there's an exhibit of jewels from India in the gallery below, and had the floor collapsed, well, I'm afraid to think of what might have happened to all those little beauties. Come to think of it…"

"Thank you again, doctor." This time, the Chief's squint silenced the doctor. "I want the results as soon as possible."

"Yes, Chief."

The Chief looked around the room. "So, at the moment it appears we have two devices. By the way, has the bomb squad finished going through the building for additional devices? Yes? Okay, why two? Both had timers, right doctor? Clearly, one was sufficient to do extensive damage, but if the other was designed to undermine the structural integrity of the building, why weren't there any others? We're confident about the number, right? What exactly was the bomber trying to achieve? Some antiquities were lost, but surely more damage could have been inflicted by placing the charges in the galleries downstairs. Do we have any sense of the worth of the antiquities that were lost? Are there any theories on the table, or is it too soon?"

"Well, sir, Agent Nesbit and Constable Thwait seem to think…," said one of the officers in the back of the room. He immediately fell silent when the Chief squinted at him, and the other officers turned to have a look.

"I am acutely aware of what those gentlemen seem to think," the Chief said as the officers immediately turned back to him. The Chief stopped abruptly, tightened his jaws, and squinted around the room, observing each officer carefully as he did so. "And where the hell are Nesbit and Thwait?"

"They're still at the crime scene," Sedgwick interjected. "I'll reach out to them after the meeting."

The Chief exercised his jaw slightly as if to loosen it up and resumed tapping his pencil against the desk. "Thank you, Inspector Sedgwick." He again glanced at the officer in the back of the room before turning back to the others. "Okay, I presume you've all had a chance to go over the case file Inspector Sedgwick compiled. It has just about everything that we know about the bombing except the forensic evidence, which I'm sure the doctor will kindly supply when it's available. Now, can anyone tell me why someone would target the museum? I realize the building's still smoldering, but we might be able to focus our investigation if we had some sense of why the building was targeted."

Sedgwick looked around the room. When it was clear that no one was going to respond, she turned back to the Chief. "If I may, Chief, I think we could be misinterpreting the intent of the extortion letters. My initial assumption was that they were directed at the museum – that is, 'give us money or we'll take out the museum' – but given the fact that the bombs were placed in or near Sir Ronald's office, I wonder if Sir Ronald was the object of both the bomber and the extortion letters."

"Chief," began the officer who had been silenced earlier, "we shouldn't rule out the possibility that the bomber was targeting the museum's art. Constable Thwait and Agent Nesbit may have been misguided on certain things, but they identified the museum, and valuable artifacts in Sir Ronald's office were destroyed. Dr. Fellows noted that a lot more could have been destroyed had the second bomb detonated as planned. Chief, if the bomber had only been after Sir Ronald, why were the bombs set for after hours when he was gone instead of during the day? Really, if Sir Ronald was the target, why not a bullet to the head while he was at his desk or in the lavatory? Look, I'm not defending Agent Nesbit, but he and Constable Thwait may be better positioned to solve this case than we are if we stick to the standard assumption that the object of the exercise is the leading figure of whatever, the Colonel Mustard of the museum."

"I don't know from Colonel Mustard," said another officer, a rather angular individual who had just come in and was now sitting on the floor by the door with his legs crossed. "But since we don't know who's responsible, we can't be certain about the intent, and I believe it would be a mistake to investigate the case on the basis of something we don't know. I think we're putting the cart before the horse. Let's apprehend the culprit or culprits and then assess their motives and intentions."

"Rubbish...," someone else began to say but was immediately silenced when the Chief held up his hand. Reaching for the ringing phone, he listened intently while the caller continued speaking for another two or three minutes. When the call was over, the Chief placed the handset back into its cradle and sat quietly for a few seconds, clearly rolling something around in his mind. Without an explanation, he stood up and headed toward the door, stepping between officers who were quickly scooting out of his way. "Keep talking. I'll be back in a few minutes," he said as he left the office, closing the door behind him.

During his absence, several officers hotly debated the usefulness of trying to divine motives at this stage in the investigation, while several others argued over the possibility of assigning motives without first identifying the culprit or culprits. "The extortion letters only confuse matters," one officer insisted, having just asked another to stop assuming that they were intrinsic to the case. "We don't even know if they're connected…," he said, but was cut off before he finished his thought. "Connected? Connected?" another shouted. "What does it take for you to see the connection?" Officers, male and female, on both sides of the room immediately chimed in with their considered opinions, making it difficult to tell which side was winning or losing. Another officer, a thickset older man whose black mustache hung limply on either side of his mouth, had just leaped off the floor and was shouting and shaking his fist at someone when the Chief came back into the office. Looking around when everyone suddenly became quiet, the officer closed his mouth and quickly sat back on the floor when he caught sight of the Chief, who was standing only inches away from him. The Chief silently stepped around him and sat down at his desk, after which he placed a single sheet of paper on it in front of him and picked up his pencil.

He squinted at the officers, most of whom turned away or looked down when he focused on them. Having had his eyeful, he turned toward the paper and began talking as if he were addressing the paper. "HQ faxed the complete wiretap. Let me qualify this. They faxed everything they had, but it's still technically incomplete. Without going into details, this was the only part that was recorded, and they assured me that it represents everything they have with respect to the wiretap." He paused and, for a couple of moments, appeared to be mentally debating something. "Before I read you this," he continued, finally breaking the silence, "I have to say I am troubled as much by what the wiretap says as by what it doesn't say. I don't think anyone is going to change their theory because of it. But, at least for now, I want any theory you develop to tie together the wiretap, the extortion letters, and of course the evidence gleaned from the bomb site – and that includes the forensic evidence, whenever we get it."

The Chief picked up the paper and seemed ready to begin reading, but he suddenly stopped and squinted again at the men. "I'm willing to concede that the Gray Ladies could be artworks like Nesbit and Thwait assert, but…," he began and then tightened his jaw. One of the officers was going to say something but the Chief squinted at him, and he backed down and tried to blend in with the other officers around him. "But, as I was going to say," the Chief started again, although this time with a tone that appeared to brook no interruptions, "given recent events, we are also going to have to factor in Sir Ronald, who may or may not have been the object of the blast. Incidentally, I have just placed a twenty-four hour detail on Sir Ronald in case someone tries to have another go at him."

"Oh, God, not Nesbit and Thwait...," someone mumbled.

The Chief hesitated, gritted his teeth, and pretended not to have heard the remark. "Okay," he said at last while carefully observing his officers, "I'm talking too much about the wiretap before giving you a chance to make up your own minds. But let me make a couple things clear before we go any further. One, the suspects (and I don't know if we have one, two, or a multitude) – they are, for some reason, out to get one of our officers. Two, the suspects might be having a spot of fun with this bombing business, and so we might expect them to continue until they get the officer in question or until their activities cease to be amusing. Three...oh, let me just read it." He cleared his throat several times before reading.

[male voice number one] "It's going to rock this bloody town, I promise you. Once we get the Gray Ladies, I'll let our favorite constable in on the big secret. He's always mouthing off about big cases, but he's never seen one as big as this. The government will fall – [male voice imitating the voice of an old woman] *We trusted 'em to protect our country's bloody treasures!* – [male voice now speaking normally] and Scotland Yard, Interpol, and all the rest of them buggers will be scurrying around like roosters with their heads bit off. Know what? He'd never figure it out on his own. Even if he did, it'd be too late."

[male voice number two] "Why do you want to do that? That's going to make them come after us. I thought the purpose was to make [unintelligible], not bring the jailor to our bloody doorstep."

"Are you a bleeding pansy or something? He's a fool. Don't you get it? He wouldn't know what to do even if he had brains. It's completely free. I'm going to rattle his cage, then make the rest of the world believe the result was his fault. We'll date the ladies, but he'll take the fall for trying to love them. He'll take the fall for bleeding everything."

"How're you going to do that without revealing our identities? And once he knows who we are, it's all over and every Tom, Dick, and Archibald will be splashing our mugs all over the place. Hey, that's

217

pretty good, huh? Every Tom, Dick, and Archibald – I sound just like you, don't I?"

"Shut the [expletive deleted] up. I'm only going to let him identify me."

"What?"

"Don't be a sod. I'm going to tell him a few things, casually and over time, that will make him think it's me, while not being absolutely sure."

"So why wouldn't he take his suspicions to Scotland Yard or whatever?"

"He's not going to do that. Nothing's going to happen, except we mess with him for a while and demand some readies for everybody's peace of mind. Trust me, you sack of [expletive deleted], he isn't going to let his only begotten [unintelligible] take a fall. It would ruin his reputation and wreck his precious career. It might even hurt his feelings, if he has any. Brother, can you imagine the headlines if it gets out? Every one of them Tom, Dick, and Archibalds' going to shout, [male voice pretending to street seller of magazines] *World famous detective linked to major crimes. Is he protecting you know who, or was he in on the crime? Did he fail in his duty to Queen and country? Is this another one of his* [unintelligible]?"

"Okay, after we mess with him for a while, then what?"

[male voice number one in his normal voice] "Then we get the readies and the last Gray…" [End transmission.]

"Once again, this is all of it. Now, any questions?"

The officers were silent for a few moments. A few ventured to look around to the room to see if anyone was going to ask a question, but they quickly looked up at the ceiling or down at their laps when it became painfully clear that no one was going to venture the first response. During this short time, the Chief scanned their faces and then looked at Sedgwick, who appeared as perplexed as the others. After a few minutes of silence, the officers slowly started whispering among themselves about the wiretap and only one of them volunteered a question to the Chief.

"Chief," Sedgwick began, and the Chief held up his right palm to silence everyone while she was speaking. "HQ said that we now have everything with respect to the wiretap. But isn't there an audio version? Do you know if they were planning to include that, too? It might be useful."

The Chief looked at Sedgwick as if he were surprised by the question. "Inspector Sedgwick, that's a very good question. Given their reluctance to give us this much, I never gave it a thought. I'll ask them about it, and get back to you." The Chief turned and squinted at Fellows. "Now, unless you have any questions, Dr. Fellows, I want you to get some of your forensics staff to take a look at the wiretap. Maybe there's something here – words, phrases, patterns, I don't know – that might tell us something about the suspects. Maybe there's something in the words that might help us connect the suspects to the officer being referenced or to a part of the city. It's a long shot, of course, but we don't have much else to go on right now."

"I'll get on it right away. But, Chief, what about…"

"You don't need to say it. HQ didn't supply anything else with respect to the wiretap, not numbers, locations, not even the assurance that there are only two speakers. If HQ has done any investigative work, they haven't said a word about it. But I'll ask them about this, too."

"I can see why they wouldn't. Too easy to get unnecessarily bogged down in the courts," one of the other officers interjected.

"You're telling me," said the officer with the mustache. "I had a case once the bleeding courts threw out…"

"I remember that one…"

"Okay, okay," the Chief said, again raising one of his hands to silence the talk. "Let's not worry about this until the courts are actually involved. Now, unless there's something else of relevance, let's meet tomorrow morning to review new evidence."

Chapter 18

Ten minutes later, the Chief walked into Sedgwick's office unannounced and sat down in a chair in front of her desk. The office was much smaller than the Chief's, and, unlike his, there were photographs on each of the walls, mainly of noted sprinters (male and female). There was also a book case, though much smaller than the one in the Chief's office, and it was packed with books and magazines on law enforcement and running. Sedgwick was at her laptop sending instructions to various officers in the field when the Chief entered unannounced and sat down.

"The whole thing bothers me."

"Chief?"

"So the suspects attacked Sir Ronald's office, and I don't think it's unreasonable to assume that they were trying to get Sir Ronald, too. On the other hand, if we accept the wiretap at face value, the speakers are going to have a spot of fun pursuing one of our officers – but how is this compatible with the bombing of Sir Ronald's office? And this business of going after one of our officers – how do we locate one disgruntled psychopath out of the millions of other disgruntled psychopaths that cross our paths every day? And how do we reconcile all of this with the extortion letters? I'm at a loss to understand any of this."

"I agree, Chief, it's all rather confusing. I'll do some digging through our case files to see if I can find anything that stands out."

"I don't need to tell you that since HQ gave us the rest of the wiretap, they are going to be all over us until this case is closed. At the same time, we have to be very careful how we handle it. They're right to be concerned about anything that would embarrass Her Majesty's government. But they're starting to panic because of the adverse media surrounding the bombing, that and of course the inconvenient fact that the suspects are still at large." The Chief paused and pawed at something in his left eye.

"Maybe things could have been a little different if they hadn't sat on the wiretap for so long," Sedgwick noted, taking advantage of the momentary silence. "Do you know if there's anything else they're keeping from us?"

The Chief grimaced slightly. "You know as much as I do. But the problem is that they can delay or withhold things all they want, since we're the ones that are going to take the heat if this investigation takes too long, especially if the suspects are planning something else and we don't catch them in time."

"Excuse me, but what about the threats to one of our officers implied in the wiretap? Have they said anything about that?"

"Not in so many words. They're right that Her Majesty's government is higher on the scale of importance, and therefore I don't have a problem with HQ focusing on this aspect of the investigation. But I can only hope that someone there understands that protecting our officers is crucial to this and every other investigation."

"I understand, Chief. But let me ask you another question." She glanced at something on her computer screen and then turned back to the Chief. "Why did HQ insist on bringing in Agent Nesbit to help us work this investigation? I'm not criticizing Agent Nesbit. I'm simply trying to understand why they would bring in someone from the outside while they were holding onto the wiretap. Is there a connection here, or is this simply a coincidence?"

The Chief shook his head and leaned back in the chair. "You got me. Even if the man was the greatest thing since animal crackers, nothing at all explains his presence here."

Sedgwick tightened her lips and looked intently at the Chief. "There's something else, Chief. I was going to send you some notes about it later this evening, but since you're here now…well, what I mean is, one of the speakers in the wiretap mentions the phrase 'his only begotten.' Of course, the next word is garbled, but do you think it could refer to a father/son relationship? Here's a poor bugger who's so mad at his officer/dad that he decides to avenge himself by committing a crime. And the term 'brother' – are we supposed to take it literally, as in a pair of brothers going off the deep end? It's happened before, you know."

The Chief sat upright and absently picked up the only pencil on Sedgwick's desk. Tapping the pencil against the edge of her desk, he nodded and said, "you make a good point about the father/son business. But the brother stuff just sounds like street slang. Why don't you see if you can find something about a father/son relationship going south? Naturally, we're only concerned with a father who's still on the force, which I think the wiretap implies. Do you agree? If you want to add a brother to the mix, that's up to you."

"Yes, Chief."

The Chief hesitated and placed the pencil back on Sedgwick's desk. Briefly rubbing the back of his neck with the palm of his right hand, he added, "make sure Constable Thwait and Nesbit see the rest of the wiretap. I don't want to leave them in the dark about anything, not that I think it'll matter."

"Chief, they're not completely in left field. They're probably wrong about the purpose of the bombing, but, as Jonson noted, they certainly pegged the right museum. You have to admit it's pretty impressive, given all the possible buildings the suspects could have hit in this city."

"A good guess, maybe." The Chief hesitated. "Sometimes when I hear about what he and Thwait are doing, I...but, like I've said before, it doesn't matter what I think. Nesbit has shown that he can come up with a good lead now and then, which probably gives HQ a reason to hope. Regardless, we might as well use him while he's here."

"I agree, Chief. I was planning to meet with them in a little while. I've got a few things I need to tidy up first."

The Chief glanced at Sedgwick's desk and for moment seemed surprised that he wasn't sitting on the other side. Standing up, he eyed Sedgwick and informed her that he was going to Sir Ronald's residence "to hold his hand again" and then "swing by" HQ. "They don't seem to understand there's an investigation underway, and instead they want to hold another in an endless stream of pointless meetings about something or other. Okay, while I'm making the world safer for Her Majesty, I want you to keep a close eye on those two. Maybe Nesbit will pull off a miracle, but I want to make sure that we have a solid investigation, not something that's going to drag me in front of some board or committee where I'll have to justify my entire life."

"Wouldn't it be easier to assign them to the station? There're plenty of useful things they can be doing here to support the investigation. For instance..."

"No, that's too close for comfort," the Chief insisted. "As much as I'd like to reassign him to Antarctica, I think we should keep him in the field for the time being. He might be useful, and it will make HQ happy. But if he screws up just once, we'll yank him in (no pun intended) and ship him back to HQ. On the positive side, HQ said that he was working on the investigation at the station's discretion, if I understand them right. Right or wrong, do whatever you have to do to keep him in line, and I'll take care of the rest if something happens."

After the Chief left, Sedgwick contacted Thwait and confirmed their meeting at the museum. Since she still had some time before she had to leave, she sent out several more messages, added to her notes, and then began searching through electronic case files and related databases for information on father/son relationships gone bad. The difficulty, she realized, was that most of the relationships in which the father is an officer were never reported. Unless the son is in serious trouble, the father rarely wants to make his family problems public and, moreover, there were no official requirements for an officer to report such issues, even if they become serious. As for brothers, Sedgwick thought more about it and decided that the Chief was right. It was probably street slang. After sending a couple of emails, she logged off and hurried out of the station.

Chapter 19

Sedgwick met Nesbit and Thwait in the first (outside from left to right) of the gigantic loading bays at the back of the museum. The bay door was open, revealing an empty, cavernous space with undifferentiated cement walls and, at the far wall opposite the bay, a smaller, garage-like door that led to the museum proper. It was closed. The bay was practically empty, but it was brightly lit up from a chain of overhead lights and the open loading door, which at that time of day allowed some outside light to filter in along with a slight, swirling breeze.

The two men were sitting a few feet apart on the same side of a long, folding table, examining small rock-like objects and other bits of debris from the blast. The table was covered with a white plastic sheet, and the debris was spread out horizontally from practically one end to the other. Wearing loose, vinyl gloves, they carefully examined the pieces and catalogued them in a small notebook each man had at his elbow, at the same time sharing their thoughts on what this or that anomalous-looking object might represent. "Possibly something from an artifact, though I wouldn't rule out the possibility of its being a bomb fragment," Nesbit said as he carefully stuck a numbered piece of white tape on it and placed it back in the tray. "I'm tagging it with number 1-6-5." While they had yet to discover anything significant, they were confident that something would turn up, especially once they combined their evidence with the evidence from the forensics lab.

"What do you make of this?" Nesbit was saying to Thwait when Sedgwick arrived. He was holding a round, coin-like object that showed signs of melting on its edges and sides. No bigger than a two-pound coin, it was silver in color and, on one of its sides, there appeared to be a rounded smile near the edge. "I thought it might be one of Sir Ronald's antiquities when I first saw it, but now that I've got most of the soot off of it, I can't say what it is," he added when he caught sight of Sedgwick, standing a few feet off to one side. She looked clean, fresh, and official in her pressed suit, which to Nesbit suggested that she had come to interfere in their important work. Silently handing the object to Thwait, he refused to acknowledge her presence.

As Thwait reached for the object, he, too, caught sight of Sedgwick on the opposite side of the table. He was still reaching for the object, which Nesbit continued to hold, as he jumped up and uttered a feeble, "hello, Inspector Sedgwick, ma'am." Shortly after this, he dropped his arm and added, "very well, ma'am, thank you. This is the only place we could find that would allow us to work uninterrupted and away from the smell." He glanced at Nesbit, expecting him to show respect to his superior, but the Interpol agent continued working as if he hadn't heard Thwait or noticed Sedgwick's presence.

"Fine, but do sit, Constable Thwait," Sedgwick said and, pulling a folding chair out from under the table, sat down on the opposite side of the table, equidistant from both men. She was silent for a few moments as she observed the evidence spread across the table and the manner in which Nesbit handled the strange, coin-like object. Seconds earlier, after she had seen enough, she was about to inform the men that they were violating two, possibly five, station protocols for the collection, examination, and preservation of evidence when it occurred to her that it was best to save the criticism for another time. After all, the evidence didn't appear to be legally compromised and, moreover, she needed to work with the men, even Nesbit, and didn't want to begin on an antagonistic footing. "Some good finds?" she asked both men simultaneously.

Nesbit didn't respond or even turn in her direction. Thwait, however, said that they had only begun combing through the evidence a few hours ago and so far hadn't come up with anything substantial. "However, you might want to take a look at what Agent Nesbit just found," he added. "It doesn't appear to be either a museum artifact or a bomb fragment."

Sedgwick looked at Nesbit, who immediately tossed the object into the shallow tray in front of him. "Nothing of significance," he said, finally turning to Sedgwick and staring at her defiantly.

"Are you sure? I'd like to have a look, if you wouldn't mind."

Nesbit continued staring silently as if he expected her to shrink back. When she didn't, and instead yanked out a pair of gloves from an open box on the table and began pulling them on, Nesbit picked the object out of the tray and tossed it to her just as she had the last glove in place.

Sedgwick easily caught the object. Balancing it between her thumb and forefinger, she carefully examined its shimmering surface and then ran a gloved finger over the bubble-like texture on one side and across the rounded smile on the other. She turned it on edge and studied the undulations from one point to another. Having held the object for more than a minute, she shrugged her lean shoulders and tossed it back to Nesbit, who failed to catch it even though it was aimed squarely at his chest. The object ricocheted off his shirt and bounced edgewise onto the floor, where it caught an outside breeze and began rolling away from the table. Nesbit jumped up and awkwardly chased it for a few yards before reclaiming it and sullenly placing it back into the tray.

Smiling pleasantly to both men, Sedgwick told them that she didn't know what it was, either. "I agree, it doesn't look like an antiquity, but I'm no expert on antiquities. Looks like a button, if you ask me."

"Actually, I didn't...," Nesbit began after readjusting himself in his chair, but Sedgwick interrupted him.

"Actually, Agent Nesbit, Constable Thwait, the reason I wanted to meet with you wasn't just to find out how things were going since the last time we talked or even to find out if you've discovered any button-like objects. I wanted to inform you both personally that there's been a slight change to how the Chief wants to handle things with respect to this part of the investigation. That is, he's placed me temporarily in charge."

"Actually," Nesbit replied in a slow, almost insulting tone. He leaned back in his chair and smiled at Sedgwick. "I'm on loan from Interpol at the behest of Scotland Yard, and so I'm afraid you aren't in charge of me."

Sedgwick was quiet for a moment, while Thwait practically shuddered at Nesbit's words.

"Yes," Sedgwick finally replied, graciously, "you certainly are. I suspect the Chief was concerned about the multiple responsibilities – to Interpol, to Scotland Yard, and to our station – and so he suggested that I should inform you that you're free to return to Interpol or Scotland Yard anytime you choose. If, however, you want to remain part of the station's investigation – and the station, I should also point out, has sole responsibility over this case – you will be advised to follow my lead. Oh, yes," she added, as recalling something, "The Chief spoke to HQ about authorities, and they seem to agree that you are working with the station at the station's discretion. Please feel free to discuss this with either the Chief or HQ, or maybe Interpol. But if you wish remain on the investigation, it will be under my direction. Otherwise, I will have to ask you to leave the premises immediately." Sedgwick glanced at Thwait, who was staring open mouthed at both Sedgwick and Nesbit, and then turned back to Nesbit, observing him unflinchingly.

"All right," Nesbit responded a few moments later. His voice was pleasant, but it was obvious from both its tone and the strained look on his face that he wasn't happy. "Have it your way. What's our next move, boss?"

Sedgwick was calm and unruffled. She reached down to the bag she brought, which was resting next to her chair, and retrieved a page of what appeared to be printer paper. Placing it face down on the table in front of her, she asked for an update on anything else they found that could have a bearing on the case.

Nesbit was about to shove the tray across the table to Sedgwick but thought better of it. He lifted the stiff, gray metal sheet, which was about the size of a large cookie sheet, and carefully stretched across the table and placed it near Sedgwick, trying not to touch the sheet of paper in front of her. He noted, as he sat back down, that he and Thwait found a small cardboard box, not more than two inches by one inch by one-half inch, behind the outside door of the office. "It's rather curious," he stated in a more professional tone, "and it weathered the blast amazingly well. There's some soot and dirt on it, but that's about it." After Sedgwick slid the paper to one side and positioned the tray so that she would comfortably reach the contents, Nesbit pointed to the box, which was in the center of the tray.

Sedgwick examined the small box as carefully as she did the coin-like object, and then passed it over to Nesbit. "It looks like part of a match box," she said.

"You think it's a piece of trash?" Thwait asked, glancing at Nesbit as he spoke.

"Not at all. If it is a match box, maybe the suspect dropped it while planting the bombs. Let's have it checked for fingerprints." Sedgwick placed it back into the tray and began sorting through the other items.

"What about the rest...Inspector?" Nesbit asked, waiting for her to dismiss it or disparage their efforts as a whole.

"Very interesting, especially the small shards." She held up a small, black object that resembled a razor-sharp orange peel. "Do you think this might be part of the detonated bomb, Agent Nesbit?"

Against his will, Nesbit was pleased that Sedgwick was showing him the respect that he felt he had earned from his years on the job and especially from his success in New Orleans. "That's what I was thinking."

Sedgwick picked up several other pieces, and each time she touched something she asked Nesbit for his opinion on the object. Once she had gone through the tray, Sedgwick handed it to Nesbit, slid the paper back in front of her, and gave the men a brief update on the investigation, including what the other stations were doing. At one point, she even asked Nesbit for his insights on how the investigation should proceed and was surprised (although she didn't show it) that his views were similar to her own. Graciously, she expressed her appreciation and promised to implement many of his suggestions without, however, mentioning that she had already implemented these very same things prior to leaving for the museum. When the discussion had run its course, Nesbit and Thwait fell silent and, glancing at one another, waited for Sedgwick to say something about new rules and restrictions governing the investigation. Nesbit, while appreciating the conversation, was particularly concerned that Sedgwick would begin to micromanage their efforts, which to him would be unwarranted and could destroy the progress that had already been made.

"Agent Nesbit, Constable Thwait," Sedgwick said, breaking the silence and tossing her gloves into a trash barrel, "I do not intend to get in your way. Unless instructed otherwise, I will give you all the freedom you need to bring this investigation to a successful conclusion. But at the same time, I will need to know everything you know. I want to be able to champion your efforts to the Chief and HQ, and I won't be able to do that if you leave me out of the loop on anything. Is that fair? I should also say that we'll have to coordinate with others working on the case, but that doesn't mean ceding authority to anyone else. Finally, I will keep you informed about what I hear, and I will help wherever I can. Does that seem okay?" She looked at both men, waiting for them to respond. When they didn't, she picked up the paper in front of her and turned it face up.

Nesbit and Thwait turned their attention to the paper.

"Ma'am?" asked Thwait glancing at her and then at the page.

"I have the rest of the wiretap. I am told that this is all of it. But before I show it to you, I must ask you both to keep this closely held. The only ones besides HQ who know about it are the station officers assigned to the case." She slid the paper across the table to Nesbit.

Nesbit took the paper and positioned it so that he and Thwait could read it simultaneously. Thwait was the first to finish and, his heavy face expressing his concerns, looked across the table to Sedgwick.

A couple of minutes later when Nesbit was done reading, Thwait said to Sedgwick, "I don't get it, ma'am. Is the bombing about destroying art or punishing one of our officers, or both?" He glanced at Nesbit expecting an answer and then turned back to Sedgwick. "Let me ask another question, if I may. Are we sure the museum bombing is related to the wiretap and not…well, you know, an unrelated coincidence?"

"Good questions," Sedgwick replied, leaning back in her chair. "The simple answer is that the wiretap, the bombing, and the extortion letters are related because HQ says they are. We can disagree, certainly, but we better have solid evidence to do so. What concerns me is that someone has a beef with one of our officers and that they're going to do something about it – and we haven't identified the officer."

Thwait wagged his head, and placed his heavy arms on the table and stared into the tray, as if it might contain something that would make sense of all these details. Nesbit, though, became silent, and the dull expression on his thin face suggested that something was bothering him.

"Agent Nesbit?" Sedgwick asked, sincerely concerned about a man she had trouble warming to.

Nesbit didn't immediately reply, and this time he wasn't being insolent or demonstrating his disregard for Sedgwick. There was something in the wiretap that didn't sit well with him. Initially, it may have been a word or two, or a chance combination of words and phrases, but as he replayed portions of the text over in his mind he became increasingly troubled, particularly when he couldn't pinpoint the exact reason why any of it should trouble him. For the first time in his storied career, the rational side of his brain was drawing a complete blank. It was as if he were staring at a picture that he knew was awry but couldn't tell whether it angled to the left or to the right. 'What is it?' he asked himself over and over. 'Something's not right, but what is it?' Reluctant to disclose his concerns, he shook his head slightly and said, "I think you're right, Inspector Sink…Sedgwick. There's more to this than meets the eye." Nesbit handed the copy of the wiretap back to Sedgwick.

"I'm sorry? I just wondered if something was wrong."

"No, nothing other than the crime," he replied pleasantly. "I'm ashamed to admit that for once I'm stumped. I still believe the Gray Ladies are works of art and, if they're not the Richardson Stones, then they're something in Sir Ronald's office, assuming that the wiretap and bombing are indeed connected." He noticed Thwait staring at him, openmouthed, as if he couldn't quite believe that Nesbit had made such an admission. Turning back to Sedgwick, Nesbit added, "my guess is that the constable in question is clueless about the threats to him, although it's hard to believe he wouldn't know that someone is insanely angry with him."

"That's an interesting point."

"By the way, has anyone spoken to Sir Ronald since the blast?"

"The Chief spoke to him after the blast and was planning to see him again today."

"Maybe there's something he can add to the investigation. In the meantime, unless the station has a database of vulnerable officers we can search, I think Constable Thwait and I should continue what we're doing. Could we have a copy of the wiretap? It might prove useful as we go along. We're planning to discuss the evidence over dinner, but we'll give you a complete rundown in the morning, if that's okay."

"That's fine, and keep the copy," she replied, handing the copy back to him. Sedgwick wanted to remind Thwait about expenses when Nesbit mentioned dinner, but she decided instead to rely on Thwait's judgment and memory.

"We'll be careful with the wiretap."

Sedgwick stood up to leave.

"Officer…Sedgwick," Nesbit began but turned away, and for a few moments the troubling expression came back across his face.

"Yes, Agent Nesbit?"

Nesbit looked at Sedgwick and shook his head. "Nothing. We'll keep you in the loop."

Sedgwick's mouth seemed almost straight. "I'll see if I can find anything on threats to our officers. I'll also see if I can find anything about threats to Sir Ronald and the museum. At this point, I think we should be open for anything."

Nesbit nodded and, once again, hesitated. "You're not convinced about the art angle, are you? You think it was an attack on Sir Ronald."

Over the years, Sedgwick had come to believe that nothing could surprise her. She wasn't jaded, and she would never have claimed to possess the Chief's knowledge and experience, and yet she had never encountered anything that seemed truly novel or beyond her imagination. Stealing the Richardson Stones would be extraordinary, but then she had worked a case in which a suspect had tried (but failed) to extract the statue of Lord Nelson off the monument in Trafalgar Square. And long before that, she read about a pair of would-be robbers who tried to rob the Bank of England by tunneling under the building into the vault – they drowned in the process when they took a wrong turn and hit one of the city's water mains. However, Nesbit's apparent sincerity in posing this question, coupled with the respectful, professional attitude that he now assumed, made her wonder if she had been wrong and that there were indeed a few new things under the sun. "I'll be honest," she began, feeling a greater sense of respect for Nesbit than she did when she arrived. "I really don't know. I could make an argument either way. But if you still think it's the art, follow it until something suggests otherwise. At some point we'll have to figure out what the Gray Ladies are."

Nesbit nodded, and Thwait verbally agreed.

Chapter 20

Nesbit and Thwait spent the rest of the day quietly going through the contents of the tray, tagging the items with numbered tape and cataloguing them in their respective notebooks (they planned to combine the notebooks as soon as they completed their inventory of the evidence).   Later that evening, at a nondescript, inexpensive pub (at Nesbit's recommendation) around the corner from the hotel, they discussed the evidence, the relevance of the letters, and naturally the wiretap.   Well, perhaps it's more accurate to say that their discussion was pretty much a monologue, although this time Thwait was doing most of the talking while Nesbit absently nodded from time to time and occasionally offered a noncommittal "interesting" or an indifferent "I suppose." Something had clearly come over Nesbit since his conversation with Sedgwick, and this fact was not entirely lost on Thwait. But instead of asking his friend if something was troubling him, he decided to wait until Nesbit was ready to share his thoughts, since it didn't seem appropriate for him to ask a man like Nesbit if he needed help. At the same time, Thwait was increasingly uncomfortable sitting silently with Nesbit, and so he kept up a nervous patter, hoping that the sound of his voice might bring Nesbit back to his senses or possibly release the man's inhibitions about sharing his thoughts.

"I don't know, sir, but I can't help thinking we're missing something," Thwait was saying between quick sips of a large drink. "I mean…well, on the one hand, we have the Gray Ladies and, on the other, Sir Ronald, and somewhere in-between are the letters and the wiretap.   I'm not trying to suggest they're all separate," he started to say but hesitated when he noticed an attractive young woman in tight jeans pass by the table on her way to the far end of the pub. "I'm, I'm, I'm simply not at all, not at all, if you know what I mean…," he stammered until the woman had taken a seat at a small table occupied by two friendly young men. Turning back to his friend, Thwait fell silent when he couldn't quite recover his train of thought.

Nesbit took a sip of his first and only glass of wine. "You know something, Tom," he said, breaking the silence and smiling warmly at his friend, "we all might be wrong. The facts, and they include the letters and the wiretap, might suggest an entirely different direction. But no sense getting bogged down in the weeds before we have sufficient evidence, right?"

"Yes, I couldn't agree more," Thwait replied eagerly, sensing a slight and positive change in his friend. "You're obviously onto something…big.

No, I couldn't agree more. But tell me, sir, what makes you think so? What makes you think that we could be wrong?" He stared at Nesbit with the eagerness of a puppy.

"I don't know," he replied after a slight hesitation. Nesbit picked up his glass, but instead of draining it, he placed it back on the clean, white tablecloth. "I think it's pretty much the same with every case – you wrestle with a few ideas until you have something. Well, if I come up with something between now and next time, you'll be the first to hear it. In the meantime, my friend, it's late and I'm tired."

Thwait was thrilled that Nesbit seemed to be coming out of his funk, and it pleased him to think that the great man had listened to him expound on the investigation when he obviously had other things on his mind. "Should we meet at the museum, sir?" he asked, smiling broadly. "We've only started to comb through the material."

"Yes, yes, we've only scratched the surface. There's still plenty to be done, Tom, and let's not forget the forensics evidence, whenever that's available. Once we put that together with our work, we might have something really interesting. Well, be sure to inform Inspector Sedgwick of everything and...," he paused and a strange look came over his hard features. "Did I tell you I'm speaking with my son later this evening? No? I told you we've been planning to get together, but so far we haven't managed to coordinate the time and place. Not surprising. He's up to his eyeballs in important work (big projects, lots of responsibility), and it's difficult to find the time to get away. I can assure you, though, he regrets it more than he can say. The important thing is that we'll talk tonight, if possible, and meet some other time when our schedules allow." Nesbit signed the bill with a flourish and, winking to his friend, got up from the table. Gently adjusting his tie and then flicking a crumb off one of the lapels, he squeezed Thwait's left shoulder and left.

Thwait turned and watched the older man as he stepped onto a wire and was lifted over the heads of the patrons. Hands nonchalantly in his pockets, he walked effortlessly and unerringly across the wire to far end of the establishment where, with a slight hop, he jumped down and disappeared out the door. It felt like a dream. Uttering a soft "amazing," Thwait recalled that his friend was always doing amazing things, things that could (and often did) confound one's sense of reality. Take this evening, for instance. Nesbit listened to every word he said and, although he appeared distracted and maybe a little out of sorts, he nevertheless gave credence to his theory (which he had made up on the spot) about the possibility that there could be two, maybe three unrelated cases, or something like that. Nesbit often listened to his ideas, but this time Nesbit seemed to be playing Thwait to his, Thwait's, Nesbit.

Thwait smiled at the thought, but he couldn't help wondering if this day had happened exactly the way it appeared to have happened. Had Nesbit really listened to him, had he actually been deferential to Sedgwick, or were these hallucinations emanating from a tired and overworked mind? Prior to today, Nesbit had for some unknown reason disdained Sedgwick and belittled her abilities, and he often compared her to his ex-wife, who Nesbit claimed was a monstrous individual. But something changed at the museum, and he not only showed her respect but deferred to her on one or two things, important things, just as he listened to Thwait...

Thwait suddenly felt tired and his drooping eyelids wouldn't allow him to concentrate effectively on such weighty matters. He rolled his shoulders and then rubbed his tired eyes with the heels of his heavy hands. Standing up, he straightened his jacket and brushed something off its front, which left a broad landing strip from the lapel practically to the bottom edge of the coat, and, yanking his tie roughly to one side, trudged heavily (stumbling only once against a table of rattling glasses) out the door and somehow made his way home for the evening.

Chapter 21

Nesbit paused outside the pub and, after patting his pockets for something, hurried to the hotel. Once inside his room, he would have followed his normal routine (having a drink while watching the evening news), but he had more important things on his mind. He fished the cell phone out of his vest pocket and then dropped to the corner of his bed to wait until the agreed-upon time. Closing his eyes, though careful not to fall asleep, he unexpectedly recalled the last time he spoke to her which, coincidently, was the last time he would ever speak to her, since she died a few months after the call.

She had answered the phone with a faint 'hello' and then lapsed into a near stony silence as soon as he began talking.

'Look, I'm only asking for a few minutes,' he pleaded for perhaps the fifth time. His own voice was beginning to sound weak, and he was certain that his words lacked the qualities that Thwait had associated with the strong, successful man he worked with and admired. 'Please,' he continued, 'only for a few minutes. How do you know he doesn't want to speak to me? Look, you're right that I spent too much time away from home, you're right that I ignored him on the rare occasions when I was home, and you're right about everything else as well – I was an insensitive husband and an absent, uncaring father. You're absolutely right. But people change – I changed, and I regret everything I did that hurt you and our son. I also realize that I can't make up for the past.' Except for an occasional and faint sniffle (did she have a cold?), there was hardly a sound coming from the other end of the line.

'Okay, do you want to hear it again?' he continued when the silence was too much. 'All right, I didn't come home because I was either working or partying. Do you remember the day after we first brought him home from the hospital? I told you that I was leaving for a conference in Costa Rica – I know you remember, but there're aspects to the story that you don't know. For instance, there was no conference. I made it all up. I went to Costa Rica, but I went there because…because I couldn't handle the responsibility of a wife and newborn child. I took a vacation, and I let you deal with the crying and the diapers and all the rest, while I soaked up the sun, drank cocktails, and took long walks on the beach. There weren't any women, I promise you.

'I did it because I wanted the peace of mind to solve great cases…I just wanted to think of something other than babies and problems and all the rest. I felt confident that as soon as Ben got bigger and less demanding, I could come home and really take this father thing seriously. Maybe if I wasn't having the time of my life....' He was silent for a moment as he recalled several incidents of the past. 'A few years later,' he continued when the images faded, 'I toyed with the idea of coming home and staying there. I was more mature, and I finally felt ready to handle the responsibilities of home life. My feelings, though, changed one afternoon as I was walking home from the train station and spotted you and Ben playing in the front yard. I don't know how to explain it, but my knees began to shake, my throat began to constrict, and before either of you noticed me, I ran back to the station. I couldn't do it. Call me a coward or whatever, but I...but I simply couldn't do it.' He hesitated and then added, 'I'm telling you all this now, so that you'll see that I am done with the lies, the prevarications, and everything else that made your lives...unhappy.'

Nesbit paused and shook his head. Sure, he said to himself, he had spent a fair amount of time away from home, but that was only because he had a demanding, high-profile job, and there were lots of people, very important people, depending on him. But she didn't make it easy for him to come home. She was demanding and irritable, and no matter what he did for her, it was never enough or else it was wrong and bad. Nevertheless, he had to say these things, he had to tell her what she wanted to hear, otherwise she wouldn't let him speak to his son. It was a child's game that she had forced him to play many times in the past. 'I admit all of it,' he continued, gulping down his indignation. 'You were right, and I was wrong. At least I wasn't unfaithful, not even once, unlike so many others...you're right, it doesn't make things better or offset the damage I caused. Look, I know I can't make up for the past, but at least I can apologize directly to my son, if you'll let me. For God's sake, please let me speak to him, or at least say something to let me know that you've been listening.'

There was a slight muffled sound on the other end. She didn't hang up, which gave him a slender reed on which to hang his hope that she might eventually relent.

'Look, I'm only asking for a few minutes, a few seconds. He can control both the length and content of the call.' When she again failed to respond, he could sense his self-control beginning to slip and he bit the inside of his cheeks to keep his voice and emotions under control. 'Please,' he said again, 'I'm begging you.' His hands began to shake, and he noticed with surprise that his jaw was moving in a circular motion. Taking a deep, calming breath, he added once more for good measure, 'please, for God's sake, Ben's practically a grown man. He is a grown man. I can't fathom why he's still living with you instead of being out on his own, making his own decisions – and it's his right, not yours, to decide whether or not to speak to me. Do you hear me? Are you listening to me? Are you?'

'Yes, I'm listening to you,' she finally said. Her voice seemed stronger than it did before, as if she had unexpectedly become healthy and regained her strength. 'I've always listened to you. How could I not listen to you? But that's the problem, isn't it? On those rare occasions when you graced us with your presence, we were forced to listen to you, listen to you talk about you, listen to you jabber on about all the great things you were doing, about all the things that made you so high and mighty, and not once did you ever shut your mouth and listen to us. Did you ever ask how we were doing in your absence? Did you ever ask about our feelings? Did you ever ask how we felt about your trips to Jamaica, Jakarta, Juneau, Junk, wherever? Couldn't you have at least once...,' her voice momentarily weakened and once again she sniffed. Gathering her breath, she began to speak more calmly, albeit somewhat distantly. 'You're right, Ben is an adult, and he makes his own decisions. He grew up a long time ago when you weren't around. Ben lives with me because he wants to, and he can leave anytime he desires.'

Nesbit closed his eyes and then glanced at the ceiling. He realized that one more misstep and the call would be over, and any opportunity to speak to his son could be delayed for years, if not forever. "You're right. I admitted as much a few minutes ago. But since Ben's an adult, why don't you ask him if he'll exchange a few words with me? Let him make his own decision. Didn't you just say he had that right as an adult?'

'What makes you think he wants to talk to you? What makes you think I haven't already asked him if he wants to talk to you? Do you know what he said when I asked him?'

'When did you ask him? Just now?'

'I asked him immediately after the divorce. I asked him a few months after that. And I have been asking him on a regular basis, every few months or so. I've never kept him from you. Do you know what he always says? He says he's not interested in speaking to you. He says he doesn't give a damn about you. He says the same thing every time. I've tried to tell him that he might regret his decision. Do you know what he says? Well, he used to say he no longer has a father, but now he only gestures obscenely at the mention of your name. I don't approve of obscenities, but it's clear you're not even worth a few words to him. I can't say I blame him.'

"I don't believe you. If it's true, you've taught him that. You've filled his mind so full of your own foul thoughts that he can only puppet what you've taught him."

"No," she laughed and coughed several times in succession. "It's all in your own warped little mind. I'd like to have him speak to you, if only to learn firsthand what you're really like, if only to let him put you in your place, but he's not interested. He practically spits at the thought because you're not worth the words. You're not worth..."

Unable to bear another word from her, Nesbit slammed the phone onto the dresser, and banged it several more times after that so that she would get the point. For a few minutes, he stormed around his apartment, cursing her, cursing the British legal system, and cursing everything else that was causing him so many problems. Charging back into the living room, he threw himself onto the rented, uncomfortable sofa and began chiding his son, whose framed baby picture was ensconced in a shadow on a narrow table just out of reach. The boy didn't have a brain in his skull, he told himself, if he listened to his mother. And he would never amount to anything if he continued to live with her. He could have gone to college, he could have started a career, he could have done something with his life, and instead he chose to throw everything away for that... Even though the sun was still above the horizon, the room was dark because the curtains were tightly closed and he hadn't turned on a single lamp. Having stretched out on his back, he draped his right arm over his tired eyes and wept.

It was now nearly ten o'clock, and his hotel room was bright and pleasant. Of course, everything had been settled earlier, but he felt oddly uncomfortable calling so late in the evening. The young man was bound to be tired after a long day, he might even have had a pint or two with his mates after work, and so the conversation could be short and strained. 'Well,' he told himself to ease some of the tensions he was feeling before he dialed the young man's number, 'it can't be helped. I need to speak to him, and I'll coax him into meeting me.' Returning to the corner of the bed in the center of the room, Nesbit sat down, straightened his back and, for a few seconds, limbered his shoulders. "Don't push, don't push," he whispered to himself as if he were reciting a mantra.

The phone on the other end rang several times. Just when he thought that no one would pick up, a masculine voice spoke Nesbit's name.

"How did you know it was me? Yes, that's right, we agreed."

Nesbit paused, inhaled deeply to settle his nerves, and continued speaking. The conversation was fairly short and pretty much one-sided. Whatever was said, Nesbit was becoming increasingly agitated, although he did a remarkably good job of appearing calm and not showing his emotions. At one point, perhaps four or five minutes into the conversation, Nesbit must have said something, or the young man must have said something else, and the connection was lost. Nesbit, thinking that the connection was still live and that the young man might have a silent streak like his mother, continued to speak and at one point asked the young man if he was listening.

"Are you listening to me, for God's sake?" he cried into the dead line when there was no response. "You don't know what you're saying. I can help. Damn you, don't be a fool! And don't hang up! Don't hang up!"

When he finally realized that the connection had been lost, he immediately redialed the number only to hear it ring a couple of times before stopping. Desperate, praying that he had simply misdialed the number, he called it again, and again it rang a couple of times before going silent. Unwilling to give up, he tried the number several more times, and each time the phone at the other end rang two times before disconnecting. Flustered to the point of distraction, and realizing that it was pointless to call the number again this evening, Nesbit got up and walked around the room to calm his anger and settle his breathing, which by this time was heavy. A few moments later, he seemed fine and resigned to waiting another day before trying to reconnect with the young man. Passing by the table in the center of the room and noticing some papers on the investigation near its edge, he stopped and, raising the phone to eye level, began squeezing it as if to punish it for what had happened. An instant before it shattered, however, he had second thoughts and slipped it back into his vest pocket.

Nesbit dropped to the corner of his bed and remained motionless for several minutes. His jaw suddenly began shaking, and he brought both hands up and grabbed his head as if it were a football. Moaning and cursing incoherently, he rocked back and forth for several minutes before falling back on the bed and rolling over onto his side. He remained motionless for a few more minutes before finally falling asleep.

The following morning, Nesbit called Thwait and informed him that he was going to be out for the day and that, in all likelihood, he would probably be out for several days. Nesbit's voice was calm though distant, and Thwait began to wonder if his friend had contracted something from the crime scene, which, after all, was rather foul smelling. Just before ending the call, Thwait promised to keep him apprised of the investigation, including anything that Sedgwick or the Chief said. Nesbit thanked him with a nod of his aching head and gently pushed the off button. Still in the clothes that he had worn the previous day, Nesbit straightened his tie without consulting a mirror, absently brushed off the front of his coat and slacks, and left the room.

Chapter 22

He knew it like the back of his hand. Really, how could anyone forget the gray stone walls, the ancient-looking windows, or the narrow gable on top, which had always reminded him of a cottage in one of the fairy tales he had read as a child? There was also a white, picket fence that marked off the perimeter of the property. The fence seemed a little out of place among the low, stone walls that surrounded most of the cottages in that region, but it was bright and fresh and between the slats you could catch glimpses of a colorful garden in front and a manicured lawn in back. The flat, open fields surrounding the cottage were memorable, too, especially when the long grasses swayed back and forth in the wind as if they were under water, or when the clouds momentarily parted after a heavy rain to permit silver rays of sunlight to illuminate distant fields along the horizon. Yes, he remembered all of it and much more, including the ivy-covered, dying tree to the side just outside the fence, and the wind's constant soughing at night when the air turned cold and hard. And he didn't need a map, GPS, or anything else to find his way there.

Once outside the heaviest city traffic, Nesbit angled his car onto the highway and then carefully merged into the center lane, where he would stay for the next hour and a half. On the outskirts of Oxford, he took the first exit toward the village and followed it until he reached a narrow, two-lane road bordered on both sides by tall hedge rows, some of which were over fifteen feet tall. Thirty minutes later, after dodging a couple of lorries coming in the opposite direction, he reached the first roundabout, but instead of going halfway around and emerging in the same direction, he continued right (a natural mistake) and another thirty minutes later found himself merging back onto the highway and heading toward London. Pulling off the highway at the next exit, he attempted to make a U-turn at a narrow intersection and ended up in front of a small pub. Nesbit asked the proprietor, a heavyset individual with three days' growth on his surprisingly narrow face, for directions, and an hour later he was back on the highway and heading the right way, this time a little warmer and fuzzier than he had been for a couple of days.

The village was a good thirty miles outside of Oxford. Once he reached the main thoroughfare, a two-lane cobblestone road, he followed it as it meandered between old stone buildings, around the WWI memorial (a blackened statue of a soldier holding a rifle and jabbing at something with the bayonet), and under a thin, empty pedestrian walkway, until he came to the end of the street. Turing left (there was no other direction to turn), he pulled up in front of a small dairy and parked. The dairy was closed and, as he stood in the middle of the street adjusting his tie and getting his bearings, he noticed the small, stone church down the road. Once a popular landmark for villagers and tourists, it was boarded up and, from the looks of it, hadn't been open for years. In fact, no matter where he turned, the village appeared closed or deserted, even though it was still early in the afternoon. Scratching his head, he noticed up the street a colorless old man and his equally transparent female companion, neither of whom noticed him as they entered one of the buildings across from the church.

Nesbit crossed the damp street to another between two buildings. The road, which was now hardly more than a series of broken or uneven cobblestones, connected the village to the back road that enabled the "outsiders" to come into the town with their produce and other goods. But as Nesbit walked over the small rocks and debris, he wondered if it had gone out of commission on the very day that the church boarded up its stained-glass windows. Well, the road was short, a little more than a hundred yards at most, and it ended, as he recalled, at the main artery that would lead to his destination. But if he had been surprised at the condition of the road between the buildings, he was shocked at the condition of the artery. Once an important thoroughfare, it was now hardly more than dirt and gravel, covered here and there by small, gray puddles (wasn't it paved the last time he crossed it?). But at least it was still level, which might limit some of the discomfort of walking in snug dress shoes – and he needed to walk, because driving would announce his presence in this part of the country. Inhaling the cool, hay-scented air, Nesbit started following the dirt and gravel road, the sounds of small rocks crunching beneath his once shiny shoes, as it paralleled the edge of the village for about a hundred yards or so before angling right and burrowing into the rolling, grass-covered fields.

There were only a few signs of habitation beyond the village. Of course, the surrounding area had never been particularly populous, and yet a fair amount of traffic did enter from this side of town, and, as he recalled from the numerous drives he had taken up and down the road, there were often lively activities going on around the houses and buildings that dotted the landscape. But the road was now deserted and, while there were still houses and buildings of some kind in sight, many of them seemed to be neglected and more than a few with windows that were broken or even missing. One large, barn-like building, for example, was sheared off at one end; the rest of the wobbly structure was covered with rust and ivy, as if no one had come near the place in years, perhaps not since the demise of the church. There was also a waist-high stone fence or wall (which, for some reason, he hadn't recalled seeing before) that zigzagged across the fields before abruptly disappearing in the distance to his right. But whatever the original intent in erecting it, it was useless now because it was broken and crumbling along its entire, visible length.

As if the countryside wasn't peculiar enough, the road lost its evenness a little farther on and was scarred on either side by two deep, parallel ruts, which reminded him of the kind of marks that horse-drawn wagons leave over time. But there were no signs of horses anywhere, and there wasn't a wagon in sight, not even along the horizon. Increasingly hot and uncomfortable, although the air was cool and the sun hidden by a thick bank of clouds that stretched from one end of the sky to the other, he carefully removed his coat and, after brushing the dust off the back, he tied it around his waist, using the sleeves as a belt. Luckily, the road was still relatively straight and fairly level, just as he remembered it, and whenever the surrounding countryside rose or fell, the roadbed either cut through the offending areas or built on top of them. But contrary to both his expectations and his memories, the low hills and shallow valleys of the area soon began to increase in size and depth, and the road (or its builders) had little choice but to follow suit, reaching up one long incline and stretching down an equally distant decline, and every now and then twisting and bending around hills that looked like gigantic animal burrows.

Nesbit paused at the base of one particularly imposing hill. Looking up at its gently rounded summit, which seemed obscured by the low, heavy clouds, he breathed deeply several times to increase his lung capacity, and as he started upward he wondered what he would do if a car approached from either direction (the hill was smooth and covered with short grass, and so there weren't a lot of places to hide). He shrugged his shoulders when no satisfactory solution came to mind and continued climbing, each step more laborious than the previous one, each gasp of air more difficult than the last. When he finally reached the top, he stopped and, instead of getting his bearings, immediately bent over and tried to catch his breath. "This must be what poor Tom feels," he told himself, breathing heavily. When he was finally ready to continue, he wiped the sweat from his face with his shirt sleeve, cinched his coat around his waist, and, after taking a quick look around, began moving downward, this time taking large strides and using gravity to his advantage. About halfway down, he stopped (nearly falling over) and looked to his right where, a few feet from the edge of the road, a portion of the hill had fallen away (no doubt in primordial times) to reveal a level plain that stretched out as far as he could see. Confident that he was nearing the end of his journey, Nesbit paused to wipe the sweat from his eyes and face and then practically jogged down the rest of the hill and up the small rise that followed.

Once he reached the top, he paused to look at the plain, which was covered with short grass, ragged bushes, and a few stunted trees. He noticed, on his left, a dry creek bed that meandered toward the horizon and back along the road (it wasn't visible from the road). Pivoting to the right, he spotted a small cottage about twenty yards from the base of the rise. The cottage had been constructed out of the same rocks that littered sections of the plain, and yet it looked anything but sturdy. The building's sides looked uneven, and its gable was listing backward as if it were being pulled in that direction by the sagging roof. Scanning the area immediately surrounding the cottage, Nesbit saw what looked like a picket fence marking off the perimeter of the property. The slats, however, were lying face down, and most of them were either rotting or overgrown with weeds. What was most surprising was that the area between the edge of the slats and the base of the house was covered with mounds of trash – cans, bottles, boxes, rags, pieces of machinery, a rusted washer helplessly on its side, and an old pickup dulled and rusted with age. It looked like a dump. Nothing was as he remembered it, nothing about the cottage suggested a fairy tale (unless the Brothers Grimm had written it), and yet he was positive that he had arrived at the right location.

Stepping back and crouching down so that he wasn't quite so visible, Nesbit looked around for something or some place that would provide sufficient cover from which to observe the cottage without being observed in return. He had been scouring the area for several minutes when he spotted a large, oblong shadow in the grass near the top of the hill some twenty feet to his right. The shadow proved to be a shallow cavity in the earth, and its dimensions along with its location suited his purposes exactly. Carefully placing his coat in the cavity, Nesbit lowered himself stomach down onto the coat, and as he squirmed this way and that to get comfortable on the hard ground, he began to feel the cool moisture from the grass beneath him quickly penetrate the front of his slacks, the elbows of his shirt, and finally his coat, soaking his chest. Shivering slightly, he readjusted himself a couple more times – the first time to get a little more comfortable (even with his coat, the ground was anything but smooth beneath the grass), and the second to position his head better so that he had a clear line of sight to the cottage.

"My God, it's unbelievable. It doesn't make sense," Nesbit muttered to himself as he squirmed and readjusted himself to avoid something large and uncomfortable underneath his coat. But the instant he was free from this impediment and, once again, was able to position himself relatively comfortably, he caught sight of a slender young man coming out of the house. Dressed in loose-fitting, piebald pants and jacket, the man walked across the yard, kicking something out of the way as he did so, and got into the truck. The truck groaned a couple of times before finally turning over and, once the gears were painfully engaged, jerked out of the yard, leaving behind a rapidly disappearing plume of exhaust. Seconds later, the truck rounded the hill in front of Nesbit and bounced into the distance behind him without slowing down.

Chapter 23

Once the truck's roar and clanging had faded into the distance, Nesbit stood up and took a quick look to see if the truck was out of sight. Satisfied that it wasn't coming back in the next few minutes, he brushed off the mud and water from the front of his clothes and picked up his coat. Since his coat was completely soaked, he shook it several times to remove the water and then twisted it several more times to wring out the last sparkling drops before putting it on. He shivered slightly, adjusted his tie, and then started for the cottage.

After a few slippery steps up and away from the cavity, he was once again at the top of the rise. However, instead of trudging downward, he paused to take another look at the area around him and then at the area around the cottage. It was a professional habit. But as he observed the cottage, he couldn't help wondering why she had chosen this place after their separation. She could have lived anywhere (she could have lived in the village, for God's sake), and yet after having complained for years that she was lonely, she insisted on a solitary cottage in an empty countryside miles away from the nearest soul. It didn't make sense. Sure the area was beautiful (and who wouldn't be tempted to exchange London's leaden skies for the silvery skies overhead?), but it might as well have been Timbuktu for all it offered in terms easing her solitude. 'And the trash, was that hers, too?' he wondered, recalling how tidy she was and her horror of misplacing things. He straightened his tie again and proceeded cautiously down the gentle, slippery hill, hoping that a closer inspection of the cottage might give him the answers he needed to make sense of her, of him, and of…things.

Using the edges of his shoes to keep from falling, Nesbit stomped sideways down the gently sloping hill, slipping only once during the three or four minutes it took to come within a couple feet of the bottom. He was proud of himself for having descended so adroitly, and he stopped to readjust his footing before taking another step. But just as he was about to take one giant step to level ground, one of his shoes (probably the left) gave way and he finished the descent on the seat of his pants. Irritated but under control, he stood up with as much dignity as he could muster and brushed the dirt and twigs from his clothing. After straightening each coat sleeve and readjusting his tie, he started for the cottage, angling toward the building in such a way as to prevent anyone inside from seeing his approach. When he was about ten yards away, he turned sharply toward the side of the cottage where there weren't any windows and hurried over until he rested his back against its crumbling stones.

He held his breath and listened for signs that someone was nearby. Birds chirped, something faintly squawked, and a gust of wind arose and briefly rattled the rubbish surrounding the building. Nothing, however, suggested that someone other than himself was prowling about the cottage. Warily confident that he could continue (at the same time cognizant of the possibility of the truck driver's imminent return), Nesbit tiptoed around the corner to the back of the cottage, stepping over debris and pushing aside cans, bottles, and food wrappers with his scuffed shoes, and, with his back still against the house, made his way to the back door. The door, gray and peeling, looked as ancient as the stones of the building. Unlike the rest of the cottage's backside, it actually had a window, albeit one that was little more than a dirty, circular piece of glass occupying nearly half of the upper portion of the door. Again pressing his back against the building (next to the door) and using his fingertips against the building to steady himself, Nesbit placed his tender ear against the rough stones and listened for evidence of someone inside. There was silence, and, pushing away from the wall, he cautiously peeked through the cloudy window.

Even though the lights were out, he could see the inside fairly well because of the sunlight streaming through the window on the opposite side of the cottage. Surprisingly, he hadn't remembered that the cottage was practically a single room, and not only could he see almost everything inside but he could also see out the front windows, which could be useful if someone were on the other side of the building. Equally surprising, the cottage was just as dirty inside as it was outside. The floor was littered with trash – cans, assorted clothing, a pile of rags in one corner which appeared to be a makeshift bed, balls of paper, and some peculiar objects on the floor against one of the walls (the objects looked like animal droppings through there wasn't an animal in sight). What happened to the furniture, the pictures on the walls, the decorations, and those bloody knickknacks that she loved because of their sentiment and that he despised because of their triteness? Glancing behind him and to both sides to make sure he was unseen, Nesbit jiggled the handle to see if the door was unlocked. It was.

He again pressed his back against the stone wall. Taking a deep breath, he reached out to the handle and, while slowly turning it with his right hand, pushed the door open with the heel of his right foot. That is, he pushed it open maybe an inch or two until it stopped and wouldn't budge any more. Not expecting it to require so much effort, he cautiously reached over added extra force with the palm of his right hand. The door opened another inch perhaps, but that was it. Puzzled, Nesbit asked himself why the door should be so resistant. Was something blocking it? Or were the hinges rusted, making it all but impossible to open without removing it from the frame? Taking another deep breath, he slowly pivoted toward the window and once again looked inside. Since nothing seemed amiss with respect to the door, he placed his right shoulder against it and forced it halfway open, after which no amount of pressure would budge it any more. When it was open this much, he spotted a dirty towel or rag wedged partly underneath it, preventing it from opening fully. But because there was enough room to squeeze through, he didn't try to remove the filthy obstruction.

Once inside the dusky building, he detected a foul smell and quickly pulled out his handkerchief and held it over his nose. He couldn't tell if the smell emanated from rotting food or from the dirt and trash on the floor, but wherever it came from it was strong enough and disgusting enough to make him feel like retching (on the positive side, it did spur him to finish his business as quickly as possible). Stepping over a lump of something on the floor, he walked two or three feet farther into the room, carefully watching where he stepped and what he stepped in or on. He paused momentarily to avoid what appeared to be droppings from an animal larger than a rodent, but when he failed to spot anything resembling such a creature, he started to wonder what might be lying under some of the papers, behind some of the cans, or around a large, cardboard box, which, apart from a couple of plastic chairs and a beat-up table, was the only furniture in the place. Curiously, there was an expensive-looking laptop on the table. Nesbit tiptoed over to the unit and noticed that one of its lights was on. Tapping a key, the screen lit up and demanded a password. Since he wasn't prepared to break into the machine or take it with him, he continued looking around the room for something, anything, that would help him understand this or what might be going on in the young man's mind. Nothing, though, not even the pile of dirty, nondescript clothes in the far corner, offered a clue.

Nesbit stepped cautiously to the front window and glanced at the hill and then at the flattened dirt and trash where the truck had been parked. The countryside was as lovely from this angle as it had been from the top of the hill.

Perhaps he could understand – a little – why she had lived here, but to live like this was impossible to understand if, indeed, she had lived like this. But to live like this wasn't living. This was like squatting in a cesspool, and he promised himself that as soon as he got back to his hotel he would take a good, hot shower – maybe two of them. He turned and caught sight of something just outside the window. Craning his head, he saw a lawn chair made of wooden slats. 'Could it be?' he asked himself. She had a chair like that when they were still married. In fact, he had given it to her as a symbolic promise that he would slow down and begin spending his weekends at home. Actually, it was one of a set of chairs, and they had planned to arrange them on some back porch so that they could sit side-by-side on summer evenings and watch the sky's fading light. But he hadn't kept that promise, and they ceased living together, and so maybe it was right that there was only one left.

Nesbit shook his head and turned to leave when he caught sight of something on the floor. It was hardly more than a small, grayish smudge situated between two empty cans of food, but it looked strikingly familiar. Pulling his handkerchief away from his nose, he used it to grasp the small item. Once safely in his handkerchief, he examined it carefully, after which he wrapped it up in the handkerchief and placed both in his coat pocket. The item was a little box, exactly like the one he found on the floor at the blast site in the museum.

He didn't know how long he had been inside the stinking place, but he was beginning to fear that if the smell didn't kill him, the truck would return before he had a chance to get out – and, if the latter happened, he didn't know how he would be able to slip out and make it back to the hill without being seen. Carefully treading back toward the door, he stopped and looked over his shoulder at the room. A loud whoosh suddenly reverberated through the small place – somebody had flushed a toilet. How could he have forgotten the cottage's bathroom? Well, he wasn't going to wait another second in order to meet the resident, who had been in the bathroom only inches away the entire time he had been in the cottage. Turning back around, he moved quickly, stepping onto God-knows-what until he reached the back door, which was now almost closed. After three strenuous attempts to open the door over the vile rag, he finally managed to yank open the door wide enough to squeeze through while still retaining the buttons on his vest.

Nesbit crouched low and quickly made his way around to the windowless side of the cottage. Pressing himself flat against the wall, he could hear now some movement inside – some clanging and what sounded like a muffled voice irritably exclaiming something – and, without a second thought, he charged straight ahead, running as far as he could before stumbling into the shallow stream bed, which he followed for at least a mile until it fortuitously intersected with the road that led him back to the village. Along the way, especially as he left the hills, he began to worry that he might come across the truck, which naturally would put him in an uncomfortable position. Luckily, he didn't encounter anyone either on the road or in the village. By the time he got back to his car, it was getting dark and a handful of pale lights were fitfully flickering from some of the nearby buildings.

Nesbit was exhausted when he reached his hotel. But instead of following his normal routine, he immediately extracted his once-pristine, silk handkerchief and shook the box it contained into a plastic clothes bag and rolled up the bag and secreted it into the corner of his briefcase. Shortly afterwards, he shed all his clothes and placed them into another one of the plastic bags (he could still smell the cottage on his clothes), and placed the bag in the hallway next to his door. As soon as he left a message with the staff that he wanted everything cleaned for the morning, he took a long, hot shower (scrubbing his hands until they were practically raw) and went to bed.

Chapter 24

It was mid-day when the Chief returned from briefing HQ on his meeting with Sir Ronald. The director was upset, of course, but he insisted that he had no idea why anyone would want to kill him or damage the museum. In fact, at one point, he suggested that pursuing either theory was a waste of time, adding that if the Chief and HQ couldn't resolve this case before something else happened (he was referring to the letters and the possibility of paying an outrageous and inappropriate ransom), he would task the resourceful Miss Montague to handle matters. After expressing their concern over Sir Ronald's discomfiture, HQ nevertheless insisted that the investigation was heading down the right path and instructed the Chief to retrieve some additional files relating to the Sanders case. Luckily, they had not taken the Chief or the station to task for Sir Ronald's unhappiness.

Having sent the files electronically, the Chief called Sedgwick into his office to update her on this latest visit to HQ. He also wanted to go over certain "issues" that seemed to be floating around HQ with increasing frequency. But while they were discussing these various things, the Chief's phone started to growl angrily, a sure sign in his eyes that HQ wanted something else from him. For a couple of minutes, the Chief listened passively to the voice on the other end, although his eye was twitching and his lips had a firm, almost stone-like frown across them. When he hung up, he paused for a moment as if ruminating on the something before turning to Sedgwick.

"That was HQ. There's been another explosion."

"The Ravenswood?"

"No, the Evermore Auction House. It happened a couple hours ago. The two closest stations are already on the scene."

"What? I can't believe we weren't advised of it earlier. Any details?"

"It appears that there were two explosions, both occurring in or around the CEO's office. HQ thinks that the CEO was injured, although it's not clear at this juncture if his injuries are life threatening. HQ also thinks this event is connected to the Ravenswood bombing. Take Thwait and Nesbit and find out what happened."

Sedgwick nodded and was heading for the door when the Chief called her back.

"Solid evidence – we're not going to connect the two without it."

"Yes, of course, Chief." Sedgwick was again about leave when the Chief's phone rang.

"Wait," he said, and picked up the phone. Pressing the receiver to his left ear, he uttered "yes" multiple times (pausing once to scribble something on a scrap of paper), "no" one time, and "damn it" a good half-dozen times. At one point, after a long silence, he uttered the phrase three times in succession. After placing the phone back into its cradle, he stood up and rolled down his sleeves. "It sounds like the CEO didn't make it."

"My God, dead?"

The Chief squinted at Sedgwick. "Well, I don't exactly know. I thought that's what HQ indicated, but now I'm not entirely sure what they meant. Either way, they're hysterical."

"Okay, we're on it now." Sedgwick again stood up, but this time she was the one who hesitated. "Chief," she asked, "did HQ say why they thought this bombing was linked to the Gray Ladies investigation?"

"The what investigation?" the Chief asked, squinting. "Ah, yes, the Gray Ladies investigation." With his right palm, he massaged the back of his neck before responding. "Let me see if I can put this succinctly. I don't have any insight into their rationale, and so I don't have a clue about why they think one thing and not another. I am amazed by how quickly they came to a definitive conclusion, but don't ask me how they did it. If you have a better answer, make sure you have rock-solid evidence to back it up – and even that might not be enough."

"Right, Chief."

"Another thing. HQ thinks there may be an eyewitness to the Evermore bombing."

"An eyewitness?"

"I guess. According to what little they said (and I'm going to embellish it a bit to make the story clearer), there was an elderly woman in front of the Auction House at the time of the explosion. She was on her way home when she heard a loud clap emanating from inside the building. She seems to have been looking at the building for a spell (no doubt trying to understand what had happened) when a young man came flying outside and bounced into her, knocking her to the ground. The young man remained on his feet and was hovering over her while she was gathering her senses. When she finally had enough of her wits about her to ask him what happened, there was another piercing clap from inside and the individual turned and fled down one of the side streets. She called Scotland Yard a short while ago, but since we're leading the Gray Ladies' investigation, as you call it, HQ wants us to check it out."

"Right, Chief," Sedgwick said and paused. "I'm sorry, but did HQ say the man was running from inside the building or from the direction of the building?"

"I don't know." The Chief handed her the scrap of paper. "Here's the address. Now go see what's happening at the Evermore."

Sedgwick nodded and left without another word. Minutes later as she was speeding toward the Evermore in a police unit, she called Thwait and instructed him and Nesbit to meet her at the command post, if they had one. "If not, then let's rendezvous someplace within sight of the main doors," she quickly added. "Unfortunately, at this point we don't have an understanding of the situation, so remain in close contact."

"Yes, ma'am," Thwait responded. Despite an aching head and upset stomach that had slowed him down earlier, he was already in motion, closing the Ravenswood loading bay door behind him and heading for his car, which was parked just outside the large door. "By the way," he added as he approached his car, "Agent Nesbit isn't available. He called in sick earlier, and he said he probably wouldn't be available tomorrow, either."

There was a slight pause before Sedgwick responded. "Bad timing, I suppose, but it can't be helped. Does he know about the bombing?"

"I can't see how. This is the first I've heard of it."

"Yes, quite right. I wasn't thinking."

By this time, Thwait was on the road and driving in and around traffic, rounding corner after corner at breakneck speed. In fact, his exertions in keeping up the incredible pace while struggling to keep the car on the road left him short of breath, forcing him to end the call with Sedgwick prematurely.

They arrived simultaneously. Parking side by side in a narrow street within sight of the auction house (every other place seemed blocked off by trucks or police cordons), they immediately began scouting out the command post, which was not easy to spot in the dim light and with all the officers, firemen, and others running back and forth and making way for emergency vehicles. After several minutes of fruitlessly asking officers and others if there was an officer in charge or a command post, they spotted several bright lights about a hundred yards to their left that were faintly glowing in the dull haze that hovered above the area. Heading toward the lights, despite warnings from a couple of individuals who didn't immediately recognize them as officers, they managed to reach its periphery before being stopped and required to show their credentials. Thwait, naturally, was slower than Sedgwick, and it took him a little longer to get close enough to the illuminated area to see a knot of officers and support crew of some kind (judging by their overalls and hard hats) standing near several large spotlights that appeared to be angled toward the darkening sky.

When he was nearly within shouting distance of these individuals, Thwait was forced to stop to catch his breath and ease the throbbing pain in his right side. Trying to stand nonchalantly amid the almost frenzied movements of the others around him, he rubbed his side and scanned the building looming to his left, which was a large, two-story warehouse-like construction with a gray colonnade on either side of the front, glass entrance door. Nothing seemed amiss until he noticed the right side of the building and a portion of the structure's roof. Both sections were emitting thick plumes of smoke, as if the building itself were sitting on a large, invisible burner and being overcooked. Thwait wasn't completely surprised, he understood what was happening, but as he turned to follow Sedgwick, he caught a whiff of an acrid, electric smell floating through the air. The odor didn't last very long, and yet he got enough of it to be almost certain that it was the same odor that permeated the Ravenswood Museum. Promising himself to bring it up later, Thwait turned to locate Sedgwick and spotted her conversing with a couple of individuals in the knot of people they noticed a few seconds ago. Once again, Thwait followed as quickly as he could only this time another officer stopped him a few yards from a strip of plastic police tape that cordoned off the area where Sedgwick and the others were conversing. It was the command post.

The officer was about Thwait's age, albeit slightly taller and definitely thinner despite his heavy vest, and he demanded to see Thwait's credentials before allowing him to take another step closer. "Hey, Tom, it's me, Jerry, from L," he whispered, angling his head and cupping his right hand over the side of his mouth. "What the hell are you doing here?" He had dark, bushy eyebrows that bounced up and down when he spoke.

Thwait turned to him and stared blankly into his face. "What?"

"I'm following orders, Constable Thwait," he replied, this time loud enough so that almost anyone near the command post could hear. He winked at Thwait. "Now, if you don't mind, sir, please show me your badge and ID."

The officer winked again to let Thwait know that he wasn't entirely serious and that he would let Thwait pass as soon as the formalities were over.

Thwait obliged and, after the officer had carefully and painstakingly examined both, Thwait grabbed them back and head toward Sedgwick.

"Thank you, Constable Thwait," the officer called out to Thwait, who didn't respond as he laboriously ducked under the police tape and walked over to the individuals.

Sedgwick was speaking to a high-ranking officer and a fireman, who, judging by his appearance (he was clearly older than the other firemen, but was wearing the same overalls and helmet as all the others) and his calm, assured manner, seemed to be in charge of the fire crew. By the time Thwait reached them, the smoke from the building was beginning to float into command post, causing some of the officers to cough and turn their backs toward the building. Pulling a ball of napkins with a small piece of meat in the center from his pants pocket and placing it over his nose, Thwait looked at the officers and then quickly stuffed it back into his pocket when he realized that none of the others saw fit to cover their noses.

Standing a few feet to the side, Thwait tried to grasp what the three of them were saying, but the noise level around the scene (people were yelling, hoses and other equipment were clanging and banging, and there were some unidentified noises coming from the building) was too much, and so he pretended to listen while occasionally glancing at the commotion, as if the conversation were merely a reflection of everything happening around them.

Suddenly, Sedgwick and the other persons in the command center became silent and, as if on command, stopped whatever they were doing and turned toward the building. Thwait turned, too, but he couldn't see anything out of the ordinary (apart from of the fire crew running out of the area and heading toward their trucks), but as soon as he turned back around, the chief fireman bellowed, "clear the area!" Without another word, everyone in the group immediately merged with all the others scrambling across the parking lot and away from the building.

Seconds later, amid the crowd of people pressing toward the chain-link fence at the opposite side of the parking lot, Thwait detected several loud moans floating above the commotion swirling around him. He stopped and, instead of seeking safety near the fence, turned toward the building, which seemed to be slightly vibrating. It was hard to tell in the poor light if it was the building or his eyes, which felt raw and tired, but as the shouts and pandemonium began fading into the background, he noticed the building's windows began to shake and, moments later, several of them burst outwards, creating a rippling sound that resembled a short burst from a machinegun. By this time, everyone except Thwait had reached the fence and was pressing against it and each other as another, darker plume of black smoke burst out of the building's windows and slowly edged toward them as if it were a killer fog from a horror movie. Just as the fog approached the fence, he heard shouting and screaming as pieces from the building's side began popping out and dropping to the ground, and, shortly after this, bright reeds of flame flickering from the windows like snakes' tongues before disappearing back into the building.

Sedgwick somehow managed to locate Thwait in the ensuing pandemonium and, tugging at his coat sleeve, shouted something unintelligible to him. "Follow me," she shouted again when he failed to respond, and together they made their way out of the parking lot toward a side street across from the building. Without informing Thwait where they were going, Sedgwick moved quickly, dodging around people, cars, and what appeared to be debris from the building's wall. Surprisingly, Thwait had enough energy to keep up with her, but not enough to inquire about their destination. It was just as well, for the din surrounding the building was too great for a normal conversation, and he didn't want to sap his strength by shouting questions and responses. By the time they reached the well-lit street next to the damaged section of the building, it was clear that they were heading to their cars.

Stopping at the police unit, Sedgwick motioned for Thwait to get in on the other side and, once the doors were closed, she called the Chief.

The first thing Sedgwick said once the Chief was on the line was that they – she and Thwait – were unhurt (she glanced at Thwait, who nodded in agreement) and then described what had happened. She was about to ask Thwait if he had anything to add when they were rocked by another loud bang, this time coming from someplace behind them. Both officers were momentarily dazed (but unhurt). For a second or so, Thwait was certain that the auction house or one of the nearby buildings had suffered another explosion, but when Sedgwick spotted a car slowly passing them and weaving through the people running across the street, she correctly surmised that their car had been struck by another car. While Thwait momentarily crouched down in case something else happened, Sedgwick made a mental note of the car's license plate as the vehicle quickly left the scene.

"My God," Thwait finally gasped, when he was certain that they were momentarily safe. "Is the world coming to an end?"

Sedgwick quickly shrugged off the accident and responded to the Chief's insistent demands to know if they, Sedgwick and Thwait, were still all right.

"Yes, yes," she replied, "we're safe. We were rear-ended by another car. Would you have someone run this plate?" She listed the numbers. "I don't know if it's anything or simply someone confused by all the commotion here."

There was a short silence while Sedgwick remained on the phone. Once the Chief came back, he informed her that the car belonged to a vicar from a chapel close to the auction house. Sedgwick suggested something about meriting punishment in the afterlife, and then began talking to the Chief about what was happening and what she had gathered from speaking to other officers. Leaning toward Sedgwick, Thwait tried to catch some of the conversation, but the noises outside the car unexpectedly picked up (he could hear shouts, sirens, and faint pops of something hitting the hood), and scores of people were now running past the car and sometimes bumping into it. A few seconds later, an ambulance with a blaring siren pulled alongside of them, and four paramedics immediately jumped out and headed toward the building or the command post (it was difficult from their position to tell which).

"Yes, Chief, yes," Sedgwick was saying when Thwait turned toward her and again tried to pick up the conversation. "We are parked about a block from the command post." She added a few other directions, including the cross streets. "We got here about thirty minutes ago, and I think there's too much going on at the moment. The initial assessment was..." She hesitated and glanced out the car at something and then resumed her side of the conversation. "Yes, yes, but it's hard to gather at this point. Good, I rather think the more the merrier." Sedgwick quickly glanced at Thwait and motioned to the glove box. "Constable Thwait," she said quietly as she switched on the overhead light. "There's a small notebook in there. Would you please hand it to me? Thanks." Pulling a pen from her jacket pocket, Sedgwick balanced the notebook on the top of her leg and began writing a number of things onto its pages while still engaging with the Chief. "Yes, yes, I have it. Right away, Chief." When the call was over, she pocketed both the pen and the notebook and turned to Thwait.

"The Chief is coordinating with the other stations to send reinforcements. In the meantime, I want you to…" she added and rattled off several items of information that Thwait was instructed to obtain. "I'm going back to speak to speak to the officers at the command post. You and I will regroup and contact the Chief again in about an hour."

Both officers jumped out of the car without another word between them and began undertaking their respective tasks.

Chapter 25

The Chief met with Sedgwick and Thwait at the command post the following afternoon. When he arrived, they were standing next to a folding table and discussing the bombings at the auction house and the Ravenswood. The sky was overcast and a slight breeze was swirling around, blowing Sedgwick's hair across her face (forcing her to sweep it out of her eyes from time to time) and rustling the edges of the photographs and papers on the table. The photographs, which were kept in place by a large brick from the Evermore's wall, contained images from the crime scenes of both the Evermore and the Ravenswood. There was a large hook and ladder close to the building, but the fire from the blast had been extinguished hours ago and the men from the truck were merely double-checking the building and wrapping up before leaving.

The Chief was in a foul mood when he arrived. He had spent most of the morning at HQ, updating them on the explosion – the bomb units and the fire departments confirmed that two bombs were planted in the auction house, one in the CEO's office and one a short way down the hall from his office, although they apparently didn't go off simultaneously (the one down the hall went off approximately fifteen minutes before the one in the CEO's office, which caused the fire and after-explosions that Sedgwick and Thwait witnessed the prior evening) – and asking in return that they give him any information they had with respect to the bombings, the letters, and whatever. "I can't get a straight answer from them on anything," he grumbled as he pushed by a reporter and walked over to Sedgwick, squinting at her and then at Thwait. The breeze suddenly whipped up, rattling everything in the command post and blowing the front page of a newspaper into the face of the officer standing a few feet away from them. The Chief impassively watched the officer struggle to rip the paper off his face and then frantically search the top of his head for his hat, which came off during the struggle.

Turning back to Sedgwick, the Chief demanded to know where the officer in charge of the command post was. Upon being told that neither she nor Thwait had seen the individual all morning, the Chief shook his head, grumbled something, and informed both officers that HQ was now certain that the CEO was still miraculously alive and on his way to the Caribbean to recover. And he was expected to make a full and happy recovery. "HQ said that he suffered an injury of some kind to one of his appendages, but they didn't know what appendage or how badly injured it was," he said as he pulled a chair out from another officer sitting behind him who had just stood up to reach for something on the ground. Dropping the chair in front of Sedgwick and Thwait while the first officer crashed to the ground, the Chief sat down and folded his arms across his broad chest. "I don't know why the company officials didn't report it earlier or provide more details."

"It's rather strange, but I'm glad he's okay," Sedgwick responded while Thwait took a step back to get out of the way in case the Chief leveled some of his anger at him. "Chief, it's beginning to sound like HQ is conducting its own investigation. Is that so?"

"I don't know what HQ is doing."

Sedgwick hesitated. "Well, if they're running their own show, they clearly don't have all the facts. Someone was hit in the explosion."

"What are you talking about?"

"Shortly before you arrived, one of the units on site told us they found remnants of someone killed in the blast. There was no identification, and so we don't know if the individual was an employee, customer, or anything else. Forensics is retrieving what was left."

The Chief was silent for a moment. "I see," he replied meditatively. Taking a deep breath, he added, "the complexion of this investigation seems to be changing by the minute. Okay, if I recall correctly, the building was closed for the day, and yet the CEO and a janitor were both in the building at the time of the bombing. The janitor was also hurt in the blast or its aftermath. How is he doing? Anyone else injured or on their way to Bermuda, or whatever that place is in Central America."

"Bermuda? No, Chief, not to my knowledge. The janitor was in another part of the building at the time of the explosion and suffered only minor bruises. We won't know if anyone else was in the building until the support units have finished going through it. This could be later in the day or early tomorrow morning, because the crews are still shoring up parts that were directly impacted."

"Has the Evermore accounted for all their employees? If anyone's missing, we might have the identity of the body."

"I'll reach out to them to see if they have anything more to share, but I have to tell you that they're not very forthcoming. Some of them act as if they had been instructed not to say anything to us."

"Do you have any suspicions about them?"

"No, we don't have enough yet to be suspicious about anyone. They're probably reacting to potential legal issues."

The Chief looked around for a pencil and, not finding one, started tapping the tip of his index finger on the top of his right leg. "You and Constable Thwait were going to interview some of the management. How's that going? Did anyone say why the building was closed on a perfectly normal work day?"

Sedgwick stated that the business was normally closed on that day of the week, adding that there had been a number of difficulties in connecting with management. The CEO aside, they had reached out to several of the Evermore's principals, who were either unavailable or could only spare a couple minutes by phone. A company vice president and a member of the executive staff fell into the latter category, and, while they didn't have anything of value to contribute, they both expressed shock that someone would have targeted their building, especially because it was closed. "Their responses were fairly generic, if you ask me, but I suppose that's what we get for a couple of minutes of phone chat. That said, I didn't sense any deception or collusion – was that your impression, too, Constable Thwait?" She turned toward Thwait, who was now farther back than before. He nodded and briefly smiled. Sedgwick turned back to the Chief, who continued to squint at Thwait until the latter broke away and glanced at an officer a few feet behind the Chief dusting off the seat of his slacks. After a nod from the Chief, Sedgwick pulled out a notebook from under the brick on the table and began to give him a rundown of some of the evidence taken from the Evermore – evidence, she noted, that bore a striking similarity to the evidence taken from the Ravenswood – two bombs, of course, as well as the timing of the explosions (coinciding with times the buildings should have been unoccupied), the locations of the aforementioned explosions, and the art connection. "Evermore collects and auctions fine art. I'm told that antiquities are one of their specialties, which is what was hit at the Ravenswood." She paused when a gust of wind picked up and rattled everything around them.

The Chief, after absently glancing around to see if the officer had retrieved his hat, squinted at both Sedgwick and Thwait and motioned to the reluctant Thwait to move closer.

"Something wrong, Chief?" Sedgwick asked after he was silent for a moment.

"No," he replied, shaking his head, "it's just the wind. Let me ask you something. Do you think the two events are connected?"

"It's starting to look that way. But we'll certainly know more once we've heard from Dr. Fellows. I think he also mentioned that he's also going to have a go at the body parts as soon as they're in his shop, I mean his lab."

Thwait, who had moved closer at the Chief's urging, started inching nearer to Sedgwick once he caught the drift of their conversation. Moving his head from one to the other as they spoke, it soon became clear from the way he practically danced on his toes that he wanted to say something, but neither the Chief nor Sedgwick noticed his movements.

"The other stations are keeping in touch with Fellows and his team, right?"

"Chief?" Thwait timidly asked.

"I believe so. I haven't heard anything to the contrary."

"Chief?"

"You get in touch with me immediately if you hear of any problems along this line. The other stations were apprised that our lab is the focal point for all forensics – for both crime scenes."

"Chief?"

"Will do, Chief."

"Chief?"

"And I've spoken to Fellows. He's aware of the priority."

"Chief?"

"Good to hear, Chief."

"Chief?"

"If there's any delay on his end, you let me know this immediately, too."

"Chief?"

"And where is the bloody officer in charge? I can't believe...Constable Thwait, what is it?" The Chief looked over at Thwait, who became visibly nervous.

"I'm sorry, Chief, but...but what about the Gray Ladies?"

"What about them? Look, I'm not as convinced as you and Agent Nesbit that the Gray Ladies are anything much less a work of art. But right now I don't want you to get bogged down by this or anything else the wiretap says. Go with the evidence you pull from the crime scenes. If you find a link,

262

fine, but don't waste your time searching for something I'm not sure is even there."

"Come to think of it," Sedgwick interjected, "Constable Thwait noticed a strange odor reminiscent of burning rubber or wire at both locations. Maybe it's a coincidence, but if it was from the bombs, it might suggest the suspects used the same explosive materials."

Thwait grimaced slightly, because he didn't want Nesbit's theory of the Gray Ladies to be discarded in what appeared to be an arbitrary fashion. "No, what I mean is…"

The Chief stopped tapping his finger and stood up. As he did so, another gust of wind blew the chair he was sitting in over onto its side. "Damn," he said, but instead of picking it up and returning it to the officer previously sitting in it (the officer eyed the Chief respectfully from a distant section of the command post), he pushed it out of his way with his left foot. Briefly glancing around the command post and noticing some of the officers and others scurrying about their duties, he turned to Sedgwick and told her to inform the officer in charge, if such an individual actually existed, that he, the Chief, had been to the command post and wanted to speak to him – immediately. "This is really getting my goat. Reach out to that old woman before she has a chance to forget whatever it was she saw. And keep pushing on the Evermore people…and where is Agent Nesbit? I don't recall having seen him lately."

"He's still out sick, sir," Thwait interjected, taking a step back. "I'm not sure when he'll be back."

The Chief squinted briefly at Thwait. "Inspector Sedgwick, HQ for some reason expects me back in an hour or so. Text me if anything urgent comes up."

The Chief turned to leave, squinting at the officer in the far corner as he did so, but hesitated and turned back to Sedgwick. Glancing again at the officer, who quickly turned away, he looked back at Sedgwick and said in a subdued voice, "I was supposed to keep this confidential, but it doesn't make any sense now. HQ tells me that they have reason to believe there are going to be more bombings. Before you say anything, Inspector Sedgwick, I was not privy to their reasons, and I have no idea why they aren't more forthright with something as significant as this." He paused and intensified his squinting. "Look, if there's another bombing, connected or not, it could very well undermine the public's confidence in the ability of Her Majesty's government to keep and restore order. If this is what somebody's after, they could very well get it."

"I don't know what to say. If HQ truly has more information, then just give it to us and quit playing these…these cat and mouse games," Sedgwick uttered angrily. "I'm sorry, Chief. I'm sure everyone's doing the best they can."

"No, your comment's well placed. When you and Thwait and the phantom Nesbit are not at your day jobs, I want you to find out of there've been any threatening letters sent to the CEO – and I don't care if he's dead or alive. If there were, that could help cement the connection. If there weren't, we could be looking at something else entirely."

"Let's hope we don't have any additional surprises."

"I agree." The Chief turned to Thwait. "Constable Thwait, I would like to see Agent Nesbit back on the investigation as soon as possible. Get in touch with him. We need all hands on this, and I have a sneaking suspicion that he's going to be instrumental in resolving a few things here."

While Thwait was smiling because of the importance that the Chief placed on Nesbit's help, the Chief leaned over and casually whispered into Sedgwick's ear, "Boot Nesbit off the investigation if it becomes necessary."

"I don't think it'll be necessary," she replied out Thwait's hearing. "Right now, he's functioning part of the team."

"I'll take your word for it," the Chief replied as he straightened his coat. "I want everyone to keep in mind," he said loudly so that Sedgwick, Thwait, and the officer at the far end of the command post could hear, "we are now dealing with a possible homicide."

Chapter 26

Sedgwick managed with some difficulty to obtain the CEO's office number. His assistant, who answered the phone, confirmed that the CEO might still be out of town but promised to let him know of her call as soon as he "checked in." In response to her query about his health, the assistant noted that "the boss" was recovering nicely after having, once again, injured his ankle playing football. "As much as he'd like to think so," the assistant added with what could only be a smile, "he isn't very coordinated. Last year, for instance, he nearly broke his, let us say, nether parts waterskiing, and the year before that..." Sedgwick thanked the assistant and, once again, emphasized the importance of her call. Having come up empty-handed with the CEO, Sedgwick and Thwait visited the elderly woman who claimed to have seen someone running from the Evermore at the time of the explosions.

The woman, Mrs. Clifton Hebert, lived alone in a large flat near the building. In her late 70s, she was petite and had long, gray hair tied neatly into a ponytail, and she smiled frequently, crinkling the rough skin around her eyes and mouth, as if she were pleased to have such distinguished guests. Judging by the size of the flat and its location, as well as by the expensive appointments in the hallway and living room (Chinese vases, old paintings), Mrs. Hebert clearly had money, significant money, and yet she dressed casually in tight-fitting jeans and wore a dark, flaccid sweatshirt emblazoned with the word "Thirsty?" on the front. As soon as she made the officers comfortable in elegant, old chairs and served them tea in elegant, old cups and saucers, she launched into an elegant, old-sounding story about the young man who had knocked her to the ground and sent her grocery bags (from Harrods, don't you know) sliding into the street only minutes after the explosion. Tapping the tip of Thwait's heavy shoe with her own pristine tennis shoe, she insisted that she couldn't identify the young man from mug shots, because she recently misplaced her glasses – "I mislaid them somewhere," she said, slyly glancing around as if they might pop up at any second. "And what with this and all the other things going on these days, I simply haven't had a chance to replace them" – and because she had only seen him for a few seconds, at best. While she was a little vague about the time at which the explosions took place, she insisted that there were several things she knew about the young man in question. He was young, obviously, and rather disheveled. "I don't believe that young man has put a brush to his long hair in ages. It was full of knots and...and dirt."

"Do you recall what time this happened?" Sedgwick interjected.

"Oh, please don't interrupt. Now, where was I? Something about my glasses... Yes, I remember, he was wearing military fatigues. Terrible shape, really. One of the buttons was missing," she noted as she leaned toward Thwait and winked at him. Reaching across Thwait to a table next to his chair, she picked up a small, framed black-and-gray photograph of a young man smartly decked out in a military uniform. "You bear a striking resemblance to my late husband, God bless him, Constable Thwait." She leaned over with a smile and patted Thwait on the wrist. "Well, if there's one thing I understand, it's uniforms and military insignia. Commander Hebert, that's what I called him – and, you two would have got along quite swimmingly, I must say, since he was such a stickler for law and order – Commander Hebert was in the military for a good twenty or thirty years, if I'm not mistaken. Oh, I do have trouble remembering dates these days." She looked at Thwait for a couple of moments and then replaced the picture on the table, lightly brushing against his chest as she did so. "Yes, well, he – I mean the dirty young man – he wasn't dressed in the least bit proper. His shirt...but where are my manners? Let me show you some more pictures of Commander Hebert. Now, he was a proper soldier. He followed every rule to the letter, wouldn't deviate an inch...oh, here's a lovely one taken when we were living in base housing. You'll appreciate this one, Commander Thwait..." Sedgwick and Thwait remained for another hour or so while she showed them pictures of the late Commander and commented multiple times on the resemblance between the slim soldier and Thwait.

Once they were able to excuse themselves (Thwait was practically forced to extricate himself from her grip), they visited several other individuals in other parts of the city who had come forward with potentially useful information. None of them, however, had seen a young man in a military jacket, but several persons described a strange, burning smell that hovered around the area after the explosions. One individual, a rather aggressive librarian planning a holiday on the continent, claimed to have seen three young men in turbans jumping up and down on the roof of a nearby car and giving themselves high fives shortly after the museum blast. According to the stocky, middle-aged man (who, unlike Commander Hebert, bore a passing resemblance to Thwait, albeit aged twenty or so years), the turbaned men immediately fled

266

the scene when the police arrived, although he couldn't say in what direction or why he had notified the police only after the bombing hit the press. The man's tense equanimity seemed strained when Sedgwick cut the interview short.

After a quick and inexpensive bite to eat, Sedgwick and Thwait went to both crime scenes to get an update on the evidence. They spoke to various police teams (and stations throughout London were now involved), as well as to forensics teams, bomb teams, and others to understand how close they were to identifying the suspect or suspects. Shortly before six that evening, they met with the Chief and after giving him an update on the investigation, they went to Sedgwick's office, where they combed through old case files for possible connections to the bombings. Since it was well after midnight before they took another break, they decided to camp out at the station (Sedgwick found a couple of cots in one of the station's storerooms) to get an early start in the morning. They were already at work when the Chief arrived, and they continued working in the station and around the city virtually nonstop throughout the day.

On a couple of occasions (once during one of the rare moments when he and Sedgwick actually took a few minutes off to stretch and to snack), Thwait called Nesbit to see how he was feeling and to update him on the status of the investigation, but Nesbit didn't answer his phone or return Thwait's messages. Forty-eight hours later, after working one particular stretch that lasted nearly nineteen hours nonstop, Sedgwick and Thwait called it a day and temporarily handed off the investigation to two capable officers.

"Take the rest of the day off," Sedgwick said to Thwait, who could barely keep his eyes open and whose tie was skewed so grotesquely to one side that it seemed to be an imitation of a hangman's noose. "Relax, go to a movie, and then come back in six hours. We're only at the tip of the proverbial iceberg."

"We're getting closer," Thwait noted as they were leaving the building, "but the suspects are as far away as ever. Should we be worried they might strike again fairly soon?"

"Our best bet is the latents, which are due back any time. Let's hope we're lucky and can attach some names to the results."

Chapter 27

Thwait planned to grab a bite to eat before heading to his flat. But on his way out of the station, he remembered his great friend and went back to his desk to call him. Thwait managed to catch Nesbit just as the latter was about to leave his hotel room. After some preliminaries, including a few choice words about the station's failure to keep him informed, Nesbit stated that he was feeling better but added that he was on his way out to run an errand. He insisted, however, that he could spare a few minutes for Thwait to bring him up-to-speed on the investigation.

"I've heard more from the media," Nesbit interjected before Thwait had completed his overview of the Evermore bombing. "Now, tell me, the Chief and Inspector Sedgwick don't seriously think the same bomber is at work in both cases? It's absurd, since the similarities you describe are characteristic of most bomb sites and therefore should not be taken as evidence of a connection."

"Well, sir, the results from the forensics taken off the bomb parts should be back soon, and maybe these will make the connection, if there is one."

"What kind of forensics?"

"We've collected fingerprints and human chemical residue..."

"Fingerprints and DNA? Tom, the bomb sites weren't hermetically sealed, and so any number of people could have touched the bomb pieces from both sites, including you. Besides that, do you have any idea of how inaccurate fingerprint and human-residue examiners are and how frequently they make mistakes? I can tell you that you wouldn't want to bet your life on the accuracy of their results – and therefore you shouldn't try to connect two events based on potentially flawed findings. No, my friend, we look at one case at a time."

"Yes, sir. I only meant..."

"I know, Tom," Nesbit interrupted. "What I'm trying to explain is that these are discrete events. One case concerns the destruction of the Gray Ladies. It was an effort to bring the government to its knees by destroying politically sensitive art. And, to forestall your question, the fact that the Richardson Stones are still intact is irrelevant, since mistakes happen even with the best of criminals. The other case is completely different in that it concerns the attempted killing of a CEO. The suspects targeted the CEO's office, meaning they were solely after this individual. And who is this CEO? Is he so special that his demise would shake the government? Look, if anyone managed to kill this character and a hundred other captains of industry, do you seriously think that their demise would amount to a hill of beans in terms of the government's stability? Why, there is any number in and out of government who would applaud such barbarism. But if you're still intent on the notion that the two are one, you'll need to bring more to the table than suspect forensics and unrelated motives."

Thwait hesitated, recalling the discussion at the Evermore command post. "No, sir. I only hope the labs will clarify…"

"Again with the forensics. Look, you have a head on your shoulders, and that's why I'm telling you that we need to proceed slowly, one case at a time. Should the inconceivable happen – should we discover something definitive that links the crimes – I'll be the first to admit my mistake. I am not an inflexible person. But let's not put the cart before the horse. Do you agree, Tom?"

"I guess so, sir."

"Listen to me, Tom. I've considered everything in the light of unemotional logic and unimpeachable scientific tradecraft, and nothing that I've seen leads me to believe that we are dealing with a single crime as opposed to two unconnected actions."

"Yes, sir. But what do I say if the Chief or Sedgwick asks me if the cases are connected?"

"You leave that to me. I will explain it to them when the time comes, when the obvious is apparent to everyone's eyes. Does that sound fair, my friend?"

"Yes, sir, I suppose," he replied, not exactly sure if he needed to say something to Sedgwick and the Chief.

"Good, good. In the meantime, I will be scouting out some clues that will break both of these cases wide open. You trust me, right?"

"Of course, I do, sir."

"You're a fine man, Tom."

"Thank you, sir. By the way, the Chief and Inspector Sedgwick want you back on the investigations as soon as possible. They understand about your illness…are you really doing better, sir? Well, we can't finish things without you."

There was a pause. "Probably not. You can tell them that I'll be back as soon as possible. In fact, I'm itching to get back in the saddle, as we say in the States. Say, did I tell you that I spoke to my son? He and I are planning to get together tomorrow, if possible. I have to tell you that I'm very impressed with that boy. Boy? He's a man in every sense. I think you'd like him."

"I'm very glad to hear that, sir. I'd like to meet him some day."

"I'd like you to meet him, too."

There was a lull in the conversation, and once again Thwait tried to find out when Nesbit might actually return. "Sir, just between us, can you give me a rough idea when you'll be back? I mean, working with me."

"Tom, I'm always working with you. Tomorrow is obviously out of the question. Maybe the following day. Let's play it by ear. In the meantime, you'll keep in touch, right? You can contact my cell. Leave a message if I don't pick up."

"I will, sir."

"Tom, keep me posted on the evidence. I don't care how thin it is. I need to know what everyone is looking at in order to solve things without being diverted by a bunch of silly theories leading nowhere and proving nothing."

"You can count on me, sir."

"Come to think of it, why don't you make a point of calling me every night? I mean, as long as I'm out and it fits with your schedule."

"Yes, sir. That won't be a problem."

There was another pause, and for a second Thwait thought the conversation was going to end, but Nesbit broke the silence.

"Say, Tom, did you or anyone else check to see if there are security videos from the buildings?"

"Not that I'm aware of. I'll check with Inspector Sedgwick. By the way, I should have mentioned earlier that we've spoken to several potential eyewitnesses. One of them…"

"Yes, yes, but remember that you can't rely on eyewitness testimony."

"I understand, sir. We've spoken to some of the staff – at both buildings, I'm afraid – and we've also interviewed an old woman who may have run into one of the suspects shortly before the second blast. Actually, he ran into her…"

"What? Tell me more."

"It wasn't the Ravenswood…"

"No, no, it doesn't matter. I need to know everything before I can make a judgment about anything. Go on, please."

"Well, the individual ran into the woman shortly after the first blast at the Evermore – I said there were two blasts at the auction house, right? – knocked her down, in fact. Once she was down, the individual scrambled to get out of the area just as the second bomb went off."

"A concussion, I thought so. Suspect testimony. What did he look like?"

"She seemed fine when we spoke to her. Maybe a little strange, but she's probably a little rattled by the whole thing. Oh, yes, the man appeared to be in his early twenties, he was unshaven, and she stated that he was unkempt."

"Can she identify him from a line up?"

"I rather doubt it. She didn't get a clear view of his face. However, she was very certain about his hair and clothing. He had long, dark hair that was shaggy and unkempt. He also wore military fatigues, the kind her late husband wore when he was in the service. There was a button missing, too. Sir?"

Nesbit was silent for a moment.

"Sir?"

"Nothing, my friend," he replied, as if he were awoken from a reverie. "Nothing. Keep up the good work, and give me a ring soon. I may have something for you, too."

"That would be wonderful, sir. Oh, I almost forgot. Inspector Sedgwick is now working with us full time. She's still in charge, of course, but she's doing the same things we're doing to further the investigations. I think you'll be pleased, sir." Thwait felt a little uncomfortable blurting this out, but he needed to make sure that there weren't any surprises when Nesbit returned. He also hoped that Nesbit's new attitude toward Sedgwick hadn't changed over the past couple of days.

There was a slight pause before Nesbit said, "excellent, my friend, excellent. Tell Inspector Sedgwick that I look forward to working with her again and that her presence will... I'm not sure she'll believe that. Just tell her that I look forward to working closely with her. She is an excellent officer, Tom."

Thwait met Sedgwick the following morning at the station. He mentioned his conversation with Nesbit (omitting, of course, his objections to the trajectory of the investigation), and noted happily that Nesbit was hoping to be back on duty fairly soon. Thwait also noted that Nesbit was available for consultation and that he wanted to be kept in the loop while he was out. "He's a little hard to reach sometimes," Thwait said, and then quickly added that Nesbit was following up on some leads of his own without, however, explaining how or why Nesbit could work while being too sick to report to the station. When he was finished, Thwait smiled at Sedgwick and was thankful that the latter didn't inquire about the leads and why Nesbit was also operating without keeping station informed. This was indeed on Sedgwick's mind, but she decided to drop it for the time being.

"I'd say that's good news, Constable Thwait," Sedgwick responded. "Last night, forensics left a note, saying that they might have some preliminary results for us this evening. Until then, we have several more people to interview."

Chapter 28

Few of the interviews that day amounted to anything particularly noteworthy. When Sedgwick and Thwait returned to the station, they wrote up their notes and then began sorting through the growing mountain of evidence recovered from both crime scenes. Shortly before seven, they broke for dinner (raiding the station's vending machines to save time and to control cost), after which they took the service elevator to the station's basement where the forensics labs were located. Once the doors finally parted, Sedgwick and Thwait confronted a long, brightly lit, featureless white hallway that was lined with evenly spaced, featureless white doors.

The labs were deserted, and there was a deathly stillness throughout the place that was relieved only by the clicking sounds their shoes made as they walked down to the farthest end of the hallway to a lab where they expected to meet their contact. Sedgwick thought nothing of the short hike, and the occasional smell of alcohol and the whiff of something unidentifiable didn't bother her, but as they approached the white lab door, Thwait was beginning to feel uneasy and slightly sick. He had never completely recovered from his first and last visit to the labs some two and a half years ago when he and another officer went to identify a body for a case they were supporting. In a small, stuffy room, the identification required lifting a decaying corpse off its tray and turning it over to locate a penny-size mole supposedly at the base of the spine or between the buttocks. Unfortunately, as they lifted the corpse, it emitted a foul odor and one of its arm bones fell out of the socket, stretching the skin covering it like a sheet of rubber. To the delight of the technicians and to the consternation of his fellow officer, Thwait dropped his half of the corpse to the floor and ran to the restroom, where he retched several times.

They were met at the door by a middle-aged man with thick gray eyebrows and an equally prominent gray mustache. He was wearing a soiled, white lab coat with what appeared to be liquid splatters across one side. This was Dr. Fellows, who motioned them into a large room that had several long tables in the center and an array of white and steel cabinets lining each of the walls. Immediately recognizing the officers, he stuck out a gloved hand to Thwait and exclaimed how pleased he was that Thwait's earlier experience hadn't kept him away from the labs. "As you'll see, we have so much to offer here," he added with a broad smile.

Turning to Sedgwick, he proffered his gloved hand again and immediately took it back. "I don't know what I was thinking, Inspector Sedgwick. I guess I've spent too much time here with the natives, if you'll pardon a poor joke. I didn't think to remove my gloves." He ripped of his glove and deposited it into a large container marked Hazardous Waste. "I'd hate to see you catch something incurable."

Thwait eyed the container and then his own hand, the one that had come into contact with the contaminated glove. While Sedgwick and Fellows were talking, he wiped his hand on the seat of his pants and, when he felt an unexpected tremor in his fingers, he interrupted the discussion to ask where the nearest toilet was.

Fellows pointed to a white door at the opposite end of the lab. As he did so, he advised Thwait to wash his hands first, since the gloves had been contaminated and, well, he would hate to see Thwait grievously infected as a result. "I'm sure you know what I'm referring to," Fellows added as he and Sedgwick silently watched Thwait practically jog to the door and then disappear behind it.

"I don't know if I should tell the poor bugger," Fellows said once the door was closed.

"What do you mean?"

"Kind of a joke, really. The gloves were clean. I put them on just before I opened the lab door."

When Thwait came back a few minutes later, Fellows greeted him with a big smile. "It's all right, my boy. Later on, I'll give you a glass of something guaranteed to cure just about anything." Turning to Sedgwick, he resumed the conversation that had been going on while Thwait was in the lavatory. "As I was saying, we are slowly piecing things together, but we do have a few things to show you." He walked over to a long, narrow table illuminated by a bright overhead light. On the table, spread out on a white cloth covering the entire table, were what looked like bent, broken, and burnt pieces of junk ranging in size from a needle to a football. None of the items, and there must have been well over a hundred assorted pieces, were immediately recognizable to either Sedgwick or Thwait.

After pulling on another pair of snug-fitting surgical gloves, Fellows picked up two small, L-shaped pieces of metal. "Evidence number 17," he announced, holding one of the pieces in his left hand slightly below eye level, "and evidence number 106," he proclaimed, holding the other piece in his right hand slightly above eye level. He carried the objects to another table, which like the first was covered by a white cloth and illuminated by a bright light directly overhead, and carefully placed them down. Taking a step back, he glanced at both officers and asked, "well?"

"I don't know," replied Sedgwick, glancing at Thwait.

"Neither do I," offered Thwait.

"Okay, number 17," Fellows replied, stepping back to the table and retrieving the item with the index finger and thumb of his left hand, "was found at the Ravenswood crime scene. If you look closely at the black smudge in its center...my God, not so closely, Constable Thwait. One false move and we're all goners!" He shoved the object under Thwait's nose, forcing the officer to lean away from the object. Fellows appeared surprised by Thwait's reaction and immediately apologized, although perhaps not entirely sincerely.

"My apologies, Constable Thwait. I didn't mean to...that is, I wasn't trying to... Really, it was just a bad joke, that's all. I don't get a lot of visitors, and, well, I'm sure you know how it is." He winked furtively at Sedgwick. "Well, as one of our lads discovered, the black smudge is actually a portion of a SKU, and, if you look closely, you can see some of the numbers (yes, Constable Thwait, it's perfectly safe). The metal is part of the armature used in the timer that set off the first explosion, that is, at the Ravenswood Museum. Naturally, it wasn't designed for this purpose. It's used most frequently in your common loo, and it can be found in almost any hardware store." While still holding the object with his left hand, he picked up the other object with his right. "If you notice 901...no, I'm sorry, 106...if you notice 106 from the Evermore, you'll see right here the very same SKU, minus the last two digits." He held the pieces side by side for a few moments, and then placed them next to each other on the table.

"I don't understand," said Sedgwick. "Are you sure the numbers match? What if the missing digits are different?"

"It's a match, all right. The manufacturer informed us that the last two digits refer to color only. However, in this instance, the last two numbers should be the same on both, since these particular items are manufactured in one color only – gray, to be precise."

"Meaning, if I understand correctly, that the same individual or individuals who bombed the Ravenswood also had a hand in the Evermore bombing?"

"I'll let you make the inferences, Inspector Sedgwick. But in my expert opinion, either the same individual acquired the same metal piece for bombs used at both crime scenes, or two disparate individuals acquired the same metal piece for exactly the same purpose at two distinct crime scenes."

"We are counting on you to make inferences, Dr. Fellows. But, okay, it looks like we have a promising link between the bombings."

"There's more to it than that, Inspector Sedgwick."

Thwait didn't respond and seemed slightly distracted.

"I'm not sure I understand," Sedgwick said.

Fellows smiled and winked. Turning to Thwait, he said, "Constable Thwait, would you kindly bring over items 19 and 109? No need to worry. They're also completely safe to handle. Yes, I'm sure. Wait, you need to put on gloves before handling them. You don't want to contaminate them, do you? Do you see that box of surgical gloves over there?"

While Thwait struggled to pull on a pair of sticky, stretchy gloves, Fellows turned back to Sedgwick and continued. "Quite a bit more, I'd say." He stated that it would be an amazing coincidence if two unrelated individuals built similar bombs for similar purposes using similar materials. "It could happen, I suppose," he added, "if they were consulting similar instructional manuals, but so far our boys haven't located such manuals. But even so, even if the suspects had watched the same how-to videos, this wouldn't account for the SKUs. Without getting too far into the weeds on this, the sequence of the numbers tells us that these metal parts were manufactured for a particular customer [he named the retailer] and that they were shipped to this customer at a particular location. The manufacturer [he named the company] also told us that, as of this date, only a handful of these items were made and shipped, since they are replacing an older version of the same part. Given all this, I think we can safely say that these parts were delivered to the customer at the same time and were most likely stocked in the same bin. Do you see what I'm getting at? Two disparate and unrelated individuals going to the same store, probably at the same time, with the same intent on their minds, and purchasing the same items – maybe even bumping shoulders in the same check-out line. I suppose it's not impossible, but I'll leave it to you officers to determine whether it makes sense."

"Please...," Sedgwick started to say, but Fellows interrupted with the gloved palm of his raised right hand.

Ignoring Thwait, who was still struggling to pull on his gloves, Fellows cleared his throat as if he were going to make a speech and continued with his analysis. "It's rather complicated, as you might expect," he said and launched into a discussion of the purpose of the metal piece in the timers and why its particular shape was less than ideal in terms of reliability. "It's not surprising that one of the Ravenswood bombs failed to detonate, and I wouldn't be surprised if the timing of the detonations at the Evermore were affected in some degree by the same little part. It was simply a poor choice of materials, especially because there are so many better options for achieving the same results. Well, I can only assume the suspects were either careless or...stupid, for lack of a better word. You know, not all bomb makers are careful about their craft, and quite a few – maybe the majority, even – don't take sufficient pride in their work. Why, I've seen a number of...yes, yes, quite so. Right, as I was saying, the individuals responsible at both crime scenes clearly used the same mechanisms..." He stopped speaking when he noticed Thwait plodding toward him.

Thwait, with grotesquely elongated, flaccid fingers, was holding the two pieces of evidence and carrying them to the table. Once he carefully deposited them as close to the center of the table as possible, he stepped back and held up his strange hands to signal that he had accomplished his mission. Thwait was about to remove the ill-fitting gloves when he recalled what happened a few minutes ago and decided to leave them on for the time being. Fellows and Sedgwick had been silently observing Thwait out of curiosity, but as soon as he waved his empty hands, they turned back to one another and resumed their conversation.

"Yes, well, at any rate, what do you think of these?" Fellows asked both officers, motioning toward the objects that Thwait had placed on the table.

Sedgwick and Thwait eyed the objects without touching them and turned back to Fellows. "Metal golf balls?" Thwait muttered, unsure of what he and Sedgwick were supposed to see.

Fellows smiled. "One-Nine (the one on your left, Inspector Sedgwick) is from the Ravenswood. One-O-Nine is from the Evermore. There may be more, to be sure, but we haven't finished going through all the evidence. At any rate, a couple of our men here tested the chemical composition of the 'golf balls,' as you term them, Constable Thwait, and determined that they are derivatives of a fairly unusual chemical compound." Fellows named the compound and sketched out its structure on a pad that he pulled from his coat pocket. He added that it was extremely unstable under certain conditions (for example, the temperature in an explosion that exceeds the chemical's normal heat tolerance) and that it had a tendency to form balls with tiny crystalline pocks on its surface as it cooled. He retrieved a couple of business cards from the same pocket and handed them to Sedgwick. "As you might imagine, it's also fairly uncommon. The same fellow who helped us with the SKUs, Terrance, I believe, informed us that there are only two places in England that sell it, one in London and the other in Oxford. I should add that both shops follow government regulations regarding the compound and therefore require purchasers to submit proper identification."

"All right," Sedgwick replied, "assuming we could get legal access to their records, how would we tell one purchaser from another? So far, we don't have anything that would give us a clue about the identity of the suspect or suspects."

"There's no foolproof way, I suppose. But since the chemical is used mainly for certain arcane scientific processes, I shouldn't think you'd have to go through a long list of customers unaffiliated with scientific institutions."

Thwait was becoming increasingly uncomfortable. "Excuse me, Dr. Fellows," he began, glancing first at Sedgwick. "Are you sure the same person planted both bombs? Are you saying that the cases are connected?"

Fellows cleared his throat and scratched the side of his lab coat. "That determination is not mine to make, Constable Thwait. Let me just say that I cannot fathom any reasonable person dismissing the hard evidence I just presented. But if you're still having doubts, I have something else that might interest you. Follow me."

Thwait nodded vaguely.

Fellows led Sedgwick and Thwait toward the door. Once back into the hallway, Fellows turned toward the elevators and, with the officers following a few steps behind, he continued to speak about the evidence. "We've pulled some good latents off the bomb housing recovered from the Ravenswood and some decent partials off various items from the Evermore. They've been sent for identification, and we should get the results fairly soon." He stopped momentarily and turned to Sedgwick. "Inspector Sedgwick, we have every reason to believe the prints will return an identity, and I have a gut feeling that a single cockroach presages a large family hiding somewhere in the cracks." Fellows continued down the hallway, this time remaining quiet, as if there was something on his mind. When they arrived at another faceless, white door,

Fellows reached inside to switch on the lights and ushered them inside. This lab, like the other, was large and fairly empty, but unlike the other there was a bank of stainless steel cabinets at the far end of the room.

Fellows headed for the cabinets and positioned himself a few feet away with his back to the doors. Sedgwick stopped once she reached Fellows and faced him expectantly. Thwait, however, stayed back a few paces from Sedgwick and, with his arms at his sides and his gloves dangling from his thick fingers, stared uneasily over Sedgwick's right shoulder. His face became pasty, and glistening beads of sweat began appearing on his smooth forehead.

Smiling and nodding at the officers as if they had just told him to proceed, Fellows turned toward one of the cabinets and, grasping a shiny handle, opened the door and pulled out a long, stainless-steel tray, which emitted a low, metallic hiss as it appeared out of its dark chamber. Fellows immediately stood to one side of the tray, while Sedgwick stepped to the other side, and for a few moments the tray appeared to hover between them like a ghastly magician's prop. Determined not to look, Thwait slowly lowered his eyes toward the tray and its contents, which were covered with a white cloth that seemed to have been made of the same material as Fellows' lab coat. Thwait was relieved that the contents were not visible. But as he stared at the lumpy cloth, he began to detect the smell of alcohol and, shortly after that, a faint scent of rotting stew. Tired of waiting for another cue, Fellows suddenly grabbed one corner of the cloth and yanked it off the tray from top to bottom, revealing a barely-recognizable pile of body parts, raw meat, and hair fragments.

"Officers, take a look at these babies," he proudly announced, draping the cloth over his arm as if it were an overcoat. "These are all that remains of the individual killed at the Evermore. He (and, before you ask, we are certain that it is or was a he) – he was found in a hallway barely a hop, skip, and a jump from the CEO's office. It appears that our fellow was at the heart of the blast."

"Heart? What do you mean?"

"He and the bomb appear to have been at the same place at the same time. If you ask me, I'd say that he was carrying the bomb when it went off, accidentally, I'm sure. But I'll leave the conjectures to you officers."

Thwait immediately looked away. Trying to appear casually interested in other things, he glanced at the cavernous hole from which the tray was extracted and then searched the faces of Fellows and Sedgwick, after which he closed his eyes briefly as if he were concentrating deeply on something – but in the end, he couldn't keep his eyes away from the contents on the tray even though the putrid, stew-like smell was slowly becoming more and more insistent. For a moment, he was certain that he was going to retch right there, but he somehow managed to control himself by recalling the time he handled the decaying body.

Sedgwick took it all in stride. She appeared genuinely curious about the once human-looking items on the tray, and she followed Fellows' disquisitions on each piece with obvious interest. But what intrigued her most was that the individual was not associated with either the auction house or the companies that cleaned and serviced the premises. Fellows stated that one of his assistants had been able to connect with the HR department at each organization (Sedgwick, however, was still waiting for information from the Evermore's HR department), and everyone had been accounted for. Fellows noted that he initially assumed the individual in question was merely a visitor who had happened down the wrong hallway at the wrong time. But this was unlikely, he pointed out, because the building had been closed for some time before the blast. Fellows also added in response to Sedgwick's slightly drooping, questioning glance that the remains were of a single individual. "Look here," he said as he picked up some of the remains and put them together like a jigsaw puzzle, "nothing extraneous or unrelated. Would you like to try? No?"

Like a proud parent, Fellows pointed out the pile of rags at the end of the tray where the victim's feet should have been resting. "This is what's left of his clothes," he said, glancing at Thwait, who appeared distracted and a little unsteady on his feet. "We removed them to examine the fabric separately from the body. I should say most came off rather easily [he made scissoring motioned with his index and middle fingers over the torso] though a few pieces had to be scraped off because the heat melted the nylon and plastic bits to the poor bugger's skin. If he felt anything, I can't imagine that it lasted very long." Fellows now made a scraping motion with his right hand to indicate the physical efforts to remove those sections of clothing. "At any rate, we're currently undertaking an analysis of the material. Naturally, we won't be doing anything with the fingerprints. As you can see, Constable Thwait [he said Thwait's name loudly to get his attention], the fingers and the hands are missing, disintegrated by the blast, though I should imagine some bits are clinging to what's left of the ceiling or tucked into a corner or two. Once they dry out, they'll probably be sucked into the ventilation system and circulated throughout the entire building. But by that time, they'd be fairly useless for our purposes." Shaking his head slightly, Fellows contemplated the remains on the tray for a few seconds while nodding his head. "We've also got good blood samples, which will come in handy when we get more information concerning the identity." Fellows turned to Sedgwick, who was visually examining the small, torn fragments, and asked her what she thought about their drab color and curious patterns.

Sedgwick shrugged her shoulders. "The pattern suggests camouflage. Constable Thwait and I interviewed a woman who had a run-in with someone dressed in military jacket, but I don't see how there could be a connection. The young man was clearly alive and ran away before the second blast."

"Right, well," Fellows said and promised to check with the military for any missing men.

When the meeting was finally over and they were all standing in front of the first door that Sedgwick and Thwait had entered, Fellows took their gloves and shook their hands, and reminded them that many of the findings were still preliminary. "Not that it will change anything," he added with a wink. Thwait, however, was certain that preliminary or not, there was now sufficient evidence to connect the two cases, and therefore someone would have the unenviable task of informing Agent Nesbit of the findings. Taking a deep breath before leaving, Thwait didn't relish the idea of being in the same building when Sedgwick or the Chief set him straight.

Once back at the station, they ran into the Chief in the hallway. After a few brief words, he led them to his office, where they gave him an update on their findings and Fellows' information.

When they finished, the Chief silently retrieved his briefcase from the floor and placed it on his desk. Standing up, he pulled his overcoat on, having taken it from the nearby rack, and adjusted the collar and cinched the waist. He grabbed his briefcase to leave but then hesitated and turned to Sedgwick.

"Inspector Sedgwick," he said, squinting at her, "I was planning to brief the media on my way out. Why don't you and Constable Thwait take my place? Mind you, don't give them out everything you've told me. Tell them…tell them that we've connected the two cases and that we'll keep them posted as the investigation progresses. Now, don't dawdle. They're waiting as we speak."

"Right, Chief," Sedgwick said. "Should we take questions?"

"No, keep it simple. You can mention the body at the Evermore, but make sure it's clear that it isn't the CEO. I'll be looking for you both on tonight's news – and if anything else breaks, contact me at home." He stopped and turned to Thwait. Squinting at him, he noted that he had been informed that a request was made for the buildings' security videos. "It's a reasonable request," he added, "but because of the sensitivity of the issue, it should have originated with the station and gone through proper channels." He squinted silently at the officer for a few seconds, noticing the beads of sweat forming on the young man's puffy forehead and his strained efforts to loosen his increasingly uncomfortable collar. "I'll let you know if and when they're available," the Chief finally said, and walked away from the officers.

Sedgwick and Thwait hurried downstairs in the opposite direction to meet the media.

"Shouldn't we contact Agent Nesbit," Thwait asked as he struggled to keep up with Sedgwick.

"No time, I'm afraid. Ring him tonight, and convey our apologies for not having updated him before speaking to the media."

Chapter 29

Nesbit was sitting directly in front of the TV. He was flipping through the various news channels, hoping that nothing earth-shattering would be said about the investigations while, at the same time, knowing that sooner or later someone would put two and two together and prove that the two were indeed one and that the bomber of Ravenswood was the bomber of the Evermore. 'It's bound to happen,' he told himself, 'but if they can hold off a little, maybe...'' He stopped. He couldn't go on. He wasn't concerned that the investigation might be getting ahead of him, and he didn't care how the connection would affect his theory of the Gray Ladies. Nesbit was troubled by something deeper, more fundamental than these issues. There were moments when he could almost convince himself that if the suspect accepted responsibility for the Ravenswood bombing in which no one had been killed, then the Evermore bombing might be explained away or maybe even waved off in plea agreement...and yet at the same time he realized that the odds of this happening were slim at best. It was an intractable situation, but he was willing to grasp at any promising straw. Suddenly, all the news channels switched to the same feed.

Sedgwick walked into view from the left amid the sounds of feet shuffling and people calling out questions, and immediately stepped behind a makeshift podium in the station's lobby. The podium had five prominent microphones on it, each one pointed at her nose, while in front of the podium were at least twenty or thirty reporters, cameramen, and media personalities, most of whom were holding cameras, cell phones, and other devices over their heads and angling them in her direction. Sedgwick appeared to be calm, although her body was still and her movements wooden. After moistening her gently drooping lips and clearing her throat prior to speaking, Thwait mysteriously appeared behind her on the right, his cheeks fuller on the screen than in real life.

Speaking with a tone of voice that was both authoritative and slightly monotonous, Sedgwick began by saying that although the investigation was still ongoing, some important evidence had been uncovered over the past few hours. "We now have," she stated as firmly as a politician denying something that everyone else knew to be true, "definitive proof the bombings at the Ravenswood Museum and the Evermore Auction House were the work of the same individual or individuals. The two events are therefore linked." She paused to clear her throat. "We have not yet apprehended those responsible for these senseless and cowardly attacks, but we are following a number of promising leads and will have more to say about these leads fairly soon. We should also emphasize that we have no indication that these were terrorist-inspired acts. To suggest otherwise could negatively impact our ability to close this case and protect innocent people." Once again, Sedgwick cleared her throat. "We have also confirmed that an unidentified individual had been killed in the Evermore bombing. Thank you." Sedgwick took a step back from the podium and appeared ready to leave the building when she suddenly stepped up to the podium and announced that the CEO of the Evermore Auction House was doing well and had not been injured in the blast as previously reported.

The crowd behind the television cameras spontaneously erupted with questions and demands for additional information. Slightly taken aback by the response, Sedgwick once again leaned forward and, speaking directly into the microphones, stated that neither she nor the station were taking questions at this time. "We will keep you informed as the investigation progresses," she added and turned to leave. Together, she and Thwait headed for the elevators pursued by shouts and barks for questions and clarifications.

Nesbit, too, was shouting and demanding answers and clarifications. He gritted his teeth and jumped to his feet, stomping on the floor several times like a child having a tantrum.

"What the hell is going on?" he hollered at the television after the news shifted to other stories. "No, you can't do this. I told you that the two cases were different and unrelated. Why didn't you listen? What are you trying to do to me?"

Nesbit shook his fist at the screen as if that would accomplish something or force Sedgwick to come back and retract her words. When nothing happened and the station began a series of commercials for intimate health-related items and services, he staggered backward and dropped onto the corner of his bed. Leaning forward and cradling his head in his hands, he was mumbling incoherently when the hotel phone began to ring. It was Thwait.

Nesbit switched off the TV with the back of his fist and picked up the phone. As soon as Thwait said hello, Nesbit took control of the conversation. "I don't understand it, Constable Thwait. I told you the cases were separate, there are two different and unrelated perpetrators, and now you and what's-her-

284

name pull this...this, and without informing me ahead of time. It's a stab in the back."

Thwait was shocked by Nesbit's reaction. He had never heard or seen his close friend and mentor behave in such a way, not even to a bad guy, and yet Nesbit was acting as if he, Thwait, were the worst of all bad people. Thwait was also certain that there was no circumstance in which he would have behaved like this, even if the great Nesbit deserved it. "I...I...sir, no, it wasn't like that."

"Then why don't you tell me what it was like, Constable Thwait. I have ears, and there was no mistaking what was said – and there shouldn't have been any mistake about what I said, either."

Sniffing and clearing his throat, Thwait did his best to remain calm and not break down. "With all due respect, sir, the Chief instructed Inspector Sedgwick and me to speak to the press. We came back from the meeting...Dr. Fellows, and he presented irrefutable proof the same individual was connected to all the bombs, and all the bombs were made in exactly the same way with the same materials. His team pulled SKUs from bomb parts, and..."

"What? You based your assumptions on part numbers without first giving me a chance to weigh in?"

"No, sir, it wasn't like that, believe me. We met the Chief in the hallway on our way back and...well, I was going to call you, but he said the media were waiting and there was no time. We were ordered to go directly to them. If anything changes, I'm sure..."

Nesbit paused and, cradling the phone between his shoulder and left ear, stepped over to the bar and poured himself another drink. After downing it in a single gulp, he breathed deeply and reconsidered what he had just said to his friend. "Okay, if I understand what you're saying, I suppose it wasn't your fault, Tom. I apologize for jumping at you like that. I know you – and Inspector Sedgwick – too well for that." There was another pause, but before Thwait could think of anything to say, Nesbit continued on about the investigation. "Nonetheless, you still have it wrong. There are two distinct events, two separate and unconnected suspects, and one of them isn't responsible for anybody's death. He shouldn't be facing a whole-life order. Have the security videos arrived?"

"No, sir, but the Chief said we would get them as soon as they're available. I don't think he was happy with how the request was made."

"The Chief isn't happy I asked someone for evidence that could have a material impact on the case?" Inhaling deeply, Nesbit tried to control his rising temper. "I see. Tom, please try to expedite the delivery of all the evidence, as long as it's okay with the Chief." Nesbit paused and remained silent for a couple of minutes while he tried to temper his anger. He knew that Thwait had no control over the security videos, if they existed, or over the Chief's reaction, which at this moment seemed incomprehensible. But while Nesbit was putting himself back in order, Thwait was becoming increasingly concerned that his friend was refusing to speak to him.

"Sir?" he uttered, his concern evident in the high pitch of his voice.

"What?" Nesbit replied as if coming out of a reverie. "I'll show everyone just how wrong they are about this case." Nesbit was again silent for a few seconds.

"Sir?"

Nesbit closed his eyes and shook his head. "I guess I'm a little tired. I'm not quite ready... Tom, do me a favor. Push for the security videos, and let me know when you have them."

"Of course, sir. May I ask when you're coming back? May I tell Inspector Sedgwick you'll be back tomorrow? She'll certainly be pleased if you are."

"Sure," Nesbit said, "tell her anything you like. No, wait a minute. Not tomorrow. I may be seeing my son tomorrow. We were going to meet earlier, but something came up, on his side. I spoke to him again last night (by phone, of course), and I think we finally hammered out the arrangements. It's been touch-and-go for quite some time."

"You must be very happy, sir."

"Words cannot explain...oh, but he is something, Tom. His job sounds great, he sounds great, and – have I said this before? – I suspect the young man has a sweetheart."

"That's good news, sir. Do you know anything about the young woman? Do you think it's serious?"

"Well, to be honest, I don't really know. When we were talking, he made a vague allusion about someone close to him, but he immediately changed the subject when I tried to get more information. He accused me of prying. I don't know what it could be if not a woman. You know, I have a feeling he's a real ladies' man who's finally trying to settle down." Nesbit coughed and cleared his throat. "He probably doesn't want me to know. You know how kids are these days. I'll bet he'll tell me all about it when we meet. He might try to spring it on me by bringing her to tiffin. That's the right word, isn't it? Yes, we're having tiffin, Tom, my son and I, at some nice place outside Oxford. I'm sure it's close to his office. Say, do you think he'll show his office to me? Wouldn't that be something?"

Nesbit was unexpectedly silent for a few moments. "Tom," he finally said, this time assuming a slightly humbled tone, "I suppose this wasn't exactly how things went. You see, my son…"

"Sir?"

"Yes, my son. Well, he leaves something to be desired. All this stuff that I said…"

"I understand, sir. Maybe things will be better after you've had a chance to sit down and speak with him."

Nesbit again breathed deeply and told Thwait that he was probably right. "Tom," he added after another short pause, "there's no need to tell Inspector Sedgwick or the Chief any of this, not just yet. Let me speak to my son first, and, depending on how things go…do you know what I'm saying?"

"Of course, sir, I won't say anything."

"Thanks, Tom. Say, why don't you tell Inspector Sedgwick I'll be back in another day or so?"

"I will, sir. Everyone will be pleased."

"Tom," started to say but again fell silent. Thwait was beginning to sense that the conversation was over when Nesbit started talking again, although this time his voice sounded strange, completely unlike his normal self. "Tom, I'm really sorry for…you know."

"No need to apologize, sir. It was completely understandable."

"You're a good man, and you're one of the few people on this earth that I genuinely admire."

"Sir? I…I really don't deserve…"

"Nonsense. You deserve more than I can express. Sometimes, I wish you were my…but enough chatter. You go back to work, and keep me updated."

"Yes, sir. Absolutely, sir."

Thwait was elated. He would have been pleased had anyone claimed to admire him. But this was something more, something almost unbelievable, and for some time he debated with himself as to whether he had heard Nesbit correctly. 'Did he really say that? Did I misinterpret or, or…or mishear? Was he joking?' Over and over, he reconsidered the older man's words, interpreting them this way and that, until, eventually, for the sake of his sanity, he decided that Nesbit had indeed accorded him this rare and special praise, although he wondered if Nesbit would still feel this way once he saw the evidence connecting the two events. Shortly before bed that evening, Thwait replayed the conversation in his mind, and he was suddenly struck by Nesbit's strange humor – he was angry one moment and happy the next, and the conversation ended with an apology, of all things – and he couldn't help fearing that his great friend was still ill.

Once the conversation with Thwait was over, Nesbit poured himself another drink from the bar and stepped over to the bed. Again straddling the corner, he let his slippered feet rest comfortably on the floor while he mindlessly sipped another drink and stared at the blank television. When his glass was empty, he got up and poured himself another one, but instead of sitting back down he reached over to the phone and dialed a number. The person on the other end responded promptly this time and, unlike previous conversations between the two, Nesbit and the individual spoke in a calm, almost civilized manner, even though there wasn't anything particularly warm and pleasant about the topic.

"I will," Nesbit assured the voice on the other end. "I will, but...but promise me you're not involved..." Nesbit was quiet while the other spoke at length. "Okay," he responded when the other end of the line was quiet, "okay, I understand, I understand. I'm not trying to do something that...no, I simply want to understand..." Once again, he waited until the other had finished talking. "Yes, yes, you're right. I'm sorry; I just get that way sometimes. It goes with the territory."

The speaker on the other end spoke at length for several minutes and then hung up before Nesbit had a chance to say goodbye. With the phone still to his ear, Nesbit added to himself, "I believe you. I know you wouldn't lead me astray. My God, I love you..." Despite everything that had been said or denied, he couldn't shake the feeling that something terrible was going to happen either to the individual or...or to something else. Holding his glass at eye level, he was surprised that it was empty ("I must have spilled it," he told himself) and poured another one, emptying the last of the bottle into his glass. Shortly afterwards he went to bed.

Chapter 30

The following morning before the sun rose, Thwait met Sedgwick in the station's conference room, which was now serving as their temporary command post. Sedgwick had been going over various papers (descriptions of evidence, eyewitness statements, photographs and diagrams of the crime scenes, and so forth) when Thwait arrived and stood at the other end of the table, waiting for her to finish reading a page of something. Noticing his presence, Sedgwick looked up over her shoulder and spotted Thwait. Smiling, she said "good morning" and told him to take a chair.

Thwait went around to the other side of the table and, after draping his black coat on the back of one of the chairs, took a seat directly across from Sedgwick. Without any preliminaries, he mentioned his conversation last night with Nesbit and excitedly informed her about the great man's imminent return. Naturally, he didn't say anything about the unpleasant side of the conversation, since he didn't feel it was germane either to the investigation or to Nesbit's fitness to support the investigation.

"I'm pleased to hear that, Constable Thwait," Sedgwick replied, smiling indulgently at Thwait.

Thwait also didn't tell her about the kind words Nesbit said about him. He wanted to, but he didn't like bragging, and he would never have said anything that might make him look better than anyone else at the station.

"Well," Sedgwick began, changing the subject, "we may have a busy day. Dr. Fellows sent word that the results from the fingerprints and DNA samples should be in any time. I hope there's something we can use."

"Excellent, ma'am."

"I've been going over the eyewitness statements to find commonalities, anomalies, whatever. So far, I haven't come up with anything interesting. Maybe you can find something in them that I haven't."

"I'll certainly try, ma'am."

"Good, and while you're doing that, I'm going to take a look at some of the evidence that came in during the night."

Once he completed this task (and he didn't find any smoking guns, either), Thwait spent the rest of the morning with Sedgwick going over the new evidence, examining various items and trying to come up with something that might help them understand the attacks and identify the perpetrators. Later in the day, they reached out to other officers to discuss the investigation and to get updates on the work being done at both crime scenes. Shortly after each interaction, Sedgwick and Thwait were confident that they were inching closer to solving the crimes. But later, as they discussed the work and evidence, they were at a loss to say why they were getting closer – were they actually on the verge of uncovering the suspects' identities or simply approaching the means by which they could come up with the names? But while Thwait continued to worry about what Nesbit might think when he found out what they were doing, he was nevertheless increasingly confident that he and Sedgwick were on the right path and that the bombings were the work of a single individual or a related group of individuals who were working together to achieve some common, ghastly goal. He was certain that sooner or later they were going to solve the case, and he wanted Nesbit to hurry back because nothing would make him happier than to see his important friend taking center stage when the resolution was announced to the media.

Later that afternoon, the officers got a call from the Evermore Auction House, informing them that the company had received a threatening letter. The letter was apparently addressed to the CEO, although it didn't refer to him by name or title. What was even stranger – the letter arrived after the destructive event, as if the author of the letter was either unaware of the event or the letter had been delayed in the post. The CEO's personal assistant, who made the call, informed the officers that the CEO would be back in town any day and would be happy to meet to them at their convenience, but that they would have to make an appointment first. "Currently, Mr. [she stated the CEO's last name] is tentatively free on [she stated a numerical date]. No, I'm sorry, I didn't mean tomorrow. I meant next month. And he's willing to squeeze you in only because of the urgency of your investigation. He is, after all, a very busy man." When Sedgwick demurred, the assistant suggested speaking to the company's publicist, whose schedule was quite a bit freer, adding that this individual (she gave the name and number) knows just as much about it as the CEO. "I don't think he actually read the letter, but the publicist certainly did and has the letter as we speak." The assistant offered to set up an appointment with the publicist, noting two possible dates, one in two weeks and another in six weeks. Sedgwick selected the earlier of the two, but instead of waiting for the appointed day and hour, she and Thwait immediately left the station and within the hour were at the publicist's temporary office.

The office was located in a warehouse-like building down the street from the auction house. The publicist's assistant, an outlandishly-dressed young man with bright, unruly hair and black, painted nails, met them at the door and stated, in an affected manner, that he was surprised to see them, since he and the publicist had expected them in six weeks. "She's, like, extremely busy, you know," he replied when Sedgwick pleasantly insisted that they wouldn't be long. "So are we," she added, noting that if now wasn't a good time, she and Constable Thwait could come back later in the day, although if that were necessary it would behoove the assistant and publicist to have good legal representation with them when they did. Without a word, the assistant flipped his head to one side to clear a shimmering wisp of hair out of his left, mascara-lined eye and contacted the publicist from a cell phone that he had retrieved from his hip pocket. After an obscure discussion with the publicist regarding the timing of the visit, he finally led the officers through the main floor of the building toward her office, explaining as he went that the office was only temporary. "Basically, like, most of the executive offices were located in the auction house, but with all that, like, destruction, we can't get into them at the moment, as you guys know." He glanced at Thwait over his left shoulder and silently raised his right eyebrow. Without saying anything to Thwait, he turned back to Sedgwick and looked directly at her. "Girl, did you ever have a, like, stroke? And if I were you, I'd replace those flats with some, like, heels, and I'd wear some, like, brighter colors, if you know what I'm saying."

The publicist's space was located in what was termed the appraisal room, an area where auction house subjected art works to a variety of tests to determine their authenticity and value. The room looked like a large, windowless artist's loft. Several huge, wooden easels were stacked together against one white, featureless wall, while on the opposite wall were six or seven gunmetal-gray filing cabinets, each one labeled according to its contents. The drawer of one of the cabinets sported a sticker that proclaimed "oils and balsams," while the sticker on the drawer below it offered "hard and soft resins," and the one below that mumbled "turpentine and mineral spirits" (the letters on this drawer were small and poorly written). At the center of the room was a long, wooden table (the publicist's makeshift desk) covered with oil and paint stains, the far end of which held a microscope, a teetering stack of used artist's pallets, and a mass of paint tubes, bottles, brushes, and so forth. The publicist occupied the center section of the table that she or her assistant had carefully cleaned and cordoned off from the artists' materials by several stacks of business papers. A slender laptop and small printer were situated on the table in front of her and to her right, respectively.

The publicist nodded to the officers when they were led into the room. Without getting up, she asked them to sit down on the chairs on the other side of the table.

"I'm a little surprised to see you here," she said, glowering first at Sedgwick and then at Thwait. "You should have made an appointment."

"I did," Sedgwick replied as she sat down.

The publicist was in her late thirties and, in Thwait's eyes, quite attractive. Like her assistant, she was heavily made up, especially her lips, and had a full head of sparkling hair which, unlike the assistant's, was tightly curled and flowing over her narrow shoulders. Dressed casually, she wore six-inch stiletto heels, tight-fitting jeans torn at the knees and back pockets, and a sheer white blouse that revealed the color of her skin. "That's funny,' she replied, her voice slightly strained. "You're not on my calendar today." She turned toward the assistant, but he was gone.

"It wasn't today," Sedgwick replied, "but I didn't think you'd want to wait."

The publicist leaned back in her chair and folded her arms across her chest. "Okay, I'll give you a couple minutes, but not a second more. I'm snowed under because of all this bombing business."

Sedgwick didn't show any emotion, but Thwait looked nervously from one woman to the other.

"All right," the publicist began abruptly, "I'm sure someone told you we didn't get the letter…you're here about the letter, right, or is it something else? Okay, we didn't get the letter until after the explosion, this morning, in fact. It's probably nothing, just some crap from one of our dissatisfied clients, or would-be clients."

"Have you received extortion letters from other clients?" Sedgwick asked.

"No, but we get complaints now and then when someone's treasured keepsake doesn't sell or sells for less than expected. And we ruffle feathers when we explain that the masterpiece from dear old Aunt Minnie is a bloody fake. As for the letter, I'm a little dubious because of its vagueness."

"I see." Sedgwick crossed one leg over the other. She had a small, black bag with her and, after retrieving a notepad and a pen, placed the bag on the floor next to her chair. "If you don't mind, could we see the letter?"

"I suppose." She walked over to one of the gray cabinets and retrieved a manila folder from a drawer labeled "mediums and mixtures." Passing both officers as she went to and from the cabinet, she returned to her chair and, placing the folder in front of her, slid it across the table to Sedgwick.

Thwait was silent as Sedgwick opened the folder and pulled out a single sheet of paper. It was a typed extortion letter and practically identical to the letters that the Ravenswood museum received. "Hand over 10 million pounds or else," Sedgwick summarized. She passed the letter to Thwait, who tried to look at it as carefully as Nesbit might.

"So, what do you think?" the publicist asked Sedgwick. "Did some creep bomb our business because we didn't pay out?"

"It's unclear at this point. We need to examine the letter before we can say if it's connected to the explosion." When Thwait finally handed the letter back to Sedgwick, she placed it carefully back in the folder. "Do you mind if we keep it?" she asked while her hand rested on top of the folder.

"I suppose. Is there any reason we should retain it?"

"No, but it might be evidence."

"Then you think there's something to it?"

"We won't know until we've had a chance to run some forensics against it. If it's unrelated, you can have it back, or we can open up an investigation into one of your disgruntled clients. Can you tell me how it came into your possession and who else may have had access to it?"

"It came in the mail just like any letter. I believe the CEO's executive assistant opened it and alerted him and several others, including me, to its existence."

"This gentleman?" Sedgwick noticed that the assistant had reappeared and was now sitting on the other side of the table, near the corner.

"No, this is Manny," she replied, not in the least surprised at his return.

"Where is your CEO, by the way?"

"Personal business. That's why I'm speaking to you."

"I see. Please continue."

"That's pretty much it. If it hadn't been for the explosion, we might have trashed it like we trash all such correspondence. Manny brought it to me. Do you have any suspects? You don't think Manny had anything to do with it, do you?"

Sedgwick and Thwait both glanced at the publicist's assistant, who looked back at them without any emotion.

"No, not at all. We don't suspect anyone at this point. Can you or Manny tell us who might have touched the letter besides yourselves? By the way, do you still have the envelope?"

"Only the people I mentioned. The CEO might have touched it. You'll have to ask Manny for his thoughts. What did you want? Yes, the envelope." She reached under the table for a cylindrical trash container and pulled it out of a mass of tissues and papers. "I didn't think it was important. There's no return address."

Sedgwick took the envelope and glanced at Manny, who shrugged his lean shoulders as if to say that he didn't have anything to add. She glanced at the envelope's front and back, and then handed it to Thwait, who did the same. She deposited it into the folder when Thwait handed it back.

"Okay, did you notice anything else out of the ordinary around the time of the explosions? By the way, why was the auction housed closed at the time of the explosion? It was a normal business day, wasn't it?"

"What do you mean? The auction house is always closed that day. As for anything unusual, I didn't see anything. We get angry clients from time to time, as I've said, but I didn't hear from any that day. Do you know what I think? I think one of our competitors could have engineered it to get an edge over us."

"What? You think one of your competitors planted a bomb in the building? Do you have any proof?"

"No, it's just a supposition. But you never know what some firms will do to increase their market share."

"Which one, for example? Are you having trouble with one of your competitors?"

The publicist was silent for a moment while she looked directly at Sedgwick. "There's a couple of them [she named two firms], highly competitive. The CEOs are scoundrels. One of them is a personal friend of mine. I can assure you he'd stop at nothing, or very little, to get ahead in the market."

"A personal friend? Would you mind giving me his name?"

The publicist looked at Sedgwick for a moment before providing the name (Manny briefly turned away as if this were none of his business). "You will keep this confidential, right? I mean, it would be slightly inconvenient if his wife found out about the relationship. You've been in the same position, I'm sure."

"No, but I'll keep the name confidential unless there's a valid reason not to. By the way, do you know anyone associated with your company that wears military fatigues or military gear? An employee, or maybe a customer?"

"Not an employee. We have a strict dress code."

Manny unexpectedly leaned forward. "Male or female?"

"Male, in his early twenties. He has light-colored, stringy hair. Do you know him?"

Manny leaned back and shook his head.

After a short, slightly tense discussion with the publicist about speaking to the human resources manager (not available) or even taking as peek at employee records ("a violation of our privacy policy"), Sedgwick inquired whether she or the CEO was ever in contact with the director of the Ravenswood Museum.

"Sir Ronald?" Manny blurted out, surprising both Sedgwick and Thwait. "We're not exactly in the same line of work," he continued. His rough accent was now gone, and in its place was an educated, cultured tone. "Sure, we've been in touch from time to time. But what are you getting at?"

The publicist silently looked at him, but didn't evince any surprise over his words or his accent.

"Nothing, really. I was just wondering if he had reached out to the Evermore after the Ravenswood bombing. The museum received similar extortion letters."

"What bombings?" the publicist asked, surprised that something other than the Evermore was hit.

Manny again leaned back in his chair and draped one arm over the back. "Girl," he said, resuming his slang tone, "it was in all the media. Like, half that place is rubble, do you hear what I'm saying? What kind of publicist are you?"

The publicist's face reddened slightly.

Manny leaned forward again and looked at Sedgwick. "He hasn't called since then. He isn't hurt, is he? I'd hate to see that happen."

Sedgwick and Thwait were both taken aback by Manny's changing attitudes.

"He's doing fine," Sedgwick replied. "I was curious, that's all. Both organizations had similar experiences."

Sedgwick directed a couple more questions to the publicist, who now seemed increasingly reluctant to say anything other than to ask if there was a legal basis for their "inquiries." Feeling that she wasn't going to get any more out of the publicist, Sedgwick started to stand (with Thwait following suit) when it occurred to her that she had forgotten to ask about the Gray Ladies. Sitting back in her chair (with Thwait following suit), she glanced at Manny, who was now eying her although he hadn't changed positions, and, turning to the publicist, asked, "one more question, if you don't mind. Do you know anything about the Gray Ladies? Perhaps it's a work of art by that name your firm evaluated or maybe you have something by that name on display. Was something by that name destroyed in the blast? A lot of works were destroyed, am I right?"

"Which question do you want answered first, Inspector Sedgwick?" Once again, it was Manny who responded.

Sedgwick hesitated. She couldn't understand this strange turnabout in Manny's personality or why the publicist wasn't objecting to his intrusion. Looking directly at the assistant, she asked, "I'm sorry?"

"Let me see if I can rephrase this. Hmm, which question do you want answered first?"

"I don't understand why you're responding. Do you have something to do with the inventory?"

Manny glanced at the publicist and burst out laughing. "Do I have something to do with the inventory? Of course, I do. I'm the CEO."

Chapter 31

"What?" This time Sedgwick and Thwait turned in unison to the publicist, who nodded in affirmation.

Manny stood up and pulled his chair closer to Sedgwick. Keeping his eyes on her, he motioned with a slight movement of his head for the publicist to leave. Once she was out of the room, he relaxed and leaned back in his chair. "I'm a little on edge because of the bombing," he said, his voice now deeper and bearing little resemblance to Manny's. "If someone's out to get me, I'm not going to make it easy for them. Sure, I saw your IDs, but you of all people know how simple it is to impersonate an officer."

Both Sedgwick and Thwait eyed Manny, as if they couldn't quite believe their eyes. Indeed, as they looked at him his shimmering hair became dull and gray, and his once youthful face now looked older, wizened, and wrinkles of various sizes seemed to rise across his pasty skin, especially beneath the eyes where they looked like small cow's udders. Smiling briefly, deep lines radiating from the corners of his eyes like flames, he suddenly turned away and rubbed at something in his left eye, smearing the black mascara. Turning back to Sedgwick and Thwait, one eye blackened as if it had been punched, he pronounced his name, adding "the third" after it, and placed his thin arms and bony elbows on the table.

"Okay, Mr. [she stated his full name]," Sedgwick began after regaining her composure.

"The third," he added, smiling again and this time revealing darkened, grayish teeth.

"The third. Let me ask you, do you concur with everything your publicist said?"

"I would have corrected her if I didn't. I did correct her about the museum attack. I can't believe that idiot hadn't heard of it. She's a publicist, for God's sake, and it's her job to be watching the news. Well, maybe she's still a publicist. She's only been with us for a couple years. Yes, apart from that absurd misstatement, everything she said was more or less accurate."

"By the way, you were in Bermuda, weren't you?"

"No, I just got back from Belize. I missed all the action," he added, again showing his old teeth.

"What, if I may ask, were you doing in Belize?"

"Vacationing. What else do you do in Belize?"

"I suppose. And you came back and assumed a disguise."

"Of course, I assumed a disguise. What would you do if a bomb went off under your desk? Yes, I suppose the cleaning crew could have left it there by mistake, or maybe someone delivered it to the wrong office (the publicist's office is down the hall), or possibly a client left it with the expectation that I would authenticate it. Are you kidding me? There were two of them. What else was I supposed to assume if not a disguise? Someone's after me, and I'm not going to make it easy for them to find me. Come on, tell me, what would you do in my shoes?" He reached under the table and gave his left shoe a tug. "Uncomfortable pieces of designer crap."

"We don't yet know who's responsible and so we can't tell if the bombs were meant for you or..."

"Or what? What else could they be meant for?"

"Okay, why do you think someone is trying to kill you?"

"Weren't you listening? Didn't you hear my former publicist? We get all kinds of morons who want to get rich off junk. That's not the way we do business here. We only deal with the finest pieces, genuine pieces, and that means we are very careful about authentication. Our clients know that when we put something up for auction, it has the Evermore seal of approval behind it. Our reputation is everything, and so, yes, we piss off a few people to protect our lifeblood. Clear?" The CEO muttered something about allergies and pawed at something in his right eye, smearing the black mascara around that socket.

"Your publicist said that other CEOs in your market are pretty aggressive characters. Do you have bad relations with any of them?"

"I don't know what she's talking about. Can't you see she's a numbskull? I get along fine with all of them. We're competitive but not homicidal."

"She appears to have some special insights into at least one of them."

"Dah, she's sleeping with him. Since you're going to ask – no, my relationship with her is strictly professional. We got tattoos, that's all."

"She mentioned disgruntled clients or angry potential clients. Are there any in particular that might be, let us say, problematical?"

"I don't know how many different ways I can say it. Yes, we get nutcases from time to time, everyone does, but there's a lot at stake and so it's not surprising." He leaned forward on his skeletal elbows and, because of his pale complexion, black eyes, and dark mouth, his head unexpectedly resembled a skull with a grizzly wig set on top.

"Anyone in particular?"

"Not off the top of my noggin."

"Do you have any enemies?"

"Enemies? Of course, I do. You don't think my friends bombed the building, do you? What kind of stupid question is that?"

"Fair enough. I was just wondering if there was somebody in particular..."

"Again, I don't know. You're the one who's supposed to tell me."

Sedgwick felt that it was pointless to purse the line of questioning, and so she went back to an earlier question. "Let's talk about something else. I mentioned the Gray Ladies earlier. Do you have, or have you come across, anything by that name or description?"

The question elicited a strange transformation in the CEO, and for a few moments he seemed to be Manny again. After centering the publicist's laptop in front of him, he glanced at Thwait while he logged into the machine. "You really should lose some serious weight," he said, adding without looking at Thwait, "It'll make you feel better about yourself." Seconds later, he was paging through what appeared to be a catalogue in search of a particular image. After a couple of minutes of fruitless paging, he paused and looked at Sedgwick. "Nothing specifically by that title," he said and turned back to the screen and continued paging with an occasional input as if he were refining his searches. "Nothing by that description, either. Maybe you mean the Three Graces?"

"Are they gray?"

He turned back to the computer and did some additional searches. "Not one," he replied, shaking his head, which bobbled loosely on his rickety shoulders.

Sedgwick was now beginning to think that the interview had run its course. "So, tell me," she asked casually, grabbing her bag from the floor, "is this your temporary office or your publicist's?"

"Mine," he replied. He was silent for a moment while he dug something out of one of his crooked ears and flicked it away. "She has a cubby down the hallway. The executive offices were destroyed in the bombing, and we're temporarily camped out here until we can get back inside. Say, maybe there's something you could do for me. I need to get into the building to retrieve some important papers. They pertain to the pieces in the storerooms here. But your officers or the fire crews or whatever won't let me in until they finish doing whatever they're doing to the building. I need these papers. I'm going to have trouble setting up the next auction without them."

"I understand," Sedgwick replied, "but I'm afraid it isn't up to me. I'm certain that once the building is declared safe, you will be given full access..."

"How long will that take? And in the interim, how do I know what's in the basement here and who owns it?"

She glanced at Thwait who shrugged. "Wait a minute. Are you saying that your inventory's in this building, not in the auction house?"

"Those are just offices, and of course the auction floor. All the art's stored in this building."

"The suspects didn't attack the art, just your office..."

"What planet have you been on? Gee, officer, those crazy people attacked my office. To my knowledge, nothing of any artistic significance was scratched."

"But the clients bring their works there..."

"What? Absolutely not. They bring them to this building to be appraised and, later, we'll move the ones slated for auction to the other building. And after the auction, we'll bring them back here for storage or removal. Luckily, we weren't open, and so we hadn't set up for the next auction."

Sedgwick was silent for a moment while the CEO or Manny looked back and forth between Sedgwick and Thwait.

"Anything else?" he asked, rising to escort them out of the building.

Sedgwick shook her head and was about to stand up when Thwait suddenly spoke up.

"Excuse me," he said before Sedgwick was fully on her feet. "One more question, if you don't mind. I noticed a strange look on your...your face when we asked about a young man with stringy, blonde hair wearing military garb. You seemed slightly nervous. Tell us again, do you know anyone like that?"

Sitting back down, Sedgwick was pleased that Thwait had taken the initiative.

The CEO cast off Manny and once again leaned forward. "It happened before that fool of a publicist arrived. Two men came in from time to time. The older one looked relatively normal, suits and all that, while the younger one, his son, if I recall correctly, like to pretend that he was some sort survivalist. Anyway, they generally brought in junk to authenticate, but occasionally they had some nice or at least average pieces. We sold a couple for them, but had to stop doing business with them once their shop was raided and one of them, maybe both of them (I haven't seen either of them for some time), was arrested for selling stolen antiquities." Once again, he glowered at Sedgwick, as if she had been the one who had asked the question. "Look, we didn't sell anything stolen or illegally acquired. We are very careful about that. And so we ceased all dealings with them, because we can't associate with people who have that kind of reputation. Legitimate buyers wouldn't trust us, and we depend on trust to conduct business. "

"I see. Go on."

"Well, a year after all that, the young punk came by with something else, a book or something, but we refused to have anything to do with it. I told him about our reputation, and he gets all huffy and starts yelling a bunch of stuff and threatening to put out somebody's eyes."

"Did you ring the police?"

"No, I understood where he was coming from. I'd respond the same way if I were in his dirty shoes. But nothing came of it. Do you think he's involved? It's hard to believe."

"I don't know. Can you give us the names?"

"Maybe. It'll take some time, though. We'll have to comb through our archives, which are stored in another building."

"Not online?"

"Don't have the bandwidth."

"Okay, ring us when you've found something. Do you think we could take a peek at those records when you do find them?"

"As long as you bring the legal help you mentioned earlier."

There was some more talk, mainly about Belize, after which Manny led them to the main doors of the building. "I'd consider that weight," he said to Thwait as he and Sedgwick were leaving, "but you, girl," he said to Sedgwick, "are, like, just right. Except the hair and the clothes, if you know what I mean. If you need, like, a good stylist, let me know. And, paleeeeeeze, do something about that frown." He blew them a kiss as they walked away from the building.

Back in the car, Sedgwick and Thwait started to discuss the interview. Thwait was about to express his reservations regarding the CEO when he noticed that Sedgwick was leaning forward and that her shoulders were visibly shaking. Concerned, he was about to ask her if she needed help, but she burst out laughing before he could utter a word, and she continued laughing for another minute or two. Finally bringing herself under control, she apologized for her unprofessional behavior and insisted that it had nothing to do with Thwait. With a slight smile still on her lips, she asked Thwait to continue.

Not knowing what to think, Thwait smiled briefly and continued speaking about what they had learned from the CEO and his publicist. There were two main issues, he said. The first concerned the young man who was peddling antiques and books. By itself, the information didn't appear particularly relevant, especially since the auction house seemed to have a number of disgruntled customers. But because the description was similar to the description the old woman provided, the CEO's criminal customer shouldn't be dismissed out of hand. "Maybe if the auction house provides...," he started to say but stopped when he noticed Sedgwick's thin shoulders shaking. Once again, he wanted to ask if something was wrong, but she quickly motioned for him to continue while she turned and stared out the driver's window. "Well, I guess we'll know then," he mumbled. Inhaling slightly, he continued and noted that the second issue concerned the absence of art at the auction house. This was interesting, he insisted, since it suggested either that the suspects didn't know where the art was housed (which seemed strange, since they had gone into the building shortly before the blast) or, more likely, that whatever the Gray Ladies are, they had nothing to do with the art at the Evermore. "If the Ravenswood and Evermore bombings are indeed connected," he continued, "we almost have to conclude that Sir Ronald and the CEO were the targets."

Sedgwick turned back to Thwait and once again apologized for her behavior. "Something amusing came to mind," she said and then stated that she agreed with him completely.

Throughout the rest of the afternoon, Sedgwick and Thwait followed up on other leads and, by the time they were back at the station, the Chief had already left for the evening. Sedgwick told Thwait that she would stay to write the report and insisted that he take the rest of the evening off. He went to his desk to retrieve a black coat that he had left on the back of his chair, and as he passed by her office on his way out he could hear her laughing loudly about something.

Chapter 32

On his way home, Thwait tried several times to reach Nesbit. He called his cell and then the hotel number, leaving messages on both – nothing too specific, since he didn't want to upset his friend before he had a chance to speak to him directly – but he felt that it was imperative that he speak to Nesbit before the night was over. The case was changing rapidly, and even if Nesbit didn't agree with some of the assumptions (one as opposed to two cases), it would still be good to hear his reasoning, his wisdom, on the matter. Not only that, both Thwait and Nesbit would be disappointed if the case were solved without Nesbit's input.

Ten minutes from his flat, Thwait suddenly turned around and headed back across town to Nesbit's hotel. Naturally, there were any number of reasons why his great colleague wouldn't answer his phones – he was napping, he was in the lavatory, he was filling his ice bucket, he was face down in an overflowing bathtub – yes, there was an infinite variety of legitimate reasons, most of them perfectly normal and happily benign, and yet he didn't feel entirely comfortable waiting until the great man was on his deathbed before undertaking a simple check on him. Moreover, assuming Nesbit was in the peak of health – he had probably just stepped out for a drink or two – Thwait was beginning to feel that it would be better to speak to him face to face (as opposed to a phone call) to explain what had happened that afternoon (omitting Sedgwick's strange behavior), and he was fairly confident that Nesbit would take it all in stride once he calmed down.

But apart from the urgent necessity of bringing Nesbit up-to-speed (and how he wished that Sedgwick were the one breaking the news), Thwait longed to see his old friend again. He wanted to see his wise face, feel the touch of the older man's soft hand on his broad shoulder, and hear his strong, confident voice discussing the investigation and pointing out the flaws in everyone else's reasoning. Of course, Thwait also enjoyed working with Sedgwick and, if he were forced to choose one officer at the station to work with, it would have to be Sedgwick, whose fairness and dedication were second to none. Nesbit, however, was in a slightly different category. He, too, was totally dedicated to his work, but he also had the kind of experiences and successes that Sedgwick couldn't hope to have until she, too, had spent more than half of her life on the job. Nesbit was a legend, and nothing made Thwait prouder than having Nesbit choose him over all the other deserving officers at the station to work with and mentor. Sure, the Chief assigned him to Nesbit, but it was at Nesbit's request, and it was clear that if Nesbit found his presence tedious or a drag on the case, he could easily request Sedgwick or someone else to take his place. That hadn't happened. After he pulled into the hotel's parking lot and then walked down the hall toward Nesbit's room, Thwait wondered if Nesbit saw something of himself in Thwait. But perhaps that was a bit too much to hope for.

Thwait paused before knocking on the door and took a deep breath. He was slightly uncomfortable arriving unannounced, and he also didn't want to seem too eager to meet his friend, which could be slightly annoying to someone who expected the utmost professionalism from Her Majesty's officers, junior or otherwise.

Thwait knocked three evenly spaced times on the door, and waited. There was no answer. Perhaps Nesbit hadn't heard. He knocked three more evenly spaced times, each instance a little louder than the previous one in case Nesbit hadn't heard any of the foregoing knocks. Inclining his head a little toward the door, he listened for signs that his friend was stirring inside, possibly coming to answer the door. Nothing – there was complete silence. Just to be on the safe side, Thwait waited a few more seconds before knocking again. Maybe Nesbit was already walking to the door, his thick slippers cushioning his footsteps and making them all but impossible to hear. Maybe he was tired or sick, and he wasn't moving as quickly as he normally did. But if he was still sick, maybe he wanted – maybe he needed – to stay in bed, and the constant racket on the outside of the door was not only interrupting his much needed sleep but quite possibly robbing him of the peace of mind needed to regain his strength. Not knowing what to do next (Should he leave? Should he stay? Should he knock again? Should he call out Nesbit's name or simply keep his mouth closed?), Thwait glanced up and down the hallway, scanned the floor near the door, and finally turned back to the door where he noticed the peephole, which was slightly above eye level. Everyone knows that peepholes are essentially one-way devices, but Thwait also knew that if you angled your eye and head just right, you could sometimes detect movement on the other side, possibly a bed with an indistinct shape stretched out on it. Standing on his toes and pressing his fleshy eye socket over the peephole, Thwait was beginning to focus in on something interesting when two men in black overcoats came up behind him and tapped him roughly on each shoulder. Surprised, Thwait turned so quickly that he nearly crashed into one of the men.

"Sir, would you like to come to the office so we can all be comfortable while you explain what you're doing?" the taller of the two men asked. He had a thick mustache and a large nose, which were about the only features visible in the deep shadow cast across his face by the brim of his black fedora. The men displayed identifications. They were hotel detectives.

"Oh, my," Thwait mumbled and chuckled slightly. He was embarrassed for having been caught doing something that was reasonable under the circumstances but that could easily be misconstrued as something illogical and maybe, given the wrong impression, even criminal.

"Quite so," replied the detective. "You are a guest here, I presume?"

"Oh, no, no, no, it's nothing like that. I'm not a guest..."

"Why am I not surprised? We see this sort of thing from time to time, and it's our job to put a stop to it in order to keep our guests safe, secure, and unmolested. I'm sure you understand."

"No, it's not like that. I'm not a guest. I'm..."

The second detective, whose face, like the first detective's, was masked by the shadow created by his fedora, quickly stepped behind Thwait and pulled Thwait's arm behind his back while placing his own around Thwait's neck. Tightening his grip, the second detective leaned forward and whispered into Thwait's ear, "mate," he said, his breath smelling of cheese, "we can do this the easy way or the hard way. It's your call."

"You don't understand. I'm not..."

"We understand," the first detective said. "You've made yourself very clear. You're not a guest." While he didn't attempt to help the second detective, he stood directly in front of Thwait, blocking him from leaving.

"I'm here to see Agent Nesbit. This is his room. He might...might...," Thwait struggled to say, but the second detective's grip was making it extremely difficult to speak. "He might be...be in trouble. He's sick."

"Yep, there's a lot of that going around these days," the first replied. "Why don't you come with us, anyway?"

The second detective, who continued to hold Thwait with a vice-like grip, began dragging him backward as the first stepped out of the way. Despite being relatively thin, the man was extraordinarily strong and the pressure he was able to exert against Thwait's throat was intense and almost unbearable. But something inside Thwait (maybe a combination of instinct and police training) made him resist, and he started dragging and repositioning his heels to make it more difficult for the man to move him anywhere. When the detective tried to strengthen his grip, Thwait somehow maneuvered his right elbow under his ribcage and began jabbing him with all his strength.

"Give me a hand," the second detective said in a loud voice to his partner. "This bloke's making it hard on himself. Get a cable, quick!"

Before the first detective could intervene, Thwait managed to force the second off and away from his neck. Now standing with his back to the hall wall, he put out both his hands as if he were going to shove the detectives away and said, "wait, wait, I'm a police officer. Stop and I'll show you my badge."

The detectives paused but remained standing directly in front of Thwait. The second detective was breathing heavily from the encounter and, tightening his fists, he was ready to have another go at Thwait. The first detective was calmer, and he stood quietly as he twirled a nylon cord in his hand in case they needed to tie Thwait's wrists together.

Stretching one hand out toward the detectives, Thwait cautiously reached into his coat to retrieve his badge and then held it out to the detectives. "Now, do you believe me?"

The second detective, the one who had grabbed Thwait, didn't respond. The first detective, though, smiled briefly and shook his head. "You look the part, but you never know what people are up to these days," he said. "But just because you're one of London's finest doesn't mean…"

"Listen to me. Check out the occupant of the room. He is Agent Nesbit of Interpol. He and I are working an investigation together. It's imperative I speak to him. He wasn't answering his phone, and so I came to see him directly."

"He won't speak to you," the first detective replied, "but you insist on speaking to him anyway? This isn't some kind of lovers' spat, is it?"

"No, no, please verify the name of the occupant. He was ill, and I think he may need some help. I guarantee he'll want to talk to me. Please, this is important."

The first detective glanced at the second and then walked a few steps down the hallway and pulled out his phone. After a short conversation, during which Thwait and the second detective stared at each other, the first detective returned and nodded to his colleague, who still didn't move.

"Our apologies, sir," the first detective said, speaking as if he didn't truly mean it. "Things happen, as I'm sure you know in your line of work. No hard feelings, right?"

"Right," he responded quickly. "Since you're the house detectives, would you open the door and check on my friend, the Interpol agent? I just want to see if he's okay. He was ill, as I told you."

The first detective smiled pleasantly. "I'm afraid not, sir. The front desk called the occupant, but there wasn't an answer. We'll have to presume he's out for the moment. We can't do any more without official papers."

"What? You saw my badge. Isn't that enough for you to take a look in his room? I told you he could be seriously sick."

"I realize that, sir, and we are both sympathetic to your predicament. But we don't even know if you're supposed to be here; legally, I mean. Sure, your badge and credentials seem to be in order, but how do we know if it's official business or something else that brought you here? I hope you understand our position. I wish we could help, but our hands are tied."

Thwait was about to respond, but the first detective held his hand up to silence him. "You're a lucky man today, Constable Twit. Since you're not a guest, it would be better if you went home now, and we'll pretend this day never happened." He nodded and tapped the bill of his hat as a signal for Thwait to leave, while the second detective took one begrudging step to the side.

Thwait squeezed between the detectives and, as he started toward the exit, one of the detectives, probably the one who had put a chokehold on him, gave him a light kick in the seat of his pants. Thwait paused without turning around, and then continued directly toward the exit, listening to the farting sounds the same man was making and the gales of laughter both men were emitting. On his way to his flat, he continued to call Nesbit's cell without success. The following day, while he and Sedgwick were back working on the case, Thwait again tried to reach Nesbit, and like every other time there was no answer.

Chapter 33

The Chief spent the morning at HQ on one of the hard, black benches lining the pale, blank walls of what was termed 'the waiting room.' He had been told to report to the fifth-floor conference room at nine sharp for an urgent meeting, but when he entered the waiting room at 8:45, the conference room door was closed and didn't open once during the ensuing three hours. The Chief was certain that he was on time, he was confident that he was at the right location, and he was comfortable with the fact that when dealing with HQ, one had to deal with it on its own terms.

Two-and-a-half hours after the Chief arrived, Slim walked into the waiting room and appeared to be looking for someone. Slim, whose real name was Martin Fizzel, was in his mid-forties and had a youthful face that was slightly offset by his gray, thinning hair, his rumpled suits, and his wide hips. He was an analyst whom the Chief had known for quite a few years. But while the Chief respected Slim's analytical skills, he generally avoided the younger man because of his overly pleasant, demonstrative personality. As soon as Slim spotted the Chief (who had turned away when he noticed Slim), he walked over to the empty chair next to him and sat down. Without even a perfunctory greeting, Slim quietly informed the Chief that a "high-level personage" had summoned him to present certain "analytical findings" at the meeting. He nudged the Chief familiarly in the side with his elbow and added with a confident, youthful smile that his findings would blow the lid off the investigation. Naturally, he wasn't at liberty to divulge these findings before the meeting. "It's all hush, hush, you know," Slim said, but couldn't resist whispering out the side of his mouth that he had identified one of the suspects. "You'll never guess who it is, although you'll know the name once you've heard it."

The Chief stated, without looking at Slim, that he was prepared to wait until the formal announcement. He glanced impatiently at the conference room door.

"I guarantee it'll knock your socks off," Slim added, leaning against the wall and nonchalantly crossing his arms across his gray jacket.

The Chief silently nodded.

"Of course, you can guess, but I will neither confirm nor deny your guess."

"Then it's pointless for me to try," the Chief responded, and he crossed his arms over his dark suit and stared at the door. The Chief's coolness should have signaled that the conversation was over, but Slim didn't notice and leaned toward the Chief.

"Look," he whispered, glancing at the conference room and then cupping his hand partly over his mouth, "I'll give you this much, but you have to promise not to tell anyone you heard it from me. Okay, here it is," he began without waiting for the Chief to respond. "I pulled a name from the fingerprints Dr. Fellows collected and ran it through a series of databases. You wouldn't believe how much came up – crimes, stolen antiquities, extortion, and a heap more, including the entire name." Slim smiled and once again leaned against the wall.

The Chief turned toward him and squinted. "What's the name?"

"I can't disclose that," Slim responded, wagging his head and eyeing the ceiling.

The Chief squinted for a few more seconds before turning away and staring at the conference room door.

A few moments later, Slim turned back to the Chief and said out the side of his mouth, "all right, the last name's Sanders. He's a bad dude. But you didn't hear this from me."

"What did you say the first suspect's name was?" The Chief sat up and looked at Slim.

Slim again glanced at the conference room door and then turned back to the Chief, who involuntarily leaned away from him. "Sanders. But I think you'll be more interested in some of the other stuff I found." He reached inside his coat and retrieved a neatly folded sheet of paper. "It's all here," he added, holding the sheet in one hand and tapping it with the index finger of his other hand.

The Chief started to reach for the paper, but Slim pulled it out of reach and slipped it back into his pocket. Patting his pocket, he said, "soon enough."

"Okay," the Chief said, squinting at him, "so what was his first name?"

"Yes, indeed, interesting stuff," Slim said as much to himself as to the Chief as he made himself a little more comfortable. He paused and stared at the opposite wall as if contemplating something significant.

The Chief was about to ask again for the first name when the conference room door burst open and several officials in gray suits began filing out. Most were silent and didn't look at anyone as they passed through the waiting room, although the last two were discussing something in hushed voices as they walked by the Chief and Slim. A minute later, a small, ovoid-shaped man with a shiny head and a paisley bow tie appeared and positioned himself in the doorway. After silently inventorying the people in the waiting room, he clapped twice and motioned everyone into the conference room with a flip of his slender right hand. While people were filing into the room, the man went quickly to the far end of the room and positioned himself behind a podium.

"Sorry to keep you waiting," the man said in a strong baritone to the people now making themselves comfortable in the heavily cushioned chairs around the long conference room table. He was in his late fifties, and he was also one of the high-ranking officials at HQ with whom the Chief often conferred about the investigation. The Chief, though, wasn't particularly fond of the individual, because he was also one of the officials who refused to confirm that HQ had more evidence than they were doling out. "We'll get started in a few minutes."

He glanced around the room, and thirty seconds later when he was satisfied that everyone was there (mainly high-ranking officials from HQ), he began speaking. "Right, then," he began, "I want to bring everyone up-to-speed on the latest evidence from the Gray Ladies' investigation. We have a lot of material to cover, so please hold your questions to the end. Now, as we all know, the bombings at the Ravenswood and the Evermore were the work of the same individuals. The extortion letters, the wiretap, and other evidence confirm this. Ladies and gentlemen, less than twenty-four hours ago, we were able to identify one of the suspects in the wiretap."

He paused and pinched the tip of his round nose. "Before I go any further, I should like to note that Mr. Slim, who graciously volunteered to attend this meeting, was instrumental in the discovery of the suspect's identity." Slim rose partway out of his chair to acknowledge his introduction. "Right, well, the named subject is the individual in the wiretap called 'male voice number one.'" There was a slight susurration among the attendees, which the official silenced with his raised palm. "Please note that some of the details are contained in the case summary on the table in front of you," he added, pointing to a stack of papers in the middle of the table.

While the papers were being passed around, the official noticed Slim's raised hand and eager expression. He turned away for a few moments, hoping that the hand would disappear, but when he turned back to the table the hand and expression were as insistent as ever. "Is this important?" he asked Slim.

"I believe so, sir. I have some additional information on the subject that could be very useful for our discussion," he said and pulled the folded paper from his breast pocket. After quickly unfolding the paper, he held it across the table toward the official.

"That's fine, Mr. Slim," the official responded without reaching for the paper. "There will be a few minutes at the end for questions and comments."

Slim sheepishly glanced around and then lowered himself back into his chair, refolding the paper and putting it back into his pocket.

"Now, unless there's anything else, I'll begin by providing background on the investigation to help you understand the significance of what I'm going to present. Pardon me – I forgot to mention that Dr. Fellows had planned to give a summary of the forensics evidence, but he can't attend today because of a rash he recently contracted. He sends us his regrets and wishes us all the best."

The Chief glanced around for a pencil and, not finding one, began tapping his index finger against the table top.

"Oh, yes, I was planning to hold a small ceremony to honor the officers who contribute to this investigation, but instead of waiting until it's resolved, I'd like to take a couple of minutes before we start to mention their names and contributions. Right, in no particular order..."

"Excuse me," the Chief interrupted, squinting at the official. "Could we back up a moment? Would you mind giving us the first and last name of the suspect? We're speaking about a young male, right?"

"Not again," he muttered, shaking his glisten head. "Can this wait a few minutes? There's some general information on the summary page."

"It's important now," the Chief replied, speaking as forcefully as the official.

"Oh, all right," he sighed, "if you want to slow things down. The suspect's name is Charles Sanders, Jr. He has a rather extensive record for petty crimes, most recently for the theft of antiquities. I presume that rings a bell?" he pointedly asked the Chief.

The Chief stopped tapping his finger and squinted at the official.

"Oh, I suppose it wouldn't hurt to go through some of this now for everyone's benefit, though it was scheduled for later." He glanced at his notes. "Right, then, Sanders Jr. and his father, Sanders Sr., ran an antique shop in

London that fronted for their illicit business in stolen antiquities. Officers from the Chief's station arrested both of the Sanders about three years ago and closed their shop." He raised his invisible eyebrows at the Chief. "Sanders Jr. was given a light sentence of two years, while his father died eighteen months into what was a multi-year stretch at another facility. The Sanders were close, and we believe that upon hearing of father's demise, Sanders Jr. hatched a scheme to punish the institutions he believed ruined the family business and caused his father's untimely demise, namely, the police and the organizations the Sanders were trying to use to authenticate their contraband. Regarding the police, Sanders Jr. seems to have fixated on one particular officer."

The Chief started tapping his index finger again. "So that's why you wanted the case file. What's the name of this officer?"

"Agent Nesbit of Interpol."

"Nesbit? He didn't have anything to do with the investigation. He's not even an officer."

"I agree his involvement was minimal, but he was helping your officers with the case."

"Minimal doesn't begin to describe it."

The official grimaced slightly. "For the benefit of the others," he added with emphasis, "Agent Nesbit and Constable Thwait from the Chief's station were working another investigation when they came across Sanders Sr. and interviewed him as a possible suspect. They were mistaken, but they were correct in concluding that Sanders Sr. was up to something nefarious and so they alerted the station. Agent Nesbit, rightly or wrongly, was mentioned in the press as one of the officers responsible for taking down the Sanders. Let me add that we cannot account for Sanders Jr.'s rationale with respect to Agent Nesbit or anything else."

"Can you provide the evidence for this?"

"Let's table this for now. We're getting off track..."

"Who's getting off track? You brought it up, and I need to see the evidence so the investigation doesn't get off track."

"Please, you'll have it in due time..."

"When's that?"

"When it's appropriate."

At the outset of the meeting, the Chief hoped that HQ would finally disclose the evidence that was being withheld from him, and therefore he had been doing his best to remain calm in the face of the official's pointless objections. But for some reason, the even sheen of the official's glimmering head seemed to be laughing at him for his misplaced hope – laughing at him for all the past times he had hoped for something from HQ – and at the moment it was more than he could take. "Look," the Chief practically shouted, "you and everyone else here have been keeping secrets since this investigation started. You feed me pieces of a wiretap without giving me any other details. You foist Nesbit on me without explaining why. You hand me this tidbit without a shred of evidence to support it. And all the while Her Majesty is supposedly in danger. Well, I've had enough. Unless you give me everything right now, this investigation is going nowhere – and it will be your fault, not mine."

"You're disrupting the meeting..."

"And you're disrupting the investigation."

"I will ask you to..."

"He's right," the woman sitting next to the Chief said, immediately silencing everyone in the room. As if on command, they all turned to look at her.

"What?"

The woman who had spoken in defense of the Chief had narrow, sharply-defined features, and a full head of practically silver hair that flowed over her thin shoulders. She was a senior representative from Her Majesty's government, as well as the most senior officer in the room. Turning to the Chief, she said, "you're right. But there were some good reasons for doing what we did. So, what do you want to know?"

The Chief was as surprised as everyone else, but he quickly recovered. "Everything you have. But you can start by telling me how you know all this about Sanders Jr."

"Interpol told us."

"Interpol?"

"Yes," she replied in a calm, confident tone. "Interpol has been interested in Sanders Jr. for some time. Shortly after he was released, they received word from a former cellmate who claimed that Sanders Jr. had told him that he, Sanders Jr., and an accomplice were planning to bomb several buildings in London to settle scores and get back at a certain 'Constable Nesbeth.' The cellmate, I should point out, is a French national who was seeking to trade information to prevent his extradition to Tunisia. Unfortunately he didn't know the name of Sanders Jr.'s accomplice, and Interpol lost Sanders Jr.'s trail about five months ago without finding out."

The representative leaned forward and placed her folded hands on the table. "Interpol picked up Sanders Jr.'s scent about two months ago and, in their eagerness to get the goods on their man, they mistakenly tapped into a line on British soil. They ended the wiretap when they discovered their mistake, after which they notified Scotland Yard. Given the information, I think you can see why we were interested in the wiretap but reluctant to share it."

"Interpol was conducting a wiretap?"

"Yes, and since it wasn't legally sanctioned, we are now on rather thin ice because of it. If it were simply a question of legality, we would have moved the issue through proper channels and let Dr. Fellows, Slim, and the rest do their jobs."

Slim sat up and acknowledged the representative's confidence with a brief salute with his right hand.

"But why did you ask for Nesbit's help?"

"Isn't it obvious?"

"Did you have to assign him to me?"

"We requested Agent Nesbit's presence to protect him, and we felt that we could do a better job of that if he were close to the station leading the investigation. Admittedly, we also hoped that if Sanders Jr. knew that Agent Nesbit was in the country, he wouldn't try to leave and we wouldn't have to deal with official requests, extraditions, and all that, which could put him out of reach for years."

Pausing momentarily to consider what the representative said, the Chief absently scanned the summary sheet in front of him when something caught his eye. While the official used the Chief's silence to continue speaking (this time about the evidence Fellows uncovered), the Chief turned back to the representative and demanded an explanation. "No one mentioned this," he said pointing to a highlighted section at the bottom of the page. "It says that Interpol thinks Nesbit's son was one of the conspirators. Is this true?"

"Can't we postpone...," the official sighed and then fell silent in deference to his superior.

"That's correct," the representative said. "Interpol told us they heard Sanders Jr. referring to the other individual on the line as Constable 'Nisbet's' son."

"Are you talking about the phrase 'his only begotten'?"

"No, this reference wasn't recorded. They picked it up just prior to turning on their equipment. It certainly fits with the rest of the wiretap."

"We sure seem to be dependent on Interpol. Okay, assuming there's some validity in this, why would Nesbit's son want to target his father?"

"Are you sure you read the summary?" the official at the podium interjected as if he had had enough. "His son was a petty criminal, and his crimes were probably the result of the estrangement from his father. I don't think it's hard to imagine a young man like that nursing a grudge against him. Sanders Jr.'s arrival – and Interpol informed us the two met in Oxford – must have occurred at exactly the right moment for both men."

"Just because he's estranged from his father doesn't mean he's going to fall for some psychopath that shows up on his doorstep."

"What?"

The Chief turned to the representative. "Has anyone spoken to Nesbit about this?"

"No, we didn't want to spook him. It's your call how you use him, but I'd hate to see Agent Nesbit leave and the investigation stall as a result. We want Sanders Jr., and we don't relish the idea of knowing he's somewhere outside of the country living it up. If Agent Nesbit's son is involved, we want him, too."

"One more question…"

"Of course."

"Since Sanders Jr. is presumably still living, are we to assume that Nesbit's son was killed in the Evermore explosions?"

Slim reached for the paper in his breast pocket but stopped when the official shook his ovate head at him.

"I don't know," the representative said. "We can't yet discount the possibility of others being involved."

"Was Interpol tracking his son?

"Not to our knowledge."

The Chief glanced at the official, who was now grimacing because of the continued interruption, and turned back to the representative. "One last question – is that everything? Is there anything else you're not telling me?"

Several of the people around the table either stared open-mouthed at the Chief or gasped, while the official seemed to hover above the podium ready to strike the Chief.

The representative shook her head without speaking.

The official took a deep breath and resumed speaking. The Chief, however, fell into a studied silence. Moments later, the Chief got up and left the room, leaving the summary sheet on the table.

Chapter 34

Sedgwick and Thwait were out of the station when the Chief returned. Sitting behind his practically empty desk, he made a couple of notes on loose sheets of paper and then slipped them into his top drawer. Dropping his pencil to the desk, where it came to rest against the stack of folders, he made two quick calls (one to Sedgwick's desk and the other to Thwait's) and, not getting an answer, he dialed Sedgwick's cell.

"Hello, Chief," Sedgwick said, as she and Thwait were leaving after having finished another interview. "I trust all went well and that you got the information we needed."

"Do you know where Nesbit is?"

"No, he's still out on sick leave."

"Has Constable Thwait heard from him recently?"

"He tried to contact him last night but Agent Nesbit wasn't answering. Constable Thwait's left several messages, but he hasn't received any responses. Is there a problem? It does seem unusual for Agent Nesbit to be out of touch."

The Chief was silent for a moment.

"Chief?"

"I'm not sure. But what I heard from HQ makes me a little concerned that he could be in trouble."

"Chief?"

The Chief paused and then provided a short overview of what he learned at the meeting. "Here's what I want you to do," he said as he reached for his pencil and began tapping it against the desk. "If Nesbit doesn't pick up his phone, go to the hotel and bring him back, and I don't care if you have to use an ambulance or cuffs. If he's not there, then find him. I want him here by the end of the day."

On their way to the hotel, Thwait tried several times to reach Nesbit. Like his previous attempts, there was no answer, and he was unable to leave a message because the mailboxes were full. He contacted the front desk to see if they could be of help, but since they were no longer allowed to give out information regarding the guests without management approval, he made an appointment to see the manager. Upon their arrival, they checked Nesbit's room (without luck) and then went to meet with the manager.

Dressed in a gray business suit and tie, the hotel manager had a smooth face (somewhat puffy under the chin) and a black, ill-fitting toupee. As

Sedgwick and Thwait made themselves comfortable in the well-cushioned, black leather-covered chairs that lined his office (which reminded them of an elegant hotel room, replete with framed lithographs on the walls and a bar at the opposite end next to a file cabinet), he dialed a number and summoned the detectives. Putting down the silver-edged phone, he turned to the officers and explained in a slightly affected voice that the detectives would arrive in five minutes or so. In the meantime, he asked Sedgwick and Thwait to clarify their request and help him understand why he should allow them to violate the sanctity of a guest's room, especially since they didn't have a legal justification.

Sedgwick offered some background details – Nesbit was an Interpol agent, the station was concerned about his safety, and so forth – and then pleasantly responded to a series of pointless, repetitive questions from the manager regarding the peace of mind of the establishment's guests. After assuring the manager that they would do everything they could to avoid disturbing the overnight guests, she noted as an afterthought that the station's ability to avoid troubling anyone hinged largely on the manager's willingness to help in this matter. "I'm sure you understand," she added, the left side of her mouth drooping slightly.

The manager stared at her for a few moments as if he were churning something around under his mismatched hair, and then asked to know how far the investigation into the Nesbit's stay at the hotel needed to go. Glancing at the file cabinet without trying to move his head, he added that if he helped in this instance, his help wasn't a charter to search beyond the room or to query more than a few staff personnel – and it certainly wouldn't allow the officers to search the records of his other, valued guests.

Sedgwick smiled and, crossing her legs, added that "our only concern is Agent Nesbit, and the sooner we understand his status, the sooner we'll get out of your hair."

The manager tugged at the back of his hair and reluctantly nodded. "I can assure you we will do everything we can to help as long as others aren't disturbed." He lifted the phone and was about to call the detectives again when there was a knock on the door. The detectives entered, and they looked exactly as Thwait had seen them the other evening. Without a word, they took a seat on the empty sofa on the other side of the manager's desk.

The first detective took off his hat and carefully placed it on his knees. When the other officer failed to follow suit, the first nudged him in the ribs and motioned to the hat on his knees. The second detective reluctantly followed suit. Once the heads of both men were uncovered, Thwait could see their faces clearly for the first time, and he was somewhat surprised to see that both were non-descript looking individuals, the kind you might see on a bus or in the Underground and never remember them again. They glanced at Sedgwick and Thwait, but didn't make any connections until the manager introduced the officers and noted that they wanted information about Agent Nesbit in room (he provided the number).

"Oh, hello, sir," the older man said, looking carefully at Thwait. "We're happy to help you officers in whatever way we can." He tried to smile ingratiatingly, but he couldn't quite pull it off with Sedgwick, the hotel manager, especially Thwait looking at him. In fact, he looked slightly uncomfortable, and he hoped that their earlier interaction with Thwait hadn't come up in conversation. The second detective remained silent and impassive.

Before Sedgwick and the hotel management could add anything, Thwait glowered at the second detective while speaking firmly to the first detective. "We would like to see if Agent Nesbit is in his room. We would also like to know if you have any information regarding his whereabouts, his movements in and around the hotel, and any guests he may have had while staying here."

Both detectives insisted that they didn't know Agent Nesbit, and they emphasized that they had not been monitoring his movements at the hotel, or anywhere else, for that matter. Furthermore, they claimed that they hadn't seen anything suspicious near his room (omitting their encounter with Thwait). Nesbit's floor was one of the quietest in the hotel, and so they had little reason to be anywhere near his room on a regular basis (again, keeping mum about Thwait). Without being asked, the first detective suggested that they go to Nesbit's room and check it out, after which if they failed to find anything concrete about his whereabouts, they should speak to the clerks at the front desk. "Three shifts work the desk throughout the day, but the evening shift is the best place to start as they're are the most experienced."

Everyone agreed and, as they started to leave the office, the hotel manager unexpectedly demurred and stated that he was going to stay behind in case anything came up. "I'll be here in the office for at least two more hours should you need me." He tugged at the back of his hair and then extended his right hand to both officers. "Please," he added, "if there is any problem, reach out to me day or night. We are concerned about your man, certainly, but as you know we have to be mindful of our other guests, too."

After leaving the hotel manager's office, Sedgwick and Thwait and the two hotel detectives walked silently to Nesbit's room. It was as if they all feared the worst but were reluctant to divulge their feelings. Of course, the reasons for the detectives' fears were vastly different than Sedgwick's and Thwait's fears.

"If you don't mind," the first detective said when they came to Nesbit's door. He was looking directly at Thwait as if he, not Sedgwick, were in charge. "I am required to ascertain if there's anyone inside before entering. Standard policy, which I'm sure you understand." He winked, as if everyone understood the absence of sense in official policy.

Thwait didn't reply but waited patiently as the first detective knocked several times and called Nesbit's name in a loud whisper (he didn't want to bother the other guests by shouting). When it was clear that no one was going to respond, the first detective pulled a keycard from his coat pocket and unlocked the door. Holding the door open and stepping to the side, he allowed Sedgwick and Thwait to enter first. As soon as Thwait came along side of him, the detective whispered in Thwait's ear, "no hard feelings about the other day, mate? Just doing our job. You understand, right?" Thwait stopped and eyed the man carefully. Noticing the somewhat impassive expression on the man's face, he shrugged his thick shoulders and entered the room.

Sedgwick quickly determined that Nesbit was neither in the neatly made bed nor in any other part of the room, and so she and Thwait systematically scoured the place from top to bottom for anything that would help them locate their friend or provide information concerning his whereabouts. Beginning with the central portion of the room, they looked under and around the bed (since the bed was nicely made, there was no sense in pulling down the covers), under the central table and inside and behind the dresser and entertainment cabinet, and, with the help of the first detective, unlocked the door connecting Nesbit's room to the one next door, which was unoccupied at the time. They checked the closet, pushing aside Nesbit's suits to check the wall and feeling the floor for anything unusual; they checked the bathroom, peering behind the opaque shower curtain and going through both the drawers under the sink and Nesbit's duffel kit (touching the intimate items that the great man handled on a daily basis thrilled Thwait and momentarily clouded his vision when he considered the possibility that Nesbit might never handle the same items again); and they checked the balcony, noting its narrowness but agreeing that it was more than wide enough to shelter two or three men, if necessary.

Nothing. They couldn't find a single thing to suggest foul play, a quick exit, or unwanted guests. And there was no point in dusting the place, since they already had Nesbit's identity and they knew that any number of people had been in the room before and during his stay – not excluding the two detectives, who stood back by the door and let Sedgwick and Thwait do their work. Since it was clear that the room hadn't been occupied for at least a day, Sedgwick and Thwait decided to leave after having spent nearly an hour there with nothing to show for their time and effort.

Sedgwick was the first to leave, and she walked briskly and without hesitation between the two detectives who were now stationed on either side of the door just inside the room. The first detective followed her, and once they were in the hall they began conferring softly about something. Thwait followed shortly thereafter, but when he approached the second detective, who had remained in the doorway, he couldn't help noticing a slight smirk pressing down the top of the man's thin lips. Stopping sideways in front of him, Thwait glanced at him out the corners of his eyes and waited for the smirk to disappear. When that didn't happen (in fact, it was getting broader and more pronounced the longer he stood there), Thwait nodded and shoved the detective against the door frame with a blow from his thick shoulder. The man's impact against the door and wall created a loud thud, making Sedgwick and the first detective turn in unison to see what had happened.

"Any questions?" Thwait asked, now standing directly in front of the second detective, ready to knock him back again if he moved or said the wrong thing. When the detective didn't respond (and, luckily, his smirk was absent), Thwait smiled and said, "I thought so." No one said another word as Thwait caught up with Sedgwick.

Before they returned to the office to speak once more to the hotel manager, Sedgwick, Thwait, and the detectives met with the associates behind the front desk and members of the evening housekeeping staff. Several employees from both groups knew Nesbit by sight, and a young woman at the front desk mentioned that Nesbit often left a tip for no reason. However, none of these individuals had any idea of his whereabouts, and one of them, an elderly woman with a dark moustache, thought that she might have seen him a few days ago but not since that time. Even the maître de of the hotel restaurant where Nesbit dined at least once a day couldn't recall having seen Nesbit in several days. Sedgwick and Thwait gave out their cards to all the staff in case Nesbit returned. Handing his card to the 'junior' detective, Thwait smiled broadly and then slapped him so hard on the back that he nearly fell over. He promised the now wide-eyed man that he would return someday, after which he followed Sedgwick out the door.

On their way back to the station, Thwait tried to reach Nesbit again, but the result was the same as it was the previous time, and the time before that and the time before that, and...

They met the Chief in the hallway outside of his office (he was on his way to meet with some other officials about a different case). Squinting at each officer, he listened to their news and shook his head. "Okay," he said as he gripped a slim, black notebook in his right hand, "I want you to continue looking for him. He's your top priority right now."

"Yes, Chief," Thwait said loudly, and for a brief moment the Chief could see the glitter of moisture in his large, innocent eyes.

"Chief, I'd like to expand the search to borders, and contact the States, if necessary."

The Chief had been about to leave, but he stopped and looked at both officers, his eyes narrow slits. "One more thing – customs officials at Heathrow reportedly received an extortion letter. From what I gather, it's similar to the letters sent to Ravenswood and Evermore. Find Nesbit first and then look into this."

Chapter 35

Two days prior to the hotel search, Nesbit managed to contact his son again and practically begged him to meet some place where they could talk. "I understand. Things happen," Nesbit was saying, "but we can work out something that'll be convenient for you. I've wanted to see you for so long, Ben, but in the past that mother of yours…no, no, I'm not going to talk about her. But honest to God, Ben, I would have given her anything for a few minutes with you. I'm not, I'm not…it's just that you can't imagine what she…no, believe me, I'm over all that. Ben, what matters now is that we work something out to get together, talk over some things, and…please, Ben, whatever works for you. And I won't say anything about, you know, the events. Please don't say such things. Say, I'll bet you don't know what I look like. You've seen my picture in the papers?" The very idea that his son had seen his image in the media filled his eyes with tears and, for a few moments, Nesbit held his breath to keep from breaking down. He didn't want his son to think he was weak, certainly not at this point in time. He and his son needed to speak like adults, and they would need to confer like adults when they finally met, since there were so many things needing to be resolved that couldn't be resolved if he started crying like a baby. A few minutes later, the day (that very day), the time (three hours from the second they hung up), and the place (a café in a small town not far from Oxford) were established for their meeting. Cautiously optimistic, Nesbit had begun mentally preparing for the meeting when Thwait called and updated him on the case.

He felt horrible after the call. He had been abrupt with one of his closest friends, and he wasn't certain that a simple apology was enough to make up for his shameful behavior. The reason was due to the unsettling conversations that he had been having with his son and, of course, with the evidence, which was pointing in the direction of the one person he loved more than anyone else in the world. Nesbit was fairly confident that his son was innocent of all crimes, and he was also fairly convinced that his son had told him things during their last conversation merely to set him off, to punish him for neglecting him throughout his life; and yet the things that he said were shocking, especially because they came close to what he, Nesbit, knew about the bombings. But even if there were some merit to the young man's claims (telling Nesbit, for example, how such a bomb could be constructed and explaining how easy it was to place them in the offices of directors, CEOs, and so forth), Nesbit refused to accept them, and he refused to let his only son take the fall for something that others had to be involved with as well. But if worse came to worse and he was unable to protect his son, Nesbit was hopeful that with the right legal team his son's complicity might be explained away (mistaken identity, tainted evidence, the rush to judgment). Complicating matters was the young man himself – he was uncouth, at times defiant, and nothing at all like Nesbit expected – and yet even this, which was clearly his mother's handiwork, was not enough to make him abandon his son to the legal system. 'That woman,' Nesbit mused, 'that pathetic fool, slandered me and did everything she could to keep Ben from making something of his life.' Ben was young and there was still a chance to help him, and yet the way he spoke – the crude words, the snide, insensitive comments, especially those about Nesbit and his profession – made him wonder in passing if a psychologist might be needed, especially if things continued on their current trajectory.

Once Nesbit was on the road, something the young man said floated around in the back of his mind, half remembered, half forgotten. It might have been the man's foul language (at times, every other bloody word was an expletive), and yet even this didn't seem enough to account for his increasing uneasiness. Then again, maybe it was simply his voice, which was so different than his mother's (although there was no reason why it should have resembled hers in the least), or something else entirely. Of course, it wasn't until recently that they had spoken after years of silence, and so a lot had obviously changed or evolved during this time, and yet he couldn't shake the feeling that the boy had forgotten all the things that he should have remembered growing up with or without a father. It's natural to forget unpleasant things, but did he have to forget everything, or practically everything? Well, given the boy's mother, he couldn't be entirely surprised that Ben's memory was a little weak, even when it came to the early years when father, mother, and child all lived under one roof.

The traffic was light for this time of day, and Nesbit was surprised at how quickly he reached Oxford and then skirted around the city on his way to the village where the pub was located. For most of the trip, he couldn't help thinking about the possible associations and the incongruities surrounding and threatening to color his perceptions of the young man, but when the village was practically in sight, his thoughts suddenly turned to the young man's living conditions and he couldn't fathom why he or anyone else would choose to live in such a pigsty. Even if he were broke, he could have cleaned up the place a little (that wouldn't have cost a thing), made it fit for a self-respecting human being instead of... 'My God," Nesbit thought, "how could it have been worse? Even if he didn't have a job or money for food, he didn't have to be this way. He could have come to me before degrading himself in that fashion. Didn't his mother leave him anything more than this dump when she passed away? Why didn't he sell it if he was desperate? Then again, could he and his mother been living this way before her death? She had her problems, but...but it makes no sense at all."

Nesbit came to a narrow street running through the center of the village and, after making the appropriate right, he wound his way through the narrow cobblestone streets, around low buildings, up small hills, and down narrow, curving paths. Finally, when he had come to what appeared to be end of the road, he spotted a small open area for cars and at its edge, the pub. 'I'm finally going to see and speak to my son,' he said to himself. 'By God, I'll get to the bottom of things. We'll put aside all that prior nonsense, and after I set him up on some self-respecting path, we'll spend a jolly good afternoon together, maybe more.'

After locking his car, he walked across the parking area to a cluster of old, stone buildings. Before he stepped on the walk that led to the pub and beyond, he took a good look at the direction from which he had come. There were a couple of beat-up cars on the opposite side of the road, half on the road and half on the sidewalk, and there were a couple more cars near the place where he parked, but he couldn't see anyone in the cars or on the street. The village was deserted except for the handful of people in the dirty windows of the restaurant across the street. Nesbit was on the verge of looking at his watch (he didn't want to be late) but decided not to. He knew he wasn't late, and so the exact time didn't matter. Time itself didn't matter. The only thing that mattered to him now was seeing his son and reconnecting with a life that he thought he would never recover after it had been ripped from him nearly sixteen years ago. Buttoning one of the buttons on his suit coat because of the cool breeze that had swept up, he started walking down the street toward the sign on the left, which hung over the door announcing a place to get cheap food and warm beer. The gray sky was darkening as he reached the establishment and, as he cautiously looked inside before opening the door (for some reason, he wanted to see his son before his son saw him), he noticed four men, each holding a drink.

There were two old men in French berets sitting at a small, round table in the corner, underneath a faded poster of a bull goring a bullfighter. Clearly, neither man was his son. But there were two other men standing at the bar, one a respectable-looking young man in his early twenties that, judging from his appearance, had a good job (businessman, attorney, doctor, veterinarian?), and another a few feet farther down the wet bar dressed in ragged khakis and a dirty hunter's jacket. He, too, seemed to be in his early twenties, but unlike the other his hair was long and stringy (a sign that he rarely combed it) and he lacked the confident self-composure of the businessman. He appeared jumpy, and he didn't seem to be connected with anyone in the establishment, suggesting perhaps that he was down on his luck (Nesbit watched him moisten his lips several times as if he were nervous or needed another drink). Since he hadn't seen his son in years, Nesbit couldn't tell if either of the men was related to him; but unless his son hadn't arrived yet, one of the men had to be the boy. Nesbit earnestly prayed that it wasn't the big game hunter or whatever he was.

Striding resolutely inside, Nesbit expected the open door to set off the delicate tinkling of a bell to announce his presence to everyone there. Instead of a bell, however, he was greeted by loud, garish music, the kind of trash he thought he left behind in New Orleans, and not a single person looked his way. Nesbit paused just inside the door, hoping that someone would notice his arrival, and when that didn't happen he continued moving deeper into the narrow, dark, foul-smelling place, praying that the businessman or veterinarian would eventually recognize him and invite him over for a drink. No one turned. The music continued while the two old men silently drank their beers, the businessman drank his glass, and the militiaman fiddled with an empty glass. Since there was no other alternative to introducing himself to the clientele, Nesbit steered away from the old men (who, because of their appearance and age, couldn't possibly be related) and stopped at the damp, steel-covered bar, a few feet away from the businessman. Taking a deep breath, he was going to approach the young man when a barman in a dirty white apron appeared out of nowhere and demanded to know what Nesbit was having to drink.

Nesbit stared at the barman for a moment not quite grasping what the man was saying. Finally shaking his head, he turned back toward the young man, who was now leaning against the counter and inscribing something into the surface with his index finger. The young man seemed about average in height, but the rest of him was anything but average – he was handsome, well-dressed, and his high, smooth forehead suggested a powerful intellect. What's more, there was something in his movements – the way his finger played with the moisture on the counter, the manner in which his smooth jaw moved while he was doubtless thinking about his father – that almost convinced Nesbit that he was watching himself some thirty years ago. It had to be him.

Reaching over, Nesbit lightly tapped the young man's shoulder. When the man turned and somewhat unsteadily faced him, Nesbit said with pride and confidence, "sorry to bother you, but I'm Agent Nesbit...no, I'm sorry, my name is [he offered his first and last name without the professional designation], and I wonder if you know me?"

The man groggily placed a non-existent glass on the counter and leaned toward Nesbit, squinting at him in a way that made him wonder if the man was related to the Chief. When the young man had seen enough, he shook his head slowly and said no. "Are you lost? What's his name might be able to help." The motioned vaguely over his shoulder and smiling fatuously, patted Nesbit on the cheek and went back to his drawing.

Nesbit nodded and, somewhat dazed, he turned to look for the hunter, who was now at the opposite end of the bar. When Nesbit lifted his eyes to focus on this young man, the young man was looking back at him, and there was a disdainful smile stretching his crude lips as if he had caught Nesbit in the act of doing something shameful.

The young man's clothes were dirty, and there was a rip in his coat near the collar where a button used to be. His face had a week's growth of stubble, his hair was messy and matted, and his face was dirty. It was oily, and there were some dark smudges next to a circular pattern of small pimples. He looked like a bum and, as he came closer, smelled like one, too. Nesbit was ready to push him away when he got within arm's reach, but before Nesbit could respond the young man said, "well, daddy, recognize me? Ain't I your spitting image?"

Chapter 36

The young man motioned to a table near the window (the old men were gone). After he and Nesbit sat down (Nesbit's back was toward the window), the young man held his empty glass in front of Nesbit's nose and turned it upside down. "Want one?" he asked Nesbit.

Nesbit smiled wanly and shook his head.

"Mind buying me one?" he said, wiping off his dry lips with the back of his jacket sleeve and exposing a mark on his wrist the looked like part of a tattoo. Before Nesbit could respond, the young man turned toward the barman, who was leaning against a sink behind the counter eyeing the two men, and hollered, "hey-a, buddy, another beer. My daddy here's paying." Laughing, he turned back to Nesbit and said, "you don't mind, right?"

Nesbit shook his head. While the young man waited for his beer, glancing first out the window and then staring at the barman to make sure he was moving with the requisite speed, Nesbit couldn't help examining him. He couldn't stomach looking at the young man's long, dirty hair, but he had little problem observing his narrow, oily forehead, his heavy, pimple-covered cheeks, and his dry, thin lips. Doubtless, there was something special there, Nesbit assured himself, but it would require some significant cleaning and possibly a dermatologist's care. But as much as he tried, he couldn't discover anything in the man's appearance that might suggest a relationship to either himself or his ex-wife – and, despite his current circumstances, if he had grown up eating as sensibly as his ex-wife (if she had a single virtue, it had to be her eating habits, which stressed balanced meals and plenty of fruits and vegetables), then surely there would be some signs of it in his overall shape, his facial contours, and even in his hair, which would have had a pleasant sheen to it. Well, he told himself, perhaps something would become apparent in his personality. Children can often be as different as night and day from their parents, but they can't escape personality.

"I hope we didn't put you out," the young man said when the barman brought over the beer.

"Keeping a tab?" asked the barman, an overweight man whose dirty apron couldn't hide his protruding stomach.

Nesbit nodded. He felt his phone vibrate, and, when the young man's head was turned, he pulled it halfway out of his pocket (his movements obscured by the table) and saw that it was Thwait. Before the young man turned back around, Nesbit shut off the phone so that it wouldn't interrupt anything. He would contact Thwait later on this evening or the first thing in the morning.

The young man turned and stared at Nesbit, moving his grubby head up and down. "Something wrong? You look good in your fancy-ass suit, but I seem to bother you. Don't I look good like you, or you got something against me?"

Nesbit was surprised at the young man's aggressiveness, which seemed even more pronounced than when speaking to him by phone. Shaking his head, he muttered "no."

"Then what is it, man? If I don't smell good, it's 'cause I ain't had a bath in..." He paused and began counting out something using his long, dirty fingers. "...I guess a while," he laughed, the sound of his voice seeming unusually loud and offensive when the music suddenly ended. "Man, they don't play this stuff long enough." He was going to demand more music from the barman when Nesbit touched him lightly on the forearm and uttered his name.

"Ben," Nesbit said gently, "it's not that. I'm happy to see you, and I don't care whether you had a bath or not."

"Daddy-o, neither do I."

"So," Nesbit began, trying to engage the young man, even though he wasn't quite sure what to talk about. "What have you been doing lately?"

The young man took a deep sip of beer. With foam on the corners of his lips, he said, "what do you think I been doing?"

For a moment, Nesbit thought that if he offered the young man some money, he might calm down a little. But he decided to wait until he got to know him a little better. "I was just curious, that's all."

"Yeah, I'll bet." He turned his head and snorted.

Nesbit glanced out the window and noticed that the street was deserted. Turning back to the young man, he said, "this is an awfully quiet town. I don't recall having seen anyone on the streets."

"I wouldn't have it no other way."

Nesbit wanted to ask him if his desire for quietness was the reason he kept the cottage, but he realized that if he mentioned the cottage, it might expose his visit to the place. "I guess that's why you stayed with your mother. She appreciated the solitude, too, in the countryside, if I recall correctly."

The young man stared as if Nesbit had committed a social blunder. "Nah, she didn't like it. She was lonely and didn't have no one to take care of her. I done what I could."

Nesbit was going to praise him for helping his mother, but the young man suddenly seemed eager to say something.

"She was alone, you know what I mean, except for me. She didn't have no one. You certainly didn't give a crap about her, or for me, neither."

Nesbit straightened in his chair. "Excuse me?"

"Man, you know what I'm saying. You deserted her, you deserted me, and all that stuff. But, hey, that's your business. You want to know something? I admire your coolness, man. You don't give a crap about nothing. You're pure ice."

"What? Wait a minute. I never said…"

"Hey, chill out, man. You did what you did, so live with it."

Nesbit was silent for a moment. He had expected more out of a face-to-face conversation with the young man, but this was starting to become more unpleasant than the worst of their phone calls. "Listen to me, Ben," he began, more forcibly than he had intended, "I agreed to all that…that stuff she said in court, because I wanted to spare you, and I wanted to make sure I had visitation rights. I also didn't want you to see your parents acting like…like… But let me tell you something – I didn't desert her, you, or anybody else."

"A little hot under the collar, huh?"

Observing this pathetic individual, recalling his ex-wife and everything that happened between them, Nesbit could barely restrain himself from saying certain things in his defense that he knew would come back to haunt him. "It didn't happen that way, and if she told you that…well, then she was lying to you, just as she lied to the court."

"Wait a minute, daddy-o. Are you now telling me you lied to the court, too? If that's so, how can I believe what you're saying now is the truth?"

"It's not the same thing. I wouldn't lie to you, not now."

"Come on, you did it before. Even if you didn't admit it, your absence was based on a lie and hence was a lie. Who's the biggest liar here?"

"Look, you have it all wrong."

"You're a liar, aren't you?"

"No, of course, not…"

"No? Have it your way. You didn't lie when you lied, and now you're telling the truth, though you sound like you're lying. I guess you're sparing my feelings, just like you did when you never came home. That's heavy stuff, man, but I get it."

Nesbit gritted his teeth and stared at the young man. "I made mistakes, sure, but whatever I did, I did for you. You have to believe that."

"I don't have to believe nothing." He turned around and looked at the barman. "Hey-a, buddy," he called out to him, "I'll have another, if you can spare the time. Get an extra for my friend here. If he don't drink it, I will." When the barman nodded, the young man turned back to Nesbit and smiled briefly. "Lousy service, but there ain't much to choose from in this pit. Probably better where you're from." He paused while the barman placed two drinks in front of him. When the man left, he took a long drink, although this time he licked the foam off his lips. "So, as I was saying, I don't have to believe nothing, 'specially stuff that ain't true."

"Look…"

"Come on, man, spare me the crap. Just say you did what you did, and leave it like that."

"No, you don't understand…"

"I understand plenty. You think 'cause of your fine clothes, I can't understand nothing or can't see through your subterfuge – that's a good one, ain't it? You think just 'cause you're some kind of hotsnot Constable, I don't know squat?" The young man took another pull from his drink, but this time some of the liquid dribbled down from the corners of his mouth. He practically dropped the heavy glass to the table where it landed with a loud thud, and stared at Nesbit as if the latter's thoughts were written on his face. "I can't believe you come in here thinking you better 'an me and I don't know nothing." He took another hard pull and appeared ready to leave, but Nesbit quickly raised his right hand and motioned for him to stay.

"I didn't come here to argue, Ben, and I didn't come here to…to show off. I don't think that way at all. Yes, I made mistakes, more than I care to admit. And I can't begin to tell you how much I regret my mistakes. I'm not perfect…"

"Man, that's an understatement. What do you think my old lady would say to that crock of…"

"Listen," Nesbit interrupted, practically shouting. But he controlled himself, barely, because he didn't want a fight with his son, especially not now when there was a chance of reconciliation and when there were other issues riding on his relationship with the young man. "Listen," he said again, more calmly this time, "I'm just saying that I know I can't do things over and that I can't make up for the past. But you need to understand that I didn't set out to hurt you or...or your mother. My God..."

"If that's true, I can't imagine what would have happened if you tried."

"Please, none of it happened the way you think."

"Are you telling me I can't think? My old lady couldn't think neither?"

"Either."

"What? Now you're telling me I don't speak good? Is that how you treated my mother?" Leaning forward, the young man smirked as if he had just turned the tables on the great Interpol agent, who had tried and failed to turn the tables on him.

The attitude, the clothes, the smell (Nesbit was beginning to wonder if the young man had ever bathed), and the smirk – the smirk more than anything else – weakened Nesbit's resolve to remain calm and set a civilized example for his wayward son. "All right, Ben, I've heard about enough. Do you want the truth? Do you want to know what really happened?"

"Why don't you enlighten me, daddy-o?"

"You mother ...," he hesitated, "my wife was a manic depressive who couldn't 'handle' life. She couldn't 'handle' making decisions, she couldn't 'handle' the decisions I made, and after a while there was nothing that she could 'handle.'"

"She told me her life was hard 'cause you were never home. You're not going to tell me she was lying, are you?"

"You have it all wrong. In the beginning, I was home every night. I took a position in Oxford to be close to home, and for years I refused to work overtime or travel for work. Back then, your mother was beautiful and charming and, I swear to God, our first couple of years together seemed like a dream – and when you came along, the dream came true. Life couldn't have been better until a few months after you turned a glorious two. For some reason, your mother started to have spells of depression, generally for a day or two at a stretch. But over time, these spells began lasting longer and longer, sometimes for weeks on end. There were periods in which she either slept all day or constantly cried and begged me to end something. I never understood what.

"When her depression reached a peak, I took her to a specialist and, between counseling and meds, she gradually started to get better. She slept normally, she stopped crying, and for a while she was practically normal. But it didn't last, because she started drinking. It didn't take long before she was drinking herself into a stupor practically every night. I tried to stop her. I tossed every bottle I found. I even cancelled the accounts she was using to buy the stuff, but nothing worked. She always managed to find enough to get drunk – sometimes, I suspect, to show me there was nothing I could do to stop her. Once the drinking started, she stopped taking her meds and refused to see the specialist. 'I don't need a specialist,' she would scream, and 'the meds don't work. They make me sick.' Alcohol was her solution. You must have seen that, too."

Nesbit adjusted his tie, which for some reason felt out of alignment, and continued. "I put up with the drinking, I continued to do everything I could to help her, and yet nothing I did seemed to work. She went from bad to worse. She was angry all the time, blaming me for everything that went bump in the night. Within a couple of years, she was practically a stranger – furious, abusive, suspicious, and, shortly afterwards, suicidal, or at least she threatened to kill herself whenever the mood struck her – and no matter what I did (I even took a month off from work just to care for her and you), she began telling me to leave. I tried to stay, but her demands became so violent that I had to leave."

Nesbit inhaled deeply to control his emotions. "Yes, I left, and she moved to a cottage in the boonies. I didn't leave, though. I rented another flat in Oxford, and from time to time she allowed me to visit you and help out around the place. Everything seemed to be going fine until there was a knock at my door, and I was served with divorce papers. She was charging me with desertion. I did everything I could to stay engaged, and she accused me of deserting her. Can you believe it? Maybe you can, because she poisoned your mind against me like she poisoned her own mind with alcohol. To top it off, she demanded sole custody. Well, I went to court without representation, because…because I didn't want to upset her; I didn't want to turn something ugly into something even uglier. Besides, I thought if I agreed to everything, both she and the court would soften and guarantee my rights."

Nesbit stood up and walked over to the window and looked out across the deserted street. When he came back to the table, he sat down and stared at the young man's unpleasant face in a blank way. "The courts sided with her; on my word, they sided with her and denied me custody. I tried to fight it, but it was too late – she moved, and I spent years trying to find her, and you. Seven years ago, I found her number and then traced her address. It was the same...she'd moved back to where she'd been before. Well, I called her several times just to speak to you, and each time she denied me for one reason or another." He glanced briefly around the pub. Again looking at the young man's cold, impassive face, Nesbit explained that he didn't press the issue because...because by then it was too late. He was afraid that if he showed up out of the blue, it might destroy whatever home life "you could have had. I made a mistake, no question, but it seemed that I couldn't change things no matter what I did."

Yes, he continued, he started to travel more frequently, but there was never a moment when his heart and mind weren't on his son. After a period of hollow, pointless meandering, he decided to break through the impasse and contact him, especially because the young man was finally old and experienced enough to understand what had happened, but his mother refused to help and he was never able (until recently) to find the phone number (she kept changing it). Once or twice he came close to reconnecting, he said, but "you were either out or, as she claimed, refusing to speak to me. Trust me, I understand what happened to you, and if I had been in your shoes, I probably would have felt the same way." When Nesbit finished, he continued to look at the young man, hoping to see something positive in those coarse, insolent features.

Naturally, he didn't expect to see the dawn rising on his son's consciousness, but he thought it reasonable for the young man to feel something positive about his father and to be a little sympathetic for what he had gone through at the hands of that woman. Good God, he wasn't trying to tug at the young man's heart strings, but his son could have listened courteously, maybe feigning an understanding nod or two, even if he wasn't ready to jettison the lies his mother fed him. He had to have undergone his own trials with his mother. Instead, the young man was impassive, though proffering a snide smile now and then, and when Nesbit had finally finished, the man sucked in his lips as if he were feeling guilty about something.

"So," the young man finally said, speaking slowly with a smirk on his lips, "you lied to judge."

"No," Nesbit responded, shocked that the young man should suggest this after everything he had just said. "No, I was protecting you."

Without responding, the young man stood up and motioned to the door with his head. "You got a car?" he asked, now speaking in a pleasant tone.

"Yes," Nesbit replied, nodding his head at the same time.

"Good. I want to show you something. Interested?"

Nesbit again nodded and, after laying money on the table, he followed the young man out the door. Once outside in front of the pub, he felt a chill from the cool air and was immediately struck by the young man's size. He had always remembered the boy as being lanky and taller than practically all his friends, and yet the young man didn't appear to be any taller than his mother, and, unlike his ex-wife, a little on the stocky side. Of course, the man wasn't anything like Thwait, but Nesbit couldn't help thinking that his eating habits (and everything else about him) must have gone to seed after the woman's death. Sad, he thought, and, as they began walking toward the car, Nesbit noticed for the first time that his son had a slight limp, as if he was suffering from a congenital defect of some kind. He couldn't recall any such problem with his Ben, but then any number of things could have happened to the boy over the years.

When they got into the car, the young man slouched down (where did that sort of behavior come from?) and rested his knees against the dash. "What are you waiting for?" he demanded without looking at Nesbit.

"I don't know what you mean."

"Come on," he began in a sarcastic tone, "don't you know the Queen's bloody English? I suppose you're still an American. Okay, let's not stay here. Get going."

Nesbit started the car, but before he put it into gear, he turned again to the young man and demanded to know where they were going. "Can you at least give me some directions?"

"Out of town; to my place; it's only a short drive from here."

"Okay," Nesbit responded and then turned into the street. "You'll have to tell me which direction when we get to the corner."

The young man looked at him and laughed. "You know the way, man. You said you came there all the time. Hey, you were there only a couple days ago. Sorry I didn't greet you, but I was in the can and all that. You knew that, right?"

Nesbit didn't say anything, and after maneuvering through the town streets, he took the correct turn and merged onto the road the led to his wife's cottage.

Chapter 37

The road felt especially rough this time, and, even though he was going slowly, the car bottomed out several times, emitting a loud, painful thud each time. The road was also narrower; in several places, particularly as it stretched around a hill, the two lane road turned into a single lane, replete with deep ruts and objects unexpectedly jutting out of the ground where the wheels needed to move or where he was certain that the transmission was located (the hard bangs underneath the car troubled him, because he didn't want to get stuck in this wilderness). When they had just crested the final hill and the cottage was in sight, the young man sat up and, leaning over, stomped on the foot Nesbit was using to control acceleration. The car lurched, banged into a deep rut and, on its way out, practically became airborne, while Nesbit fought to hold onto the wheel, apply the brakes, and retrieve his foot out from under the young man's heavy boot.

After one particularly loud and painful bang, the car's occupants, tethered by their constricting seatbelts, were stretched unmercifully upward, after which they were jerked back down and then thrown violently to one side, while the car began to careen sideways and appeared to be on a collision course with the junk in front of the cottage and after that the cottage itself. Somehow, and his mind was a blank about it afterwards, Nesbit managed to get the car back under control and stopped before entering the yard, although it sent a couple of paint cans and other rubbish flying before it finally came to a rest in a slight cloud of dust and debris. Once stopped, the car shuddered before shutting down, and the young man, who had immediately hopped out of the vehicle, began laughing, bending over to relieve some of the pressure on his sides as he did so.

Nesbit didn't immediately move. He wasn't hurt, but he was furious with the young man for having pulled such a dangerous stunt. Breathing deeply to calm his nerves, Nesbit continued staring at him, trying to understand was going on in his head, trying to fathom his inexplicable and perverse behavior. Finally opening the door, he got out of the car and started walking slowly toward the cottage, with each step doing his best to control his rising anger. The young man, whose movements and behavior were so alien to him, was standing unsteadily, pointing a grubby finger at Nesbit, and laughing raucously.

"Why?" Nesbit demanded in a whisper when he was only a few feet from the young man. Without waiting for an answer, he asked the single-word question again, since it was the only thing at the moment that he could safely articulate.

When his laughter subsided, the young man rolled his shoulders and stretched his back and, still smiling, looked at Nesbit and asked, "What did you say? Come in here," he added as if Nesbit had answered, and walked toward the front door of the cottage. "You don't have any objections to going in through the front door this time, do you?" He glanced back at Nesbit and then opened the door into the foul-smelling building, having first pushed it open with his boot.

Once inside the place and confronted with the visible filth and horrible smell, Nesbit wanted to vomit, but this time the sensation had little to do with the unkempt state of the cottage. The young man motioned for Nesbit to take a seat in the family's old garden chair, which for some reason was now in the center of the room. Settling into the chair, he noticed that the young man was now at the far side of the room, reaching down into a large, cardboard box, with only the top of his head and his rounded shoulders showing. As he observed the young man and waited for him to finish, Nesbit couldn't help wondering how his son could have fallen so low, and he couldn't understand why his mother had taught him so little about life. Could she herself have become more useless than she seemed to be? Or was it a defect of some kind that led the man to live like this, as if by any stretch of the imagination this could be called living, and to act as if every mindless thing he said or did was perfectly reasonable and acceptable?

While the man continued searching for something in the box, Nesbit couldn't control himself and said loudly to get his attention, "why do you live like this? I can't imagine your mother condoning..."

The young man immediately looked up and glowered at Nesbit. "Sorry, man, but the skivvy had the day off. I live like this cause I got no choice."

"What do you mean you have no choice? We all have choices. If it's a matter of money..."

"You did this to me. Did you really think I had a choice in the matter? Did you ever consider the consequences of your actions? And now you got the jones to ask me why I live like this? Well, genius, I owe it all to you."

"Didn't you hear what I said about your mother and my efforts to stay with you?"

The young man didn't respond and, when Nesbit started to stand up to go speak to him, he stood up and screamed at Nesbit to sit back down. "Don't move!" he shouted, as Nesbit slowly sat back down.

For a few seconds, there was almost total silence in the room while the young man rummaged through the box. Every now and then, however, the silence was broken by shuffling and scraping sounds originating from inside the box. Under different circumstances, Nesbit would have asked about the sounds, but he was momentarily unable to utter a single word, much less a coherent question. He was shocked by the young man's behavior, and a heavy blanket of guilt settled over him because of the way his beloved child had turned out. There was a time when he had such high hopes for the boy. The lad had talent, intellectual curiosity, and the kind of adroitness with small objects that a skilled artisan would envy; and when Nesbit left him with his ex-wife, he had every reason to believe that the boy was emotionally mature enough to handle both the loss of his father and the predatory instincts of his mother. Naturally, he didn't expect the boy to walk in his father's footsteps. But was it wrong to have expected him to make something of his life, something that might have illuminated both of their lives in history books? 'Ben's father was of course Nesbit, who had done a thing or two in his own right.' But this – a dirty, useless, possibly violent individual who preferred squalor to decency – this was too much; this was beyond the pale. This was a parent's worst nightmare. This was something, all right.

"Another minute, and we'll be set," the young man said, glancing out of the box at Nesbit, a tender expression covering his otherwise vile features. He appeared to be holding something under his coat.

The almost pleasant sound of the young man's voice momentarily softened Nesbit's heart – this was his son, after all, and one can't divorce a son like one can a wife – and he promised himself that he would do everything he could to turn the young man's life around – money, connections, he would do it all, and for a few seconds he imagined the young man's gratitude once he was a productive member of society and able to look everyone, especially his father, straight in the eye.

Nesbit had just begun to imagine how far his son could go with a little help when the young man abruptly straighten up and tossed a thick, coil of rope at Nesbit's feet. The rope was slightly tangled and frayed in spots.

Smiling at something, the young man thrust his right hand into his coat pocket, and it was then that Nesbit thought about the tear near the buttons and recalled the strange coin-like object recovered at the scene of the first blast. Before the young man spoke, Nesbit noticed the strange crossed swords at the bottom of each button, and asked him about the jacket. "How did you lose your button?"

The young man looked at him and craned his head to one side as a dog might when it noticed something curious or unexplainable.

"Your top button. See," he said, pointing to the top of the man's jacket.

The man looked down at the tear in his jacket. Once he understood what Nesbit was talking about, he looked back up and smiled. "Got it caught in something." As if changing his mind, he suddenly shoved his left hand in his left pocket and pulled out a pack of cigarettes. Since the pack was already open, he yanked a cigarette out with his lips and then tossed the pack to Nesbit.

Nesbit didn't flinch as the pack bounced off his head and landed on the floor next to the rope. Without taking his eyes off the young man, he said, "I don't smoke."

"Suit yourself, pal," the man replied and fished in the same pocket for something else. It was a small box of matches. He slid it open and retrieved the last match. Striking the match against the side of the box, it flared briefly and the man brought it to the end of his cigarette, after which he tossed the match and the box on the floor in Nesbit's direction. Once again, fumbling with something in his right pocket, he looked at Nesbit, his left eye squinting when a slender plume of smoke hovered briefly below his eyebrow on its way to the ceiling. Without taking the cigarette out of the side of his mouth, he asked Nesbit again if he was sure.

Nesbit shook his head slowly. "Why did you ask me here?" He glanced around the room and then looked back at the young man who hadn't moved an inch.

"You really don't know?" he asked, as he blew smoke out of both nostrils.

"For a while, I thought you wanted to come to an understanding. But I really don't think that's what you want, unless you have a different meaning for the word than I do. So why don't you just tell me what's on your mind."

The young man smiled broadly and blew more smoke out of his nose. Without moving from where he was standing, he replied that what he had in mind was indeed an understanding of sorts, "but, like you said, not the kind you're expecting, Constable."

"I don't know what you're talking about?"

"How come you're so dense? You really don't know why you're here?"

Nesbit slowly shook his head.

"Because I told you to come."

"We spoke on the phone, but…"

The young man laughed and spit out his cigarette, which also landed a few inches from Nesbit's right shoe. "Man, it's got nothing to do with shooting the breeze."

Nesbit didn't move this time.

"I sent you a message. You still don't get it? You, the big constable and all that crap?"

When Nesbit didn't move or acknowledge his statement, the young man jabbed his right hand deeper into his coat pocket and retrieved a black handgun. Pointing it directly at Nesbit, he asked him to open his jacket. "You're not packing, are you?"

Nesbit slowly opened his coat to expose his vest. He didn't have a weapon.

"Sorry, man, I had to check. It's just professionalism, you know." He took a couple of steps forward and, locking his eyes on Nesbit while pointing the gun at his face, he slowly reached down and recovered the rope. Smiling, he asked Nesbit to put his arms and hands behind the chair.

Nesbit complied without showing any inclination to do otherwise.

The young man quickly stepped behind him. Slipping his gun back into his pocket, he wrapped one end of the rope around Nesbit's neck and tied his hands behind the chair with the other. He went about his business quickly, securing the rope on Nesbit's wrists while periodically adjusting the noose around his neck. Nesbit was beginning to have trouble swallowing, but something inside forced him to be pliant. If the circumstances had been different, he would have resisted; he would never have let the situation go this far without putting up a good fight. He had the training and the experience to handle situations like this and young men like this one. But this was different; this situation was unlike anything that in all his years in the police business he had been led to believe could happen. He was facing his son, the child he loved more than life itself, the very being that he had so cruelly abandoned years ago, and so he couldn't bring himself to hurt the young man (and if he resisted, the young man would surely be hurt, possibly killed). Besides, he probably deserved what his son was now doing to him.

Nesbit started to close his eyes and let the young man finish his work when it occurred to him that, as the rope was being cinched against his chest, this would be as good a time as any to find out if his son was involved in either or both bombings. He had tried to protect the boy, and he had hurt Thwait's feelings in doing so, but he couldn't help fearing the worst then and especially now, while the rope was constricting his neck and parts of someone's body were lying in a morgue.

"Tell me," Nesbit gasped as the rope was again adjusted against his neck, "you weren't involved in the bombings."

Chapter 38

The young man didn't say anything for a few minutes. He somehow managed to connect Nesbit's legs to the same system, which meant that whenever Nesbit moved his legs (and they now only moved in unison, not separately), the rope would pull on his neck. When the man was done, he stepped around in front of Nesbit and eyed his handiwork.

"Man, I ain't half bad, if I say so myself." He turned away for a moment and went to the other side of the room to retrieve a white, plastic lawn chair that seemed to appear out of nowhere, which he set in front of Nesbit, barely a yard away. Sitting down, he momentarily eyed Nesbit as if he couldn't help admiring his masterpiece and, when he had seen enough, he asked the older man if that was a serious question.

Nesbit, who couldn't move any part of his body without hurting his neck, practically whispered, "tell me."

"Tell you what?"

"Tell me you didn't have anything to do with...the museum bombing..."

"Man, I want some of what you been sniffing. Of course, we did, Constable."

"Why?"

"Why? We thought you knew. Okay, I'll tell you something kind of funny." The young man relaxed his posture, clearly pleased to be letting Nesbit in on the details. "We planned it from the beginning. We thought it would encourage you to come here, to the UK, to solve this big crime thing."

"But I told you over the phone I...I was coming on a case..."

"It was the plan, man. We figured you wouldn't come otherwise. But once you showed up – and I got to tell you we was both surprised – we did it anyway. We didn't want you leaving too soon, and it was on our roadmap."

"I don't understand."

The young man suddenly stiffened and shook his head. "There's a lot you don't understand, Mr. Constable. You weren't coming to talk. You were working a case. It was convenient, and now you're right here because of a case – the bombings, right?"

"Look, I would have come to talk. Honest to God, my arrival...had more to do with you than the..."

"You lie," the young man burst out, his face flushing and his pimples momentarily disappearing. "You always lie. You only came here only for a bloody case." He briefly looked away and, gritting his teeth, turned back to Nesbit. "He told me. One excuse after another. But it don't matter, since you're here now."

"Tell me you weren't involved in both bombings."

The young man stared at Nesbit as if he couldn't quite believe his ears. "Are you a parrot or just deaf?"

"Tell me," Nesbit gasped as the rope tightened around his neck. Nesbit had no doubt about what the young man was saying, but he was hopeful that he could get the young man to retract his statements, or contradict himself, if he kept him talking. Of course, this was becoming tricky, because the young man was becoming increasingly agitated. "Tell me you weren't involved, and I...I can help..."

"He said it'd be useless." He shook his mangy head and spit on the floor near Nesbit's right shoe. "We done them, fool. And we planned to do them whether you was here or not. We planned some others, too."

"I don't believe it. This is senseless..."

The young man leaned forward and pressed his red lips against Nesbit's left ear. "It don't have to make sense," he shouted. "You're here. You're in this chair. And now you and everyone else is going to know what a fool you are." He dropped back into his chair, breathing heavily as if the short exchange had robbed him of his energy.

"I can't believe...the art and everything else..."

"Who gives a crap about art? You still don't get it, man."

Nesbit was silent for a moment to ease the raw throbbing in his throat and the ringing in his ears. During that moment as he struggled to control his own emotions in the face of his angry, criminal son, his agent training suddenly came back to him and he decided that if he was going to expire (he couldn't bring himself to utter the word 'die') at the hands of his son, he wanted at least one more mystery resolved. "What are the Gray Ladies?"

"What?"

"The Gray Ladies, what are they? The Richardson Stones, right? You...and your friend spoke about them and how once they were destroyed...government would fall."

"The Richardson what? Is that a group? Are you messing with me? How do you know about gray ladies?"

Nesbit tried to smile. "I have sources. The Gray Ladies are the Richardson Stones, aren't they?"

"What are you talking about?" He stood up and began pacing back and forth in front of Nesbit, occasionally kicking something out of the way and occasionally pausing to turn his firey face to Nesbit. A few minutes later, he stopped and walked toward his chair, kicking it aside as he planted himself directly in front of the Interpol agent. Motionless, his carotid artery visibly throbbing, he glowered at Nesbit for a few moments before speaking. "I don't know nothing about Richard's whatever. And I don't know who told you about the gray ladies. But since it don't matter now, the gray ladies are all them museum directors, appraisers, and so-called experts – all of them gray old ladies – who were mouthing off about our antiques as if they were the only ones who knew anything. They're national treasures we're supposed to call 'sir' and bow our heads when they walk by. We lost sale after sale because these national treasures butted in and told our customers our goods weren't good or authentic. A couple of them told customs we were bringing in stolen goods, which mucked up our supply lines. Now, how can you make a decent living when all these gray ladies badmouth your inventory just to make themselves look smart?" He paused, although this time he didn't seem tired or out of breath. On the contrary, his own words seemed to rejuvenate him. "And you didn't help things. You and all the rest of them will be singing a different tune when I get done."

"I don't understand…"

"Don't try to lie to me. It was his idea to hit the museum first. He thought it would make you look stupid. Man, he wanted to get you real bad for all that crap you pulled. Me, I didn't care who got it first as long as we got everyone else – and I'm going to get everyone else, plus a few others."

Nesbit carefully angled his face toward the young man. "What did I have to do with your business, if that's what…this is about?"

"Are you messing with me? Three years ago, you and that fat friend of yours brought the poleese on us. We had a decent antiques business until you two idiots barged in, shoving my old man around, talking to him like he was garbage, and before you left you made sure the poleese would come and finish us off. They shut us down and sent us on an unpaid vacation. My old man wasn't done with two out of the fifteen when he dies in that stinking hole. You knew, Mr. Constable, you and all them other Tom, Dick, and Archibald's, and you're all going to pay."

"What?" Nesbit demanded, barely able to choke out the words. "I don't understand!" He coughed several times.

The young man looked at him for a moment and then began to laugh. Stepping back a couple of feet, he continued to laugh for two or three more minutes, at times holding his side and pointing at Nesbit. When he was finally under control and his almost pleasant smile was again a dour grimace, he planted himself once more in front of Nesbit and balanced himself on outspread legs like a soldier at rest. Pulling the gun back out of his pocket, he pointed it at Nesbit, holding its dull, impassive barrel only a couple of inches from his nose. "You twit! Don't you know who I am?"

"You're my son…"

This time the young man didn't laugh. He gritted his teeth and his hand began to shake slightly. "I ain't your son, fool. The name is Charles Sanders Jr. Charles Sanders was my old man, and you and that fat…by the way, I forgot to tell you. I'm going to get him, too. He don't look like a gray lady now, but he will before I'm done."

Nesbit recalled the case that had made him famous. Prior to arresting Charlie Saunders and his infamous female accomplice in New Orleans, he and Thwait had worked the case in London and had interviewed a number of suspects, including Charles Sanders, who ran an antique shop a few blocks away from Saunders' antiquarian business. He knew Sanders was dirty the second he and Thwait entered the shop, but since Sanders wasn't connected to his case, he and Thwait (actually Thwait) passed the lead to the station. Maybe Sedgwick arrested him. He didn't know that the creep had a son or that the son was the creep's partner in crime; and he certainly didn't know about Sanders' death in prison. Well, good riddance, Nesbit thought, and he couldn't help smiling at this strange turn of events, even though he knew that his smile wouldn't help his situation.

"You're Charles Sanders, not my son," Nesbit said slowly, feeling lighter, almost happy. So there was a reason why his recollections didn't match this pimple-faced degenerate standing insolently in front of him. "Where's Benjamin?" he asked, hoping against all odds that his son wasn't mixed up with this individual.

The young man stared at Nesbit as if he couldn't understand why anyone would ask such a question. "He's gone."

Nesbit shuddered at the finality of this statement. He was going to demand a clarification, but noticing a peculiar expression coming over the

345

young man's face, he decided to wait for a more propitious time to discuss the status of his son. Still, he wasn't ready to end the conversation. Experience had taught him that most criminals unconsciously revealed exploitable vulnerabilities if kept talking long enough and on the right topics. "Fine, so what do you intend to do with me?"

The young man didn't respond. He eyed Nesbit as if he were trying to make him tremble, or so Nesbit thought.

Nesbit was certain that the situation would degenerate unless he did something quickly. "You don't know? Well, you don't mind…if I make a suggestion, do you?"

The young man growled and then struck Nesbit in the face with the back of his dirty, left hand, the one not holding the gun.

The blow happened so quickly and unexpectedly that it wasn't initially painful. Seconds later, though, Nesbit could feel his upper lip tightening, and moments after this he detected a metallic taste on the inside of his mouth near the same lip.

"I don't need your suggestions," the young man snarled. "I don't need nothing from you except your life and reputation. But let me make things clear to you since you don't seem to understand much. I'm going to finish you off for my old man, and I'm going to humiliate your memory for my bud Benny. You think you're some kind of special gray lady? Just wait till I'm done, and you'll be the laughing stock of your profession, of this entire bloody country." He tried to laugh, but his anger made it sound forced and artificial.

Nesbit's upper lip was now throbbing, and he could feel the skin expand and tighten. Keeping his eyes on the young man, he tried to ease the discomfort by touching the most sensitive section with the tip of his tongue. To his surprise, the young man unconsciously mimicked his movement with his own tongue, a sure sign to Nesbit that he was hesitant to take the next step without provocation.

Sensing an opportunity, Nesbit said in his best fatherly voice, "you don't want to do this. I can still help you." He was careful not to overplay it, for the young man might overreact if his nervousness got the better of him.

"Shut up!" The young man scowled and took a step back. "Just shut up!" he shouted again a few moments later as if Nesbit had said something else to affect his concentration. The man angled his gun shakily at Nesbit's face, and he gritted his teeth like an animal ready to tear something apart. "It ain't just what I wanted. It's what we both wanted. Do you get it now? We both wanted it."

Nesbit tried to nod, but the rope stopped his movement and made him cough twice. Recalling the Chief's intimidating mannerisms, he squinted at the young man as if something important had just occurred to him, although he was in fact desperately searching for something that would calm the young man and divert his attention from undertaking his next, possibly fatal move. "Hey," Nesbit coughed out and asked why the young man came to this cottage, of all places, since it was once his ex-wife's residence, if he wasn't mistaken. "It wasn't a dump then," he added with a faint smile.

The young man warily observed Nesbit. "A dump, huh? I got it from my bud Benny. I think his old lady died or something. He was living here, too, after he got kicked out of his other place. Say, is it true you kept changing numbers, addresses, and all that?"

"That's not true," Nesbit gasped, the rope tightening around his neck as he squirmed to loosen it. "He could have looked me up any time he wanted."

"I didn't say it, Constable."

"Where's Ben? What...have you done with him?"

The young man glowered at Nesbit and then spit on him. The saliva hit Nesbit's nose and cheeks, and its slow-moving drops fell from his left cheek. "Fool, he was planning all this. We met last year at a pub, and it only took a few for him to open up about you and his mum. I told him about me and my old man and what you done to us, and he gets this funny look and says you was his old man. Could have knocked us on our asses. It was his idea to work together. That's when he let me stay here – I didn't have money 'cause of you – so we could work it all out. I'm an expert, but Benny was something else. Dumb as crap, but he reads all this stuff and watches the videos, and pretty soon he's got it all down. Man, together we could of had some fun at Heathrow Customs." The young man became rigid and the muscles in his jaw tensed. "Poor sod, didn't work out like we planned. But I got you, and in a few you're going to meet Benny face to face. You only get second chances once in your life."

"What are you talking about? Where is he?"

The young man stepped forward and pressed the gun's muzzle against Nesbit's moist forehead. "'Where is he, where is he?'" the young man replied, mimicking Nesbit albeit with a high, childish voice. "You ass, he's waiting for you."

"Where?"

The young man glowered at Nesbit, his body stiff and motionless. He started to turn, which to Nesbit was a sign that he was backing away from taking immediate action, and then with a motion that was little more than a blur, he struck Nesbit on the temple with the butt of his gun.

Chapter 39

Nesbit awoke with a throbbing head and a sensation that one side of his skull was monstrously distended. It took several minutes to remember where he was and several more to recall what had happened, both of which were complicated by the pressure against his windpipe and by the crepuscular light, which cast the room in a deep shadow. He blinked several times to clear his vision (tears filled his eyes from the rope's pressure and the banging inside his skull) and then glanced around the room. He was alone, and nothing suggested that the young man or anyone else was in the cottage, unless of course the bathroom was occupied. Nesbit closed his eyes and tried to listen for sounds emanating from that room or anywhere else around the place, inside or outside, but he had trouble hearing anything because of the persistent throbbing inside his head, which at times obliterated all but the loudest noises around him.

Fearing that he only had a few minutes before the young man returned, Nesbit began stretching his shoulders, spreading his ankles, and moving his arms and hands to try to loosen the rope (without cutting off his oxygen, because the rope around his neck was getting tighter and tighter). When it was clear that he couldn't spread the rope wide enough without strangling himself, Nesbit relaxed and considered using his toes to help rock the chair over, which with his weight might be enough to break or deform the chair and hence slacken the rope sufficiently to wiggle out of it. But when he angled his eyes downward to get an idea of how much he would have to push, Nesbit momentarily froze and sweat began to drip off his forehead. There was a large bomb at his feet. What's more, the bomb appeared to be tied to his chair (shoestrings?), meaning that any undue movement of the chair would likely rattle the bomb and... He didn't want to follow the logic very far.

Angling his head to one side to get a better look at it, Nesbit observed the coffee-can housing (he recognized the brand of coffee), the gray wires running in and out from both ends, and a section of a large, glass vial that probably contained the explosive material. Even though most of the device was out of sight or under the chair, he was convinced that it was the same kind of bomb found at the first site and the same kind of explosive devise detonated at the second and, unfortunately, the same kind of thing that would do away with him unless it failed like one of the bombs at the museum. Nevertheless, Nesbit couldn't help momentarily smiling, for he was now certain that he finally had all the evidence he needed to connect Sanders's son to the crimes…and, shortly after this, he began to think about his own son.

How could his son have been involved in something like this? How could he have done even half the things that the lying swine claimed he did, even if his ex-wife had been a worthless parent and had raised their child in a household filled with hate? It didn't seem possible. And yet the Sanders boy seemed to know a great deal about their personal lives, and he was living (if one could call it that) in his ex-wife's former cottage. Why, he, Nesbit, was even roped to the very chair that he and his wife had purchased years ago, which ironically was the last time they had been a family. Did Nesbit's own son know that? Maybe, Nesbit told himself, recalling some of the young man's comments, his son met Sanders in the pub and, over a few drinks, uttered some drunken statements that wouldn't stand the test of a bright, cloudless day. Sanders took those drunken slurs, illegally camped out in the abandoned cottage (Ben probably told him about the cottage, too), and used everything to further his wretched scheme. If any part of this were true, Nesbit surmised, it might be enough to lessen the charges and, with any luck, his son could be free in a few years. After that, he would see to it that the boy got the treatment he needed to get him back on his feet. Nesbit's smile quickly faded, however, when he recalled Ben's absence, the anonymous body found at the auction house, and the manner in which Sanders referred to Ben, speaking as if he were…somewhere else. More to the point, he couldn't understand why his son, drunk or not, would tell that piece of scum such hateful, disrespectful things about his relationship with Nesbit.

"My God," Nesbit said out loud, "did he really hate me? Was I that bad as a father?" Nesbit immediately glanced down at the bomb, which was becoming less distinct in the shadows, to make sure he hadn't done anything to speed up its timing.

Breathing a temporary sigh of relief that the bomb was quiescent for the time being, Nesbit couldn't help ruminating on his son's relationship with that monster. Even if he was close enough to Sanders to lend him this house, this didn't have to mean that his son was a participant in the man's despicable plans. Still, Sanders did know some things that went beyond mere pub talk. Was this the real Ben, a person who would not only associate with the dregs of society but who would also participate in the worst kind of crime?

"What have I done?" Nesbit said to himself and immediately checked the bomb again.

But where was his son? If he were indeed party to the crimes, if he had wanted to torture him as Sanders intimated, then where was he now? Surely, if he were the animal that Sanders described, he would have been front and center, haranguing him, planting the bomb under the chair, and doing whatever else to make his, Nesbit's life, miserable, if indeed that had been his goal. But he wasn't there and, since he wasn't, wouldn't it be reasonable to assume that... Nesbit hesitated and, once again, looked at the bomb. Then again, there was the body from the second blast, which apparently was not connected with either the auction house or its clients. While the media provided some compelling clues, he had learned from Thwait that the body probably (did he say 'most likely'?) belonged to one of the suspects, the poor wretch having stumbled over a pucker in the carpet or tripped on his own shoelace and 'that's all, folks.' If Ben were waiting for him, as Sanders intimated, then... "My God," Nesbit whispered, "could it be...?"

Nesbit let his eyes drift downward, and once again the bomb came into view, a dull, dark object malevolently chiding him for the fragility and finitude of his flesh. Realizing that time was of the essence, he put aside thoughts about his son and instead tried to concentrate on a strategy to extricate himself from this 'predicament.' He reminded himself that he had been in tougher positions (although he couldn't recall a single one), and so he was determined to survive this one like he survived all the others, whatever they were. Slowing his breathing to remain thoughtful and in control, Nesbit decided to start off by enumerating all his options and then evaluating each one according to its likelihood of success; but after staring blankly at the smooth outer shell and the strange vial for several minutes, he couldn't come up with a single option. Unless Sanders had a miraculous change of heart and returned to free him (and what were the odds of that happening?), he was stuck waiting for the bomb to go off.

With nothing else to do, Nesbit speculated on the length of time he could endure sitting in the chair if the device failed to detonate. One day, two days? He might be able to last three days but not much more, given the throbbing in his head and the competing pain in his backside (the chair was every bit as uncomfortable as he recalled). But as he gloomily contemplated what endurance might look like in this context, it occurred to him that someone might walk by the cottage and either rescue him or call the authorities. Straining his eyes to peer outside the window, he observed the dark, faceless hills and remembered that the cottage was isolated and that the nearest building could be several miles away. Nesbit was on the verge of giving up and counting off the hours, minutes, and seconds until it was all over when he remembered that a postman would eventually arrive (no place in this country is without postal service, he told himself, forgetting post boxes and places not directly connected with standard mail service) – and, as soon as he spotted the genial, longsuffering postman, he would holler out and explain his situation. Unfortunately, the darkening sky meant that no one connected with the postal service was likely to arrive this late; but there was always tomorrow, and, when the jovial Santa Clause-like figure began stuffing letters into the mailbox's maw...but where was the box? Okay, so perhaps one couldn't see it in this light. But as he searched his memory, he became concerned that he hadn't seen it earlier when he was walking around the house in broad daylight. Was it possible that among all the other pathetic deficiencies of this lousy dump, there wasn't a single mailbox...somewhere? "No," he whispered to himself, "every building has to have a mailbox. Surely, there's a law somewhere that dictates this, in addition to the box's size and shape." Satisfied with the legal side of the issue (especially because he didn't have any other reed to grasp), he decided to put aside everything else, especially the bad things, and make himself as comfortable as possible while he waited for the kindly old Saint Nick to deliver him from his bondage.

Nesbit was half asleep when he felt something strange happening, something that forced his eyes open and sharpened all of his senses. It was impossible to describe this sensation, but as it continued he was convinced that he was finally approaching the beginning of the end.

Chapter 40

It started with a vibration in his left breast pocket and, when he squeezed his arm against it to stop the movement, it ended with a muffled voice.

"Sir?" the voice asked. It seemed to be originating from a great distance away. "Sir, are you there?"

Nesbit immediately recognized the voice. "Tom, I'm here, in this bloody house. Come inside and untie me. Be careful, there's a bomb at my feet."

"Sir, I'm glad we found you. Where are you…wait, what's this about a bomb?"

"I'm inside the cottage. There's only one room, except for the bathroom, which might be occupied. Come inside, but be careful. The place is…well, hurry, man. I don't know how much time I have left."

"Sir, where is the cottage? I don't entirely understand what you're telling me. Did you say cottage?"

"Damn it, man, the place is right in front of you. There isn't another for miles. Come get me. I've solved the case."

There was a slight pause. "Sir, we're at the station. Where exactly are you?"

Nesbit was about to respond when he felt the small, rectangular box in his breast pocket and immediately realized that he was speaking to Thwait through his cell phone. He was certain that he had turned it off at the pub, but it was now obvious that he had either failed to turn it off completely or that he somehow managed to turn it back on while strapped in the chair, and some slight movement that must have made enabled him to respond to the call. Wasting little time, he told Thwait where he was located and he insisted that Thwait waste little time in coming to free him. "Tom, I don't know how much time I have left on the battery – and, for God's sake, be careful when you enter. I can't tell if the detonator is connected to the door or something on this filthy floor. My God, this place gives me the creeps."

Police and bomb-disposal officers arrived from Oxford about forty minutes later and were able to free Nesbit without mishap. When Sedgwick and Thwait arrived, about two hours after this, they spotted Nesbit in front of the cottage, standing next to a flood light and speaking to a couple of officers from Oxford. The large bomb disposal truck stood in front of the cottage, its immense size blocking nearly half of the dark building from their view, while there were three other vehicles (an ambulance, the lights of which were still flashing and reflecting off the cottage walls, and two police vehicles) either on the property itself or on the dirt road that ran in front of the place. Outside the remnants of the fence stood a few people, all dressed casually and somewhat grubbily, who had appeared out of the darkness to observe the spectacle. Spectacles of any kind were extraordinarily rare in this part of the country. Sedgwick parked her car on the road beside the ambulance and walked quickly over to the center of the yard, where Nesbit was speaking to one of the officers. When Nesbit and the officer spotted Sedgwick and Thwait approaching, they turned in unison to face them.

"Don't worry," Nesbit said without looking at the officer, "they're from the station." Smiling broadly, Nesbit took a couple steps toward them and held out his right hand. "My God, it's good to see you," he said, as if he hadn't seen Sedgwick and Thwait in quite some time. Indeed, for although it had only been a few days, his experience in the chair made it feel like an eternity since the last time he laid eyes on them.

For a few minutes, Sedgwick and Thwait bombarded him with questions about his health (did he sustain any injuries?), whether or not he needed any additional services (the implication being mental health professionals without exactly saying it), and how he was able to endure – how long was it? – his captivity. The questions seemed to peter out naturally, and what followed was an odd moment of silence, as if what had happened was so momentous that words were merely an encumbrance to a true understanding of Nesbit's situation. Thwait broke the silence moments later when he stepped up to Nesbit and gave him a bear hug, which Nesbit reciprocated. But when Thwait stepped back, he noticed for the first time that Nesbit didn't look his usual self despite his smiles and pleasant demeanor. For one thing, his face was dirty (there was smudge of something running from his lips to his ear) and slightly puffy; and, for another, his pinstriped suit was wrinkled and covered with what looked like dried mud, and one of his pants legs was ripped. Thwait felt sorry for his great friend and angry that he of all people should have to endure such indignities.

"My friends," Nesbit added when he noticed tears glistening in Thwait's eyes and unexpectedly felt the same welling up in his own. "I owe you both my sincerest thanks. You cannot imagine what…what…," Nesbit was saying when he suddenly paused and ran to the front edge of the property. "He stole my car." He stared at the cottage as if he were surprised that it was still there, and then turned back to Sedgwick and Thwait, his pleasant demeanor having evaporated. "Good God, why didn't I get it earlier? We don't have much time," he said to no one in particular, and walked quickly over to the lead officer from Oxford. After a short but animated conversation (animated on Nesbit's part), Nesbit walked quickly over to Sedgwick and Thwait and informed them that they needed to leave. "We need to go now," he said loudly, "we don't have a second to spare."

Sedgwick and Thwait looked at each other and then at the lead officer, who nodded reluctantly, raising his almost nonexistent eyebrows and lowering the corners of his thin lips. Sedgwick unexpectedly hesitated as if she, too, had something on her mind, and jogged over to the officer, handed him her card, and immediately headed to the car just as Nesbit and Thwait were getting in. Nesbit, though, was behind the wheel, and soon as Sedgwick's door closed, the car took off, leaping out of holes, diving into others, and swerving and banging into rocks, sticks, and whatever else lay in the road. Once the headlights were on, Thwait felt a little more comfortable with Nesbit's seemingly erratic driving, but seconds later as the vehicle began rocking back and forth over the uneven road, he began to feel sick and, for a few moments, he wasn't certain that he could last the entire trip, wherever Nesbit was taking them.

Sedgwick tried several times to speak to Nesbit while they were speeding along the dirt road, but every time she tried to say something the car would either spring madly into the air or wallow and tailspin in mud or soft dirt, making it all but impossible to have a calm talk about where they were going and why they needed to go so quickly. After a while, Sedgwick resigned herself to waiting until they were on firm ground to get answers from Nesbit, while Thwait, hanging on for dear life in the back seat, couldn't have uttered a word if he wanted to, not even to beg to pull over so that he could empty the contents of his stomach.

Once they were back on solid ground, which occurred with a shuddering thud and a series of nervous rumbles, Sedgwick tried to communicate with Nesbit. "Where exactly are we going?" she asked, trying to keep her tone calm and rational. "We need to communicate our status and position to the Chief."

Shaking his head as if to say he didn't have time to speak, Nesbit charged recklessly onto the highway and, pressing down on the accelerator, careened around slower cars and squeezed between towering lorries that seemed intent on preventing him from passing. Sedgwick regretted not having taken a car with a siren, while Thwait regretted not having taken a paper bag with him. "Tell him...tell him...," Nesbit shouted a few minutes later as he hurled onto the side of the highway to get around a slow truck carrying live geese, "tell him Heathrow Customs is next. Tell him...my God, can't that fool pull over more...tell him the bomber is driving a [he described his car] and...my God, tell him I know everything now. I'm not going to let that worthless...achieve his goals."

Nesbit concentrated on the road while Sedgwick relayed the information to the Chief, and when the Chief demanded more details, Nesbit would only say, "no time, when we're there, when we're there." Seconds later, Nesbit shuddered, rounded another slower moving car, and shouted to Sedgwick to tell the Chief to send bomb-disposal units, ambulances, and the police to the airport. "There's no time...," he tried to add, but immediately fell silent as he slammed the car to a screeching, smoking halt. In front of them, stretching from one side of the artificially lit highway to the other, was an mountainous mass of motionless cars so tightly packed that it was impossible to drive between or around them. Some of the cars appeared to be parked, nose to tail, as if the road were an enormous parking lot, while others were positioned at strange angles, several emitting gray smoke from having rear-ended or collided with other vehicles. There were even two jackknifed lorries, the trailer of one reaching off the road and penetrating a solid wall of gray hedges. Beneath the pale, flickering street lights, dozens of people were out of the vehicles and talking to one another, observing the carnage, or helping others out of their cars. And a good portion of the people were standing in the middle of the highway looking into the distance where a solid, black wall of fog or smoke rose from the horizon, blackening an otherwise clear, moonlit sky.

"My God, my God," Nesbit shouted and jumped out of the car and ran over to a knot of people speculating on the cause of the distant smoke and complaining about the possible delay they would have to endure as a result. "Out of the way," he continued shouting, waving his arms like a deranged scarecrow. "Move your damned cars. People are going to die!" When they didn't respond and merely stared at him as if he were mad, Nesbit ran to others and shouted the same thing. At one point, he leaped onto the hood of a small car and screamed directions for others to make way for his car. But when this didn't work and the owner began shouting at him and trying to pull him off his car, Nesbit jumped down onto the pavement and tried to push and shove people toward the cars, telling them that they needed to move "now! Now!" One of the individuals he shoved was a thuggish-looking young man with a Mohawk and several shiny steel rings in his nose, eyebrows, and ears. The man immediately grabbed Nesbit around the neck and threw him to the pavement. He was about to kick Nesbit, but an elderly man in an elegant suit, black derby, and silver-knobbed cane appeared out of the shadows and intervened.

The man's face was soft and smooth, and he was thin and average in height, but he had a commanding presence, and when he took off his glasses and told the young tough in precise, carefully articulated English to back away, the man obeyed, gesturing and shouting at Nesbit over his shoulder as he walked away. When the tough was finally gone, the gentleman reached down and helped Nesbit to his feet. Before Nesbit could respond (he was a little dazed from his impact with the pavement), the man put his glasses back on and informed him that the backup was miles long and, even if the matter were urgent, there was simply no way of parting such a thick sea of vehicles to allow him to pass through any time soon. Motioning with the silver tip of his cane to the cars now stacking up behind them, he added that it was also impossible to retreat even if he wanted to. "There are already hundreds of cars behind us. If I were you, I would settle my business by phone." The man lifted his hat and smiled pleasantly just as Sedgwick and Thwait arrived.

Sedgwick asked Nesbit if he was all right, while Thwait, bending over and trying to catch his breath, held his left side. After Nesbit signaled something with his right hand, Sedgwick turned toward the gentleman to speak to him about the backup, but he was gone and nowhere to be seen. The man had been absorbed back into the darkness at the edge of the road where an increasingly restless crowd of people were getting out of their cars and, standing close together, discussing the backup, the smoke, and everything else that had contributed to make their travel impossible. A stone's throw to the left of this group, several young men had climbed to the top of one of the jackknifed lorries and, with their portable radio blaring, were dancing and hollering for others to join them. When Sedgwick turned back to Nesbit, the latter seemed to have momentarily disappeared, too. Sedgwick quickly spotted him, however, although this time he was on his knees and pounding the pavement with his fists. "God Almighty," he howled like a dog frightened by the night, "why did this have to happen? Why, why, why?"

Sedgwick and Thwait helped Nesbit to his feet and together they led him back to the car, where he sat morosely in the back seat while Sedgwick spoke to the Chief.   The pale, shimmering light surrounding them was punctuated by falling stars created by the partiers on top of the lorry, who were wadding up magazines and newspapers, lighting the small masses, and hurling them into the night air, where they glowed briefly before falling to the ground in a burst of sparks.

In the distance, above the mass of black cars and trucks, a strange, unnatural glow was now illuminating the horizon, while a full moon hung higher in the sky, red and partially obscured by the distant smoke as if it suffered from an incurable disease.   An hour or so later, a strange, burning smell permeated the area where Sedgwick, Thwait, and Nesbit stood, silently watching incapacitated cars being towed to the side of the highway.

Chapter 41

Six hours later, they were among a group of vehicles slowly passing by the locus of the accident. As they approached, they saw what could only be described as a simmering, black caldron created from a tangle of cars and trucks, emitting shooting stars that quickly faded in the hellishly black night. The foul smelling air, which seemed to be a combination of burning wire and smoldering flesh, permeated their car even though the windows were closed, and the heat still being generated from the site could be felt for over a hundred yards in either direction. Sedgwick tried to attract the attention of one of the officers directing traffic around the wreck, but the stolid young man refused to look at her credentials and angrily ordered her to keep moving.

It was still dark when they arrived at the station. The Chief met them at the main door and walked them to his office. The faintly buzzing light was on when they entered, and they sat silently until the Chief took out his pencil and began tapping on the top of his desk. Looking at Nesbit, although this time without squinting, the Chief asked him if he felt well enough to talk about his experience and what he may have gleaned from it.

Nesbit described his meeting with Sanders, noting that Sanders was the son of the man who was running a London-based shop specializing in stolen antiquities. It was, he reminded the Chief, the very shop that he, Nesbit, had mistakenly visited while working on what became known as the New Orleans case. The Chief nodded, and Nesbit continued by describing the cottage, the things he had seen in the building, and what he had learned from speaking to Sanders. Nesbit glanced at all three officers at this point and, with a familiar smile on his thin lips, stated that he could prove that the bombings at the Ravenswood, Evermore, and Heathrow, as well as the letters and the wiretap, were all part and parcel of the same case. "Everything," he added, "adds up to a single, glorious case." Smiling, he turned to Thwait, and, noticing the concerned expression on the junior officer's heavy face, shook his head again as his smile faded. "Actually," he said, looking directly at Thwait, "I didn't have a clue until I spoke to Sanders." He added that there should be enough evidence in the cottage – fingerprints, bomb residue, and so forth – to make the case quite easily. Nesbit paused and once again turned to Thwait, informing him and the others that the Gray Ladies, contrary to what Nesbit often said, had nothing to do with art. He himself was one of the Gray Ladies (Nesbit didn't mention what Sanders said about Thwait).

359

By this time, Nesbit appeared tired and, leaning forward with his hands between his thin knees, he began speaking about the phone calls that eventually led to his meeting with Sanders. He stated that in retrospect he couldn't be sure if his son or Sanders made the calls – it could have been one and then the other, or simply one and not the other – but it really didn't matter because they were practically the same individual. Sanders, he noted, was residing at his ex-wife's cottage and he had intimate details of the Nesbit family, details that could only have come from one source. After Nesbit slowly enunciated his son's full and formal name, he became silent and couldn't look at anyone, not even Thwait.

After several minutes in which the only sound in the room was an occasional cough and the incessant tapping of a pencil, the Chief cleared his throat and informed Nesbit, Sedgwick, and Thwait that Sanders hadn't bombed Heathrow Customs because he had been killed in the explosion on the highway. He was on his way to the airport with a live bomb when it unexpectedly went off, perhaps in response to a bump in the road or a fender-bender with another vehicle. Nesbit raised his eyebrows when the Chief mentioned that the explosion may have saved his life. The bomb disposal unit found what appeared to be a remote detonator a few feet from the car. Since it was most likely connected to the bomb Nesbit was sitting on, the explosion probably prevented Sanders from using it. Seconds later, Nesbit lifted his head and, smiling briefly, collapsed onto the floor.

Chapter 42

The following afternoon, Sedgwick, Thwait, and the Chief assembled in a large conference room with a dozen other officers and listened to Nesbit recount for the record his ordeal and everything he learned from Sanders. Feeling stronger after some sleep, as he mentioned at the outset of the meeting, Nesbit told them most of what he told the Chief, Sedgwick, and Thwait – this time with the humility that had been lacking in the previous discussion – and added some details that might have been dismissed earlier as being coincidental or lacking evidentiary value. He mentioned, for example, the small boxes (including the one he recovered from the cottage), which, as Sedgwick rightly noted, were match boxes, and then pointed out that the coin-like object found at the Ravenswood was not a coin at all but a partially melted button from Sanders' jacket (the rounded smiles on one side were what was left of an intaglio of crossed swords). He added that the clothing remnants in the morgue were most likely hunter's camouflages. The meeting was well into its second hour when Nesbit placed his right elbow on the table and rested his forehead on his right fist. Everyone there thought that he might be having an emotional release after his ordeal, and so there was a general reluctance to break what seemed to be a necessary solitude.

Lifting his head and glancing around the room, Nesbit calmly noted that he also had the identity of Sanders' collaborator. "Sanders was not acting alone, as I'm sure you've gathered by now. But what you probably don't know is that his partner was my son, whom you'll find resting comfortably in the morgue. He conspired with Sanders to plot the whole thing out. The goal, according to Sanders – and, in this instance, I believe he was telling the truth – was for both of them to get back at me. I am the constable in the wiretap. Even though they didn't have a chance to finish their bloody job, the evidence and everything else will clearly show their intent. Sanders, of course, wanted revenge for his and his father's loss of business, their respective incarcerations, and his father's death behind bars. I will leave it to you to determine the rationality of such an enterprise. My son, on the other hand, wanted to hurt me for having neglected him and his mother. While there might be some reason to question Sanders' sanity, there can be no doubt that my son and his mother had genuine grievances." Nesbit paused and, staring off into the distance, seemed to be churning something around in his mind. Suddenly, his firm chin began to shake and, closing his eyes, he let his head sink to his chest.

The officers stared at him, some were shocked by Nesbit's revelations about his son, and others were waiting for him to say something more about the case and his son's involvement in it. Nesbit, however, was silent for at least another minute before he resumed speaking. This time, he looked downward, not at any individual, and his voice sounded unexpectedly heavy and clouded. "For the record, my son's name is Benjamin Nesbit. You will find sufficient evidence in the cottage and at the crime scenes to show, beyond a doubt, that he was the co-conspirator. He was in on everything from the beginning, before the beginning, in fact. He was, I am ashamed to say, a useless individual, but his uselessness came about only because I was his useless father. Our family fell apart because of me. The worst of it...my son, my son..." Seconds later, he added in a voice that was much louder, "My God, what have I done?" Nesbit was silent after this. He couldn't go on. Placing both arms quietly on the table, he cradled his head in his arms and, seconds later, his shoulders were visibly shaking.

The officers looked at one another and, as if responding to a silent command, quietly got up from the table and exited the room. Thwait, however, remained seated. Once the officers were finally gone, he looked at Nesbit, who began sobbing louder and cursing himself for something that he should have done but for some reason hadn't.

Chapter 43

Thwait started to put his arm around Nesbit but hesitated. It seemed wrong for him to hold a proud man like Nesbit, who in his everyday life personified strength, courage, and everything else that Thwait admired. Nesbit was the tightrope walker who had fallen and needed the kind of help that was beyond a mere member of the audience. Pulling his arm back, Thwait said, "I'm sorry, sir. If you need anything, I'm here for you."

Nesbit's heaving subsided, and for a couple of minutes he was quiet. "He was my son, Tom," he said finally without lifting his head, "and whatever he did, whatever he became, I was the cause of it." Slowly raising his head, Nesbit looked at Thwait through watery eyes. "Do you remember all those calls I claimed to be having with my son? They sounded wonderful, didn't they? I told you about his job and his prospects, and I mentioned his happiness, his girlfriend, and I don't know what else. The calls were certainly real, but the content as I described it was a complete fabrication. Our conversations were terrible, and he accused me of the most horrendous things – desertion, abandonment, cruelty – all of which were true. I said all those things, because he embarrassed me and I didn't want you to think that I was the kind of person who could have such a child. I wanted a son I could brag about, a young man who was in some small way a reflection of me at my best, and I wanted to have the kind of relationship with him that every father dreams of having with his son. I still loved him, or at least I thought I loved him. Maybe I simply loved the idea of having a son I could love. I don't know. Do you know what's really pathetic? I envy the relationship that Sanders had with his father. As perverted as he was, Sanders wanted to kill for his father, while my son wanted to kill me."

"You know," he said after a brief pause, "in the early days when my son was still an impressionable child, I really didn't care about being a father. I mean, I liked my son and all that, but I was happy to leave him in the care of his mother, so that I could gallivant around the world, working on one case after another. It was only later on, after my career stalled and the work became routine, that I realized how important my son was to me. But instead of reaching out, I sent him a Christmas card or something and waited for him to make the first move. In the back of my head, I had this stupid notion that children are supposed to be deferential to their parents, and so I left it up to him to bridge the yawning gulf that had separated us for years. God, it's hard to believe that I had such expectations. What's even harder to believe is that when he didn't reach out, I felt insulted and even more resistant to contacting him."

Shaking his head slightly, Nesbit sat back in his chair and stared blankly at the wall across from him. "About a year ago, something happened to me. I can't explain it except to say that I had, for whatever reason, come to see that all my notions about fathers and sons were wrong, and that if I were ever to have a relationship with my son, it was up to me to make the first move. He was the injured party, and he was now at an age in which he didn't need me. I, however, needed him." Nesbit turned his head toward Thwait without moving the rest of his body. "Look, I had no illusions about erasing the past or recreating the father/son dynamic that I had discarded years ago. I wanted to apologize for my failure as a father, and I hoped that if he could get beyond the past just a little, he might be willing to open the door to his life from time to time, letting me know how he's doing or offering his opinions on the issues. So I managed to contact his mother, and she informed me that he was living with her and that he didn't want to hear from me under any circumstances. Naturally, I blamed her – I always hold others accountable for my own failures – but I can see now that she wasn't standing in the way of the relationship I desperately wanted to revive. Well, I knew that I didn't deserve his attention, and I also knew that it was my own fault if I didn't get it."

Nesbit looked away briefly and inhaled deeply as if he were trying to control another surge of emotion. Turning back to Thwait, he smiled slightly and said, "Tom, when that first call came, it seemed to change everything, and my love for him was so profound and my desire to connect with him was so great that I simply lost my mind. I really thought that I could hold my little boy in my arms again..." Smiling wanly, Nesbit stood up and patted Thwait firmly on his thick shoulder. "You've been a good friend, Tom, probably the only true friend that I've ever had. Don't let me mess up your life, too." He reached down and shook the young officer's plump hand and left the room.

As soon as the door snapped shut, Thwait ran over and pulled it open. He wanted to speak to his friend, he wanted to understand what his next steps were, and he wanted to offer his assistance in some fashion, which he knew that Nesbit would do for him. Given Nesbit's obvious state of mind, Thwait also wanted to be certain that his friend wasn't going to do anything rash. But he was too late. Nesbit was nowhere to be seen.

Chapter 44

Two days later, the Chief, Sedgwick, Thwait, and the other officers assigned to the case were seated around the long table in the conference room near the Chief's office. They were discussing some of the details of what the station was planning to present to the media now that the case was more or less closed. Sure, there were still a few unresolved issues, a handful of ambiguities, that needed to be clarified before everyone could turn to other cases, but at least the perpetrators were both thankfully dead (and Nesbit had confirmed that there had only been two) and, as a result, Sir Ronald, the CEO, and Her Majesty's government could all sleep a little easier (and, based on the evidence, there was no reason to suppose that the two had planted bombs anywhere else). More importantly, the country could now get on with the time-honored processes of healing and closure.

From the outset of the meeting, nearly every officer praised Agent Nesbit for his invaluable contributions to the case, and a couple of them (Sedgwick and Thwait) went so far as to suggest that the case would never have been resolved, or at least not as quickly, if it weren't for Agent Nesbit. He was a brave and inestimable law enforcement official, and of all the people who had worked on this case, he was the one who deserved to be front and center when the media was addressed. However, that was beginning to seem unlikely, since no one, not even Thwait, had seen Nesbit since his debriefing (he left his hotel without word, and he wasn't answering his phone). The Chief also grumbled his disappointment, squinting at something in the distance and tapping his pencil against the table, but he added that it couldn't be helped because Agent Nesbit was probably back at work on something else.

But neither Nesbit's absence nor some of the unresolved issues were nearly as significant as another, much bigger problem concerning Nesbit that was looming over the case like a black cloud – sooner or later, the station would have to inform the media that Nesbit's son was killed at the Evermore and that the young man was the other conspirator in both bombings (three, if one included the attempt on Heathrow Customs). Having to pair this relationship with all the other sordid facts of the case would not only dull the luster of Nesbit's glory, as one officer suggested, but it might also make the man a laughingstock for being unable to identify and control his own criminal son. 'Couldn't the bloody sod have raised his child better than that?' someone among the media was bound to ask. Moreover, the relationship might even elicit calls to have Nesbit himself investigated, for certain members of Parliament would doubtless refuse to accept the facts at face value and do whatever they could do to profit from the man's shame and exposure. But while none of the officers at the table expected anything serious to come from such "disrespectful nonsense," they all agreed that any public and Parliamentary blather over the relationship would be embarrassing to the man and could, to the delight of a few august MPs, ruin the agent's estimable career. Since no one truly knew how strong Agent Nesbit was on the inside, no one could therefore say how well he could handle the adversity, the negative publicity, and the public humiliation.

"I've seen people kill themselves for less," one officer intoned, but shrank back when the Chief squinted at him.

"He shouldn't be condemned in the press," another said. "Of all people, he's the one who presented the facts as they were and didn't hesitate to implicate his worthless son. No, he deserves better."

"Why...I mean, why do we have to mention the name of Agent Nesbit's son? What point would it serve?" Thwait interjected. "We could withhold the name pending notification of his nearest relative. Since that would be Agent Nesbit, there would never be a reason to tell him what he already knows, and hence no cause to ever mention the son's name." Thwait wanted to say more to help his friend, but he couldn't think of another reason to keep the information from the media, which he feared would get out regardless of the officers' promises to remain silent. Could they count on HQ's silence?

The Chief leaned back in his chair and cradled the back of his head in his hands. Looking up at the ceiling, he asked of no one in particular, "are we that convinced about the identity of the second individual, the one killed at the Evermore?"

"Yes, Chief," replied Dr. Fellows, who was sitting almost directly across from the Chief. "Our lab tests confirmed the body parts in question belonged to Agent Nesbit's son."

The Chief leaned forward and, once again, began tapping his pencil on the table. "I want to be clear, Dr. Fellows," he replied without looking directly at the doctor. "We're talking about the body taken from the second site that your lab had trouble identifying, if I'm not mistaken."

"Yes, Chief, but the difficulties we faced are not uncommon when working with body parts. I mean, the process isn't as straightforward as matching a fingerprint or a facial image. Still, we were able to extract DNA and match it to an individual, after which Slim was able to connect the individual to a name in a local criminal database. We've got our man."

"Where is Slim?"

"He couldn't make it because of another case. He sends his regrets and wishes us…"

"I got it," he replied, squinting at Fellows. "So tell me, Dr. Fellows, "what's your level of confidence in the call?"

"I'm sorry?"

"I can sense that. What I want to know is your level of confidence that you've correctly identified the remains."

"Well, very confident, I suppose."

"No suppositions. Give me a number."

"A number, Chief? I'm afraid I don't…"

The Chief's face intensified and his eyes were practically slits. "Yes, statistically speaking. Are you a 100% certain you've properly identified the remains, and there's absolutely no possibility that something was missed?"

"I'm confident that everything was conducted according to proper…"

"A number, doctor."

Fellows hesitated. "Well, I would say that we are 95% certain that the remains are who we believe they are. Yes, Chief, I would say our confidence is very high."

"I see. Not 100%, though."

"I don't think we can be 100% positive about anything, really."

The Chief was silent as he nodded his head slightly. "Tell me, doctor, are you equally confident there were no signs of coercion on the remains?"

"There was nothing on the remains to suggest the individual was anything but a willing participant in the crimes. The explosion was apparently an accident."

"But there were only body fragments left."

"That's true, Chief, but there were enough of the right pieces to determine whether or not the individual had been subject to bodily distress prior to the blast. There were no signs of distress, I'm afraid. If you'd like," he added, hopefully, "I can send one of the technicians to bring up the parts in question to show you exactly what I'm talking about."

"Will the parts in question tell us whether the individual had a gun to his head?"

367

"No, I suppose not. But given the blast radius, it would be highly unlikely that anyone would have survived within fifty feet of the unfortunate individual."

"Thank you, Doctor." The Chief stopped tapping his pencil and glanced at the officers around the table. "Has anyone revealed details regarding the deceased outside of this room?"

"Not me, Chief," Fellows quickly responded, after which he immediately looked down to avoid the Chief's glare.

"Except for Slim and Agent Nesbit, I don't think anyone outside of this room knows," Sedgwick said.

The Chief silently nodded. "HQ has suspicions, but they don't have enough information right now to make a call."

"Let me assure everyone that our technicians don't," insisted Fellows, looking around the room to avoid the Chief's gaze. "They run the samples and make numerical matches – Nesbit's son was, I believe, number 1756632 (I can check my notes, if necessary) – and so they don't know John Doe from John Donne from 1756632. Perhaps Slim…"

"Thank you, doctor. I'll reach out to Slim."

The doctor flushed slightly and looked down.

"His name, however, is now in our internal records." The Chief turned to Sedgwick. "Remind me about Nesbit's son. He has a record, correct? How extensive is it?"

"Minor offenses, for the most part. Delinquency, vagrancy, shoplifting, but nothing that might be considered a precursor for what he and Sanders were doing. However, I haven't checked with Interpol, Europol, or the States, and so maybe there's something there."

"You've done enough. Drop it, unless you've got some special angle on him."

"What about possible connections?" asked an officer, who was sitting at the far end of the table.

"Connections? Do you have reason to believe that more people are involved in this case?" When the Chief responded, all the other officers at the table turned to stare at the officer who had asked the question.

"No, Chief, I…I don't think there's anything else to find," he replied timidly. "It was only a pro forma question."

The Chief turned away from the officer and looked at each of the others in turn. "Let me be clear," he began, addressing them as a group, "if you have any reason to suspect that these two men were not the only ones involved in these crimes, or if you suspect that they might be connected to other individuals or groups tangentially associated with these or similar crimes, then we are required to follow these leads. I would rather reopen the investigation than be confronted with something in the media we should have known. Now, if there are any suspicions, let's put them on the table so we can run with them. No?" He glanced again at the unfortunate officer at the end of the table. "Let me clear about one more thing. If I find out that anyone is holding back, I'm going to hang them out to dry. Are we clear?"

The Chief was silent as he squinted at every around the table. "All right," he began, ending what seemed to most of the officers an unpleasantly long period of time, "I want to clarify a couple more things about Nesbit's son and Sanders before we move to other things. According to Agent Nesbit, both men were equally involved, although Sanders appeared to be the one interested in expanding their target set. Do we have anything else on Sanders or the relationship between the two men that might shed some more light on why they did what they did?"

"Not a lot, I'm afraid," Sedgwick replied. "As you know, Sanders had connections through his father to an international crime syndicate specializing in stolen art, although he doesn't seem to have reconnected with anyone from the group after his release." Sedgwick paused, the left side of her mouth drooping slightly, while she waited for the Chief to respond. When it was clear that he wasn't ready to say anything, she continued. "I'm afraid we don't know any more than HQ or Interpol what brought the two men together. It's possible that Agent Nesbit's son was mulling over something when he heard about Agent Nesbit's role in the arrest and incarceration of the Sanders. If Agent Nesbit's son was the instigator, this may have been given him the idea of reaching out to Sanders Jr. On the other hand, if Sanders Jr. was the instigator, I can't quite fathom why he would have thought that Agent Nesbit's son would be amenable to such a criminal endeavor. I should also point out that since there are no records of the agent's son communicating with Sanders Jr. during the latter's incarceration, the pivotal meeting between the two must have come after Sanders Jr.'s release. However they came together, it seems clear that the one thing they both had in common was Agent Nesbit." Sedgwick glanced briefly around the room. "Chief, let me add for the record that we do not have an official justification for delving into Agent Nesbit's private life."

"Don't you think they had more in common than just their hatred of Agent Nesbit?" one of the officers said. "I mean, they occupied the cottage for some time. From what I'm told, it's hardly bigger than a closet, and, according to what we now know, there was only one sleeping space."

"There's no reason to assume that a closer relationship leads to, or is indicative of, criminal behavior. I suspect that the living arrangements were at least in part out of necessity. Sanders Jr. appears to have been unemployed for most of the time since his release, while Nesbit's son had a job for a few months before he was terminated. Interestingly, he was working at one of the chemical supply companies that sold the very ingredients that were used for the bombs. He was terminated shortly after an inventory showed large amounts of the chemical was missing. While he wasn't charged for theft, his record was discovered during the investigation and he was let go for failing to disclose his record when he applied. We also found evidence of his residence at a bedsit in Oxford, from which he was evicted in less than a year for being in arrears. Constable Thwait and I spoke to the manager, but he couldn't tell us much other than the young man didn't pay the rent. There isn't much else apart from the usual public records."

The Chief was quiet for a moment while he rubbed his rough chin. "Tell me, Inspector Sedgwick, did you or anyone else uncover anything related to the letters? I'm not sure how important the letters are at this point, but it might be useful if we could connect them more directly to young Nesbit and Sanders, especially if at Sanders' instigation they were planning to hit places beyond Heathrow."

"No, Chief. We haven't found any connections between the letters and our suspects. We were able to run the postmark on the envelope retrieved from the Evermore, but it led us to a station in Cambridge, and we have nothing to put either man in that city. It's very strange."

"I see." The Chief let his pencil fall from his hand, hitting the table and rolling to the other side, where it disappeared off the edge. While one of the officers scrambled under the table to retrieve it, the Chief caught sight of Fellows, who, judging by the expression on his gray face, seemed eager to say something. "You have something you'd like to add, Doctor?"

"Chief, we also got CCTV footage. It arrived only..."

"Fine, and what does it show? Were you able to identify the men from the videos?"

370

"Well, not exactly, Chief," Fellows responded, glancing sheepishly at Sedgwick. "What I mean to say is that the cameras at the museum weren't functional at the time of the explosions (a software upgrade, I believe). But the footage from the auction house clearly shows a couple of casually-dressed young men entering the main door shortly before the close of business. At first blush, they seemed to be sporting military fatigues, but upon closer examination we were able to determine that they were wearing hunters' apparel. Right, well, later on, after the first explosion, the footage shows what appears to be one of the men exiting the building from a side window. Unfortunately, none of the images are clear enough to make a positive ID."

"Can you run a facial scan against the images?"

"We tried, but the images weren't clear enough to deliver satisfactory results."

"Any way of matching the clothing to a particular seller?"

"I'm afraid not. The same clothing can be found at a number of outlets and, of course, online."

"Okay," the Chief began, frowning briefly at the officer who, having retrieved his pencil, suddenly handed it to him from under the table, "everything we discussed here remains tightly held until I say otherwise. Are we all clear?" He squinted at Fellows. "Good. I will prepare a statement for the media." The Chief pocketed his pencil, which the officers knew was a sign for them to leave. Sedgwick, however, remained seated, and she motioned for Thwait to remain while the others filed out of the conference room and closed the door behind them.

For a few moments, the Chief seemed to be unaware of their presence, but he looked up when Thwait unconsciously sniffed.

"Good, I'm glad you and Inspector Sedgwick are still here," he said, glancing under the table to make sure they were alone.

"Yes, Chief, we wanted to speak to you about what's going to be said to the media," Sedgwick replied. "What I mean is…"

"Yes, Inspector Sedgwick, I know what you mean. You want to brief the media," the Chief said, looking at each officer in turn. "I know you're disappointed that I didn't immediately assign the media presentation to you."

"That wasn't exactly what I had in mind…"

"There's nothing like presenting the wrap-up to the media. You offer the results, you answer a few questions, and you leave," he continued, appearing to have forgotten the presence of the two officers. "The great thing

371

about it is the media themselves. They hang on every word you say, and they practically give you all the credit in their stories. It's very interesting, and I think it would be a nice complement to your earlier experience."

"Yes, Chief, but what I wanted to say…"

"Yes, indeed, Inspector Sedgwick, and you deserve another opportunity of speaking to them and putting your mark on this case."

"What, Chief? No, I wasn't asking…"

"Don't be modest, Inspector Sedgwick, you've earned it. You and Constable Thwait did a great job on this case, and you both deserve to be front and center when the media are briefed. And, Inspector Sedgwick, I was quite pleased the last time you briefed them. You told them exactly what I wanted you to tell them. This time…well, I hate to say it, but this time I'm not going to let you speak to them."

"Chief?"

"It's not that I think you'll do a bad job or that you lack the experience. In fact, in many ways, I think you're an ideal candidate to do it. But this case is different than most of the others we've handled. A lot of the media are not going to be satisfied with what we say, and if we're not careful, they're going to be on us like piranha, demanding additional answers and accusing us of purposely leaving them in the dark. It's also the case that some of your answers, which will have to be the correct answers, could affect you with respect to certain colleagues and others. I don't mean Constable Thwait, but others, including HQ. I'm not questioning your fortitude; I just don't want to see these issues dogging you at this stage in your career."

Sedgwick and Thwait glanced at each other and turned back to the Chief. "Chief," Sedgwick began, "I can handle whatever…"

"Of course you can, but that's not the point. Look, I'm pleased that you're willing to shoulder some tough issues for the station. But since there'll plenty of similar opportunities in the near future, I'm asking you to stand down in this instance."

"All right, Chief," Sedgwick replied. Once again, she glanced at Thwait. "Chief, may I ask what you're going to say about the body? Once you mention its relationship to Agent Nesbit, the media will have a field day, Agent Nesbit's career will be ruined, and those two scoundrels will have got their revenge. Isn't there some way…?"

"Our responsibility is to present the facts and nothing else," he replied sternly, squinting.

"But, Chief, hasn't he already suffered enough? He doesn't deserve any more pain simply because he's his father." She could feel herself becoming flushed. Turning to Thwait, she noticed that he, too, was angry.

"Inspector Sedgwick, Constable Thwait, I expect this to be the only time in your careers that I need to say it. If we make an exception in this instance, it will be easier to make exceptions in other instances, and pretty soon we will have corrupted our integrity and lost the public's trust in our ability to do an honest, impartial job. Am I making myself understood?"

"Yes, Chief," Sedgwick said, and Thwait quickly nodded.

"Look, I'm not happy about the way things turned out, but nobody promised to make the job palatable to my sensibilities. Now, unless you have anything else that requires my attention, our media friends are in the lobby waiting for me."

Chapter 45

Amid the clicking and snapping of cameras, the Chief entered from the left and walked over to a makeshift podium practically in the center of the station's lobby. The podium held three prominent microphones, each one angled more or less at the Chief's stern mouth, while in front of the podium were nearly a hundred reporters, cameramen, and media personalities, most of whom were holding recorders, cameras, phones, and other devices over their heads and angling them in his direction. The Chief's brisk movements as well as his trim physique, straight back, and closely cropped hair reminded one of a military officer about ready to make a formal presentation to his troops, even though his furrowed forehead and hard cheeks sparkled from the camera flashes and overhead lights. Clearing his throat, the Chief adjusted the position of the podium and the microphones and, when everything was just right, Sedgwick and Thwait mysteriously appeared behind him to his right.

The Chief squinted directly at the media and, speaking in a forceful, quasi-military tone, he informed them that the bombings at the Ravenswood Museum, the Evermore Auction House, and the crash on the highway have been solved. While some minor details were still being mopped up, he noted, "we are nevertheless confident that the individual responsible for the bombings was Charles Sanders Jr., a petty criminal who had been released less than a year ago. Sanders Jr. was also responsible for the recent multicar highway crash, and forensic evidence proves that he was killed in the same crash. We have also identified the individual killed at the Evermore...," he began but paused to clear his throat. Glancing at Sedgwick and Thwait, he turned back to the media, cleared his throat again, and momentarily gritted his teeth. "As I was saying, we have identified the individual whose remains were found in the building. However, we have not connected this individual to the bombings or to Sanders Jr. Given the forensic evidence, he was most likely a hostage. We will release the name upon official notification of his nearest relative." The Chief added a number of additional details regarding the case and finished by thanking Agent Nesbit of Interpol, "whose assistance was instrumental in solving this case."

<<<◇>>>

Endpoint?

"My dearest Tom,

"It's been a long time since I've spoken to you (has it been six months already?), and I'm ashamed I didn't reach out sooner. It has nothing to do with you, my friend. It was simply me being me, me being self-centered and inconsiderate. I hope you'll forgive me.

"Tom, I want to express my sincere gratitude to you. Without your insights and hard work, this case wouldn't have been solved, or at least it wouldn't have been solved quickly enough to save my worthless skin. More importantly, I cannot express how much your help and friendship meant to me in the aftermath of all our work. If it weren't for you, I might never have got over the loss of my son or the heavy burden I bear as a fallible human being. I will never be able to repay you adequately for all you've done.

"As for my son, I have reconciled myself to the fact that he was a worthless individual and a detriment to society. While I appreciate everything that you and the station did to keep his name unsullied, there is no doubt in my mind that he was heavily involved with Sanders and that the two of them conspired to commit unthinkable crimes against humanity. In fact, my son was the worst of the two, because he would have become a parricide had he not been so careless with that bomb.

"But, God help me, Tom, there are still moments when I feel something less that utter disgust for that pathetic individual. No, my friend, I will never forget or excuse what he did. But now and then there are moments when I can't help feeling sorry for him because of his pathetic childhood, and there are many more times when I consider how different he might have turned out had I been a present and attentive father. Perhaps these feelings are nothing more than a guilty father's desire to find something redeeming in a child he can't stand to remember but is unable to forget. I know this doesn't make a lot of sense, and yet, God help me, I can't entirely hate him, not when I still have vivid memories of the little boy who used to run to the door and greet me with smiles and hugs as I tromped inside and made excuses for my absence. And I can't completely dismiss his memory when I remember that this same little boy never had anyone who might have helped him grow up well-adjusted and socially responsible. He needed a man, my friend, which he didn't have. Do you want to know something funny? The other night I got down on my knees and prayed for a chance to do everything over again. I told the Almighty that I had learned enough not to repeat the same mistakes and that if I had this one opportunity, I would make sure that my son turned out differently. I promised that he would become that kind of man that anyone on earth or in the heavens would be proud of. It's absurd how far someone will go when he's at his wits' end, and it's laughable to think that I could change something the second time around when I destroyed it the first time I had the opportunity.

"I know what you're thinking, but your heart is kind and generous. Believe me, Tom, I am at least partly responsible for the pathetic choices my son made (and let's not forget my wife), and I deserve all the pain and more for what he did to those innocent people in London, Oxford, and in England itself.

"But enough; I'm not trying to make you feel sorry for me, and I'm not hoping that you'll understand my past behavior. You weren't responsible for any of this, and so it would be grossly unfair of me to ask you to shoulder some of the emotional burden, which you would be doing if you felt even a twinge of sympathy for me. No, my friend, this isn't my purpose, and I apologize most heartily for having brought it up. Truly, the reason for this message is simply to get back in touch and tell you a little about what's going with me on these days.

"However, before I begin, I must offer you a couple of additional and related apologies. Once again, I am sorry that it has taken so long to get back in touch with you. It would be an insult if I were to offer any excuses, and so let me just promise that I will never again let such a long span of time separate us. I am also sorry for not responding to any of your recent messages. I listened to every one of them, and I can't tell you how moved I was by your heartfelt words about my loss (which, I have to admit, was the world's gain) and your repeated requests to meet for lunch or dinner. I was deeply touched by your generous offer to select any restaurant in town (London, of course) and it would be on you, since it most strongly suggested that the request was not a professional obligation. I will indeed take you up on your offer, and fairly soon, too, but I cannot allow you to pay, nor will I ask Interpol to foot the bill. Tom, I owe you more than I will ever be able to repay for your friendship, and I also suspect that you had to bear some of the expenses of our comestible outings, and so I will be the one shelling out for this meal and many more to come. Is that a deal, my friend?

"As for other things, you probably already know that I've been on an extended leave from Interpol. The separation was voluntary, of course, it wasn't meant to be permanent, and I requested it because I needed some time to think about the past and what comes next. Something always comes next, and I didn't want to sit back and wait for it to happen. I wanted to take control of my life while I still had time. Well, I think I've used these days wisely, because I have come to a couple of important decisions.

"The first is that I'm going to leave England (yes, I'm still here), perhaps forever. I had been toying with the idea of seeking a permanent position here, but then everything happened and…and now I'm going to return to the States. This wasn't an easy decision, for I have come to love this country and its people almost as much as I love my own, but I can't stay here any longer and still retain my sanity. Some of my greatest achievements occurred in this wonderful country, and yet I can't imagine walking along Oxford's storied streets without recalling the abomination that was once my son or remembering the little child that I deserted when I was still proud to call him my son. And London – my God, Tom, in London, you and I solved two of the most important cases ever to beset these golden isles. But where could I go in this city to escape the stench from the burning buildings, and where could I hide to avoid all the once beautiful faces staring at me because of my son? No, it's impossible, not without risking a flight to the tallest building and howling at the moon from its rooftop. So, yes, it is with a heavy heart that I am returning to the United States, but not to New Orleans (it, too, holds unpleasant memories) – I've secured another posting with Interpol at the Chicago office.

"The second is far more important, and it was certainly the easiest to make. Tom, my dearest friend, I want you to come to Chicago. While you have a great future ahead of you no matter where you are or what kind of work you do, I feel certain that you would realize your enormous potential if you took a position with me in the States, where you would feel most at home. I have already conferred with the higher powers at Interpol, and they are pleased as punch to bring you on board as an Agent at the Chicago office. Naturally, you will have to resign your position at the station, but you could keep your citizenship while working with me on more cases than ten of your seasoned officers could possibly handle. Tom, we would be a team, a great team, and together we could solve half the world's problems. What do you say, my friend? There will be more pay, more responsibility, and more benefits. (We can discuss these at your convenience.) You may have to lose a couple of pounds, but that's only a minor inconvenience, while in the greater scheme of things you and I will be having the times of our lives. Have you ever been to

Chicago, my friend? It is a stunning city, with small pubs, grand restaurants, shimmering skyscrapers, wonderful museums, and no end of alluring young women waiting for a young man just like you. This is the opportunity of a lifetime. Once you give me the word, I will get the ball rolling and you'll be over here before it reaches the end of the alley (a bowling metaphor).

"Do you still need convincing? Then let me add this: Tom, you and I have already been asked to take on a case involving political intrigue, royal families, beautiful women, and assassinations (at least two of them!). I can't provide a lot of details, but I can say that a certain South Asian country wants to know who recently murdered two members of the royal family. The elimination of royal members is not uncommon in this backward country, but what is setting the royal family on edge is that the two recent assassinations concerned princes who were direct heirs to the royal throne. If this isn't interesting enough, suspicions are currently revolving around one member of the family, a young gadabout who was conveniently in Monte Carlo at the time of the murders, losing half his fortune on the roulette table. The old king is staying out of the fracas, but his youngest daughter (a twenty-something princess of a favored wife who was murdered a few years ago) has succeeded in galvanizing Interpol and others to bring the culprit to the kingdom's royal court of justice. If you believe our young princess, the only one who had the motive and the opportunity was the Monte Carlo chap, who has not yet returned from his vacation and refuses all communication with the royal family. Parenthetically, I am not surprised by his reluctance to return, since we're dealing with a family of backbiters who value human life less than I do the change in my right pocket.

"Tom, this case has all the convolutions of a Shakespearean tragedy – and, if I may say so, all of his comedies' dependence on actors to make them interesting – plus a few contortions that so far remain unaddressed. So, here's what I'm thinking. I'm not convinced that our Monte Carlo royal is the culprit. Sure, he was out of town at the time of the murders (and everyone knows that you leave town to deflect suspicions), but he isn't eligible for the royal crown, and it doesn't make sense for him to eliminate the very people who might have been able to replenish the money lost at the table. The princess, on the other hand, seems particularly hot and bothered to implicate our Monte Carlo friend. Since she surely understands the line of succession as well as I, one has to wonder why she would point the royal finger at Monte Carlo instead of someone else who stands in the way of her royal ascendance to the throne (the head princess, as it were, or the queen herself).

"I've done some preliminary background on the royal family, and as a result I wouldn't be surprised if the princess were involved in something untoward that came to the attention of the deceased royals, who were therefore dispatched before they could render judgment on this activity. Now, what could this lovely young lady have done that would have induced her to follow the family's time-honored method of sweeping unpleasant things under the rug? How about a torrid affair with a commoner? This would not only violate the sanctity of the royal line, but it would also mirror what other disreputable family members have done over the years. Keep in mind that if such a relationship were to come to the light of day, her eligibility to assume the royal tiara would be rendered null and void in a wink, and the all-important doors to the not inconsiderable royal coffers would be closed to her and locked – forever. She may even lose her crown in a rather unpleasant way. Yes, she looks good for it in my eyes, but what are your considered thoughts, my friend? Do you buy this line of reasoning or do you have something better that would fit the facts as we know them?"

Nesbit paused and ran a quick playback to make sure he got the image and sound quality perfect. To his chagrin, he noticed that he had positioned the camera in such a way that only the top of his head was visible. Grumbling, he was about to re-record his message to Thwait, when he decided to let well enough alone. The sound quality was first rate, he told himself, and being completely in the picture at the end might provide some rhetorical force to his message. Unfortunately, the realignment of the camera wasn't quite as effective as planned, for his head was now completely out of the screen and the only image captured was open door of his hotel bathroom.

Taking a deep breath, he started speaking again. "Tom," he said, looking at what he thought was the camera's lens, "I apologize for the quality of this video, but I hope you understand how much I want you to come to Chicago with me and how much I need your expertise on this and every other case. You are my dearest friend, and if you decide against such a move at this time, I will understand. You have your wits about you, and if you decline my invitation, I will know it was only because you have seen and understood things that I haven't. I'll respect your decision however it goes, and I promise you that even if you remain in England, I'll not fail to keep in touch. I will not do to you what I did to my son.

"So there it is, my friend. Let me know one way or another as soon as you can. Send my sincerest regards to the Chief and Officer Sedgwick, and tell them that I owe them both my deepest gratitude."

- - - -))) - -)) – ((- - (((- - - -